THE NEWCOMER

Laura Elizabeth Woollett is the author of a short story collection, *The Love of a Bad Man* (Scribe, 2016), and a novel, *Beautiful Revolutionary* (Scribe, 2018). *The Love of a Bad Man* was shortlisted for the Victorian Premier's Literary Award for Fiction and the Ned Kelly Award for Best First Fiction. *Beautiful Revolutionary* was shortlisted for the 2019 Prime Minister's Literary Award for Fiction, the Australian Literature Society Gold Medal, and the Kathleen Mitchell Award. Laura was the City of Melbourne's 2020 Boyd Garret writer-in-residence and is a 2020–22 Marten Bequest scholar for prose.

THE
NEWCOMER

LAURA ELIZABETH WOOLLETT

SCRIBE

Melbourne • London

Scribe Publications
2 John St, Clerkenwell, London, WC1N 2ES, United Kingdom
18–20 Edward St, Brunswick, Victoria 3056, Australia

Published by Scribe 2021

Typeset in Adobe Garamond by the publishers

Printed and bound in the UK by by CPI Group (UK) Ltd,
Croydon CR0 4YY

Scribe is committed to the sustainable use of natural resources and the use of
paper products made responsibly from those resources.

978 1 913348 38 0 (UK edition)
978 1 922310 23 1 (Australian edition)
978 1 925938 92 0 (ebook)

Catalogue records for this book are available from the National Library of
Australia and the British Library.

Supported by the City of Melbourne Arts Grants and Creative Spaces
programs.

scribepublications.co.uk
scribepublications.com.au

OVERDUE

Just like grief, waiting had stages. And by two o'clock, Judy Novak was well and truly in the anger phase.

Thirty years old! And still bloody selfish. Well, whose fault is that?

The Mutineers' Lodge cabins had been renovated for high season. Marine-blue carpet. Brochures swimming under coffee-table glass. Drapes so red they hurt her eyes. 'You have to stay at Mutes'!' Paulina had insisted, months back. 'I'll make your bed and serve you breakfast!'

So proud of the fact that she could finally make a bed. Making an appointment — not so much.

Two hours late! Island time be damned. It's selfish, bloody selfish.

Judy had called — how many times? Enough. She'd call again. Just once. On the bedside phone, so plasticky-new it looked like a toy.

NOVAK, PAULINA

The only 'Novak' in the Fairfolk Island phone book. Almost, it gave Judy goosebumps, seeing her daughter's name so alone in that forest of Kings, Carlyles, Stevenses, Greatorexes.

Pick up! For chrissakes, Paulina. Pick up!

Each ring like a screaming newborn. Torture. She slammed the phone.

'Fine! You're a grown woman. So am I.'

Judy stared at the phone for a long moment, like it was a snake slithering into a bush. Then she picked up her beach bag, threw a challenging glance at her pink-faced reflection.

'I'm fine.' She swiped a tear. 'You're fine.'

'Excuse me. If you see my daughter—'

He didn't remember Judy, the fat clerk in the mutiny-red shirt. His smile said as much: a crocodile smile that didn't quite meet the sea-glass eyes with their curiously beautiful dark-brown lashes. A man her age. It was one thing being invisible to young blokes, but had this man really lumped her in the same category as all the nearly-deads with their coach tours and activity calendars?

'I'm Paulina's mum,' she reminded him.

'Of course you are!' Patronising. 'What can I do for you, ma'am?'

Judy's eyes wandered down to his name tag: *Bazel.*

'Well. She was supposed to meet me at my cabin two hours ago. At least, that's what we agreed? After her walk. Paulina said we'd go to the beach.'

Bazel cupped his chin in his hands and frowned. 'Is that right!'

A gold ring glinted in his right ear. His desk was shaped like a prow, the wall behind it painted with half-naked Polynesian women and rogue British sailors, looking out to sea at a burning ship.

'That one's my ancestor, Samuel Stevens.' Noticing her looking, Bazel pointed out one of the sailors. 'I made sure the artist gave him lots of muscles.'

'Which one's his wife?'

'Your guess is as good as mine.' He shrugged sheepishly. 'That one there with the white flowers is Gideon King's bride, Puatea.'

'Very … historical.' Sighing, Judy straightened the strap of her beach bag. 'If you see Paulina, tell her I've gone for a drive. I'll be back in an hour or so. She can call me then, if she likes.'

Judy didn't wait around to listen to Bazel's reply; she had things to do, goddamnit. Although, once behind the wheel of her rented Hyundai, she wasn't quite sure what.

Where are you, Paulina?

There'd been no rental cars when she and Marko honeymooned on the island thirty years ago. Just hiking. Horseriding. Men cracking onto her every time Marko left her side — asking *what's a girl like you doing with that old bloke with the funny accent?* Even so, Judy felt a pleasant sense of déjà vu, easing onto the sleepy palm-lined road.

The Pacific peek-a-booed from the bottom of the hill. For a moment, Judy thought the car might roll straight into it. Instead, the road twisted and flattened out to a disconcertingly British expanse of fields, ruins, grim Georgian architecture. Pine trees tall as skyscrapers. Judy slowed as she neared King's Pier, parking behind a cluster of trucks and utes. On the horizon, dockers in hi-vis shirts bloomed like hallucinogenic flowers.

'Afternoon!' A bloke, half-hidden by the truck he was loading up, startled her as she exited the Hyundai. He was old for a labourer, with a skinned-seeming head, hair so colourless and closely cropped it looked more like a film of sweat.

'Afternoon.' Judy smiled. 'Working on Good Friday? You poor things!'

'First supply ship in six weeks, all hands on deck. See these boxes?' He motioned Judy closer, deftly sliced through the cardboard. 'I've been telling the grandkids to expect chook eggs in this year's Easter-egg hunt. Better late than never, eh?'

'I miss those days.' Judy looked down at the bright-foiled chocolate eggs. 'My daughter won't go anywhere near chocolate. She's thirty this Sunday.'

'Mother–daughter birthday trip, eh?'

'I'm just visiting. She's here on a work permit.' Already, Judy felt annoyed with herself for talking about Paulina — who, wherever she was, surely wasn't talking about *her*. 'She's … working now, actually. So much for the easy, breezy island lifestyle!'

The bloke winked. 'You need a local to show you some of that.'

Was he cracking onto her? Judy didn't stick around to find out — just squeaked a laugh and drifted away from the pier, toward the grassy clifftops. She could almost hear Paulina cackling at her back: 'Told ya! Fairfolk men are *desperate*!'

Judy stumbled upon a plaque, bowed her head to read:

After six torturous months at sea, the mutineers and their Polynesian wives found shelter on Fairfolk's paradisiac shores, and set HMS *Fortuna* on fire.

Judy walked on, until she reached a cemetery where elderly couples were wandering around like reanimated corpses. She knew there was a beach just beyond the cemetery, a beach Paulina loved. But when the wind picked up behind her, bringing with it a fresh, earthy smell, she took it as a sign.

By the time she got back to the car, her carefully blown hair was stringy, the powder on her nose dissolved. But worst of all was the tender thought rattling through her brain:

Wherever you are, Paulina, I hope you're safe from the rain.

Judy drove into town. Everything was closed, including the pubs, which had been her greatest hope for finding Paulina. She parked and sat behind the wheel, hopelessly watching the miserable strip of shops being rained on. A cow wandered past. A *cow*. No people. Not for a long time — until she saw a blonde woman bustling across the road to let herself into a shop: *Tabby's Treasures*.

'Sorry? Are you open?' Judy knew it was a desperate thing, barging muddy-footed into this woman's shop on a public holiday. 'Sorry — I was just wondering? Could I use your phone?'

She could see the woman's face forming a 'no'. It wasn't a kind face. Pretty once, maybe. Young once. Still youngish in a pert, freckle-nosed sort of way — or younger than Judy's, anyway. She had the eyes Judy kept seeing everywhere: pale with dark lashes.

'I'm sorry. Just quickly, I was hoping — could I just call my daughter?'

'Is there not a phone where you're staying?' the woman asked, in that accent Judy had just now decided she hated.

'There is, but … Look, I'll be *quick*.'

The woman relented. Judy apologised for her muddy feet, followed the woman like a sniper, eyes trained on the fat spilling over the outline of her bra. There was a scrunchie in her rain-frizzed hair. A *scrunchie*. 'What pretty things,' Judy murmured. 'What a pretty shop.'

The phone was behind the counter. 'I'm just here for some paperwork,' the woman explained. 'The supply ship's arrived. I'm expecting a big delivery tomorrow.'

Judy picked up the phone, tried to dial.

'I'm sorry. I should know it by now. My brain's not working.'

With a hissy little sigh, the woman dumped a lean phone book on the counter, stood back with folded arms as Judy fumbled, dialled.

Hey, I'm not here. Sorry! Leave a message or see ya when I see ya. Whatever! Bye.

'I'm coming over, Paulina,' Judy said, in her sternest undertone. 'Okay? I don't care … what state you're in. I'm coming over. Okay?'

The machine beeped. Judy hung up, lost her nerve. Her eyes latched onto the closest thing: a tray of pale-aqua business cards on the countertop.

'Oh, are you "Tabby"?' She picked one up: *Tabitha King, Custom Designs.* 'Like the shop? You design everything, do you?'

'Just the jewellery,' Tabby said, in a distant voice. 'Everything's Fairfolk-made, though. I export, too.'

'Oh. Lovely.'

'Take as many as you like.' A saleswoman's voice edged in. 'I'm open tomorrow. Monday, too. Please, do come back, when I'm open.'

'Of course …' Judy's eyes scanned for something else: fastened on a pendant in the nearest cabinet. 'The angelfish! The little angelfish. Oh, I *have* to get her that!'

'The angelfish?' Tabby looked over her shoulder. 'I'll put it aside.'

'Yes — no!' Judy panicked. 'Please, you don't understand? It's her birthday. Her thirtieth. I'll be a terrible mother if I don't get it now.'

In fact, Judy had already bought far too many presents: a new Sony Discman, headphones, pedometer, Reeboks, and enough batteries to last the year.

'Cash,' Tabby demanded. 'One hundred and fifty, cash. Our EFTPOS machine isn't working.'

Judy knew this woman, this *cow*, was screwing her over. She also knew she would've paid any amount for the little angelfish, in that moment.

'Of course,' Judy replied, with hysterical poise. 'Thank you very much. And please — if you can — please gift-wrap it.'

Pulling onto the gravel-and-mud of Tenderloin Road, Judy had the feeling she was trespassing. A downcast Fairfolk flag, dripping against its pole. A bathtub murky with rainwater. A miniature plantation of palm trees, their bases sharp with rat traps. Then she noticed the letterbox: shaped like a cow, with a slot for a bum-crack. She laughed, louder than it warranted. Paulina had told her about the letterbox, and the lady it belonged to — her landlady, Vera.

Judy parked in front of the main house.

It was a white clapboard house with an olive-green tin roof. Wraparound porch cluttered with fishing gear and mismatched furniture. Judy wondered if she should knock before proceeding to the cottage. Then she spied Paulina's little blue Mazda parked outside.

So she is home! Unless—

The windows of the Mazda were open. Carpet drenched. Upholstery drenched. A puddle of water on the dashboard, flecked with dirt and stray pine needles.

'Oh, Paulina!' Judy cried, and shivered all over.

She crossed the yard to the cottage — a smaller, boxier version of the main house. Banged on the flyscreen. 'Yoo-hoo! Paulina!'

No answer, except the jingle-jangle of a cat, scampering out of the bushes and winding its fluffy, toasted-marshmallow-coloured body around Judy's legs.

Judy grimaced. '*You're* not Paulina.'

She tried the door. Unlocked. This wasn't *so* strange, was it? Paulina was always saying nobody believed in locks here.

The cat dashed inside.

Right away, Judy could tell two things: Paulina wasn't home, but had been. Car keys on the counter. A half-empty water glass. The cat leapt onto the counter, sniffed the water.

'Shoo!' Judy cried. 'Get down.'

She peeked inside the pantry. Canned soup. Canned veg. Alcohol — a lot of it.

'Oh, Paulina,' Judy repeated, noticing a stack of empty goon boxes by the bin.

The bathroom, though, made her proud. No dirty clothes on the floor. Only a single long brown hair in the sink. Towels hung from a rack on the door, the hooks shaped like seahorses. Even a wicker hamper for her laundry.

Judy looked through cabinets, heart hammering. Found Paulina's blow-dryer, plugged it in, and puffed her hair back to life.

Her heart was calmer, entering Paulina's bedroom. *Not snooping. Just checking.*

The bed was made. Good girl. Cobalt-blue damask covers she knew Paulina had ordered from a catalogue, waited weeks for.

A copy of *Anna Karenina* on the bedside table. Judy opened the bedside drawer.

Phone book. Birth control. Diary.

She should've known better; she'd read Paulina's diary once when she was a teenager, and they'd fought bitterly about the contents. But surely things were different now?

March 21, 2002
Hangover. Fat pig. Sick of this shit, wish I was dead already.

Judy shut the diary away, fought the tears. *Oh, Paulina!* 'Mrep!' The cat slunk into the room, pounced on the bed, and stalked toward Judy's lap. Judy jumped to her feet. Snatched a tissue from the box by the bed, blew her nose — then wondered how often Paulina used those same tissues to clean up after men.

That's what you get for snooping!

Crossing the room, Judy paused to check her hair in Paulina's vanity, to spray Paulina's perfume. Picked up the framed photo Paulina kept of herself, taken by her ex, Vinnie, outside Marko's village in Croatia. Judy had never seen the village. Didn't especially want to. Still, she'd envied Paulina — twenty-five and zipping off to Europe with a 65-litre backpack and the Greek boy she almost married.

'Knock, knock!' a cheery voice — not Paulina's — called from the front door. 'Fresh-laid Easter eggs.'

The cat sprinted to meet the voice. Judy followed it, face burning; she was sure the snooping would show on her face. 'Hello? I'm just looking for—'

'You must be Judy.' The woman, previously just a silhouette in the flyscreen, let herself in, and, in one fell swoop, set down a basket of eggs and scooped up the cat. 'I'm Vera. I see you already met the Queen of the World, Miss Katie. Paulina's out, is she?'

A tall woman, wide-hipped, brown as toast, older than Judy — but not so much older that she'd call her 'old', like Paulina did. *I'm renting from this old lady now. Vera, the old landlady. The old bitch next door's on at me for smoking again.* Vera's dark-grey hair was short as a man's, her clothes also mannish: boots, jeans, grey flannel. Slanted, very dark eyes. One of the few Islanders Judy had seen who looked typically Polynesian, instead of like a run-of-the-mill sunbaked Anglo-Australian.

'I don't know where she is. She told me she'd meet me at Mutineers' Lodge, but that was hours ago.' *Don't cry. Do. Not. Cry.* Judy looked determinedly at the couch. 'Maybe I should go back to the hotel?'

'Absolutely not.' Vera's face smoothed in sympathy. 'Come up. I'll make some calls.'

The cat squirmed in Vera's arms as she led Judy across the yard. 'I wait on Miss Katie hand-and-foot, but she prefers Paulina. Every time she hears her come in — *whoosh.*'

'Cats love Paulina,' Judy played along.

'Cleopatra reincarnated,' Vera quipped. A border collie lazing on the verandah grumbled as she side-stepped it. 'Don't mind Jake. He's just lovesick.'

The house was busy with weekend clutter: a leaning mop, draped rags, splayed newspapers, and, on the kitchen table, a bowl of fish-guts. Vera dumped the cat, moved the bowl to the floor. 'Rocky!' she called. In response, a beetle-browed older man shuffled into the kitchen and shook Judy's hand, shuffled out again.

'Pacific Games re-runs.' Vera rolled her eyes. 'Coffee, tea, Milo? Or you can have a beer with Rocky.'

'Milo. Thanks.'

Vera nodded toward the lounge. Obediently, Judy went and sat on the weathered navy-blue couch across from Rocky's armchair.

Weightlifters grunted in a grainy gymnasium. Vera returned with a mug and a plate of Scotch fingers, nudged Rocky's ankle with her boot. He lowered the volume. Sitting beside Judy, Vera reached behind the couch for a directory and an off-white corded phone.

'Yorana, Kymba.' Vera listened for a moment, brow furrowed — then started speaking rapidly in a funny, old-timey almost-English.

'Sorry,' she told Judy, after she hung up. 'It's just easier speaking Fayrf'k, if you want to get to the point.'

'Oh, don't mind me.' Judy waved her hand. 'You can speak Klingon for all I care.'

It was disconcerting, though, as more conversations rushed by, seemingly varied in detail and nuance, yet all with the same result — no Paulina.

'Camel?' Rocky suggested after his wife hung up again.

Vera dialled a new number. Judy nibbled a Scotch finger. Stale. Dipped it in her Milo. Why had she asked for Milo?

'He's nay home,' Vera muttered, hanging up.

'Eddy?' Rocky suggested.

Vera scowled. '*Nay*, Rocky!'

Rocky shrugged, chuckled. Vera dialled. 'Yorana, Eddy …'

Miss Katie leapt onto the couch, kneaded Judy's thigh. Vera's face was red when she finished her call. She muttered something vicious at Rocky in Fayrf'k, didn't translate. Rocky chuckled again, drained his tinnie, and shuffled out.

Judy finished her Milo. Vera dialled. 'Merlinda … ?' Jake loped into the room, followed by Rocky, who offered a cold-beaded can to Judy.

'No. Thank you.'

Vera thrust out her hand. After finishing up the call, she cracked it open and swigged. 'Merlinda saw Paulina driving.'

'Oh?' Judy perked up.

'Around eleven am.'

Judy's heart sank. 'Oh.'

Jake whimpered and lay on the rug. Miss Katie's tail lashed. 'Toa?' Rocky suggested, and it was suddenly horribly clear to Judy that he was no longer interested in the faded footage.

Judy stood up. 'Excuse me. Mind if I—'

'Right down the hall,' Vera pointed, already dialling.

The bathroom was done up in peaches-and-cream tiles, daisy decals on the walls. Judy ran the taps. Washed her hands; washed her face; wept. Washed her face again. 'You're fine,' she reassured her reflection. 'We're both fine.'

Lifting the fuzzy peach toilet lid, Judy unbuttoned her shorts, tugged aside her swimsuit, and peed a stinging trickle. *UTI? Wonderful.* On the wall above the toilet was a picture of a dreamy-faced fairy squatting on a toadstool, bloomers around her ankles, thought-bubble at her head:

Sometimes I sits and thinks
And sometimes I just sits.

'Gawd!' Judy despaired. 'Get me out of here!'

When Judy returned to the lounge, she found Vera and Rocky huddled and talking quietly in Fayrf'k. Across the room, the mantel clock struck seven.

'Shame on me! It's your dinnertime.' Judy sucked in a lungful of stuffy air. 'Thanks for your help, but I really should get back to Mutineers' Lodge. Maybe she's left a message.'

'I tried Mutes'.' Vera said. 'Tried everyone we could think of; it's *strange ...*'

A splitting pain shot through Judy's chest. She closed her eyes, leaned against the mantel. When she opened them, Vera was standing before her, lips pursed white.

'It's real strange, I have to tell you. The sort of place Fairfolk is ...' Vera gestured. 'You sneeze in your backyard, five people shout "bless you". You buy a bunch of flowers, ten people ask who you're trying to impress. Everyone's always looking over each other's shoulders.'

Nodding, Judy tried not to think of the main street, deserted in the rain.

'And Paulina: she's eye-catching. I guess you know that. It's strange, no one seeing her in so long.' Vera glanced at Rocky. 'I hate to say it, but ...'

Don't say it! Don't.

'I think we should call the police.'

Like a slap: this thought Judy had been avoiding, so clearly articulated.

'Oh! No. She's just ...' But Judy had no justifications. 'Please. Do you really think—'

'I *do*,' Vera cut in. 'Mother to mother? I think it's for the best.'

As Vera dialled, Judy's throat tightened. To hide her hot, broken face, she examined a little clay jar on the mantel, a line-up of framed photographs.

'Jake as a puppy.' Rocky came up behind her, pointed. 'Katie as a kitten.'

Judy nodded politely. He pointed at another picture: a beautiful girl with waist-length black hair. 'Vera as a puppy, kitten?'

'Gorgeous,' Judy mumbled. 'Are those your kids?'

'Vera's kids.' Rocky grinned. 'Nothing to do with me.'

'He said to come to the station.' Vera stood, dusting cat-hair from her jeans.

'The *station*?' Judy cried, affronted.

'It's close. Five minutes.' Vera avoided her eye. 'I'll drive.'

Rocky went to the coat rack for windbreakers, whistled at Jake, who ran ahead to the door.

Outside, the sea breeze licked Judy's cheeks. They hopped into Vera's jeep: Rocky in the back with Jake, Judy shotgun.

'Some tourists aren't prepared for how cold it gets at night.' Vera started up the jeep. 'Of course, that's how it goes when you've got the sea on all sides. Big temp drops.'

You bitch, don't you dare talk to me about the weather. 'I know. I spent my honeymoon here. Did they say why they want us at the station?'

'Didn't say much.' Vera rolled onto Tenderloin Road. 'Your honeymoon? Really.'

'1969,' Judy said, her willpower like a punctured tyre. 'I wanted to go to the Central Coast. But Marko wanted to take me somewhere exotic.'

Only when they got to the station did Judy realise that she didn't mind the small talk; didn't want it to end, actually. As if reading her mind, Rocky fished a flask from his pocket.

'That's a good idea,' Vera said, then waited until Judy drank.

It was cold inside the station, despite the liquor, despite the windbreaker. A pimple-faced young cop stood to attention.

'Hank!' he called into the office behind him.

An older man appeared: square black crew cut, square florid face, watery eyes the same light-green that so many of the Islanders had.

'Mrs Novak, thanks for coming down. I'm Detective Sergeant Hank Turner.' The man offered a meaty handshake. 'I believe your daughter's been missing since midday. Can you describe her?'

'Pretty,' Judy blurted out.

'Can you be more specific? Height, weight, hair colour, things like that?'

Did it mean anything that he wasn't wearing a hat?

'Dark brown hair, with a fringe; probably in a ponytail, if she was exercising,' Judy chose her words as carefully as birthday gifts. 'Dark eyes. Medium height — 167 centimetres, I think.' *Don't look at him. Keep talking.* 'Slim, very slim … I always tell her, she doesn't need to diet so much, but she never listens.'

The man opened his mouth. *Don't look! Keep talking.*

'Thirty years old. She's thirty this Sunday. *Hates* it. I've been telling her, though, she shouldn't worry; thirty is still young. It's still so young …'

Don't look! He wants me to look, the bastard, but I won't—

'Mrs Novak. I'm sorry to tell you—'

Don't! Bastard. Don't you dare!

'Mrs Novak. A body has been found.'

Y2 KILL ME NOW

Paulina started drinking at midday, but so did *all* the bridesmaids. Mimosas, gulped between mud wraps, facials, bikini waxes, and mani-pedis at the Nirvana Spa in Mosman. After that was the Dom Pérignon while they were in their movie-star chairs for hair and make-up. Another bottle of champers was chilling in the limo. 'Shame to waste it!' Paulina popped it, and three of the other chicks cheered. But Carli and her boring cousins said no thanks, they didn't want to smudge their lippie.

By the time they boarded the *Stella Maris* an hour before sunset, Paulina was buzzed enough to trip a little in her kitten heels, to wolf-whistle in the general direction of the prime minister's residence as they pushed off from Kirribilli Wharf.

'Missed ya chance, Johnny-boy! Carli's taken!'

Later, milling around on the deck, waiting for the sun to go down, she nicked a glass from the tray one of the cute boys in white was carrying. 'Wait till you see Carli,' she told Kyle, the groom-to-be. 'She looks just like Rose DeWitt!'

Someone took Paulina's drink away for the photos. Bridesmaids and groomsmen, all posed against the prow of the yacht.

'Geez.' Paulina smiled up at the guy she was paired with. 'You're *tall*.'

A little while later, she stood on the guy's foot and said, 'Oops!', patted his pocket square. A little after that, she touched his shirt. '*Love* these black shirts! So dashing!'

Kyle's sister Adrianna poked Paulina in the ribs. 'He's *seventeen*.'

'Oops!' Paulina winked a glittery eyelid. 'Gotcha!'

She couldn't see any more boys in white, after the photos. Anyway, it was time to get in position. Her dress itched. She scratched the flatness between her tits, right below where the cowl-neck cowled.

'Paulina!' Kirsty hissed. 'You're like a bloke with his balls!'

Then there was a sudden hush that made her giggle, then the three-piece band started up, and sure as Paulina's ballooning bladder, there was Carli on her dad's arm, and even if Paulina did someday find another bloke willing to say *I do*, she'd never have that moment. Thinking this, she got all teary, started sniffling almost as much as Carli's mum.

'Shhh.' Kirsty reached and stroked Paulina's arm. 'Shh, Pauls. S'alright.'

Paulina gave a big, ugly sob — big and ugly enough to attract death stares — then turned off the waterworks. She was giggly again once Carli and Kyle were at the altar.

'Psst!' She brushed a fleck of sea spray from Carli's veil. 'Carli!'

Carli swivelled her neck minutely. Cut her eyes at Paulina.

'All good!' Paulina mouthed, thumbs up.

But really, she was dying for a drink.

Paulina wasn't *that* drunk. It was the lighting!

So dim and flashy, blue-and-red, and strobes wandering like floaters in and out of her field of vision. How was she to know who was age-appropriate and who wasn't?

'Life isn't fair!' she moaned, as yet another bloke flitted in and out of the men's, wiping his hands on his suit pants. 'Why's life so *unfair*?'

'You can try your luck in there.' He nodded. 'Wouldn't recommend it, though.'

He made as if to go. But Paulina saw him throw a glance at her neckline.

'Hey.' She grabbed his arm. 'For real, I'm *busting*. Can you guard the door for me? Please?'

The guy looked at her French-tipped manicure. 'Wouldn't recommend it, love.'

'Yeah?' Paulina took a step back into the line. 'Who are you? What would you know?'

'Who are *you*?' The guy rejoined. 'I know — you're one of the bridesmaids. I saw you up there. You girls looked beautiful, in your beautiful dresses.'

'Yeah?' Paulina swished her skirt, stumbled on some chick's foot. 'This dress?'

'Beautiful.'

'Yeah, nah. The material's kinda itchy.'

'Itchy?' He ogled her as she scratched herself. 'Looks nice and silky to me.'

'Ha-ha!' Paulina threw her head back, felt her undies dampen. 'Oh! Shit.'

She crossed her legs, lost her balance a bit. The guy steadied her; took the opportunity to caress the silver satin at her hip. Paulina giggled. 'That *tickles.*'

'Bride coming through! Bride needs the loo!'

It was Kirsty yelling, jumping the queue with Carli. The guy made himself scarce.

'Pauls! *No.*' Kirsty grabbed her hand. 'That was Carli's *godfather.*'

'Godfather?' Paulina fanned herself. '*Mio dio!*'

Carli's face looked profoundly unhappy, pores starting to show through her makeup. Paulina changed tack. 'How're you gonna piss in that dress? Need help?'

Carli nodded.

'Bride coming through!' Paulina shouted. 'Bride needs the loo!'

'You looked so beautiful up there,' some old lady at the sinks told Carli. 'Such a beautiful couple. Congratulations to you and Kyle. I hope—'

Paulina started banging on cubicles. 'What, are you drowning?'

A girl with smudgy makeup and a velvet dress emerged, abashed. The three of them stuffed themselves inside the cubicle. Paulina got to the toilet first.

'Ohhhh!' Her eyelashes fluttered. 'It's better than sex!'

Carli and Kirsty both gave her the stink-eye.

'Your turn, babe.' Wiping, Paulina scooched aside. 'Let me get your skirts.'

Carli settled on the loo with a frown. 'Did you eat, Paulina? Please tell me you ate.'

'Yeah-hh.' Rolling her eyes, Paulina handed Carli a wad of paper. 'Course!'

The bride clearly didn't trust her though, since she personally fetched a tall glass of water and a plate of croquembouche.

'Thank you, *Mrs* Portelli!' Paulina gulped the water, took a bite of profiterole. 'Mmm! Sure you don't want some? Hey, wanna come for a smoke?'

Carli had quit months ago, *of course*.

Paulina tripped up to the deck, spitting into her napkin as she went. She chucked her profiterole in the ocean and laughed. A boy in white looked at her.

'Hey.' Paulina smiled. 'Got a light?'

He was *cute*. 'Caterers are always cuter than the guys in the wedding. Why is that?' she asked, lighting up. 'I've been to *shitloads* of weddings this year. Guess you must too? Gawd, I hate them! Did you see the banner? *Y2 Kyle and Carli?* Y2 kill me now! Ha-ha.'

He smiled. Cute! Stubbed out his ciggie. 'Better get back to work.'

'Hey!' she called as he made for the stairs, but the look he gave her, like she was a bit of gum on his shoe. '… Is there a phone around here?'

'That way.'

Paulina found the payphone, in a nook full of ropes and lifesavers.

'Vinnie. I know you said not to call anymore, but since it's New Year's I just wanna tell you I'm a new person now; that person who screwed up isn't me; I've changed; I've tried so hard to change — please, just, I don't think you really understand how sorry I am? I'll be sorry till I'm dead. Till you forgive me and love me again, I feel like I could die; I'm so sorry …'

She wept into the machine's beep. Hung up and banged her head on the glass.

A bunch of smokers appeared on the deck.

'What's the time?' she asked the nearest one. 'When's this millennium gonna end?'

Paulina wasn't looking for a fight. She just wanted to dance!

Dance her troubles away — to music that wasn't completely crap.

'You again,' said the DJ.

'Yeah, listen, I know you said Nirvana's like the most alternative thing you got, but I think maybe you're just thinking about grunge when there's so much we haven't talked about. Like obviously *you've* never heard of post-punk but howabout some classic punk? "Rock the Casbah"? "Blitzkrieg Bop"? I can compromise! Bloody hell, play some Britpop. Bowie. *Everyone* likes Bowie! Work with me, mate. C'mon.'

'What are you, a muso?'

'I'm a financial advisor.' She squinted, leaned over the turntables and arched her back. 'Look, babe. Maybe it's easier if I just come over there and—'

'Pauls!' Kirsty said. 'Come here.'

'What? Gawd, this guy's shit. I know he's a second cousin or something, but bloody hell. Where's my drink?'

'Let me fix your hair.' Kirsty fixed her hair. 'Let me take your photo.'

Obligingly, Paulina posed for the disposable camera. As soon as they were done, she made for the DJ again, but Carli had taken her place. Like it wasn't enough she was *married*.

Paulina veered toward the bar. To her surprise, though, Carli turned around and looked at her; a smile spread across her face like jam on bread. A new song started.

'Gunners?' Paulina cried. 'He had Guns N'Roses this whole time?'

Carli grabbed her hand, pulled her into a slow dance. 'That horrible concert at Eastern Creek, remember? It was so hot.'

'It was *brilliant*.'

'Remember how they charged $2 for those tiny cups of water?'

'Remember that bogan you hooked up with? Oi, why aren't you hooking up with Kyle now? Don't tell me you're waiting till you get to Fiji!'

'Fiji?' Carli looked confused. 'Our honeymoon's on Fairfolk Island.'

'Pffft! Isn't that place for old people?'

'It's actually really—'

'*Paaatience*,' Paulina sang, closing her eyes. Then they started leaking. 'I'm gonna die alone.'

'Patience, babe.' Sighing, Carli patted her back. 'Patience.'

'I called Vinnie.'

'No, babe. You can't be doing that. No.'

'But I'm sorry! He needs to know I'm so sorry.'

Carli sighed. 'You need to leave him alone.'

'Please, can't you tell him? I feel like I'm dying.'

'You're just drunk. It's worse when you're drunk.' Carli broke away from her. 'It's a bad thing, what you did. I don't know how else to say it. If Kyle did that to me, I don't think I could—'

'What? So, you reckon he's only gonna have sex with *you* forever?'

'Stop it.' Something passed across Carli's face, like she'd just got a whiff of dogshit. 'It's my wedding night.'

'Please, just. Tell Vinnie I'm sorry? Maybe if *you* call—'

'Kirsty! Can you take her? I can't do this!'

Carli left Paulina wet-faced on the dancefloor. Kirsty took her place, and Adrianna with her; both of them pinching Paulina's arms and telling her to shush, drink some water. In the bathroom, they got her to drink from the tap, cleaned up her mascara. While she was locked in a cubicle, she heard them bitching. 'She's a disaster.'

'I know. Totally desperate.'

Paulina flushed, walked out of the cubicle, and rinsed her hands with deeply feigned composure. 'Better?' Adrianna asked. Paulina nodded, got out her lip gloss and reapplied it. She looked sexy. At least there was that.

'I wanna dance,' she said.

They danced. To some R'n'B crap, bubblegum crap. Danced long enough for her to feel like she *looked* normal, though the hate was thrumming in her brain like bad music.

'Wanna smoke, Pauls?' Kirsty asked.

'Nah! Dancing!'

'Want more water, Paulina?' Adrianna asked.

'Cheers, babe!' As soon as Adrianna's two-faced back was out of sight, Paulina tiptoed up to the DJ.

'You know you're shit, right? You must know.'

'I'm not talking to you.'

'I'm just saying what everyone's thinking. You know a monkey could do your job?' She leaned closer. 'Hey, have you heard of Smashing Pumpkins? Everyone's heard of them. "Bullet with Butterfly Wings." C'mon!'

The DJ bowed his spiky blond head.

'Hey. Play some Sonic Youth?'

'Who?'

'Sonic Youth!' She clapped her hands. 'Bauhaus! Play Bauhaus. Have you heard of Peter Murphy, you stupid shit—'

'Paulina!'

'Oh! Cheers.' Paulina smiled sweetly and accepted the water. 'Didn't see ya there.'

Adrianna turned to the DJ. 'Tommy, I'm *so* sorry.'

'So sorry, Tommy!' Paulina parroted.

Then she chucked the water at his head.

Paulina had been back at work three weeks when she got the email. Three weeks on best behaviour: up at five-fifty to chuck out her bottles from the night before, then *Aerobics Oz Style* in her room, jumping away her hangover. Showering and leaving the house in a pencil skirt, pastel shirt, plastic clip in her hair, sunnies on, and Discman clipped to her waistband for the hour-long bus ride. Swallowing two Panadol with Berocca at her desk and resisting the urge to spew whenever some fat-arse walked past with a crumpet or tub of yoghurt. Doing her time, day in, day out.

Till she got Carli's email:

OUR FAIRFOLK HONEYMOON!

There was a photo attachment of Carli and Kyle on a white-sand beach with sky-scraping pines in the background. Carli was grinning so much she had dimples. Paulina zoomed in on Carli's love-handles, stretch marks, cottage-cheese thighs. She zoomed out again, hovered over the trash icon. But there was something about those pines.

That lunchbreak, instead of smoking as she power-walked around the block, Paulina stubbed out her cigarette in front of a travel agency.

'I wanna go to Fairfolk Island,' she told the chick at the counter.

'Fairfolk Island.' The chick furrowed her brow. 'Is that near Tonga?'

'Dunno. But that's where I wanna go.'

'Let me see if I can find a holiday pack—'

'Babe.' Paulina crossed her arms. 'I don't want a holiday. I wanna live there.'

COOKIES

'It's her,' Vera said. 'She's my tenant.'

Cows lowed in the hills around them. Cook's Falls trickled laboriously, like an old man pissing in the middle of the night. The grass was still damp from the storm, the earth soft as putty.

Dr Jimmy Greatorex nodded his thanks, pulled the plastic back over Paulina Novak's face.

Vera took a deep breath and walked back to the mother.

Already, the mother was a wreck. Had to know, already, that it could only be bad news.

And yet, seeing Vera, her eyes shone hopefully — as if it were still possible for all that knowledge to be undone.

'It's her,' Vera repeated.

There was a silence, like the world had simply ended. Then the worst sound Vera had ever heard in her life.

By far the worst. Worse than a Mutiny Day domestic. Worse than a cow giving birth. Worse than the Great Rabbit Cull of '65. Whatever sound Paulina had made when she went through the hell she went through, the sound the mother was making had to come close.

When it stopped, their relief — well, maybe they didn't move as quickly as they should've.

For like a woman possessed, the mother lurched toward the black plastic, which was shining like seawater in the floodlights.

'Let me see her. I have to see her one last time. I don't care.'

They got to her before she got to Paulina. But she'd seen enough.

Not as much as Vera, but *enough*.

The foetal huddle under the plastic. The coy peek of a sneaker, its angle all wrong.

'You did it, you finally did it.' The mother sobbed. 'Baby. Poor baby. I'm sorry.'

Vera wondered if it'd be kinder to let her keep believing it had been Paulina's choice.

It was Sergeant Hank Turner who explained it wasn't. The mother just shook her head.

'No. You're wrong.'

The nature of her wounds. The position of her clothing, he continued to explain.

'No,' the mother argued. 'Tell me the truth.'

Vera longed to get away from the mother. Get away from her, and the sickly, sticky dark of Cook's Falls. 'We'll know more after the autopsy,' the Sarge compromised. 'But her clothing. It was cut clean.'

Somehow, that got through to the mother. 'Somebody hurt her?'

'We'll know more after the autopsy,' the Sarge repeated. 'We'll find answers.'

The mother started sobbing again, hyperventilating, until Rocky got the flask in her mouth. 'She was just going for her walk.' She swallowed, red-nosed. 'She walked every day.'

'Aye.' Rocky fed her more liquor. 'Same time every day.'

The Sarge turned to Vera, lapsed into Fayrf'k. 'She's staying at Mutes'?'

'Aye.' Vera shook her head. 'But look at the state of her.'

'Nay husband. Single mother?'

'Widow.'

'Nay other children?'

'Jus' Paulina.'

'Poor ulvini.' The Sarge frowned. 'Nay people at all?'

'Paulina mentioned an auntie. Rich.' Vera rolled her eyes heavenward. 'Nay flights till Tuesday, but. Easter.'

The Sarge cussed under his breath. 'Can you take her till then?'

'Don't have much choice.' Vera glanced at Rocky, over the top of the mother's fair, bedraggled head. 'I'll put her in Miti's old room.'

Normally, the Sarge would've blushed at that. This time, he just nodded. 'Jimmy'll give her something. For sleep.'

'And the rest of us?'

'Want something?' The Sarge looked surprised.

Vera waved her hand. 'I'll be fine; I've been up since dawn. You've got some sleepless nights ahead, but.'

The Sarge grimaced. 'The mainland can have this, eh. Mainie girl, mainie problem.'

Vera inclined her head towards a plot of land just over the hill. 'Bes' tell the mainland police to pay a call to Mister Minister of Culture, up there. She had him over, other week. Got him pretty riled up.'

By the time they got the mother back to the house, whatever Jimmy Greatorex had given her had worked its magic.

'Alice in Wonderland?' she asked, eyelids sagging as Vera pulled the cartoon-covered bedspread over her. 'Why Alice?'

'My daughter Miti chose it. This was her room.'

It was possibly the cruellest thing Vera could've said, under the circumstances. But the mother just nodded and closed her eyes.

'It's nay "Novak".' Vera shook her head at Rocky, as they sipped their beers and picked at their Lent fish. 'That's the dad's name. If she's got people, they're nay Novaks.'

The phone rang; Vera reached for it mechanically. Kymba Burney-King. Somehow already she'd heard Paulina was dead, was asking *was it an accident?*

'Nay.' Vera sighed. 'Looked deliberate.'

Next time the phone rang, Vera didn't touch it.

'Funny pine?' Rocky offered, nodding toward the clay jar on the mantle.

'Nay. I bes' call Miti.'

Rocky shrugged. Struggled out of his armchair, legs knotted with veins and thin as fishing poles, and got a green nugget from the jar.

Vera had to ask. 'Anybody see you fishing today?'

Rocky inclined his head in Jake's direction, gave her a wonky smile. Vera couldn't smile back. After replacing the lid, he added, 'Some surfers, too.'

'Go on, then.' Vera waved him outside. Picked up the phone to call her daughter in the time zone where she was living now; still living.

———

Vera woke even earlier than usual. She went out to the woodpile in her boots and bathrobe, gazed across the orchard at the little blue Mazda parked outside the cottage. Probably, The Car Kings would buy it back at a discount. Unless the mainland wanted it for evidence.

She got the hot water system fired up, nice and early. When the officers arrived to go through Paulina's things, she was ready to take their orders. 'Coffee, tea, Milo?'

Miss Katie got underfoot as Vera was bringing the tray of mugs to the officers, snuck into the cottage and started sniffing around.

'Probably thinks she's getting a feed,' Vera apologised, taking back the squirming cat. 'Paulina was always feeding her. More often than she fed herself.'

A little later, Rocky hauled his boat from the garage. Snorkellers. He'd promised to take a group of them out to the reef, cheaper than the tour companies did it.

'She up yet?' she asked, nodding back at the house.

Rocky shook his head.

Vera didn't have much appetite, but she made herself some porridge, flicked on the TV. The news hadn't reached the mainland, yet.

Later, the burly chef from Mutes' came by with a shiny hard-shell purple suitcase, which looked crushable in his huge hands. His eyes were bloodshot.

'You know her well?' Vera asked.

'Saw her every day.'

'So did a lot of people.' She looked at his hands, wondered if they could've done all that damage. 'Take care, eh.'

The mother was still under her pile of blankets when Vera wheeled the suitcase down the hall and into her room. Her eyes fluttered as Vera entered, opened their milky-grey glaze just long enough to confirm there wasn't anything in the world worth seeing. 'There's fresh towels in the bathroom, when you're ready,' Vera mumbled, and gently made her retreat.

———

The Sarge swung by a bit after eleven, asked the million-dollar question. 'Is the mother up?'

'Nay yet.'

'We need her to make a statement.'

Vera knocked softly on the mother's door, peeked inside without looking. 'Judy?' The name felt strange on Vera's lips, like the name of someone else's child, suddenly put in her care. 'Sarge wants you to come to the station. Make a statement.'

The mother didn't move. After a while, though, she made a creaky sound, and a little later, quavered, 'I'm coming.'

The Sarge was by the mantle, sniffing the contents of Rocky's clay jar.

'Thought you said this was a job for the mainies?' Vera crossed her arms.

'Gotta look busy or there'll be mass hysteria.' He recapped the jar. 'The way the vinis are carrying on, you'd think she was one of our own.'

'Couldn't've happened to one of our own,' Vera humoured him. 'They all fly the coop as soon as they hit eighteen.'

'Modern women, eh.' He stuffed himself into Rocky's armchair. 'You told Miti yet?'

'You here to talk about Miti, then?'

'Jus' making conversation. We can talk about the mainie girl, if you rather.'

'Paulina.'

'How long's she been your tenant?'

'Since June, thereabouts.'

'Any trouble?'

'She liked her music loud. Smoked inside the cottage, sometimes. I told her off.'

'I can imagine.' He shook his head. 'Still remember you calling me a kuka plana when you busted me and Miti.'

'You'd do the same if you caught a married tane climbing in your daughter's window.'

Reddening, he drummed his fingers on the armchair's scratched-up fabric. 'She do drugs? The mainie?'

'Nay. Drank, but.'

He nodded at the window. 'Good view.'

'Nay much to see, verly.'

'You saw Ric White.'

'Jus' that one time. He left in a hurry. Slammed the door. Jake barked at him.'

The bedroom door creaked open; bathroom door clunked shut. Vera ducked into the kitchen and made Milo and toast; laid them out with a selection of spreads. When she returned, the Sarge was standing at the window, looking out.

'Good view,' he repeated. 'Must see all her visitors.'

'Nay many, verly.'

'Girl like that? They'd be pounding on the door.'

'I must be going deaf.'

'Heard she was pretty friendly with a nephew of yours.'

'Eddy?' Vera shrugged. 'Aye. I heard that too. Second-hand.'

'Never seen him around, then?'

'If I did, I'd get him to fix that on his way out.' Vera nodded at the cracked wall socket behind the TV. 'She's friendly with Joe Camilleri's boy.'

'Boyfriend?'

'Only ever saw them smoking on the porch and blasting music. I'd tell them to turn it down and he'd go home. Never spent the night, far as I know.'

'Girl like that? Why wouldn't he?' The Sarge stroked his double chin. 'Butcher's son. He'd have all the tools.'

Paulina's cut-up face rose up in Vera's mind like a curse.

'She was gone a few days, last spring,' Vera heard herself say. 'Came back with bruises.'

He raised his eyebrows. 'She say how it happened?'

'Said she fell. Looked like Fairfolk chivalry, to me.'

'Any visitors?'

'Jus' me. I brought her food. Seemed like she needed it.'

'Scared?'

'Never admitted it.'

'She with Camilleri's boy, then?'

'Nay. He only started coming a few months ago.'

'How many months?'

'You should ask her diary.'

His pale-green eyes widened. 'How'd you know she kept a diary?'

'She accused me of reading it.' Vera laughed. 'Like I've nay got enough to do, around here.'

The Sarge laughed too. Stopped short.

The mother.

'There's some breakfast on the table,' Vera switched from Fayrf'k to Queen's English.

The mother pulled out a chair, slowly, like it was made of lead. Sat in it stiff-backed and stared at her food like it was rotting flesh.

'If you want something else, let me know. I can fry you an egg. Porridge.'

The mother picked up a piece of dry toast with the slow movements of a stroke patient. Bit into it, getting more crumbs on her lips than in her mouth. The white of her scalp was visible beneath her straggly damp hair. It was too painful to watch.

Vera sat on the couch and waited. The Sarge joined her.

After a few minutes, the mother seemed to give up on her toast. Vera cleared the table. The Sarge cleared his throat.

'Alright, Mrs Novak.' He touched her shoulder gently. 'Ready when you are.'

The mother turned and looked at him, at Vera, with pure hatred.

Rocky got home while Vera was repairing a TV in the garage. 'How were the snorkellers?'

Rocky shrugged. 'Went to Cookies instead.'

Vera grimaced. 'Fairfolk Tourism nay dead.'

The Sarge dropped the mother off late that afternoon, looking like she'd been on the worst date of her life. She didn't want food or drink, just bed. They left her to it. When Vera finished fixing the TV, though, she got Rocky to help her lug it into the bedroom. Miss Katie tagged along, getting in the way again. Vera stepped on Katie's tail and, offended, she bolted under the bed — wouldn't come out, no matter how they coaxed.

'Hope she's not allergic.' Vera frowned, looking from the mother's lumped form to the glowing eyes.

They left the remote on the bedside table, along with a jug of water and a toastie.

Around seven, Rocky put on his good dark flannel shirt and told her he was going to the bowls club. A little after that, a shrill-voiced woman rang, calling herself Judy's sister.

'*How* can you tell me there's no flights till Tuesday? *How?* she interrogated Vera. 'My niece is *dead*. My sister's *stranded*. Is this how you treat grieving families on that godforsaken rock?'

'We're a tiny island.' Vera measured her words. 'Two thousand people. Nothing like this has ever happened here before.'

'Two thousand! And not one of you can give me a straight answer.' The sister inhaled raggedly. 'I know *for a fact* there's a charter flight from Canberra arriving tomorrow night.'

'Bes' talk to someone in Canberra, then.'

'What I want,' the sister said haughtily, 'is to talk to my *sister*.'

But the mother wouldn't.

'No!' she cried, eyes firmly shut, like she was having a nightmare. 'No! Go away.'

There was nothing for Vera to do but let the sister give her another earful. By the time she hung up, she was ready for a stiff drink, and bed.

She was woken a few hours later, though, by Barry White calling her to come get Rocky from the RSL. 'He's been fighting with Kobby.'

It was a sorry sight, pulling up to the bowls club and seeing Rocky, shirt untucked, squinting into the headlights.

'You miggy ul'tane.' Vera looked askance at his welted jaw. 'Kobby's twice your size.'

She started up the engine. Backed out. Rocky's chest started shuddering.

'He talked bad on ...' He gestured, struggling to remember the name. '... That girl.'

Next morning, getting ready for the Easter Sunday service, Vera bumped into the mother coming out of the loo. She bugged her bloodshot eyes at Vera's skirt, woven hat.

'Church,' Vera explained.

'UTI.' The mother winced. 'Have you got any ibuprofen?'

'I'll check.' Vera rushed back to the mother's room a couple of minutes later with a sleeve of pills and a fresh jug of water. 'I'll swing by the doctor's after church. Get you some antibiotics.'

The mother popped some tablets into her mouth. Sank deeper into her nest of tissues and bedding and stared at the TV's low-volume flicker.

'Shouldn't take those on an empty stomach.' Vera eyed the cold toastie on the bedside. 'Can I get you something else?'

The mother shook her head, then changed her mind.

'Cranberry juice, if you have it. And maybe … chocolate?'

Vera hurried to the kitchen. Returned soon after with a carton of apple juice and some Delta Creams. 'This's all we have. I'm sorry.'

The mother looked at the biscuits with disinterest. 'It's her birthday today. Did you know that? She's supposed to be thirty.'

'I'm sorry,' Vera repeated. Then: 'Your sister called last night? Caroline?'

'Caro.' The mother sighed. 'She probably thinks she can fix this. She can't.'

The mother raked her fingers through Miss Katie's fur.

'That stupid girl. She didn't want to be thirty. She was so *stupid*.'

'Sharp as a tack, mind,' Vera offered. 'Witty. Cracked me up, the things she came out with.'

The mother's face distorted, a savage mask of grief.

'Please go away now.'

Vera scurried from the room; barely had time to shut the door before the wailing started.

Something. Something had to be done. If not for the mother's sake, for Vera's — that sticky, dark grief that was entering her lungs like a contagion.

It wasn't a crime scene, the cottage. Easy to think of it that way, but whatever had happened hadn't happened there — and whatever they'd wanted for evidence, they'd taken. All that was left now was a sad mess of things belonging to a girl who wasn't alive to put them back in order.

Vera snatched up a pillow. A band T-shirt, soft and fragrant with old sweat. A perfume bottle, which had somehow made its way onto the bedroom floor. Last of all, a photo.

Too much? Even for Vera, looking at the photo was hard. But then, the mother hadn't seen Paulina's face.

'Some things from the cottage.' Vera averted her eyes as she re-entered the bedroom. 'Perfume. Pillow. Just some things of Paulina's.'

The mother looked up. Tentatively, Vera sprayed the perfume.

'Give them to me,' the mother demanded.

It was a muggy sort of day; Vera could feel it already. The hot-box stuffiness of the van, sweat-pits forming under the sleeves of her blouse. But it wasn't just that. It was the curve of Klee Welkin Road, cuddled by hills and sea, lined with police tape.

Paulina walked here.

How many times had she seen Paulina walk here? Paulina Novak, like clockwork. Busy, narrow hips in lycra. Dancing ponytail. Discman clipped to the band of her shorts. Seen her and thought — well, all sorts of thoughts.

That girl is deranged.

That girl likes being looked at.

That girl will get herself killed someday.

The road, though. She could have tolerated the road on its own; even the police tape. It was the people clustered at King's Lookout that really brought it home. The people, pointing not at the view, but something spray-painted on the tar.

Vera parked. Got out of the van to look at what everyone else was looking at.

HAPPY BIRTHDAY PAULINA

'They're saying this is where that girl was taken,' a woman with a baby, familiar to Vera by sight, clued her in. 'It's her birthday today.'

'I know.'

'You knew her?'

Vera nodded. 'I was her landlady.'

In the distance, church bells chimed the resurrection, for whatever it was worth.

HONEYMOON

'As a matter of fact, one of our waitresses at Great-O's is heading to the mainland for uni next month,' the lady on the phone, Merlinda Carlyle, told Paulina when she called Fairfolk Tours. 'If you're interested, I'll get Mick Greatorex to phone you, and you can work out terms.'

Paulina decided to forgo the gym that day, and get two rum and Diet Cokes after work instead, in addition to her usual trip to the bottle-O.

She got off the Cherry Hill bus smiley and starry-eyed, loving the blobby look of the trees in the twilight, the blurry people watering lawns. Her mum had bought a roast chook.

'Guess what?' Paulina plonked her wine on the kitchen counter. 'I'm moving to Fairfolk Island!'

'You're moving *where*?'

'Fairfolk Island.' Paulina kicked off her heels. 'You've probably never heard of it. It's this beautiful paradise island in the Pacific, between New Zealand and—'

'I *know* where Fairfolk Island is! I went there on my bloody honeymoon.'

'Oh yeah, you did, didn't you? Ha-ha-ha. Anyways, that's where I'm moving.'

'Does Westpac know this?'

'Nup.' Paulina skipped over to the cupboard for wineglasses. 'I'm gonna tell them to get stuffed first thing tomorrow, though. Don't worry.'

'Paulina!' Judy sighed. '*Please*. Not the good glasses.'

'It's a celebration. Dad'd want us breaking out the good stuff.' Paulina placed two wafer-thin crystal glasses on the counter, then got distracted by the tennis on TV. 'Ooh, who's he in the red shorts? I like him.'

'Sit down.' Judy sighed again. 'Let me do it.'

Paulina sat eagerly, giggled as the guy let out a loud, carnal grunt.

'Oh, he's *nice*.' A plate appeared in front of her. 'Ugh, Mum. Why'd you get chicken? You know I'm vegetarian.'

'Half the time you're vegetarian, half the time you're not. Half the time you don't even eat.' Judy griped. 'Fairfolk, Paulina? What are you on about?'

'I'm moving there.' Paulina peeled the skin off her chicken breast, put it to the side. 'This March. I got a job.'

'A job? On Fairfolk Island?'

'Yeah. Waitressing.'

'*Waitressing?* Judy gulped her wine. 'On *Fairfolk Island?*'

'Oi, where's mine? I bought that wine with my own money.'

'Eat some chicken first.' Judy hawk-eyed Paulina as she chopped her chicken into tiny pieces, mixed it into her salad, ate a dainty mouthful. '*More*, Paulina.'

Paulina obliged. 'So, the thing is, you keep telling me I need a change. So, I was talking to Carli today. She just came back from her honeymoon and says—'

'I thought you said Carli was a c-u-n-t.'

'I was *joking!*' Paulina clicked her fingers for wine. Judy shook her head. Paulina forked up the last of her chicken, swallowed without tasting. Clicked again.

'Be careful.' Judy brought her glass. 'Those glasses have seen more of the world than I have.'

'Like *that's* hard.' Paulina smirked. 'Anyways: I talked to this lady Belinda Carlisle at the Fairfolk Tours place, and she says even though it's minimum wage, every dollar I earn is *tax-free*. Also, there's loads of jobs not even advertised so really I just need to get my foot in the door. Also, they have the *best* beaches. Palm Beach is shithouse compared. Also, more importantly, you keep saying it's time I moved out. So? I'm moving to Fairfolk!'

Judy clutched her temples. 'I don't feel good about this.'

'Ugh! You're such a *hypocrite*.' A hot tear slid down Paulina's cheek. 'You're always saying how I've overstayed my welcome since the womb, and you wanna turn my room into a sewing room? Well, here I am trying to be master-of-my-own-fate, captain-of-my-own-soul, and you can't even say *one nice thing*!'

'No need for Shakespearean drama, Paulina.' Judy cringed as Paulina stomped to the kitchen for a refill. 'Calm down. We've both had long days at work.'

'Ugh! *You!* The thing with you is, you're only happy if I'm *miserable.*' Paulina emptied the last of the bottle into her glass, scrabbled in her gym bag for the second bottle. 'You were *ecstatic* when I told you me and Vinnie were broken up! You *love* having me here, washing my sheets, making me eat meat. Mum, you *know* I'm vegetarian—'

'Careful.'

'You just want me to be miserable with you. Well, too bad. I'm gonna have the best life on Fairfolk and there's nothing you can do!'

'*Careful.*'

'Whoops! He-he-he.' Paulina licked up the wine that had sploshed on her hand, then slit her eyes at Judy. 'Excuse me, mother? Fuck you.'

'Oh, come off it!' Judy yelled as Paulina stormed out, bottle in hand.

In the privacy of her bedroom, Paulina cried hysterically. After that, she scrawled in her diary and, after that, turned on the TV and giggled at the tennis players making sex noises. A little while later came her mum's soft knock.

'Piss off!'

'Just let me in for a minute,' Judy pleaded. 'Let's just talk.'

Paulina opened the door warily, and there was her mum, looking so daggy in her PJs, photo album tucked under one arm and holding a bowl of choc-ripple ice-cream.

'I thought you might like to see some pictures,' Judy said. 'Since you're so serious about this.'

As it turned out, the waitressing job fell through.

'There's been a fire at Great-O's,' Merlinda Carlyle told Paulina, three weeks before she was due to leave. 'The whole place is gutted. They'll be out of commission for a while. I'll let you know if something else comes up.'

'Oh, geez,' Paulina said, absolutely gutted herself. 'Keep me in mind, hey.'

When a week passed without any news, Paulina called Fairfolk

Tours. 'Nothing,' Merlinda said. 'Unless — do you have a forklift licence?'

'Nah, not really. Don't you have anything in the finance area? Banking? Sales?'

'It's not a good time for retail.' Merlinda sighed. 'I'll let you know.'

Merlinda never called and didn't answer the messages Paulina left. 'This Merlinda Carlyle's a lying bitch!' Paulina told anyone who'd listen — which, now she'd quit her job, was mostly just the housewives at the Cherry Hill Fitness Centre and her smug cow of a mum.

'Why don't you cancel your flight, while you still can,' Judy suggested, fifty times a day. 'You can work with me at the Student Help Desk till Fairfolk gets its act together.'

'I'd rather scrub toilets, thanks.'

Five days before Paulina's departure, Merlinda finally phoned back.

'I'm sorry. You seem very eager. But high season's winding down; I don't expect there'll be much till Mutiny Day in August. Why don't you call back then, if you're still keen.'

'*Merlinda.*' Paulina clawed at her eyes. 'Help me out. I'll do anything! I'll scrub toilets. I *have* to get out of this city, it's killing me.'

'Oh, really? I quite like Sydney. I can't wait to get over there for the Olympics.'

'Merlinda!' Paulina took a deep breath. 'I dunno if I ever told you this, but my parents *honeymooned* on Fairfolk Island? All my life, I've been hearing how it's the prettiest place on earth, then my dad got cancer and made me promise I'd go there with my own husband someday? Only, I met the most perfect guy, but he broke my heart, Merlinda. I'll never love again. Then the other week I was sitting in my office I had this epiphany, like: you don't have to wait around for the life you want, Paulina. It's the new millennium; you're an independent woman. So I said to myself—'

'Okay,' Merlinda interrupted. '*Okay.*'

'Okay?'

'Look: this is strictly under the table, okay?' Merlinda groaned. 'My dad's been a bit dotty since Mum passed, and god knows I'd rather not be putting out any fires at *his* place. I hope to inherit it someday! Why don't you go stay with him? Meals and board and a small allowance, and maybe you can help out here at Fairfolk Tours now and then.'

'Small allowance?' Paulina said meekly.

'Fifty dollars a week. Tax-free.'

Paulina bit her fist.

'Alright.'

Paulina moved to Fairfolk carrying as much liquor as she could in her 65-litre backpack — and more in her 30-kilo suitcase, and also bags of duty-free. 'Bloody hell, Paulina, you're going to Fairfolk, not the Prohibition era!' Judy complained as they packed the car for the airport, and again while unpacking it, and again when messing around with the luggage trolleys. Then it turned out they were in the wrong terminal — domestic instead of international — and Paulina cried, and Judy laughed at her. When they finally got in line for the flight to Fairfolk, Paulina was happy to see it was shorter than all the others — but dismayed seeing the other passengers.

'*Mum*, they're all *ancient*.'

'I told you. Newlyweds and nearly-deads.' Judy smirked. 'I guess wedding season's over.'

They argued again after going through security check. 'I'm almost twenty-eight! I can have a beer for breakfast if I want!'

'No, Paulina.'

'Last drink together! Live a little, Mum.'

'I'm having a coffee, and so are you.' Judy looked concerned. 'Honestly, you *worry* me. How do you expect to hold down a job over there if you're drinking round the clock?'

That hurt, bad. Stiff-backed, Paulina walked to the counter, told the girl:

'Two flat whites. But make mine skinny, alright?'

The girl nodded, got out two coffee cups and a texta. 'My name's Milica,' Paulina volunteered. 'Need me to spell it? M-I-L-I—'

Judy sighed loudly at Paulina's back. Smirking, Paulina swished her ponytail in Judy's direction. 'She's Ljubica. I'll spell that too, when you're ready.'

Shaking her head, Judy stormed off to find a table. The coffees took ages, tasted like shit. 'This tastes like shit!' Paulina proclaimed, loud enough for the girl to hear.

Judy sipped fastidiously. 'Are you trying to make me not miss you? Because it's working.'

'You're the one who took the day off to drive me — Susan from the gym would've done it.' Paulina tried her coffee again. 'Blergh! I'm gonna buy some magazines.'

Of course, her mum still cried at boarding-time. 'Call me as soon as you get there!'

'I'll try. Not sure if this old man's place has a phone, to be honest.'

'If he's creepy … Paulina. Don't even stay one night. I *mean* it. I don't care if you have to go to a hotel, I'll pay. Trust your gut, okay?'

'Yeah, yeah. Okay.'

'Love you. Gawd, I love you.' Judy sobbed. 'Finally — quiet time!'

'Yep. Whole house full of yarn. Love ya.' Paulina hoisted her duty-free bag onto her shoulder, blew kisses over it. 'Bye! Stop crying. You're embarrassing me. Bye!'

On board, there were so many empty seats, Paulina got a whole row to herself. She got out her magazines and Discman. The flight attendant told her off for stretching out before take-off, and Paulina said, 'Sorry!' to her face and, '*Bitch*,' to her arse. At take-off, her hands gripped the armrests, white with fear. She was happy above the clouds, shoes off, magazine in her lap — especially when bar service started.

'Rum and Coke,' she told the flight attendant. 'But make it Diet, okay?'

'Diet!' A white-haired lady across the aisle teased her. 'You young girls!'

'Ha-ha!' Paulina giggled. 'You're funny!'

'Excuse me, but you're so pretty, my husband and I were wondering—' The lady lowered her voice, like she was asking for a threesome. 'Are you an *actual* Fairfolk Islander?'

'Uh … yep? Sure am!'

'You're a *descendant*?'

'Descendant?'

'Of the Mutiny on HMS *Fortuna*! Gideon King and his swashbuckling men and their beautiful Polynesian wives!'

What the fuck! Paulina giggled. 'Yep. That's me.'

'Oh! How *exciting*! Bob, did you hear—? Oh, he's snoozing.' The lady lowered her voice another octave. 'May I ask — your *surname*?'

'Novak!'

'Novak?' The lady screwed up her face. 'That sounds … Slavic.'

'Yep!' Paulina beamed. 'See, my *mum's* an Islander. Only, she married a Slav, so Novak's my name? But we're totally descendants of that other guy, King. Yep.'

'Oh!' The lady clapped her hands. 'Slavic and Fairfolk! How exotic!'

'He-he-he.' Paulina sipped her rum and Coke. 'You're *funny*.'

Then she slipped her headphones back on, before she got in too deep.

The flight took three hours. She only got scared twice: when the ceiling of the plane shook, and when she accidentally flushed the toilet with her back and had to get up fast so her intestines wouldn't get sucked into the sky. She wasn't too scared when the plane started descending: the sea was so gorgeous and glittery, then out of nowhere these green-green cliffs, and creepy old buildings, and loads of pine trees, so dark green they looked black.

'Cows!' Paulina squealed. 'Aw, baby cows!'

'Has it been a long time?' her friend across the aisle asked. 'Since you were here?'

Not this shit again! 'Yeah, yonks!'

There were people on the tarmac, some holding signs. Paulina saw her name on a sign and felt excited — and then scared shitless. It had just occurred to her how small an island could be.

The person with the sign wasn't Merlinda Carlyle, like Paulina expected. It was a chick called 'Kymbalee'. That's how it was spelled, on her name tag. Paulina *tried* to be polite.

'Kymbalee! Is that how youse spell "Kimberley" here?'

'Oh … no. My mum just wanted to give me something different.' Kymbalee looked embarrassed. 'You can just call me "Kymba".'

'Kimba, the White Lion!' Paulina sang.

'Just "Kymba" is fine. Kymba with a "Y".'

'Kimba, the White Lion!'

Kymba turned bright red. Paulina tried harder to be *polite*.

'You don't have to help with my bags. They're heavy, hey.'

'It's my job.' Kymba's face turned redder when she felt how heavy Paulina's backpack was. 'It must be hard, deciding what to bring.'

'Not really. I made sure to pack lots of booze, but. I heard it's way expensive here. And Merlinda's pretty stingy, no offence. Where is she, anyways?'

'Oh, Auntie Merlinda thought it'd be nice for you to meet a young person.'

Paulina didn't realise those two were related. She also didn't realise Kymba, with her chubby body and granny glasses, was *young*. Paulina reminded herself to be polite.

'Here's my car. Merlinda thought it might also be nice if I, um, gave you a tour before taking you to Merle's. Um, I don't *have to* though. I mean, if you're ... tired?'

'Tour!' Paulina skipped to the car. 'Thanks, Kymba-lee!'

'Just Kymba is fine. Really, I prefer Kymba.'

'Ooo, Kymba, forgot to tell ya.' Paulina slipped into the suicide-seat. 'Scariest thing happened on the plane! When I sat down to piss, yeah? I accidentally pressed the flush with my back, and it flushed while I was sitting! It was soooo scary.'

'Oh, no.' Kymba, behind the wheel, finally cracked a smile. 'That *is* scary.'

'I know, right? Almost lost my intestines! Then there was this lady across the aisle; she was off her rocker, hey. Asked if I was part Polynesian and if I was related to some guy Gilligan King? I told her yeah and she *loved* it.'

'Oh.' Kymba lost her smile. 'I mean, you probably shouldn't ... *do that*. King's a big name here. It might upset some people, if a mainlander pretends — also, it's "Gideon", not "Gilligan". You mean you've *never* heard of the mutiny on the *Fortuna*?'

'Yeah, that's the one she said.'

Even so, Kymba told her this long story. Paulina sort of listened, sort of just stared out the window at the thickets of palms, splashy-bright flowers, cows, *whose* cows? When Kymba finished, Paulina whistled. 'Geez, those sailors must've been horny, chucking their captain overboard and kidnapping those Polynesian chicks like that. Why didn't they just bugger each other?'

'Well, anyway.' Kymba smiled tightly. 'That's some Fairfolk history.'

Later, Kymba added. 'Just so you know, I'm a descendant.My surname's "King". Actually, "Burney-King" now. I married an Englishman—'

'*You're* part Polynesian? No way!'

'I know, I don't look it.' Kymba sighed. 'A lot of us don't. A lot of us are named "King" here. Lots of things are named after Gideon King. It's a big name. I don't personally mind … but some people take it very seriously. Our tourist trade sort of depends on it.'

After that, Kymba drove her into town. It was so bloody small and ordinary-looking, like the main strip of a seaside village where people came to die.

Next was 'King's Lookout'. Paulina liked how the ocean looked, spread out into eternity like a sparkly blue blanket. But it scared her, too. She could see the island's edges.

Next was 'King's Pier'.

'Geez, I see what you mean about all the Gideon Kings,' Paulina said uneasily.

'It's a big name.' As they hopped out of the car, Kymba added brightly: 'Anyway, you chose a good day to come. The supply ship's arriving.'

'Supply ship?'

'It's very exciting. It only happens every month or so.'

There were some people standing around on the pier already, mostly old. Kymba pointed out a big ship on the horizon, then some smaller boats rippling towards it.

'Our men go out on the lighters to get the supplies. Because of the reef and the cliffs, big ships can't come any closer.' Kymba spoke with great passion. 'All large freight comes in this way. Building supplies. Livestock. Cars!'

The boats moved slower than snails. A tour bus full of old people pulled up to watch, oohing and ahhing and taking photos. Paulina was chilled to the bone.

'No offence,' she said, very politely. 'But is this what youse do for fun here?'

Some exciting things happened later, though. The first was when they passed a restaurant with a sign in the shape of a great white shark, jaws wide open.

'That's Great-O's. The Great-O White Shark Grill,' Kymba said. 'They had a big fire last month. They've had to shut down for repairs.'

'Ohh, Great-O's!' Paulina's heart swelled. 'That's my great white whale!'

'Great white shark,' Kymba corrected her. 'It's a shark.'

'It's *my* great white whale.' Paulina clutched her heart. 'Like, the thing I want but can't have? Oh, I love it!'

'They had a big fire,' Kymba repeated. 'They'll be closed for a long time.'

The other exciting thing was when Kymba took her to the bowls club for something to eat. 'Nah, I'm full of plane food.' Paulina poked her tummy. 'Let's get beers.'

They had to walk past a table full of blokes in hi-vis to get to the bar. The blokes were, miracle of miracles, not old. They all checked Paulina out.

She leaned over the bar extra-sexy, back arched and singlet crawling up to reveal a stretch of skin. When her beer came, she tasted the foam and glanced over her shoulder.

'Whew! New mainie in town,' one bloke said, and all his mates laughed.

Kymba steered her toward the door. 'It's nicer outside.'

The only blokes outside were old coots playing bowls. But the sun was nice, roasting Paulina's ponytail against her nape. She pulled up her trakkies, stretched her legs on a chair, glanced at the tinted-glass windows. 'What's a "mainie"?'

'Oh. It's not exactly a nice word,' Kymba said delicately. 'It comes from "mainlander", as in mainland Australian. But it can mean ... lots of things.'

'Like ... sexy things?'

Kymba sighed. 'Look. Can I give you some advice?' She had that mum-look, which told Paulina she was getting advice, either way. 'Don't get involved with any Island men. At least until you know who everyone is. Other mainlanders, that's fine. But try not to get involved with *Islanders*.'

'All them in there are Islanders?'

'Yeah, and they're all married. They'll act like they're not, if they see you as a "mainie". Then when it all hits the fan, they'll pretend it was all you, and you'll get the blame, and a reputation. A lot of girls have gone home in tears.'

Paulina didn't want to go home in tears, not yet.

'Thanks, Kymba,' she said sweetly. 'You're a really good friend, hey.'

Still, Paulina folded and unfolded her legs, smiled towards the glass every now and then. No harm in being looked at.

GOOD NEWS

'The good news is, she wasn't raped.'

That was the detective from Canberra; Judy had already forgotten his name. Something Polish. He'd made a big fuss about being Polish, assuming they had this in common — until she told him, actually, her late-husband was *Yugoslavian*. Judy didn't know how to keep new names in her head; anything new, really. All new things smelled like death. She yearned to be back in bed, with the T-shirt that smelled like Paulina.

'Oh. Wonderful.'

That was Caro. She thought she could fix anything with sarcasm. She couldn't fix *this*.

'I suppose …' It was like Judy's lungs were full of lead, how hard making words was. '… It's good she wasn't. But. *Why*, then?'

'We haven't ruled out a sexual motive,' the detective spoke slowly, as if to match Judy's leaden speech. 'The way her clothing was tampered with, along with the … *frenzied* nature of the attack. And Cook's Falls — "Cookies". It may not be significant, but locally it's known as a place for … couples.'

Judy couldn't help it; she was crying again.

It kept happening, the crying. Involuntary as bleeding.

The detective nudged his tissue box her way, though she already knew it was there.

'Ms Novak. We can stop anytime.'

Earlier, Caro had jumped down the detective's throat for calling Judy *Mrs Novak*. Caro was almost as bad as the detective. Judy thought some more about the nest of things she wanted to get back to: the pillow, the T-shirt, the photo of Paulina on the hillside in Croatia, looking more beautiful than anything in the universe.

'No,' Judy mumbled. 'Go ahead.'

'I want you to know, we're looking into all avenues, all motives.' He was still speaking slowly. A slow, drippy voice — like Chinese water torture. 'The nature of this case … it's unique. We're talking about an isolated population of less than two thousand. It had to be someone who was on the island that day, and still is—'

'You said *locally*, Mr Wozniak,' Caro interrupted. 'Locally, Cookies is known as a sex place. So, surely it had to be a local?'

'As I said, we're looking into all avenues.' Detective Wozniak splayed his fingers. Pale and stubby, with a too-tight gold wedding band. 'Which brings me to the next point: fingerprints aren't as reliable as other forms of DNA, but we've lifted a pretty solid profile from the sheet of plastic she was found under. Best-case scenario: we identify the fingerprints, we identify the perpetrator. As such, we're strongly encouraging everyone on the island to come forward for fingerprinting.'

'"Strongly encouraging"?' Caro bristled. 'Can't you *force* them? As if the killer's going to give up his DNA because you *encourage* him.'

'We can't force anything without a warrant. But we're working with the Island Administration to put it out there as a matter of civic duty.' Wozniak nudged the box of tissues even closer to Judy; it'd fall into her lap, at this rate. 'Ms Novak. If you'd like to take a break—'

'No!' Judy flapped her hands. 'Just get on with it, please.'

'As I was saying … we're asking everyone who was on the island that day. It's just a formality, Ms Novak. But, I wouldn't be doing my job if I didn't—'

Caro jumped in. 'Mr Wozniak! Can't you see how much pain she's—'

'Shhh, Caro. I don't care.' Judy closed her eyes, held out her hands, as if for shackles. 'Take my fingerprints. Take my blood. It's all gone anyway. What do I care?'

It reminded Judy of kindergarten, the ink on her fingers. Paulina in kindy, with her fingerpaintings, her pretty homemade dresses. There was so much to cry about.

'She was always bossy. Even when she was a tiny thing,' Judy volunteered, when it was time to sit down with Wozniak again. 'Her first report, in kindy. It was so silly.'

She faltered, hands twisting.

'Something about how her husband would be henpecked,' Caro supplied. 'I remember. I was a teacher, too. I thought it was so silly and old-fashioned.'

'It was the *silliest* thing.' Judy shook the tears from her face. 'I wasn't a bra-burning feminist, but I thought it was so silly, worrying about husbands when she was just this tiny thing. So what if she liked her own way? She was an only child. She was used to getting it.'

'Judy had some trouble conceiving,' Caro explained. 'She never *spoiled* her, though.'

'So what if she *was* spoiled? She was the beautifullest, smartest, funniest girl; she deserved it.' Judy was crying hard again. 'She had her own mind. I wasn't going to change it.'

'The "henpecking" comment,' Wozniak ventured. 'Was there any truth in it?'

'No!'

'No?'

'Men strung her along. Men used her.' Anger was almost a nice change. 'She had low self-esteem. She didn't *henpeck*.'

Caro nodded. 'My sister's right. Boys were always stringing Paulina along. That Greek boy? She worshipped him, and he just threw her away like rubbish.'

'Vinnie.' Judy shook her head. 'She was practically suicidal with guilt, and he wouldn't forgive her. She never got over that.'

Wozniak took notes. 'This "Vinnie"? He was before Fairfolk?'

'He's in the Air Force now. He went away for basic training and she ... well, they'd never been apart like that, and she was stressed at work and got drunk one night, and some prick took advantage. That's all. She was *twenty-six*. They'd been together five years, they'd been *backpacking*, and suddenly this separation? Of course she was confused!'

'You couldn't pay me to be twenty-six again.' Wozniak's wrinkles deepened. 'The drinking. Was it a problem, before—?'

'She was stressed,' Judy repeated. 'She didn't know how to be without him. Then he dumped her. It was hard for her. Things sort of spiralled.'

'It's helpful, Ms Novak, if I can understand who your daughter was, the kinds of relationships she had, even before Fairfolk. The bloke she cheated with—?'

'She didn't *cheat*. He took advantage.'

'My mistake. But any relationships, serious or casual—'

'Paulina didn't have many relationships.' Judy resented his implication. 'Everyone thinks … just because she flirted. She was very inexperienced, before Vinnie. A late bloomer. Naïve.'

Caro smiled wryly. 'More than we were, at that age.'

'Thank you for your candour.' Wozniak kept writing. 'You mentioned "suicidal" feelings. Would you describe Paulina as suicidal?'

And just like that, Judy's righteous indignation jumped off a cliff, into the saddest, coldest depths of the ocean.

'I apologise, Ms Novak. I don't mean to imply your daughter didn't want to live. There are defensive wounds that prove she did, she absolutely did. I know it's cold comfort — but the extensive nature of the defensive wounds proves beyond all doubt. She fought for her life.'

Judy cried herself blue in the face. Blew her nose, loud as an explosion.

'I *know* she fought.' She glared. 'She thought about suicide, yes. But she always fought. I know better than anyone, how hard she fought.'

'You did well,' Caro reassured her, driving back to Vera and Rocky's. 'You did very, very well. He knows who's boss now.'

Judy clutched her head. 'You're giving me a headache.'

'I'm just saying, good on you. They're always trying to turn it on the victims — or the *mothers*, god forbid. It's always somebody else's fault besides the bastard who did it. You told him, Judy.'

'All I did was tell the truth.'

'Well, that's what they need to hear. Look: I know this Wozniak seems pretty stodgy, but maybe that's the best thing, for a place like this? And he's very experienced. Better an older guy than some cocky young thing straight out of the academy.'

Caro slowed for a lilac cow, dawdling across the road.

'I *hate* cows,' Judy seethed. 'Gawd, I hate them.'

'Want me to run it over?' Caro scrabbled inside her handbag for a cigarette; she was smoking again. 'I hate this *whole island*. It's barbaric. I half expect them to start burning wicker men.'

'Don't be racist,' Judy said listlessly.

'How's it racist?' Caro honked at the cow. 'They're no darker than me after a day by the pool!'

As they reached the scenic bend where that horrible graffiti was, Judy held her breath. A couple were standing at the lookout, innocently looking out — but nothing was innocent anymore. They were standing on Paulina's name.

Caro read Judy's mind. 'Want me to run *them* over?'

Judy closed her eyes. 'I just want to go to bed.'

Bed was where Judy felt closest to Paulina. Bed, where there was no life or death. She swallowed some pills, changed back into the T-shirt.

'You look fifteen going on a hundred-and-fifty,' Caro told her.

Judy buried herself under the Alice bedspread. Reached for the perfume on the bedside table, sprayed a bit inside the bottle-cap, sniffed, and started sobbing.

'Oh, god, Jude.' Caro grimaced. 'You're a mess.'

'Leave me alone.'

Instead, Caro got under the blankets with her. Caro's arms were bony, her feet. 'Shh,' she whispered, stroking Judy's hair until she fell asleep.

Caro was gone when Judy awoke. She could hear her shrill voice outside the room, though; and other voices — Vera, Rocky? Judy turned on the TV to drown them out; an evening news program. All news was bad. She switched to a gameshow, head-hurting glitz and buzzers.

It wasn't long before Caro came to the door with a mug of Milo and more toast.

'That woman seems to think Milo's your preferred beverage,' Caro sneered. 'I guess it's better than coffee, though, if you're planning to sleep tonight. Just don't take too many pills; you'll get addicted. Do you want something proper to eat or are you still on your invalid's diet? I had some fish and chips before; they weren't bad, considering.'

'Toast is fine,' Judy murmured, watching the lights and laughter.

'Anyway, if you'd rather be alone, alright. But there's this boy here who's saying he's a friend of Paulina's. He wants to meet you and — give his condolences, or something.' Caro gave an impatient jerk of her

45

shoulders. 'I just thought, what the hell, every man's a suspect. Maybe you'll get some sort of vibe from him. Mother's intuition blah-blah-blah.'

Judy didn't feel intuitive, just groggy. She took a sip of Milo. 'I don't know.'

'Should I tell him to rack off, then?'

'I don't know.' Judy looked down. 'I'm not even dressed.'

'Have you seen the way they dress around here?'

'Should I brush my hair or something?'

'I'd embrace the hag look, personally.'

Judy raked her fingers through her hair.

'Fine.' She shook her head. 'Bring in the suspect.'

FOODFOLK

Every morning around eight-thirty, nine, Paulina went to Foodfolk for Merle's copy of the *Fairfolk Daily*, then hung around to beg for a job as a checkout chick.

'Hey, it's my birthday. Can I have a job?'

'It's your birthday?' Flick looked up from her magazine. She was a mainie too, but Tasmanian, so she fit right in on Fairfolk. 'How're you celebrating?'

'Looking for gainful employment, *obviously*.' Paulina rolled her eyes. 'Then either slitting my wrists or going to the beach. Haven't decided yet. Wanna come to the beach?'

'I'm here till six.'

Paulina fake-wept against the till. 'But I don't wanna be *alone*.'

Flick rung up Paulina's purchase. 'Ask Rita.'

'To the beach? Fuck no!'

In the bakery section, Rita was spreading out the loaves so it'd look like there were more of them.

'Hey, Rita.' Paulina slipped her rolled-up *Fairfolk Daily* into her waistband and started helping. 'Can I have a job? It's my birthday.'

'No it's not.'

'Wanna see my ID? It's bloody depressing, but I'll show you.'

'Shouldn't you be throwing yourself a party? Asking the boys at the bowls club for free drinks?'

'I'd rather celebrate my new job, thanks.'

'Well, as I said yesterday: no jobs. Ask me when the next supply ship arrives.'

Instead of asking when the ship was due, Paulina ducked into the fridge section.

She'd just seen Eddy's wife.

As Paulina studied the label on a can of Diet Coke, a guy came up beside her, picked up a carton of choc-milk. 'You'll get fat,' she muttered, since she was in that kind of mood, done with men. The guy looked at her and she changed her mind. He was wearing a Bauhaus T-shirt.

'You like Bauhaus?' Paulina grabbed his arm; it was tattooed and muscly and dark. 'No way!'

'Um …'

'Hey, I was just joking about you getting fat.' She led him away from the fridge; Eddy's wife was rolling closer with her toddler and trolley. 'You must work out *loads*. I like your tattoos, by the way. What's that one, a Camel-cigarettes camel? Is that your brand? I just smoke rollies. Shit, I'm almost out. Let's ask Flick if I can have some for my birthday.'

'Um,' the guy said as she steered him toward the checkout. 'Happy birthday?'

'*Unhappy* birthday.' Paulina was too depressed to say her age. 'Oi, Flick. Rita said I can have some ciggies for my birthday.'

As Flick went for the tobacco, Paulina moistened her lips, toyed with her rolled-up *Fairfolk Daily*.

'I come here every morning. For the *Fairfolk Daily*.'

'Oh,' the guy said. 'Cool.'

Flick handed over the tobacco, scanned his milk. 'Hi Camel.'

'"Camel"?' Paulina grimaced.

'Yeah.' The guy got out his wallet. 'It's my nickname.'

'No way am I calling you *Camel*. If you think that's happening, you can get fucked. Ha-ha.'

'Um.' The guy passed Flick a handful of coins. 'Okay, then.'

Then he walked out with his choc-milk.

After Foodfolk, and after installing Merle in the shade with his *Fairfolk Daily*, Paulina put on her exercise clothes and sunglasses and went for her walk. After her walk, she showered and changed into her beach clothes, then phoned her mum to say what a shithouse age twenty-eight was, and when was the supply ship with her birthday presents arriving? After that, she flung herself across the bed and cried her eyes out. Then she put her sunnies back on and sat in the shrinking shade with Merle.

'Hey, Merle,' she chirped, slathering sunscreen on her arms. 'Did you know it's my birthday?'

'Birthday?' He looked confused. 'Whose birthday?'

'Me!' Paulina pointed at herself. 'Twenty-eight. Almost as old as *you*.'

Somehow Merle heard this and found it hilarious. He stopped laughing, though, when she offered her sunscreen. 'I'm not a mainie.'

'Yeah, I know! Geez.' Shaking her head, Paulina recapped the bottle. 'Lunchtime?'

Merle squinted at his watch, at the sun, then gave her the thumbs-up.

At the bowls club, Paulina told Barry the bartender, 'We'll have our usual, only *two* "salads" today. It's my birthday.'

Barry began pouring two pints of Pine Brew. 'Happy birthday.'

'Cheers.' Paulina glanced at Merle, sitting under an umbrella outside. 'Listen, do you have any jobs going yet?'

'Sorry.' Barry passed her the beers.

Paulina sighed. 'Yeah. Me too. Don't forget my receipt, okay?'

The first beer lasted her till Merle's Hawaiian ham-steak and chips arrived. She didn't like the smell, so she took her second beer over to where Woody and Kobby were playing bowls. 'Guess what?' she recited. 'It's my birthday.'

'Happy birthday!' the old men enthused, and looked at her like she was the sun, or the sexiest thing on earth. Then Kobby inclined his head in Merle's direction. 'Boyfriend taking you somewhere special?'

'Nah, same old, same old.'

They guffawed. Paulina sipped her beer, slunk back into the shade to roll some ciggies.

It was boring in the shade. She went into the sun again, but it felt sleazy against her skin. The lawn's edges were blurring, the ham's stink still strong. She smoked a ciggie to cover it.

Her beer went warm.

Paulina gulped the beer down, cringed at the vomity taste. Then she walked back to Merle, trying not to let the booze show in her walk.

'Hey, Merle, can I have a Fisherman's Friend?'

Merle dug the packet from his pocket. She popped three lozenges in her mouth. 'Thanks, Merle.' Patted his bony shoulder. 'See ya later, okay?'

Merle gave her the thumbs-up.

Around the corner from the Bowls Club, Paulina smoked and paced, re-tied her ponytail. Fanned her cheeks and told herself: *don't be shit. Stop being so shit.*

'Guess what?' Paulina smiled like a flight attendant. 'It's my birthday.'

'Oh really?' Merlinda munched a handful of salt-and-vinegar chips, without glancing up from her notepad. 'You should celebrate at the Fortuna fish-fry tonight. My nephew Tony "Tunes" Carlyle is performing.'

'Can't really afford it, hey.' Paulina slipped her receipt across the desk. 'Need help with the books? I was a financial advisor once upon a time.'

Merlinda shook her messy steel-grey bob. 'I'm working on a poem for the new edition of the *Fayrf'k Songbook*. Not really your area of expertise, dear.'

'Yeah ... guess not.' Paulina indicated her bikini-straps to Kymba, who was on the phone, and mouthed, 'Beach?'

Kymba shook her head apologetically, cupped the phone closer to her mouth. 'I'm really sorry. I'll let you know if anything comes up.'

'Geez, you're still getting mainies calling?' Paulina marvelled as Kymba hung up. 'Beach, Kymba-lee? It's my birthday.'

'*Birthday?*' Kymba looked horrified. 'Why didn't you say—?'

'Twenty-eight. Big whoop. Should've joined the twenty-seven club when I had the chance.'

'Is that like the mile-high club?' Merlinda's hand squeaked inside her chip packet.

'Nah, it's more exclusive.' Paulina cringed at the scrunching packet. 'Fuck, I may as well be thirty. Twenty-eight is so depressing.'

'Watch your mouth.' Merlinda smacked her lips. 'I'd kill to be twenty-eight.'

'There's nothing wrong with twenty-eight. Or thirty,' Kymba reassured her. 'Simmo's thirty.'

'He's a man. Doesn't count.'

'Well …' Kymba toyed with her wedding band. 'You've done much more with your life than *me*. I'd never quit a fancy big-city job and move to an island. You're very brave.'

'Brave enough to jump off a cliff, at this point. I'm so bored.'

'You should go to the Fortuna fish-fry.' Merlinda wiped her salty fingers off on her pants, pulled open a drawer. 'Here. Birthday bonus!'

'Yeah?' Paulina peered at the tickets dubiously. 'Drinks included?'

'Beer, wine, and sparkling.'

Paulina smiled at Kymba.

'I don't know,' Kymba started. 'The kids—'

'Aw, bring 'em. Bring Simmo. Bring his cute mates. C'mon, Kymba-leeee.'

'Well …'

'Beach?' Paulina kept pestering. 'Auntie Merlinda, can Kymba please come play on the beach? Pretty please? Look how pale she is! She looks like a mainie.'

Kymba opened her mouth in protest.

'Go on, then, Miss Kymba,' Merlinda cut her off. 'Get some colour.'

There was no one else at Tombstone Beach. Paulina didn't mind. It was nice being almost naked, with the sun on her skin and that clear water, cliffs and pines and cemetery view. 'Fuck, it's pretty here.' She got out her ciggies. 'I get so bored I wanna shoot myself and then it looks like this. What the hell.'

'Yeah, it's like that.' Kymba shyly peeled off her shorts. 'Swim?'

'Nah. Sharks.'

'They're only on the north side of the island.'

'You think Jaws can't swim from there to here? It's like ten k's, tops.'

'They never swim past the reef. Anyway, I thought you liked sharks? You're so obsessed with Great-O's.'

'Yeah, cos it's my great white whale.' Paulina lit up. 'Go be shark-bait, Kymba-lee. I'll scream if I see any fins.'

Kymba tiptoed to the water's edge, kept walking till she was belly-deep, then plunged. Paulina lay back and puffed smoke into the clouds.

'You should swim. It's *beautiful*.' Kymba returned, dripping cold beads. 'Oh, shit.'

'What?' Paulina perked up; Kymba didn't swear often.

'Oh … this pervert, Yooey Turner. He comes here sometimes. Oh, *don't look!*'

'That guy in the golf gear? Bloody right he's a perv, dressing like that at the beach!'

'Oh, *don't look.*' Kymba covered up with her towel. 'Don't, or he'll come over.'

Paulina sat up. 'Oi, perv! What're you looking at?'

Just like Kymba predicted, the perv crept over like a beaten dog, hands deep in his pockets. He had that face a lot of Fairfolk men seemed to have: weather-beaten skin, wide lips, light eyes. He wasn't looking her in the eye, though.

'Oi!' Paulina clapped her hands. 'Up here! What're you looking at?'

'You're pretty ladies,' the perv mumbled, eyes drifting down again. 'Will you go on a date with me?'

'Who? Me? Her?'

'One of you … pretty ladies.' He looked her full in the face, curled his lip. 'Please will you go on a date with me.'

'Nah.'

He turned to Kymba. 'Please will you go on a date with me?'

'Not her either. She's married with kids and stuff. Alright?' Paulina clapped and pointed to the horizon. 'Fuck off now.'

He did, somewhere further up the beach and out of sight.

'Oh god!' Kymba groaned. 'He's probably going to you-know-what now.'

'Wank?'

'Yeah. That.'

'Well … better he gets it over with than keeps staring and ruining my birthday.' Paulina nudged Kymba's shoulder, wriggled under the towel with her. 'You should show him Kimba, give him something for the spank-bank.'

'Everything's a joke to you.' Kymba sighed heavily. 'There's a reason I married outside the gene pool, you know.'

'Don't let Gilligan King hear you say that.' Paulina poked Kymba's love handles. 'Oi, show *me* Kimba. Please? It's my birthday.'

'No! Once is enough.'

'Please? I'm so old, I don't have many joys in life. Please?'

'*No.*'

'Please, please, pretty please?' Paulina tickled her some more. 'Kim-ba, the White Li-on! Kim-ba, the White Li-on! Kim-ba …'

'Fine!' Red-faced, Kymba tugged down her swimsuit just far enough to show off the little white cartoon lion tattooed on her big white tit. 'Happy?'

'Aw!' Paulina cooed. 'Kimba!'

Next morning, Paulina woke up with scum on her pillow, a concrete-headed horror about whatever she'd done the night before. She thought about staying in bed forever. Then she thought about Merle finding her body, or not finding it, just shuffling around as her stink got stronger. Eventually, her stink got so strong she had no choice but to get up and shower.

'Morning, Merle,' she mumbled, finding him waiting at the table. 'Sorry I slept in.'

Foodfolk was busy, and only Flick and some teenagers were working. After fetching Merle's *Fairfolk Daily*, Paulina cleaned up a milk-spill, then stuck around to bag while Flick scanned. 'Was I bad last night?' she asked quietly.

'You kept saying Tony Tunes was a shit singer.'

'Duh, he *was*.' Paulina lowered her voice. 'Was I slutty?'

Flick shrugged. 'No more than usual.'

Paulina's soul ached. 'I'm never drinking again.'

She stuck to Diet Coke and water, the next few days. 'Three days without booze or ciggies,' she bragged to her mum. 'Now I'm twenty-eight, it's time I made some healthy lifestyle choices. Also, I'm growing out my fringe.'

'Oh, don't do that! You look so cute with your fringe.'

It was bad weather on Tuesday, though, and the temptation was strong, smelling the sweet, yeasty air inside the Bowls Club. Instead of hanging around, Paulina drove to the national park and took a walk among the pines and palms and ferns, then to the cliffs beyond them. But there was temptation there, too.

She was relieved when she saw some fishermen on the rocks. Even more relieved when she saw what they were looking and pointing at.

'The supply ship's here!' Paulina practically sprinted into Foodfolk, car keys stabbing her sweaty palm. 'Can I have a job now?'

'We'll start unpacking stock first thing Thursday.' Rita smirked. 'Come see me tomorrow, and we'll talk.'

'Why not now?'

'Come see me tomorrow,' Rita repeated. 'When you're presentable.'

Paulina looked down at her grubby fitness gear. 'Oh! Ha ha.'

From Foodfolk, Paulina drove one block to the liquor store, bought herself a six-pack. Then she drove to King's Pier to watch the supply ship unloading.

ULVINIS

It took a while for his eyes to adjust to the dimness of the room. Then it hit him, hard.

'You look like her,' he said.

'Oh, no,' murmured Paulina's mum. 'Not really.'

She sounded like her, too. Softer, politer. But like her. *Fuck.*

He knew it'd be a mind-fuck, coming here. He hadn't wanted to. It was his dad who made him: *you said you'd meet the mother, didn't you?* Plus, he had the present to give her — not that he could do it, right now. Right now, all he could do was stare.

'Sorry.' He dropped his gaze to the bedroom floor — but that was bad, too. It was littered with tissues, clothes, including a mumsy beige bra. He became conscious of the close smell of the room: toast, milk, body odour, and … *perfume?*

Paulina's perfume. What the fuck!

'Sorry to disturb you.' He looked at the bedcovers. Alice in Wonderland. 'You were sleeping?'

'Judy's been sleeping a lot,' said the aunt, Caro, who was guarding the door with crossed arms.

'I'm awake now.' Judy met his eyes. 'There's only so much I can sleep, before I wake up and realise I'm still here.'

'God. You really look like her,' he let slip. It was the eyes: bloodshot like Paulina's after a bender, and shaped like hers, though the blue-grey colour was all wrong.

'I *don't.*' Judy seemed almost offended. 'It's kind of you to say, but I don't. She looked much more like her father.'

'There's a resemblance,' he insisted. 'Around the — whole face. The eyes and the cheeks and the, um, mouth.'

He didn't want to insult her — these weren't things Paulina liked about herself. She liked her hair, her legs, her arse. Not her face.

'She got her father's Slavic good looks. And his nose. She didn't get my nose.'

Judy's nose was straight and thin, almost to the point of over-refinement. *Just a white lady in her fifties,* he reminded himself. *Nothing special at all.*

'Yeah, that's different,' he agreed. 'Your colouring's different, too. But everything else … You're very similar.'

'We're *not*, though.'

Caro ahemmed ostentatiously. 'Excuse me, young man, but are you going to introduce yourself? Or are you just going to stand there gawking all day?'

'Sorry …' His brain took a while to recover his own name. 'It's Jesse.'

'Jesse. Yes.' Judy smiled placidly. 'I've heard of you.'

Then she drew up her legs and skimmed her eyes over the bedcovers.

Face glowing, Jesse perched on the bed's edge. 'Yeah. We were good friends.'

'Not a boyfriend, though?' Caro cocked an eyebrow.

'Just friends. Good friends.'

'I find that hard to believe.' Caro spoke over his head. 'He's very dark and handsome. You know Paulina's type.'

Judy glanced at him. 'She did have a type.'

'You're very dark and handsome.' Caro's gaze was both lewd and accusing. 'I bet they get you to play Gideon King in all the re-enactments.'

'No, ma'am.'

'"No"? Did I say something funny?'

'Sorry.' He straightened his face. 'Just, I could never play Gideon King. I don't have mutineer blood. Fairfolk's very particular about that kind of thing.'

'But you're an Islander?' She scrutinised his skin. 'You have … the accent.'

'I'm third-generation. Dad's parents were Maltese.'

'And your mother?'

'She grew up on the mainland.' Jesse met her narrow blue eyes. 'She was Yuggera.'

'Yuggera.' Caro half smiled, like she had him all figured out. 'That's a Queensland group, isn't it?'

'It was Yuggera land before the queen put her name on it.'

'And how did your mother end up on Fairfolk? If you don't mind me asking.'

'She worked as a cleaner on a cruise ship, ma'am. Came here on a day pass. Met my dad.'

'I see.' Caro bristled at his deadpan delivery. 'Well, you're very striking. You're sure you and Paulina were *just* friends?'

'It was … complicated.'

'It's a simple question.'

'We …' He could almost hear Paulina laughing at him. '… Hooked up. Yeah. But we were better as friends.'

'Why's that?'

'It's complicated, like I said. She was a complicated chick.'

'And you?' Caro was looking at his skin again, the tattoos on his arms, in a way that made him wish he'd worn long sleeves. 'You're not complicated?'

'No offence, ma'am. But I came here to pay my respects, not to talk about myself.'

Caro didn't bat an eyelid. 'No offence, young man. But you're going to have to get used to talking about yourself, when the detective asks you the same questions.'

'Sorry, what?' Jesse looked from Caro to Judy, who was staring into her lap, eyelashes pale and lank. 'Detective?'

'The homicide detective, from Canberra. He'll want to know all the details of your complicated relationship, I'm sure.'

'Homicide.' Jesse's throat constricted. 'I thought it was … I mean, the way she was … she was so depressed about turning thirty?'

'Oh.' Judy's raw eyes lifted to his. 'You did know her well.'

Then she covered her face and wept.

Washing his trembling hands in Vera and Rocky's peach-hued bathroom sink, Jesse half expected to see blood mixed with the water. A mind-fuck. The worst fucking mind-fuck of his life. Trust Paulina to still be at it, from beyond the grave.

Jesse sat on the fluffy peach toilet lid and got out his Camels, hoping Vera would understand; surely now, of all times, she'd understand people needed to smoke inside the house sometimes?

Sometimes I sits and thinks
And sometimes I just sits

He read the quote on the framed picture of a winged little girl with her undies down, squatting on a toadstool, and thought, actually, probably Vera *wouldn't* understand. Anyone who willingly displayed pictures like that was a loose cannon.

'Paulina, you bitch.' Jesse cried into his hands. 'You wanted this.'

'Have a nice smoke-break, did you?' Caro asked, looking almost envious.

'S-sorry.' Jesse looked at Judy; her face like a lost battle. 'I'll go.'

Caro closed the bedroom door behind him. 'We're not done with you, yet.'

Then she sat on the bed beside Judy, stretched out her legs.

'Sorry.' Jesse settled on the floor among the luggage. 'I don't know what to tell you.'

'You can start by telling us where you were on Good Friday.'

'Yeah,' Jesse said, then saw what she was implying. 'Wait: you seriously think *I*—?'

'I think this is a very serious matter.'

'Yeah, sorry.' He looked at Judy again; she was picking some lint off her shirt — *his* shirt. 'Hey! That's my shirt!'

'*Excuse* me?' Caro cried.

'My Bauhaus shirt.' Jesse gestured wildly. 'Oh, wow. I was wondering where that went. Paulina must've stolen it.'

'This?' Frowning, Judy plucked at her shirtfront. 'I just wear it because … it has her smell.'

'I'm glad she took it,' Jesse choked out. 'I'm glad. It's yours.'

Judy sniffed the sleeve, shut her eyes.

'Good Friday.' Caro's voice told him he was staring too much, again. 'Your alibi?'

'Sorry. I was working.'

'On a public holiday?'

'Yeah. Um. I work for the family business; Easter's one of our busiest times.'

'And what business is that?'

'Camilleri's. The butcher's, ma'am.'

Judy let out a small sob; covered her face again. 'You're a *butcher*?' Caro glowered.

'Like I said, it's the family business. I …' He saw Judy's shoulders shaking and felt faint. 'I'm an artist, too.'

'An artistic butcher. How interesting. Drawing, painting?'

'Yeah, both. I painted the mural at Mutineers' Lodge. I do tattoos too.'

'But you were butchering on Good Friday?'

'I was helping Dad prepare the orders for Easter.'

'Just your dad?'

'It's a family business, ma'am.' Jesse hated his dad in that moment for making him come here. 'Look, do you want his phone number? Jesus, I wouldn't lie about that, okay? Paulina was a friend of mine.'

Caro looked at him for a long time; so long, he had to look down at his sandals.

'And what time did you finish work?'

'Around two.'

'Then what?'

'I went for a drive. I heard the supply ship was coming in. There wasn't much to see by then. I bummed around at home till dinnertime. It was raining.'

'Then what?'

'I went to Dad's for dinner. I live in the cottage behind his house. He fried some fish, for Lent. My sister called. She lives in Brisbane. I got the call about Paulina … later.' His nose stung. 'Toa, the chef at Mutes'. He wasn't specific. I really thought it was … self-inflicted.'

Something flashed across Caro's face, jagged as lightning. She touched the crease between her eyebrows, appeared to smooth it with her fingers.

'Well, it wasn't. She fought very hard.' She put an arm around Judy, who was tugging tissues from a box, trembling all over. 'Dozens of

stab wounds. A broken pelvis. You can't know how hard she fought …
unless you were there, of course.'

'I wasn't.' Jesse pinched the pain between his eyes. 'Jesus. I *wasn't*.'

'Then you won't have any problem giving your fingerprints?'

'Jesus, lady, how many times do I have to tell you? She was my
friend. I'd never hurt her. I …' He reached into the pocket of his cargo
shorts. 'I made this for her birthday. I was gonna give it to her; now I
can't. Here.'

Caro snatched up the CD, though he'd meant to hand it to Judy.

'"Ulvini Songs."' Caro read aloud. 'Does that mean something? In
your little language?'

'It's Fayrf'k for "old woman". It was just a dumb joke, with her
turning thirty.'

'You joked about that? Knowing how depressed she was?'

'Sorry. Just, she was always calling me a baby cos I'm younger, so I
called her "ulvini".'

'I see.' Caro frowned. 'And you drew this … album art?'

'Yeah.' He crawled closer to the bed. 'It's another dumb joke. See,
she's driving the bus, being queen of the ulvinis. And those in the bus
are all the old people on their "Nearly-Dead Tour". Um, just ignore
the guy with the rabbit ears. And, yeah. That camel behind the bus is
me.'

'Very … creative,' Caro murmured. 'You're not bad.'

She passed the CD to Judy, who looked at it vacantly.

'Sorry if it's in bad taste.' Jesse watched her hopefully. 'I just meant
to make her laugh, Mrs Novak—'

'Do you see a husband anywhere?' Caro snapped.

'*Ms*, sorry. You can keep it, Ms Novak. I want you to have it.'

Judy looked up, and he got the creeps all over again; she looked so
much like her.

'I don't want it,' Judy mumbled, shaking her head.

Jesse hadn't prepared for this.

'But, it's for you.'

'No,' Judy said firmly. 'It was for Paulina.'

'But, you're the closest one to her. I want you to have it. Like the
shirt.'

'I don't want it.' Judy shook her head again, harder. 'Or the shirt.

Please, if you just give me a minute to dress. Or I can get that woman to wash it and give it to you tomorrow.'

'No,' Jesse pleaded, though he didn't know why it mattered so much. 'Please. Keep them.'

Judy tossed the CD on the bed. 'I don't want it. Take it away. Please.'

'But, please, Ms Novak, I—'

'Oh, for chrissakes!' Caro grabbed it. 'You're lucky I don't smash the thing!'

Then she steered Jesse out the door. He tried to get one last look at Judy, from over Caro's head. Caro noticed. 'Haven't you seen enough?'

'Sorry.' Jesse winced as the door slammed, leaving him with Caro in the hall. 'You won't actually smash it, will you?'

Caro patted her pockets. Her face had that ragged, hungry look Jesse knew well.

'Here.' He offered her a Camel. 'Bes' take it outside, but. Vera hates smoke.'

Caro stuck a ciggie in her mouth. Raised her brows expectantly.

Jesse lit her up. All at once, it hit him hard again.

'What?' Caro blew smoke towards the kitchen. 'Are you going to tell me *I* look like her, now?'

'Sorry.'

'Fingerprints.'

'Yeah.'

'If you don't give them, I'll *know*.'

'Yeah.' Jesse sighed. 'I believe you.'

NICE GIRL

Paulina dressed like a nice girl for her meeting with Rita. But right after her contract was signed, she went and sat on the bench outside Foodfolk with her skirt pulled up and legs stretched out, smoking rollies like the girl she was. That's when she saw him again.

'Hey, you! What's your name? Your real name, not your camel-name.'

He stopped short. 'Oh. You.' Looked at her skirt. 'You're dressed different.'

'I know, right?' Paulina rubbed the fabric of her flowery skirt. 'I'm dressed like a nice girl today. Like a girl you'd take home to your parents. Can't say the same about *you*.'

'Yeah, cos I'm not a girl.'

Paulina cacked it. The guy shook his head, strolled into the shops. She was ready to strike again, as soon as he came out.

'Oi! What'd you buy? Choc-milk? Camels?'

He looked into his shopping bag. 'No. Just normal stuff.'

'Oi!' She patted the bench. 'Sit!'

He sat, all embarrassed. Paulina curled up her legs, turned her body towards him, and smiled sweetly. Then she made a grab for his shopping bag.

'Geez, mothballs? Chicken Tonight? Choc-ripple ice cream? That's soooo lame.'

He snatched his shopping back. 'Do you always hang around Foodfolk criticising people's shopping?'

'I do now! I got a job.' She gave him her hand to high-five; he didn't. 'Watch out. Starting tomorrow, I get to criticise your shopping every time *and* get paid for it.'

'I bet the pay's shit.'

'At least I won't spend it on mothballs, *Camel*.' Paulina poked the camel tattoo on his bicep. 'Hey, tell me your real name?'

'Jesse.'

'Girl's name!'

'No. It's only a girl's name when it's Jessica.'

'What's your surname? Ooo, let me guess, is it King? Carlyle? Greatorex? That's my favourite, cos of Great-O's. Do you know the Great-O White Shark Grill? I *love* them.'

'They burned down.'

'I love, love, love them!' Paulina giggled. 'Oi, is it Stevens? Turner? MacArthur? White? Um, that other W-one; I always forget—'

'It's not Wotherspoon. It's not a mutineer name. Don't bother guessing.'

'Aw! Fine. Tell me.'

'Camilleri.'

'Camilleri!' She bit her lip. 'Italian?'

'Maltese.'

'Maltese!' Paulina smirked. 'My friend Carli married a Maltese guy. He's a sensitive bugger like you. Can't take a joke.'

'I like funny jokes.'

'Yeah? Say something funny, then.'

'My humour's too sophisticated for you, eh.'

'What, cos I'm a mainie?' Paulina scoffed. 'Wait: if you don't have an island name, does that mean *you're* a mainie?'

'Nay. I was born here.'

'Does your mum have an Island name?'

'She was Yuggera.' He saw the question mark in her face. 'Aboriginal. From Brisbane.'

'*Really?*' Paulina leaned forward. 'So, like, you're even more of a mainie than me, if you really think about it.'

'That's not how it works, eh.' Jesse stood up. 'I bes' go.'

'Aw! Don't leave me, Jesse-Camel!'

Jesse indicated his shopping. 'Melting.'

'You're leaving me for choc-ripple ice cream?' She grabbed his hand. 'Please, Jesse-Camel. Just one question?'

Jesse sighed.

'Just one question.' Paulina gave him a gooey look. 'Do you *really* have good taste in music? Or was that shirt you had on the other day from, like, a bargain bin?'

In Jesse Camilleri's cottage, sorting through his CD collection, Paulina was happier than she'd been in weeks. Also, hornier. He really did have amazing taste.

'*Deep!* Jesse, you're *beautiful.*'

'… Thanks.'

Jesse wasn't on the floor with her. He was on the couch, watching her touch his stuff with a look of horror-struck resignation.

'What's your favourite track?'

'Uh, "Marlene Dietrich's Favourite Poem", probably.'

'Ha! Sensitive bugger.' She was blushing, though. 'Mine's "Cuts You Up", thanks for asking.'

'That's a good one, too.'

She sorted some more CDs into piles: stuff she liked, stuff she didn't know, stuff she scorned as hippie music.

'*Another* Beatle? One minute you're cool, next minute you're my mum.'

'How can you like Elliott Smith but hate The Beatles?'

'Told ya, hippies are lame! Like that air-freshener in your Camel-mobile.' She'd already told him exactly what she thought of his red Commodore, and everything in it — especially the marijuana-shaped air-freshener. 'Peace, love, groovy baby. Fuck off!'

'Uh huh.'

Paulina made a peace-sign with her fingers, stuck her tongue between them, and wiggled it around. That shut him up.

'Oh, Jesse,' she cooed, moments later, holding up *Souvlaki.* 'Beautiful!'

'Yeah, it's one of my favourites,' he said coolly — as if she didn't already want to fuck his brains out. 'Like I said, though. You're wrecking my order.'

'Like I said: *my* order's better.' She pointed at the piles. 'Cool. Lame. Borrowing!'

'You can't borrow all those.'

'I'll take some today then bring them back and take some more.'

Paulina grinned triumphantly. 'I'm coming here *every day*, Jesse-Camel.'

He didn't say anything. But he did look at her legs when she rearranged her flowery skirt around them.

'You can come over mine, too,' she said. 'Once my new stereo's set up.'

'Um. Sure.'

'I have a housemate. But he's deaf, so we can be as loud as we want.'

'Um.' He'd gone all breathless. 'Sure. Yeah. My housemate's not deaf ... but he's out surfing a lot. I have the place to myself a lot.'

Paulina moistened her lips. 'Jesse-Camel? Do you have any beer? I'm thirsty!'

'Um. I'll check.'

He got up very quickly. While he was gone, she abandoned her sorting, undid a button of her blouse, and snooped inside a nearby toolbox.

'Sorry.' He really did look sorry, too. 'My housemate must've finished them.'

'What's this box with the needles and stuff? Are you a junkie?'

'I'm a tattoo artist.'

Paulina's jaw dropped. '*No way.*'

'Yeah, um. There's not much money in it here. Mostly I work with my dad; he owns the butcher's, Camilleri's? But tattoos are my—'

'I want a tattoo!' Paulina lifted her blouse. 'Right here, above my butt. Please, please, please, can you?'

'Now?'

'Not now, *obviously*. I want a custom design. Something specially for me.'

'I can do that. I can show you my portfolio. I can do some sketches tonight, even.'

'Tonight!' She clapped. 'I'm still thirsty, though, Jesse-Camel.'

'I'll get more beer.'

'You get the beer; I'll get the music.' Ecstatic, Paulina picked up *It'll End in Tears*. 'Jess!'

'Play it,' he said earnestly. 'Play whatever you want.'

Then he whisked up his car keys, headed for the door, and smiled at her in a way that told her she had him — hook, line, and sinker.

'You're beautiful, Jess!' she called. 'Beautiful!'

And she meant it, she really did. Just, in the few minutes it took Jesse to go to the shops for beer, an even more beautiful guy walked through the door — shirtless and all drippy-wet from the surf.

'Guess what?' Paulina phoned her mum that night. 'Today I dressed like a nice girl, and I got a job and some CDs, *and* met the father of your grandkids! They're gonna be soooo good-looking.'

'Oh!' Judy was delighted. 'See what happens when you dress like a nice girl instead of a bogan?'

'Mum, he's *gorgeous.*'

'Tell me about him.'

'Tall. Dark. Cheekbones to heaven. Hot bod. Um, he surfs.'

'A surfer! Oh, that takes me back!' Judy sighed. 'You know, I probably would've married a surfer if your dad hadn't come along.'

'Yeah, yeah. Big yawn. Let me tell you about his body.'

'… Okay.'

'You know those abs when they're shaped like a V? Those abs that go down in a V-shape and it's like a sign saying "my dick's right here"? *He has those.*'

'Well, good for you. I don't think abs are relevant to my grandchildren, though.'

'They're relevant to me *making* your grandchildren!' Paulina giggled. 'Normally he'd be way outta my league, but Fairfolk's so inbred, I'm *beautiful* here. Watch out: I'm gonna marry him and have his babies before he knows what hit him.'

'Have you … yet?'

'Not yet! I'm a nice girl now, remember?' Paulina laughed uproariously. 'Anyways, I don't want Rita firing me for turning up at Foodfolk tomorrow morning in today's clothes. Patience, mother. Patience.'

'Yes, child. *Patience,*' Judy cautioned. 'May I know my son-in-law's name?'

'Pellet!'

'*Pellet?*'

'It's French-Canadian! He comes from French Canadia!' Paulina swooned. 'All his mates call him "Pellet" but it's short for "Laurent

Pellet". You're right, though. I should call him "Laurent" instead. I wanna be more than his mate.'

'Darling … it's French Canada, not Canadia. Or better still, say *Quebec*. And those T's are definitely silent.'

Judy demonstrated how she thought 'Laurent Pellet' was pronounced.

'Pfft! You're just a receptionist, what do you know,' Paulina jeered. 'Anyways, I like it with the T's. It's nice and hard … like his dick's gonna be when we make all your grandkids.'

'Oh, Jesus Christ, Paulina!' Judy cried. 'You're really *not nice*!'

PRECIOUS CARGO

'Everyone's staring,' Judy complained as they sat in the sun, waiting to board their flight out of Fairfolk. Paulina was already onboard, in the cargo hold. It was a terrible thing to be aware of on a bright Tuesday morning, drinking overpriced coffee and watching strangers in hi-vis vests loading up the baggage.

'It's because of your reverse-panda eyes.' Caro reached across the table to blend in the concealer Judy had hastily smeared under her eyes that morning. Judy slapped Caro's tobacco-scented hand away. Rummaged in her handbag.

'I lost my sunnies,' she lamented. 'Where did I lose them?'

'Somewhere in that awful woman's house, probably.' Caro offered her horrific gold aviator sunglasses to Judy. 'Take mine.'

'I want *my* sunglasses.' Judy put her face in her hands. 'I want my Valium.'

'On the plane. I don't want you falling on the tarmac.'

Judy closed her eyes, but couldn't blot out the sun's glare, the sense of being stared at.

'It's like that boy yesterday. The way they're staring. It's like I've got three heads.'

'That boy was something else.' Caro sipped her coffee. 'He really must've been obsessed with Paulina.'

Judy shifted in her plastic chair, tried to ignore the anxious sting of her bladder. She looked at her sister despairingly.

'*Again?*' Caro griped — then censored herself. 'No, it's fine. Really. We *should* go before we board.'

The bathroom was like an office bathroom, small and gloomy beige. Judy took the cubicle furthest from the door. Only a few droplets came out. She sat a long time, head-in-hands, crotch burning. Alone time.

'You should see a doctor,' Caro advised her, at the sink. 'It should've cleared by now.'

'It's just menopause. I've had UTIs before.'

'Stress makes everything worse. You could end up with sepsis, if you're not careful."

Judy rubbed her under-eyes, but it was useless. Her skin was so crêpey-thin, the concealer stubborn as super-glue. Besides, that boy was right. She *did* look like Paulina. A feeble, watered-down Paulina who didn't deserve to live while the real one lay cold.

'I wish I had sepsis,' she mumbled. 'It would hurt less.'

'Here.' Caro pressed her ugly sunglasses upon her again. 'Wear these.'

'They're ugly.'

'They're Roberto Cavalli.'

Sighing, Judy nudged the aviators up her nose. They headed for the door, just as a pair of fashionable older ladies in colourful scarves and boots hobbled in.

'Oh!' One of them clutched her chest like she'd seen a ghost. 'Excuse me: we're so sorry for your loss! We were staying at Mutineers' Lodge. Your daughter—'

'Excuse me,' Caro cut in forcefully. 'We have a flight to catch.'

But Judy's heart was racing. 'You met my daughter?'

'*Beautiful* girl. She served us breakfast the morning of — Talked about you, too.'

'About me?'

'All about how you were here for a visit. We asked, "and is Dad here too?", and she told us it'd just been the two of you for a long time. I'm *so* sorry.'

'*I'm* sorry.' Caro grabbed Judy's shoulders. 'But mind your own fucking business.'

As Caro steered her out of the ladies' room, Judy's mind clung to the image of Paulina in her Mutineers' Lodge uniform, smiling and chatting with strangers like there was nobody in the world she couldn't trust.

Outside, Caro lit another ciggie.

'This could be my last one.' She squinted at the sun like a cowboy. 'Tim'll give me hell when he smells the smoke.'

'I wish Marko was here,' Judy said. It'd been years since she'd said that.

MUTINY DAY

'Would you eat this?' Flick showed Paulina a recipe in the latest *Women's Weekly*.

'Fuck no! Looks like roadkill.'

'It's chicken.' Flick peered at the glossy page. '"Butterflied chicken."'

'Why would you want chicken to look like a butterfly?'

'Girls!' Rita huffed, hugging a big cardboard box to her chest. 'I thought I told you to set up that book display?'

'We did.' Paulina waved at the rack of Fayrf'k dictionaries and songbooks. 'Now we're doing the magazines.'

'Would you eat this chicken, Rita?' Flick asked.

'Felicity: put those away and get back to the till.' Rita pushed the box into Paulina's arms. 'Paulina: help me with these Mutiny Day decorations.'

'Geez, that's a shitload of bunting,' Paulina marvelled, looking inside the box. 'All this to celebrate your ancestors killing Captain William Lyme?'

'It's "Walter Lyme", not "William".' Rita led her to a stepladder. 'And the mutineers weren't *murderers*. They set that tyrant and his loyalists adrift, that's all.'

'Yeah, alright.'

'Mutiny Day is a celebration of our independence.' Rita climbed the ladder. 'Since the arrival of HMS *Fortuna*, we've been completely self-governing, self-sufficient—'

An old bloke in bike gear wandered over with a shopping basket. 'Alright there, Rita?'

'Oh!' Rita went as red as she'd been when she was lugging that box. 'Actually, we're just putting up this bunting, but I'm afraid … I can't *quite reach*. Would you mind, Rabbit?'

Paulina giggled. '*Rabbit!*

'Paulina.' Rita glared. 'Go help Flick.'

Paulina skipped to the tills, where Flick was once again preoccupied with the magazine. 'Check it out: Rita's on the prowl.'

Flick looked where she was pointing. 'Gross.'

'Check her checking out his tackle in that lycra. She's *frothing.*'

'Would you eat these carrots?' Flick flashed another recipe.

'I bet Rita would eat *his* carrot.' Paulina flicked a glance at the glossy page. 'Honey-glazed? Blergh, too many calories.'

They were still scoffing at recipes when the old guy sidled up with his basket, shadowed by Rita.

'Girls, what did I say? No one's going to buy that after you've put your grubby hands all over it.'

'Aw, Rita.' Paulina turned up her palms. 'My hands are clean, promise.'

'Mine too.' Flick copied her. 'Promise.'

Rita turned to the old bloke. 'I'm sorry. Service isn't what it used to be.'

Just to prove her wrong, Paulina smiled and swept up his shopping basket. 'Sorry, sir. We just got distracted by the recipes. Do you cook?'

'Uh, yes. I do.' He blushed. 'Indeed, I do.'

'Good on ya. There's some good ones in here, if you wanna try something new?'

He hesitated. '*Women's Weekly?*'

'It's a new millennium.' Paulina scanned his cereal and skinny milk. 'Chicks love a man who's in touch with his feminine side.'

'Well …' he stammered. 'Alright.'

'We've got some Fayrf'k songbooks, too? New edition?' She swished her ponytail. '*Everybody's* selling them, but ours are the best, just so you know.'

'Alright,' he said quickly. 'Count me in.'

Paulina gleefully bagged his stuff, took his cash. 'Enjoy!' she sing-songed, fingers brushing his as she gave him his change.

As soon as he'd scurried off in his lycra, she cracked up.

'Talk about easy money! Aren't you glad you hired me, Rita?'

———

Next morning, as Paulina was power walking to King's Lookout before work, Merlinda honked the horn of her van and shouted, 'I've got a job for you!'

'Geez, Merlinda!' Paulina clutched her heart.

'Get your skinny little bum in here.' Merlinda patted the passenger seat. 'C'mon.'

Paulina slipped off her headphones and hopped in. 'Can't help you, mate. My shift starts at nine.'

'Oh, I don't need you *today*. I mean *Mutiny Day*.' Merlinda grinned like a wolf in grandma's clothing. 'What do you know about Mutiny Day?'

'It's a celebration of Fairfolk independence,' Paulina recited diligently. 'Youse honour the arrival of your ancestors on the island by setting fires and getting pissed.'

'Yes, yes, excellent.' Merlinda poked around for some brochures. 'But more importantly … tourists!'

Paulina studied the brochure: old-timey costumes, burning ships, picnic tables laden with flowers and fatty food.

'Fairfolk Tours holds this picnic every year, so the mainies can feel like they're part of it. Now: I'm afraid we can't pay an hourly rate, but these retirees tip very well, and you'll get a cut of any souvenir sales, plus free lunch, drinks, *and* entertainment.'

'Tony Tunes?' Paulina grimaced. 'No offence, but I'd pay not to listen to him.'

Sighing, Merlinda dug out her wallet.

'Tell you what: if you can recruit those boys of yours, I'll include a bonus.'

She counted out two twenties. Paulina crossed her arms. '*Merlinda*. I've seen those boys shirtless. I reckon they're worth fifty each, at least.'

With a huff, Merlinda counted out another sixty.

'Nice doing business with ya!' Paulina slipped the cash inside her sports bra. 'Oi, will I get to wear a costume? I *love* dress-ups.'

'Costumes are for descendants, only.' Merlinda's face turned to stone. 'You'll get a Fairfolk Tours shirt and a name tag.'

'Oh … Okay.'

Paulina reached for the doorhandle. But before she could get out, Merlinda grabbed her arm and gasped; pointed as the old guy from the day before zipped past on his bicycle.

'Rabbit White! It's my lucky day!'

'*Him?*' Paulina looked out the window dubiously. 'Didn't know you had the same taste in men as Rita.'

'Darling.' Merlinda fanned herself with the brochure. 'He's worth more than those boys you live with, shirt or no shirt.'

Leaning against the parked Fairfolk Tours bus, shivering in the brisk sea-breeze, Jesse lit a Camel and told her, 'Fuck, I hate Mutiny Day.'

'Oi, whip off your shirt.' Paulina brandished her disposable camera. 'I want a photo of you with the bonfire.'

'Yeah, nay.'

'Aw, c'mon!'

'Get your boyfriend to do it.'

'You look more exotic!'

'Yeah, nay. Racist.'

Dismayed, Paulina turned her back. 'Oi, Loh-rent!'

'Eh?' He stirred from his vantage point further downhill.

'Photo time! Take your shirt off, babe?'

'Cold.'

'But, *babe*. You'll look so sexy with the fire behind you.'

Laurent's vanity got the better of him. Peeling off his Fairfolk Tours shirt, he posed on the hillside while Paulina giggled, and the costumed throng below sang hymns around the bonfire.

'Soooo sexy, babe.' Paulina passed the camera to Jesse. 'Take one of me and my boyfriend?'

Just as Jesse was about to click, a bit of ash flew onto her Fairfolk Tours shirt, making her frown.

'You're not gonna cry again, are you?' Jesse cracked a smile. 'Crying won't get you a pretty costume.'

'Please, don't cry.' Laurent put his arm around her. 'Not again.'

She had cried earlier, when she saw Kymba and her little girl in their long white dresses and garlands, carrying baskets full of seashells and flowers. This time, she snuggled up to Laurent, smouldered for the camera. When it was done, Laurent put his shirt back on and wandered downhill again.

'What a beautiful design!' A crone in lime-green resort-wear wandered up to Jesse and placed a hand on his camel tattoo. 'Is that HMS *Fortuna*?'

'Uh, no, ma'am.' Jesse blinked his thick eyelashes. 'It's not a ship, it's a camel.'

'A *camel*?'

'Yeah, um. My surname's "Camilleri". It meant "camel driver", back in the day.'

'"Camilleri"'? Is that ... Italian?'

'Maltese, ma'am.'

'Maltese and Fairfolk! How *exotic*.' Admiringly, she patted his brown skin. 'But why aren't you down there burning little wooden ships with the rest of them?'

'I made him help me.' Paulina winked. 'Didn't wanna be the only direct descendant of Gideon King missing out on the festivities.'

'You're *both* direct descendants?'

'Yep!' Paulina smiled heroically. 'It's a shame not to dress up this year, but sharing our culture with youse is really special, hey. Did ya get a copy of the *Fayrf'k Songbook*?'

Stubbing out his ciggie, Jesse muttered, 'Fuck this,' and went to nap on the bus till the fire died down.

In the Fairfolk Tours marquee, Paulina drank so many plastic flutes of champers, she had trouble walking straight. Also, keeping her hands to herself.

'Loh-rent!' She came up behind him at the buffet table as he filled his paper plate with roast pork and banana dumplings. 'Let's get out of here?'

'I'm eating, *bébé*.'

She stood on her tippy toes, nibbled his earlobe. 'Eat *me*.'

'*Bébé*.' He unpeeled her arms from his waist. 'There are all these people.'

'What, you're embarrassed of me?'

Laurent shrugged, placed some pork crackling onto his plate.

'Yeah?' Paulina snatched his plate. 'Well, *you're* embarrassing *me*. Pig.'

On her way past the stage, Tony Tunes gave her a pinch on the bum. She gave him the finger. Jesse found her at the bin, dumping Laurent's plate.

'That's Camilleri's meat you're wasting.'

'Meat is murder. Where's my drink?'

'You drank it.'

'Get me a new one, Jesse-Camel?'

Jesse sidled off, came back with a cup of orange juice.

'That's not a drink!'

'It's a mimosa.'

She took a sip. 'Bullshit.'

'Just drink it, okay? I don't want you spewing in some poor old lady's lap.'

'Nah. I'm saving my spew for next time Tony Tunes grabs my arse.'

'Tony grabbed your arse?' Jesse whistled. 'Touched by a musical legend.'

'Oi, ask him for his autograph. I dare ya.'

'Drink your mimosa.'

Cringing, Paulina downed the orange juice. Jesse smirked and got a napkin, meekly approached the stage, and waited for Tony Tunes to finish his song.

'Hey, brudda,' Jesse mumbled, holding out the napkin. 'Nice job. Could I get a, um …'

'Anytime, brudda.' Tony brandished a pen from the pocket of his waistcoat.

Paulina laughed into her hands as Jesse returned. 'I'm gonna wet myself!'

Jesse handed her the napkin. 'Here's something to wipe with.'

'Shit!' Paulina crossed her legs, clutched his arm for balance. 'Oh, *shit.*'

'You *didn't.* Seriously?'

'Take me to the loo, quick!'

'Seriously?' Jesse looked around. 'You can't go by yourself?'

'You made me drink juice!'

Shaking his head, Jesse walked her out of the marquee and across the too-bright lawn to the toilet block. On the left side was a mosaic banana and the word 'TANES'; on the right, a flower and the word 'VINIS'.

She went into 'VINIS', Jesse into 'TANES'. He was smoking on the grass when she emerged.

'Did you spew?'

'Yeah.'

He gave her his ciggie. When they got back to the marquee, she was ready for another drink. Tony Tunes was strumming his guitar, talking into the mic. 'This one goes out to Bill and Elsie on their golden anniversary. Fifty years, and more in love than ever.'

'Jesus,' Jesse marvelled. 'That's twice my age.'

'I can't imagine living with *myself* for fifty years, let alone getting a guy to live with me that long.' Paulina's eyes misted up. 'I'm gonna die alone.'

'Yeah. Probably.'

'I'm gonna die alone, Jess.' She pawed at his shoulder. 'Jess: do you think he'll propose if I say I'm preggers?'

'Tony Tunes?'

'Loh-rent!'

'Yeah … nay.'

'Why not? He wears a crucifix.'

'He'll just call you a "chalice" and tell you to get an abortion.'

Even so, Paulina gave it a go two drinks later, after they'd cleared the oldies out of the marquee, and herded them onto their buses, and stacked up all the tables and chairs.

'Babe?' She played with Laurent's crucifix as he sparked up a celebratory spliff. 'Sorry I called you a pig before. I've had a lot on my mind, hey.'

He shrugged. 'Okay.'

'Wanna know what's on my mind?'

He shrugged again.

Paulina made sure Jesse was out of earshot, hauling the last rubbish bag to the skip. 'I'm late, babe.'

'Late for what?'

'You know.' She grabbed his free hand and pulled it to her tummy. '*Late*.'

He gave her the exact look she wanted: like a man given a life-sentence.

'I know; it's a lot, babe.' Guilt bubbled up in her as she noticed

Jesse returning from his garbage-run. 'We've both got a lot to think about. Why don't I leave you alone for a while, and you can have a nice long think about our future, okay?'

Paulina kissed him and pranced out of the marquee to find more alcohol.

The clouds were all pebbly and pink when she stumbled into the Islanders-only picnic in the field of limestone ruins just beyond Tombstone Beach. Everyone was barefoot and lolling around on picnic rugs; the women in long white dresses and garlands, the men in breeches and billowy white shirts, with waistcoats and straw hats.

'Islanders only!' a bloke bellowed. 'No mainies!'

Paulina laughed and kept walking.

'Oi!' She noticed Kymba. 'Kymba-leeeee!'

Kymba looked up, then quickly looked away.

'What's wrong?' Paulina tumbled onto the picnic rug. 'Embarrassed to be seen with a mainie?'

'Oh … no.' Kymba's long light-brown hair was straight as a flag down her back; her little son curled up in her lap. 'Just, we're leaving soon. Hunter's got a tummy-ache.'

'Whatsamatter Hunty, did ya eat too much?' Paulina rubbed the boy's tummy, then peeked inside the nearest esky. 'Ooo, Wild Turkey!'

She waved the bottle at Kymba, who shook her head.

'Drink with me, Kymbaaaa-leeee! Whatsamatter? You preggers again?'

Kymba's pink cheeks told Paulina everything she needed to know.

'Ha!' She threw back her head. 'That makes two of us!'

Then she drank some more and told Kymba about what she'd told Laurent.

'You *lied* about being pregnant?' Kymba wrung the fringe of her white crochet shawl. 'Oh, Paulina, that's … not good.'

'Whatever!' Paulina swigged. 'It's time he took our relationship seriously.'

'Yes, but … trust is the foundation of any good relationship.'

'Trust men? Pffft!'

Kymba looked ready to cry on her behalf. 'You just need to find your Mr Right.'

Right on cue, Kymba's big ginger-haired hubby Simmo strolled across the field, holding hands with their six-year-old, Zoe. He wasn't wearing a costume like the Island men, but he'd trimmed his beard and had on a collared shirt.

'Auntie Lina!' Zoe squealed. 'No mainies allowed in here!'

'Yeah? Howabout your daddy? His surname's "Burney".'

'It's Burney-*King*!'

Paulina got out her ciggies. 'Maybe I should get myself knocked up by a King instead. Then I'd get invited to all the parties.'

Simmo looked uneasily from the ciggies to the bun in Kymba's oven.

'Sorry.' Paulina put them away. 'Oi, Simmo. Would you be pissed off if Kymba lied about being preggers?'

'Um.' Simmo looked at his wife's belly. 'She *is* pregnant. She had an ultrasound.'

'Ugh, forget it.' Paulina drank. 'Youse are really lucky. I probably can't even have babies. Mum had like five miscarriages before she had me … and look how I turned out.'

Kymba and Simmo glanced at each other. Head swimming, Paulina stood.

'Oi, Zo,' she slurred. 'Let's play chasey.'

The dark-blue air felt cool on Paulina's cheeks as she dashed across the field. Zoe shrieked after her, ear-splitting. She ran faster, like she was fifteen again, playing centre-back defence for the Cherry Hill Colts. Until the booze rose to her throat, hot and bubbly.

'You're it, Auntie Lina!' Zoe caught her. 'Eww, you spewed?'

Paulina wiped her mouth.

'Don't tell your mum and dad. Okay?'

'Islanders only!' the same bloke bellowed, when they passed his picnic rug. 'No mainies!'

'Yeah?' It was too dark to see his face, but he was big, even sitting down. 'What're you gonna do about it?'

Then she laughed and kept walking.

'Mummy, Auntie Lina spewed!' Zoe sold her out as soon as they got back to the rug.

'Oh, no!' Kymba furrowed her brow. 'Did you eat? Simmo, get her a plate.'

Simmo sighed and got up.

'S'alright …' Paulina giggled. 'I'll probably just spew again if I eat, at this point.'

It wasn't alright, though. Kymba's face had frozen.

'Islanders only.' The bloke from before was looming over them, drink in hand, his stiff black hair frosted with moonlight. 'No mainies.'

Then he crouched down to smooch Kymba and the kids.

'Yorana,' Kymba greeted him, drew Zoe closer and started fussing with her garland.

'Nice to meet you, sweetheart.' He turned to Paulina. 'I'm Carlyle King.'

'Pfft!' Paulina scoffed. 'That's not a name, that's two surnames.'

'Two *mutineer* surnames.' He had a dent in his fat chin and the typical Fairfolk eyes, like clear seawater rimmed with soot. 'My mother's a Carlyle, my father's a King. I'm a direct descendant of Gideon King and his beautiful wife, Puatea. What's your name, sweetheart?'

Paulina pointed at her Fairfolk Tours name tag. 'Duh!'

He leaned so close that his beery breath warmed her collarbone. 'Pretty name … Paulina.'

'Yeah, better than "Carlyle".'

'My friends call me "Car".'

'Ha-ha! Vroom-vroom!'

'That's right. I own The Car Kings dealership.'

'Is that s'posed to impress me?' She swigged her bourbon. 'I'm not a stupid mainie … I can see your wedding ring.'

'Let me tell you a secret …' Car leaned closer; through his flimsy shirt, she glimpsed a nautical star tattooed on his heart. 'My missus and I are on the outs. She's crazy.'

'Yeah? What'd you do?'

'A younger woman threw herself at me … and the missus blamed *me*.'

'Yeah, right.'

'Trust me. They all get crazy once they hit forty.'

Kymba muttered in Fayrf'k. Car ignored her. So did Paulina; she was having fun.

'Yeah? Well, let me tell *you* a secret: I'm already crazy.'

'Nay, you're a sweet vini.' Car fingered her name tag. 'I'm gonna take you home and show you what a man with mutineer blood in his veins can do with a vini like you.'

'Nah, thanks! I've got a boyfriend. And I don't like fat old men, no offence.'

'You don't know what you like. Till you've had a King in your bed, you'll never know.'

'She said *no*, Car,' Kymba interjected. 'Don't you know the meaning of that word?'

Car responded gruffly in Fayrf'k. Kymba snapped back at him, but her voice had a rickety edge. Hearing it, the kids started whimpering.

'Look: you've made the kiddies cry!' Car laughed and reached for Zoe. 'Don't cry, sweetheart. Come to Uncle Car.'

Kymba snatched Zoe back. 'Simmo!'

Car raised his hands and stumbled to his feet, smiling graciously at Simmo, who'd rushed over with a paper plate. 'Congratulations on your growing family.' He held out his hand. 'Kymbalee is absolutely glowing.'

'Much appreciated.' Simmo looked from Car to his tearful wife and children. 'Give my regards to Tabby.'

Once Car had staggered off, Paulina cracked up laughing.

'Bloody hell, what a dickhead. Are youse related?'

'Just a drunk cousin.' Kymba stood. 'I'm going to find Pellet.'

'I'll go,' Simmo offered.

'I'll go.' Kymba gestured at Paulina and the kids. 'Just, make sure Paulina eats.'

Kymba stormed off, round-bellied in her long white dress.

Paulina took a fiery gulp of bourbon. 'Gawd, this place is inbred.'

Simmo shoved a plate full of cold roast veggies under her nose.

'I don't know why my wife is friends with you.'

'Islanders only!' Car King bellowed. 'No mainies!'

'Chill out.' It was Jesse's voice. 'I'm just taking my drunk friend home, okay?'

'I'm not drunk!' Paulina protested, swigging more bourbon as Jesse appeared with Kymba. 'Where's Loh-rent? Is he angry with me?'

Jesse prised the bottle from her hands and gave it to Kymba. 'I guess you're not worried about foetal alcohol syndrome.'

'First trimester's a free pass!' Paulina giggled as he pulled her to her feet. 'Bloody hell, you don't have to manhandle me! I can walk!'

Jesse let go of her; she collapsed back onto the rug.

'You dropped me? Arsehole!'

'Jesus!' Jesse pulled her up again. 'Cut the crap, Paulina.'

'Bye, Kymbaaa-leeee!' Paulina blew kisses like a beauty queen. 'See ya at our antenatal class next week!'

'Thanks for looking after her,' Jesse told Kymba and Simmo. 'And … sorry.'

Linking her arm with Jesse's, Paulina zig-zagged happily beyond the ruins.

'You're with *Camilleri*?' Car King jeered. 'Let me know when you want a real man, sweetheart!'

All his mates laughed.

'That's the Car King. He wants to root me.' Paulina snuggled into Jesse's shoulder. 'Don't worry, I told him where to go.'

'Well, that's probably the smartest thing you did today.'

'Where's Loh-rent?' She repeated as they climbed uphill. 'Is he angry?'

'In the car. And not yet, but he will be. Fucking hell, Paulina. Why do you have to make everything a drama?'

'Life's boring. Gotta make some noise or the void will swallow me, hey.' She reached into the butt pocket of his jeans. 'Gimme a Camel, Jesse-Camel.'

'Fuck!' Jesse stopped. '*Don't* … don't touch. I'll do it.'

As he fumbled with his ciggies, Paulina pressed her hips against his, slid her hands inside his Fairfolk Tours shirt.

'Jesus-fuck! What're you doing?'

'Nothing …' She nuzzled him. 'I'm cold, that's all.'

He pushed her away; she fell back on the grass, giggling.

'Get up.' Jesse lit a ciggie. 'There's cow-pats everywhere.'

'Get down!' Paulina grabbed his belt-buckle, pulled him onto her. 'I'm soooo cold!'

Their mouths mashed together, tasting of smoke and stale vomit.

'Fuck!' Jesse wiped away her spit. 'I'm not Pellet! Don't play with me.'

'I like playing with you.' Paulina bit his lip. 'It's good fun.'

He kissed her back with those lovely full lips, stubble scouring like a Scotch-Brite sponge. A ghoulish moan echoed from the hills around them.

'Ghosts!' Paulina clung to him. 'Jess — ghosts!'

'It's a cow, you fuckwit.' He sat up, looked at his ciggie; it had burned out. 'Jesus. Oh, Jesus. Don't *cry*.'

Paulina snatched the ciggie from his fingertips and placed it between her lips. He lit it. Then she lay back, weeping and watching the scudding smoke and clouds.

'Is Loh-rent angry? Is he gonna break up with me?'

'Yeah, probably. If he didn't have a reason before, he does now.'

'Don't tell him we hooked up, Jess! You won't tell him, will you?'

'Fuck. No.' He took the ciggie. 'Just, stop crying.'

Paulina stopped crying; pulled Jesse back down. They kissed for a few more minutes, till the cow mooed again and she quavered, 'I'm scared!'

'Yeah, yeah.' Jesse smoothed down his stiffy. 'C'mon, Pellet's waiting.'

In the backseat of the Commodore, Laurent was sprawled out, pale and glaze-eyed. Jesse shut Paulina in the back with him, walked around to the driver's side.

'Babe, I missed you!' She smooched Laurent. 'Did ya miss me?'

Shoving his keys in the ignition, Jesse tuned the radio.

'Seurry, *bébé*.' Laurent closed his eyes. 'I'm not ready to be a fatheur.'

'Nobody's ever ready, babe.' Paulina took his hand. 'Till it happens.'

Jesse cursed and rolled the car onto the steep, pine-lined road.

'*Bébé*.' Laurent pinched his nose-bridge. 'I did not expect this. You said you are on the pill?'

'Accidents happen. The important thing is … we're in love.'

'Ergh!' Laurent loosed his hand from her grip. 'I never said that!'

'You said it!' Paulina's heart cracked. 'Loads of times!'

Exhaling through his teeth, Jesse turned up the radio.

'*Câlisse*! I never said it!'

'Don't call me a "chalice"! You said it, you lying shit!'

'You are the liar!'

'You're a liar! You said you loved me, and now you're just gonna leave me and our baby? You lying French fuck, *how dare you*?'

'Jesus, Paulina,' Jesse butted in. 'Tell him the truth already.'

'Mind your own business, Camel!'

A car full of hooning teenagers, all dressed in their colonial whites and straw hats, sped past. 'Fuck, I hate Mutiny Day,' Jesse muttered.

'Truth?' Laurent questioned Jesse. 'What do you mean, truth?'

'Don't talk to him!' Paulina clawed at Laurent's forearm. 'Talk to *me*.'

'You scratched me? *Tabernac*!'

'I'm not a "tabernacle"! I'm your pregnant girlfriend! You're really gonna leave me?'

'I will leaf you on the roadside, if you keep scratching! *Decriss*!'

'Jesus, Pellet,' Jesse intervened. 'That's not cool.'

'You'd leave me? If I was preggers, you'd leave me?' Paulina crumbled. 'Shit-pellet! You couldn't knock me up if you tried!'

'Ehh? *Câlisse*! You made it up?'

'Yeah-hh! Thank fuck. Now I know how shit you are.' As Jesse slowed for a bend in the road, Paulina pushed the door open. 'Wanna leave me here? Do it!'

'*Decriss*!' Laurent shoved her. 'I don't care!'

'Don't, Pellet!' Jesse stopped the car. 'Jesus … she'll be raped.'

'She deserves it!' Laurent pushed her again. 'Go, lying beech!'

Staggering onto the roadside, Paulina power-walked away from the Commodore through the rain of her tears.

'Oh, come on.' Jesse got out, chased her down. 'Paulina, calm down.'

'*Calm*? He wants me to be raped!' She yanked her arm away. 'You're just as bad. You're his *friend*.'

Laurent honked the horn, unleashed a stream of French-Canadian cusses. 'Go! Walk faster, beech! Camel … leaf her!'

'Shut the fuck up, Pellet.' Jesse followed Paulina as she rushed into the middle of the road, waving madly at a pair of headlights. 'Paulina! Don't hitchhike.'

The headlights slowed to a stop.

'Car trouble?' asked the old bloke behind the wheel.

Sobbing, Paulina shook her head and let herself into the passenger side of his car.

'Please, help me, sir! My boyfriend wants me to be raped!'

The old bloke squinted through the glare of his headlights.

'Camel?'

'Not him! That French fuck.' Paulina gestured at the Commodore. 'He pushed me! Please, get me away from him!'

Jesse came up to the driver's side, his face flushed.

'Sorry, Rabbit. My friend's really drunk. Can you drive her home?'

The bloke looked from Jesse to Paulina, and something clicked.

'I know you,' he said. 'You're the new checkout chick at Foodfolk.'

Paulina sniffed. 'I was a financial advisor, once upon a time.'

'I'll drive you. Where do you want to go?'

'Just get me away from that arsehole.' She sighed, closing her eyes on Jesse and Laurent and the bullshit mutiny of her life. 'Take me back to your place … I don't mind.'

ONLY CHILD

It was impossible to be prepared for everything, in the circumstances. But Caro took comfort in being prepared for most things.

'Jude, it's time,' she whispered into her sister's hair. 'Time to sit.'

Judy protested — a wrenching, girlish cry, like she'd fallen and skinned her knee. Feverishly, she kissed her fingertips, pressed them to the cool mahogany. Kissed the wreath of daffodils and white freesia.

No tears, though. Was she shedding them faster than her body could produce them? Or had the pills obstructed something — made her capable only of performing grief?

'Here, Jude.' Caro crossed herself. 'Over here, now.'

She sat her sister in the front-row pew, beside Tim. Caught his eye across Judy's lap and nodded.

Tim and the boys stood. Shuffled to the casket with sloped shoulders and bowed heads, their ears pink and exposed. She'd made them all get haircuts.

'Caro!'

The smell of him: Ralph Polo Green and something animal, pheromonal. Caro stiffened her cheek for her ex-husband's kiss.

'Gav.' She cringed at the *swick* of his lips. 'Thanks for coming on time.'

'Jude! I'm so sorry.' *Swick*, again. Bastard. 'It's unbelievable. Never seen so many coppers outside a church before. They any closer to catching the guy?'

Judy looked at him glassily. 'Fingerprints.'

'Whassat?' Gavin leaned closer.

'*Fingerprints*,' Caro supplied. 'They found fingerprints.'

'Well, shouldn't take them too long, then. They looking into her boyfriends?'

'Great idea, Gav.' Caro raised her eyes heavenward. 'Ground-breaking. Where would we be without you?'

'Wasn't she dating an older guy? I'd be looking at him.' Ignoring Caro, Gavin helped himself to Tim's seat. 'Young woman, full of energy, hard to satisfy ... You know how it is.'

Judy nodded vaguely, as she would've nodded at anything.

'Poor old Marko. Lucky he never had to live to see this day.' Gavin slid his gaze over Judy's lap. 'Not so lucky for you, though. I mean, you're *all alone* now.'

'She's not alone.' Tim reappeared with Bronson and Wyatt. 'She has us.'

'Sorry, mate.' Gavin vacated his seat. 'All yours.'

Then he turned his attention to their sons. Their freshly shorn sons with their sensitive skin and cowboy names, who wilted like flowers under his shoulder-claps.

'Caro.' Tim noticed Caro's fingers itching at her purse, the bitter yearning of her clenched jaw. 'It can wait.'

'*Can* it, Tim? Are *you* reading the eulogy?' Caro stroked Judy's hair and rose from her seat. 'Jude, honey, I'll be right back.'

All the people she had to pass, filing in to the chapel as she stalked out. It was a good sign. Paulina wouldn't be forgotten — not with a crowd like this.

'Alright?' a cop asked as she shouldered past him. Only young, Bronson's age.

'My niece was stabbed five dozen times.' Caro jabbed a cigarette between her lips. 'Do you think I'm *alright*?'

If she didn't seem so alone, Caro wouldn't have noticed her. It had been a few years. She'd dyed her hair. And, anyway, the resemblance had never been strong.

'Milly!' Caro beckoned. 'Thank *God*. Someone I can smoke with.'

Milica trotted across the carpark, tall despite her poor posture and heartbreakingly cheap flats. The bag on her arm was synthetic, too large for the occasion.

'I quit.' She looked at Caro's Marlboros apologetically. 'Sorry.'

'So you should be!' They hugged, tight. 'Thanks for coming.'

'Of course I came.'

'I didn't mean it like that.' Caro clutched her temple. 'Fuck. I didn't mean *that*.'

'I know you didn't.'

Caro waved her ciggie at the jam-packed carpark. 'You're one of the few people who actually *belongs* here. Who are all these people?'

'Lots of BMWs.' Milica attempted a smile. 'Your friends, not mine.'

'Did you get here okay? How'd you get here? Taxi?'

'Train. From King's Cross.'

'*King's Cross*?'

'I stayed in a hostel.'

'A *hostel*?' Caro shook her head, outraged. 'Tim's brother has a harbourside apartment sitting empty. I would've offered.'

'It's fine.' Milica eyed her ciggie. 'Once an immigrant, always an immigrant.'

'Once a smoker, always a smoker.' Caro held it out. 'I won't judge. God might … but he's a bastard, anyway.'

Relenting, Milica took a drag. As her features relaxed, the ghosts flew in: the unapologetically dark eyes, the shadows under them, something about the throat and ears.

Caro tried not to stare. 'How's Ljubica?'

'Oh, you know.' Milica handed it back. 'Angry.'

'Not as angry as *me*.'

'She would've come. But flying's hard, at her age. Anyway, I thought it might be overkill.' Milica winced. 'Sorry. Bad word. How's Judy?'

'Drugged to the eyeballs.' Caro drew the smoke deep into her lungs. 'It's the only way we could get her through today.'

'I saw her walking into the chapel. She's still beautiful.'

'Damsel in distress.' Caro passed the ciggie. 'Gav's been sniffing around her.'

'Mongrel.'

'You got here early? You could've come in with us.'

'And upset Judy?'

'Like I said, drugged to the eyeballs.' Caro watched Milica drawing in. 'Anyway, she has bigger things to be upset about.'

'I can't handle a repeat of Dad's funeral.' Milica shook her head. 'I'll stick to the nosebleed section, if you don't mind.'

'I *do* mind.' Caro seized the ciggie. 'Paulina would want her big sister close.'

Sniffing, Milica dug inside her handbag. 'I brought something. For her coffin.' She drew out a worn plush lion. 'Leon Lav. *Baka* — Dad's mum — made him. He used to help me sleep when I was small.'

'Oh, Milly.' Caro's brow creased. 'You know it's a closed casket?'

'Shit.' Milica's mouth quirked downward; her dark eyes brimmed quicker than she could avert them. 'Of course it is.'

'I'm sorry. I should've asked if you had anything you wanted to bury with her.' Caro flicked away the cigarette butt. 'The poor thing's been through so much. With the autopsy, then being stitched back together and flown across the Pacific; you can't *imagine* the paperwork. We just wanted to give her some rest.'

'Of course.' Milica wiped her eyes. 'I'm an idiot.'

'Jude made sure she had some of her baby things with her. And her jewellery.' Caro squashed the butt with her stiletto. 'They'd even chosen a dress, if you can believe it.'

'"They"?'

'Don't get me started.' Caro swallowed the lump in her throat. 'I'd wring Jude's neck, if she wasn't so helpless. You'd think it was Paulina's wedding, the way they had it all planned out.'

Milica blinked, uncomprehending.

'She was suicidal, Milly.' Caro held her gaze. 'Jude talked her off the ledge … God knows how many times. A lot, by the sounds of it.'

'I had no idea.'

'You wouldn't. I had to find out from the *detective*.' She sighed. 'Jude and Paulina: it was always them against the world.'

Milica's chin wobbled.

'I'm sorry.' Caro checked her watch. 'I'm due at the podium.'

Milica nodded, eyes streaming. With a rueful smile, Caro picked up Leon Lav, swatted Milica's tears with his nubby paws.

'Prrr?' She purred hopefully. 'Prrr?'

Milica choked a laugh, snatched back Leon. 'You're such a schoolteacher.'

'Takes one to know one.' Caro gave her a swift hug and air-kiss. 'See you inside?'

'Maybe if you brought binoculars.' Milica grimaced. 'I'll be right in.'

Crossing the carpark, Caro's heels clicked loudly. At the door of the chapel, though, she glanced back.

Milica was sobbing into the lion's soft fur.

RABBIT TRAP

The first thing Paulina saw, waking up the morning after Mutiny Day, was a man's billowy white shirt and breeches on the floor by the bed. Next, she saw the wiry arms of the man they belonged to, slung across her body.

'Oh.' He stirred as she disentangled herself. 'Sorry.'

'All good,' Paulina bluffed, heart racing. 'Um. I'm just gonna—'

'Oh.' He sat up, showing off his salt-and-peppered chest. 'Let me.'

He cast around for his breeches. Paulina plucked them from the ground and passed them to him, along with his shirt.

He laughed. 'It's been a while.'

'All good.' She laughed too, though her head was killing her. 'Um. Thanks for last night?'

'Thank *you*, Paulina.' His eyes were fiercely earnest. 'I had a wonderful time.'

'Yeah?' They were nice eyes, she decided; dark brown, a little slanted, deeply crinkled at the sides. 'Um. Same?'

He leaned forward shyly. 'Do you mind if I … ?'

Closing her eyes, Paulina presented her lips, hoping her breath didn't stink.

'Um.' She had to ask. 'No offence, but: how old are you?'

'Fift—' He stopped. 'Almost fifty.'

'Oh, geez.' His face fell, so she added, 'I mean, you're in really good shape.'

Bashfully, he touched her waist. 'I could say the same about you.'

'Ha!' Stuck for words, Paulina offered her mouth again.

After that, he put on his breeches and loose linen shirt and hunted for *her* clothes. Watching him cross the room, Paulina realised how high the ceilings were, how large the windows beyond the curtains.

'Geez, your room's really nice.' She accepted her black g-string. 'Spacious.'

'Too spacious, sometimes.' He picked up her Fairfolk Tours shirt. 'I'm afraid your uniform's a bit … muddy.'

Paulina didn't want to think about how it got that way.

'I can run it through the wash,' he offered. 'No problem.'

'You'd do that?'

'No problem,' he repeated. Then he gave her a look, as if she was too beautiful to be believed, and shook his head. 'It's the least I can do.'

Smiling, Paulina lazed back in bed, letting her tits catch a pale ray of sun that was crawling across the sheets. 'Alright. I'll be waiting right here.'

As soon as he'd gone, she got up and drew the curtains. The view made her gasp.

By the time the old man was getting dressed for the second time that morning, to put her clean clothes in the tumble-dryer, Paulina had decided she wouldn't mind marrying him and having his babies, whoever he was. He gave her his old-timey shirt to wear downstairs.

On her way into the kitchen, Paulina bumped into a chubby girl with braces.

'Daaaad!' the girl yelled.

'Geez.' Paulina clutched her head. 'Not so loud.'

'Oh. Bunny.' He reappeared, frowning. 'I thought you were staying at Hine's.'

'*Bunny?*' Paulina scoffed.

'It's what we've always called her, with my nickname being "Rabbit" …' he explained. 'Bunny, meet Paulina. She's … the new checkout chick at Foodfolk.'

'You brought home a *checkout chick?*'

'I was a financial advisor, once upon a time.' Paulina pawed at Rabbit's shoulder. 'Babe, Panadol?'

He fetched a packet from the cabinet atop the fridge, together with a glass of tap water. She gobbled two tablets; patted his bum gratefully. 'Thanks, babe.'

'Dad!' Bunny cried. 'How old is she?'

'Uh …'

'Twenty-eight,' Paulina supplied wearily. 'And I'm feeling it, babe. See these crow's feet? I didn't have them till last year.'

'Dad! She's half your age!'

'That's enough, Bunny.' Rabbit scolded her. 'If you can't be polite, go to your room.'

'Urgghhhh!'

Bunny stomped her foot, grabbed a box of cereal, and stormed upstairs.

'Bit melodramatic, isn't she?' Paulina laughed. 'I was like that, too, once.'

Rabbit pinched the bridge of his aquiline nose.

'I'm sorry. I thought she'd still be at her friend's.' He sighed. 'Maybe you bes' leave.'

'Yeah. Maybe!'

Paulina stood on her tippy-toes and slipped her tongue in Rabbit's mouth. His breath caught in his chest. She put her hand on his shirtfront and felt his heart, rabbiting there.

'Oh, you're gorgeous.' He stroked her cheek. 'But who am I kidding … You're too young for me.'

'I guess we'll just have to be star-crossed lovers, then.' She pushed her tongue back in his mouth, pressed up against him. 'Till you change your mind, um … *Rabbit*.'

He smiled.

'You can call me "Ric". I know you think Rabbit is silly. You told me last night.'

'Gorgeous man!' What else had she told him? 'Ric!'

'Oh, *you're* gorgeous,' he repeated, tucking her hair. 'Come on. I'll drive you home.'

Rabbit lived on the north-east side of the island, near Cook's Falls, where there were no beaches, only big grey stones and dark cliffs skirted by indigo sea. Turning onto Cook's Falls Road, they saw a line of yellow police tape, bits of smashed glass and metal on the road. Some people were standing around.

'Wait here,' Rabbit told her, getting out to talk to the people in

Fayrf'k. When he returned, he looked stunned. 'A schoolmate of Bunny's was killed in a car crash last night.'

'Oh, geez, Ric.' Paulina reached for his hand. 'I'm sorry.'

'That poor family.' He wiped his eyes. 'Local business owners, Carlyle and Tabitha King.'

'The Car Kings guy?'

Rabbit nodded and re-started the car, hands shaky.

'Drunk-driving.' His voice was shaky, too. 'Those girls shouldn't've been drinking.'

'Yeah,' Paulina mumbled. 'Not till they're legal age.'

'Too many girls start early here. I worry about Bunny.'

'Don't worry, babe,' Paulina reassured him. 'She seems like a good kid.'

Rabbit's eyes got smaller and wetter, squinting into the midday sun. 'It's hard, as a single parent.'

'I get it, hey. Dad died when I was fourteen. It was just me and Mum, after that.' She squeezed his hand. 'I reckon I turned out alright.'

Rabbit shot her a tender glance. 'You turned out beautifully.'

They held hands for the rest of the drive. Her heart broke a bit when he parked.

'This is the butcher's place, isn't it?' Rabbit asked. 'Joe Camilleri?'

'I live in the cottage out the back. It's kinda a sharehouse situation.'

He frowned. 'Lots of parties?'

'Um.' She shrugged. 'A few.'

Rabbit caressed the bauble of bone at her wrist. 'I should tell you: I'm not a drinker. I'm not going to tell you how to live your life, but I don't like what drinking does to me … to people. I've been sober nine years.'

'Oh,' Paulina puzzled. 'Congrats?'

'I hope that doesn't change things for you. I'd like to get to know you. I'd like Bunny to get to know you, too.'

'Same, babe.' She smiled. 'Same!'

Flushed with relief, Rabbit's furrowed face looked ten years younger. 'That makes me so happy. Gorgeous — can I kiss you goodbye?'

'You can kiss me.' She leaned closer. 'Not "goodbye", though.'

She skipped into the cottage with the biggest grin on her face. Jesse was on the couch playing his PlayStation. He had a bruised neck and looked like shit.

'Oh, Jess!' Paulina sprawled on the floor. 'I'm in love!'

'Great.' Jesse let himself get mown down by pixelated gunfire. 'I guess you won't mind moving out, then.'

'Did ya hear about that girl who got killed drunk-driving?' Flick asked her, sneaking a smoke before work Monday morning,

'Sad, hey.' Paulina blew smoke toward the skip. 'Did ya hear I dropped Loh-rent?'

Flick's dull blue eyes sparked. 'So he's ... single?'

'Go for it.' Paulina flicked her ash. 'Just, for your information? Guys who look like that don't try at all.'

'He's still at Camel's?'

'Yeah. And still in *my* bed.' She checked Flick's face for envy. 'Get this: Camel wants *me* to move out, not Loh-rent. Says it's too "complicated" since I've been there. Whatever! I'm done with boys.'

'You gonna move back in with Merle, then?'

'Nah.' Paulina dragged. 'I've got something else in the works.'

Rabbit came in at noon, dressed in chinos and a short-sleeve button-down shirt.

'You're dressed different!' she greeted him, loud enough for Flick and Rita and the lunchtime shoppers to hear. 'Still a gentleman, though.'

'You're dressed differently too,' he replied, more quietly. 'Different uniform.'

He passed her a plastic bag with her Fairfolk Tours uniform in it. She took it out, breathed in the crisp smell. 'Mmm! Oh, babe, I've still got *your* shirt.'

'Don't worry about it.' He looked around. 'I bes' get back to work.'

'Aren't you gonna buy anything?' Paulina rubbed the uniform. '*Women's Weekly*?'

Rabbit blushed into his collar.

'A drink for me? Diet Coke, pretty please?'

Obligingly, Rabbit strode to the fridge.

'Flick!' Paulina called out. 'Thirsty?'

'Fanta, please!'

'And a Fanta for Flick.' Paulina giggled. 'Rita?'

Nothing for Rita; she was marching off like she had more important business elsewhere.

'You're too kind, babe.' Paulina lowered her eyes coyly as she scanned the drinks and took Rabbit's money.

'Let me cook you dinner,' he blurted out. 'Friday night.'

'Geez, Friday?' Paulina ran her fingers up and down the Coke bottle. 'Guess you don't miss me as much as I miss you.'

'Wednesday,' he corrected himself. 'Wednesday?'

'You mean "hump day".' She kept a straight face, though Flick was choking on her Fanta. 'I can't wait.'

'Neither can I.' His blush deepened. 'I hope you like my cooking.'

'Babe, can you do me a favour?' Paulina leaned forward on her elbows. 'I don't have time to go to Fairfolk Tours today. Reckon you can return my uniform?'

'Uh, sure. No problem.'

She'd only drunk half her Diet Coke before Merlinda came stomping into Foodfolk, tomato-faced.

'*Rabbit?*' She tugged Paulina's ponytail. 'You're with *Rabbit White?*'

'Ouch!' Paulina laughed. 'Never knew I liked the taste of rabbit till now, hey.'

She was plucking her eyebrows on the porch after work when Jesse parked his Commodore and said more words than he'd said to her since Mutiny Day.

'Your old man came into Camilleri's today.'

'Ric?' Paulina grabbed Jesse's arm. 'You saw Ric?'

Sitting, Jesse stole a sip of her Pine Brew. 'He ordered a chicken. For Wednesday.'

'Ric's making me *chicken?*' Paulina clutched her heart.

Jesse furrowed his brow. 'What happened to "meat is murder"?'

'I'll eat chicken for Ric. No red meat, but.'

'Jesus, you really like this guy? Daddy issues, much?'

'He's a fine wine, Jess. Better with age.'

'Yeah, but. He's like … sixty.'

'He's not even *fifty*.'

'Ask my dad. They're schoolmates.'

'He's younger than Joe. And he's in way better shape.' Paulina skimmed her eyes over Jesse's midsection. 'I reckon he's in better shape than *you*.'

'He's in better shape than your eyebrows, eh. What the fuck's going on there.'

'I'm making myself perfect, for Ric.' She rubbed the pinkness where she'd been plucking. 'Not a hair out of place.'

'What hair? You plucked them all.'

'I'll wait till tomorrow to shave my legs. And my pubes. I'm gonna be so perfect. He won't be able to live without my rabbit trap.'

'Did you just call your vagina a "rabbit trap"?'

'He-he-he. Oi, why's he called "Rabbit", anyways?'

'You know that Jefferson Airplane song, "White Rabbit"?' Jesse smirked. 'He's named after that. He was a real hippie back in the day.'

'Nooo!' Paulina dug her nails into Jesse's arm. 'Please, no!'

'Jesus! Are you gonna cut those claws before your date? He's an old man; his skin's probably really breakable, eh.'

'Jess.' Paulina put down her mirror and tweezers. 'This is serious, okay?'

'Yeah, I get it. Daddy issues.'

'The way he looks at me ...' She sighed. 'Jess, he's *serious*.'

'Yeah.' Jesse shrugged. 'Okay.'

'Did he ask about me?'

'Um. He asked if you're on the rebound.'

'From Loh-rent? Pfft!'

'Yeah. Um.' Jesse rubbed the fading hickeys on his neck. 'He also asked ... about us.'

Paulina looked at him blankly. Then she laughed, loud and fake.

'Bloody hell, just cos we're housemates?' She took a nose-fizzing gulp of beer. 'Gawd, blokes get so territorial. You told the truth, right?'

'Truth?'

'Like, *obviously*, there's no us. If there was, I'd be sleeping in your bed by now.'

'Um. Yeah. Obviously.'

'Don't worry; after tonight, Ric's gonna be begging me to move in with him. I'll be out in two weeks, tops.'

'Calm down. You only just met the guy.'

'Jess. I really think he might be the one.' She contemplated the Pine Brew in her hand. 'You know, beer doesn't even taste as good, since I met him?'

The smashed glass and metal had been cleared off the road by the time she was driving to Rabbit's, but there were mountains of flowers, and a makeshift cross reading 'TIFFANY KING', and a school picture of the dead girl, blonde-brown hair scraped off her face, her neck toothed by a shell necklace, smiling like her life depended on it. Such a bloody downer. Paulina reached into the glovebox for her flask, then into her handbag for her Tic Tacs.

'Oh. *You*.' Her face fell when Bunny answered the door. 'Where's your dad?'

'He's cooking.' Bunny rolled her eyes. 'For *you*.'

'Yeah?' Paulina perked up. 'You gonna piss off to your room and give us some privacy? Hope so!'

Bunny led her to the kitchen. 'She's here.'

Rabbit stopped slicing carrots and smiled. 'Oh! Good.'

As Bunny withdrew, Paulina poured herself into Rabbit's arms, dipped her tongue in his mouth, and passed him a bottle of Sav Blanc. 'I know you don't drink … but I heard we were having white meat.'

'Oh.' Rabbit's smile diluted. 'None for me. But you go ahead.'

'Cheers, babe!'

While Rabbit fetched her wineglass, Paulina snatched a bit of carrot. 'Geez, how'd you cut these carrots so skinny? It's like a restaurant.'

'Chef's secrets.' Filling her glass, Rabbit looked at her like she'd sprinkled fairy-dust in his eyes. 'God. I didn't think you could get any more beautiful, but here you are.'

'Do you like my dress?'

He watched her pose and turn. 'Beautiful.'

'It's nice dressing up for a change. Like my shoes?'

His eyes travelled down her legs. 'Beautiful.'

'Like my earrings?' She came closer, moved her hair off her neck. 'Teardrops. See?'

'I like them.' He inhaled her perfume. 'I like everything.'

'You haven't seen everything … *yet*.' Paulina moistened her lips.

'Later, though. I went to a lot of effort, you know.'

'I appreciate it.'

Laughing, Paulina took in a mouthful of wine and kissed him. His dick went hard against her tummy. 'I'll never get dinner on the table, at this rate,' he sighed.

Paulina nuzzled him. 'Guess we'll have to go to bed hungry, then.'

He was serious about cooking, though, because soon after, he called Bunny into the kitchen. 'Why don't you show Paulina around the house.'

'But Daaaad.'

'That wasn't a request, Bunny.'

'Look at your dad, laying down the law.' Plucking her wineglass from the counter, Paulina linked her arm with Bunny's. 'I like a man who can do that.'

Bunny tore her arm away once they were in the hallway.

'That's the front door.' Bunny pointed. 'Want me to show you how to use it?'

'Har-har.' Paulina trotted in the opposite direction. 'Oi, who's the baby in that picture? She's pretty chubby.'

'… Me.'

'You haven't changed much.' Paulina smirked. Then a terrible thought occurred to her. 'Wait: Ric doesn't have any more bunnies running around, does he?'

'Just me.'

'Phew!' Paulina clutched her heart. 'Never know, though. Men are sneaky like that. I never knew about my half-sister till Dad's funeral. Oi, is this Ric when he was young?'

'Duh.'

'Gawd, he's good-looking. What's with the costume?'

'He played a redcoat soldier.' Bunny looked embarrassed. 'For the BBC.'

As Paulina cracked up, Bunny clomped ahead to the lounge room.

'Here's the bookshelf. It's where books are kept. For r-e-a-d-i-n-g.'

Elbowing Bunny aside, Paulina ran her fingers over the book spines. 'Cooking, acting, reading … Ric's pretty cultured, hey?'

'He's the Fairfolk Island Minister of Culture.'

'Yeah?' Paulina had no idea what that meant, but it sounded

impressive. 'Not too cultured for me, but.'

A black-and-white cat stalked into the room, tickled Paulina's legs with its tail.

'Aw!' Paulina scooped it up and read its collar. '"Anastasia"! She's Slavic, like me.'

'You're Slavic?'

'Why? You got something against Slavs?'

'No.' Bunny frowned. 'My mum's Russian, for your information.'

'No shit? Guess Ric's got a type.' Paulina lowered her voice. 'Oi. Why'd they split?'

'Mind your own business.'

'Whatever. Ric'll tell me, when he's ready.' Narrowing her eyes, Paulina sipped her wine. 'Let's see your room.'

'No way.'

'Yes way. Want me to tell Ric how rude you're being?'

'Ugh, fine!' Bunny led her upstairs, opened the door of her room. 'Here.'

Paulina pushed inside, headed straight for the bed.

'Comfy! Your dad's is bigger, but.' As Bunny sat at her desk and opened her school books, Paulina drank more wine. 'What's that, maths? Want help?'

Bunny didn't answer. With a shrug, Paulina dug under the mattress.

'What's this, your diary? *Dear diary: sorry I haven't written in a while* … Bah-ha-ha! Like anyone cares.'

'Dooon't!' Bunny jumped to her feet. 'That's private!'

'Pretty obvious hiding place, no offence.' Primly, Paulina gave it back. 'Oi, is that a photo of your mum? Gawd, he *does* have a type. Oooo, what are those trophies for?'

'Archery.'

'No shit? Where'd you learn that?'

'Dad's been taking me since I was six.'

'Ric does it too?' Paulina swooned. 'What *can't* this man do! Oi, what's that instrument?'

'Clarinet.'

'Lame! Why don't you play guitar or something? Oi, where do you keep your CDs? Your room's really boring, no offence. Do you even own a mirror?'

Bunny rummaged in her drawer, pulled out a compact, and threw it. 'Here!'

'Cheers, babe!'

Paulina was examining her crow's feet when Rabbit rapped on the door. His eyebrows went up, seeing her so comfy on Bunny's bed, and Bunny quietly doing her homework, and Anastasia licking her paws.

'Look at this! All the girls together!'

'Yeah.' Paulina beamed. 'I was just helping Bun with her algebra.'

The chicken was all splayed and flattened, like roadkill, but with herbs and lemon and stuff.

'Aw, you made the butterfly one?' Paulina gushed. 'Cute!'

Rabbit smiled proudly. When he saw her remove the skin, though, he frowned.

'Too much fat, you know,' Paulina explained.

'I'm sorry. I'll keep that in mind.'

'Mmm, the veggies look good! What's this?'

'Sauteed carrot and zucchini in honey vinaigrette.' He watched as she scooped some onto her plate. 'Homegrown. Except for the honey. That's Fergal's Farm.'

'You *grew* them?'

'The taters, too.' He nodded at a bowl of baby potatoes. 'This weekend's harvest.'

'Wow, Ric.' Paulina shook her head wistfully as she took up the bowl. 'You're a man of many talents.'

'Fairfolk soil.' Rabbit shrugged. 'Everything grows here.'

'You don't get pests?' Paulina shot him a sly look. 'Rabbits?'

'No rabbits on Fairfolk.' He leaned back in his chair. 'Not since the Great Rabbit Cull of 1965. That's how I got my nickname, actually …'

Bunny groaned. Paulina didn't, but she was tempted, once he got going — it was a bloody long story. Partway through, she clapped her hands and laughed.

'That reminds me! I totally have a rabbit-killing story, too!'

'Oh?'

'So, like, my cousin Bronson had this bunny, Lappy? Really cute white bunny-rabbit.' Paulina topped up her wine. 'I was maybe six and

Bronson, ummm, three? Anyways, our mums left us alone — they were probably getting high, bloody hippies — and Lappy had this cage, and every time I lifted the door, he'd try to run out and — BANG!'

She slammed her hand on the table, cracked up again.

'Oh?' Rabbit repeated.

'I guess I did it so many times he got a brain haemorrhage? Poor Lappy!' Paulina glugged her wine. 'Anyways, I blamed it on Bronson. Mum and me still joke about how he's a serial killer, they just haven't found the bodies yet.'

Bunny started coughing; hid her mouth behind her serviette.

Rabbit smiled politely. 'That's quite a ... *different* rabbit story.'

'Yeah, but kinda the same?' Paulina giggled. 'We're a match made in heaven, hey.'

'I don't think rabbit killers go to heaven,' Bunny choked out.

'Well, your dad's worse than *me*.' Paulina slit her eyes at Bunny. 'I was just a kid. How old was he when he culled all those poor rabbits?'

'Twenty-one!' Bunny recovered. 'He was twenty-one in 1965. Thirty-five years ago.'

Rabbit pursed his lips. 'Thank you, Bunny.'

Paulina felt a bit like throwing up. But the feeling passed with her next gulp of wine.

'Don't be embarrassed, babe.' She stroked Rabbit's leg. 'Age is just a number.'

Bunny stood. 'Can I go to my room?'

'Go on,' Rabbit said.

After Bunny left, they sat playing footsie, till Paulina's foot ventured to his crotch and he cleared his throat, stood to clear the table. Picking up the near-empty wine bottle, Rabbit frowned, before carrying it out with the dirty dishes.

Cheeks burning, Paulina finished her glass, then followed him to the kitchen.

'Don't do that,' he protested as she started filling the sink. 'Sit. Relax.'

'I'll wash, you dry?'

'You'll chip your nail polish. Let me find some gloves.'

Under the kitchen lights, she could see Rabbit's hair was thinning on top, and longed for her wine. But she kissed him when he rose; felt

101

giddy as he helped her into the pink rubber gloves at the sink.

'Talk about royal treatment! Those boys I live with expect me to do all the dishes … and they definitely don't own pink gloves.'

Rabbit's face reddened.

'Does that make you jealous?' she asked, sinking her gloves into the steaming water. 'Me living with those boys?'

'A little bit,' he admitted. 'Yes.'

Paulina sighed heavily — though she was smiling on the inside.

'I don't wanna make you jealous, babe. I don't wanna be living with those boys. That's not how I saw myself living, at twenty-eight.'

'Oh?' Rabbit took a soapy plate from her hands. 'Where did you see yourself?'

'Well …' She set down a bundle of clean cutlery. 'Somewhere like this. Doing dishes with a gorgeous man who knows how to take care of me. Is it too soon to say that?'

'A little bit,' Rabbit repeated, laughing. 'Yes.'

'Well, I'm saying it.'

There were butterflies in her tummy as she scrubbed the chopping board. Rabbit moved her hair off her neck and kissed it.

'Oh, gorgeous. This is all happening so fast.'

'It doesn't feel fast to me.' Paulina turned to face him. 'It feels just right.'

They kissed again, her gloved hands floating in the warmth like bath toys.

'I used to see you walking, you know,' Rabbit confessed. 'I started riding my bike that way to work, so I could see you. I never thought I'd be so lucky.'

'You noticed me?' Paulina's cheeks glowed. 'You should've talked to me, hey.'

'Darling … I should warn you.' Rabbit turned away to dry the cutlery. 'I haven't lived with a woman since Bunny's mother. Tatiana. Almost ten years ago.'

'Yeah?' Paulina went back to her scrubbing. 'Time to give it another go, I reckon.'

'She wasn't an easy woman to live with,' Rabbit continued. 'She was bored by Fairfolk, by me. Too quiet for her.'

'I like the quiet.' Paulina passed him the chopping board. 'I don't get bored easy.'

Rabbit set down the board, took her gloved hands in his. 'What would your mother say about you moving in with a man my age?'

Paulina laughed.

'Probably the same thing she said about me moving to Fairfolk: "I don't feel good about this, Paulina!"'

TROPHY

Bunny was folding the washing after school, like Rita had asked her to, when she found it. In the pocket of her dad's jeans. Right away, she knew it was *hers*.

'Ugh!' She flung the skimpy piece of black fabric across the room. 'Urghhhh!'

Anastasia stirred from where she'd been sleeping, curled up like a snail by the pillow. Bunny looked at her pleadingly.

'How *could* he, Anastasia?' She sniffed. 'Oh, Anastasia! What do I *do*?'

Anastasia blinked her green eyes, then stared at the wall, not helpful. Slowly, like Anastasia sneaking up on a bird, Bunny inched over to the g-string, pinched it between her fingertips.

It was *hers*. Definitely *hers*. But why was it in his *pocket*?

She scrunched it up quickly, stuffed it inside the junior girl's archery trophy on the shelf above her bed, then dug her diary out from under her mattress.

Dear diary, she wrote. *I don't know how to tell you this, but I think my dad might be a murderer! Verly, a MURDERER! Oh diary, give me guidance in this moment of turmoile! What do I do, what do I do???*

She kept quiet all day at school, even though her chest felt like it was full of bugs, and even though she almost cried during her maths test, and even though Hine asked why she was being so weird at lunchtime, picking at her tuna-salad sandwich under the banyan tree. After school, she met Hine like usual for the walk home, and Hine asked if she wanted to get ice cream at Jellyfish Fuel, and Bunny said, 'Bes' not,' and Hine said it again:

'Why're you being so weird today?'

'I'm not weird.' Bunny's eyes prickled. 'I'm always like this.'

'You are *so* weird! Are you on a diet or something?'

'Aye.' Bunny shrugged. 'Maybe.'

'Well, *I'm* getting ice cream.'

Hine took ages at the freezer, deciding between a Hava Heart and a chocolate Paddle Pop. She took ages paying, too; she only had silver coins.

'You're so annoying!' Bunny whined. 'Don't you ever have proper money?'

'I can't help that my dad's not as rich as your dad!'

'My dad's not rich! He just owns lots of land. It's like, verly expensive to maintain.'

'Can I have two dollars?'

Bunny rolled her eyes. 'Aye.'

Outside Jelly's, Hine grabbed Bunny's arm, put her index finger to her lips, and started jumping up and down, pointing at Jesse Camilleri filling up his red Commodore. 'It's him! The serial killer!'

'It's not "serial" if there's only one victim!' Bunny hissed. 'Duh, Hine!'

'There'll be more, eh.' Hine unpeeled her Paddle Pop and sucked on the tip. 'Look how *dark* he is.'

'Hine! That's verly racist, eh!'

Jesse glanced back at them, and Hine shrieked, pulled Bunny's arm, and dragged her away. They ran all the way from Jelly's up to Missionary Road.

'Thanks a lot, Bun! Now he knows us,' Hine fretted, when they ran out of breath. 'We'll have to lock our windows every night!'

'Duh, he knows us anyway! We've only been buying meat from Camilleri's since we were born.'

'But now he *knows* us, *knows* us. He *knows we know!*' Hine examined the dribble of ice cream down her hand. 'Ohhhh, Bunny, it's *melting*! This is the worst day of my life!'

'Don't waste it! I paid good money for that!'

They walked on, Hine lapping at her ice cream. A couple of guys in a truck honked at them as they walked, and a little after that, Kristian King pulled up in his Bongo ute and asked if they wanted a lift. Hine looked at Bunny hopefully. Bunny shook her head. 'No thank you.'

'You sure?' Kristian asked. 'It's a long way, girls.'

'No thank you,' Bunny repeated.

Hine followed her lead. 'No thank you.'

Kristian shook his head like he thought they were stupid, and drove off.

'*I* would've said yes,' Hine griped, trudging uphill. 'It's not like he's the killer.'

'You would've said yes even if he was.'

'Yeah, but only for, like, information.' Hine finished her Paddle Pop, chucked the popstick into a field of grazing cows. 'And to look at his arms. He has really good arms, eh? And … Bun, are you *crying?*'

'No!'

'You are so!'

'The sun's in my eyes!'

'Why're you being so weird?'

'Shut up!'

'Tell me!'

'It's a secret!'

Hine stopped in her tracks. 'Best friends don't keep secrets!'

'I'm not allowed to tell.'

'Then we can't be friends, sorry.'

Bunny wiped her eyes. 'You have to promise not to tell anyone.'

'I know how secrets work.'

'Pinky promise?'

'Pinky promise.'

They linked pinky fingers and, weeping, Bunny told her everything she knew about the g-string.

'It's so *small*,' Hine marvelled. 'How does it even cover her notties?'

'She shaves them, I think.' Bunny felt sick. 'Shaved, I mean.'

'Like, all of them? That's so slutty!'

'Soooo slutty!' Bunny agreed. 'That's how I knew it belonged to Loony Lina! Rita never wears undies like this.'

'Ew! I can't believe you just made me picture Rita in a g-string!'

'I can't believe it was in his pocket! Why would Dad put it in his pocket?'

'It's probably a trophy, eh. To remember her by. When he's wanking and stuff.'

'Nay!'

'At least it's been through the wash.' Hine inspected the crotch. 'Do you think DNA comes out in the wash?'

Bunny snivelled, shrugged. 'I wish they taught us this in school.'

'Remember in the news when Monica Lewinsky had the president's seed on her dress? Did *she* wash her dress?'

'I don't know. Dad always changed the channel when that story came on.'

Hine giggled, stretched the g-string. 'I wish I had the body for these, eh!'

'Ugh! You'd wear that? It's so slutty!'

'Boys like it, but.'

'But, imagine a string between your bum cheeks! How does it not get kuka on it?'

'You wipe after you go, duh! Don't you wipe?'

'I wipe!' Bunny started crying all over again. 'You're not even helping, Hine!'

'I'll help!' Hine's hand flew to her heart. 'I swear on our friendship, I'll help you, Elena White! Even if it makes me an accessory to murder. That's what best friends are for.'

'I can't keep it in my room. It's giving me nightmares.'

'Why don't you just put it back in your dad's pocket?'

'Because! It's *gross*.'

'Or you could put it with Rita's things?'

'She'll lyme him!'

'I know! Why don't we sneak into Jesse's place when he's at work and hide it there?'

'Nay, Hine! He's innocent. And he's verly cute, eh.'

'Or someone else? Yooey Turner! *He's* a perv.'

'Nay, Hine.' Bunny dashed a tear. 'It doesn't matter if Yooey's a perv. If they test for DNA, they'll know he's not the culprit.'

'Then there's only one solution,' Hine said solemnly. 'We need to destroy the evidence.'

———

They were sitting in front of the fireplace, whispering to each other, when Rabbit got home, wearing his bike gear.

'Hello, girls,' he said. 'What's with the fire? It's twenty degrees out.'

'Sorry, Dad.' Bunny shivered. 'We got cold.'

Hine shivered too. 'Brrrr!'

'You might think to put a jumper on, next time.' Rabbit frowned at their bare arms and legs. 'You didn't think to put your jumpers on?'

'Sorry, Dad. Want me to chop more wood?'

'Nay, I'll do it. It'll be good stress-relief, after the day I've had.'

When Rabbit said that, Hine gasped and clutched Bunny's arm, terror-struck. Rabbit looked concerned. 'Is … everything alright, Hine?'

'Yes Mr White,' Hine squeaked. 'I'm good, thank you.'

'Are you staying for dinner? I'm making seafood mornay.'

'Aye. If that's not too much trouble, Mr White.'

'Nay trouble.' Rabbit smiled. 'There's always room for you at our table.'

Then he moseyed out of the room, whistling a tune.

'No offence,' Hine whispered, once he was gone. 'But your dad's verly creepy, eh.'

Bunny was offended.

Two days later, Bunny and Hine were buying ice cream after school when they found themselves standing in line behind that podgy old detective from Canberra with the Polish name and the big round head like a soccer ball.

'Elena White, isn't it?' he greeted her.

'Aye,' Bunny mumbled. 'Nobody calls me "Elena", but.'

'Don't you get hot, wearing that suit?' Hine blurted out.

'A bit, yes,' said Detective Wozniak. 'But I like to look professional.'

Hine smirked. 'You look like a mainie.'

'Well, the cat's out of the bag, now.' Wozniak looked at Bunny's ice cream. 'Cornetto. Good choice.'

Bunny burst into tears.

'I don't know anything, okay! Leave me alone!'

OFF THE ROCK

'Being a mother is hard,' Paulina moaned. 'I see what you meant, all those years.'

'You're not a mother!' Judy scoffed. 'Sounds to me like you enjoy fighting with the girl more than you enjoy that old bloke's company.'

Judy always found a way to bring it back to how boring Rabbit was. 'I don't! I'm a calm person, essentially. Bunny just shits me.'

'Yes, child. You're calm … like a boiling kettle.'

Judy chuckled at her own joke, way more than it deserved. All at once, Paulina was filled with an envy as white-hot as the bulb of the reading lamp she was quietly burning her hand on.

'Muuuum. Are you drunk?'

'What? No!' Judy chuckled again. 'Oh, I had a couple of wines with the girls from work. Renee turned in her thesis on Georges Bataille! Just a couple, though. I didn't want to cramp their style.'

'You don't seem to mind cramping mine.'

'*You* called *me*.' Concern edged into Judy's voice. 'Are you really that bored?'

'I'm not bored!' Paulina cried, so loud that Rabbit stirred in the reading chair where he'd dozed off with *The Charterhouse of Parma* in his lap. 'Just … shitty. Bunny shits me.'

'Darling, are you getting your period soon? You always get so moody before.'

'Ugh. I dunno.' Paulina cooled her hand on the windowpane. 'It's hard keeping track. They're so irregular.'

'If you gained a bit of weight—'

'I'm eating! Gawd, all I do is eat.' Paulina lifted her shirt to examine her after-dinner bloat. 'I ate so much of this pesto pasta Ric made tonight. I look *gross*.'

'Oh, come off it.'

'You can't see me. I reckon this is the fattest I've ever been in my life.'

'I'd like to see you, Paulina. Any time you want to visit, just say the word. Have you thought any more about Christmas?'

'Yeah,' she spat. 'I'm spending it with Ric.'

'Well … I'll miss you,' Judy murmured. 'And not just me. Aunt Caro. Uncle Tim. Bronson. Even Wyatt's flying over from the States with his girlfriend. Look, you can even bring—'

'I'm *not* bringing Ric. Bloody hell. I'm not putting him through that.'

'I'll be nice. I'll make Caro be nice,' Judy bargained. 'I *know* it's awkward, but if you're serious about this old man — and it sounds like you are — I'll have to meet him eventually.'

'We don't need your passive-aggressive bullshit. We're happy on our little island.'

'Oh yes. Just like *Blue Lagoon*.'

'Gawd, you're a cow!'

'Oh, Paulina.' Judy sighed. 'I *worry* about you.'

'I worry about *you*. You need to get a life.'

'You have nothing in common with that man.'

'Racist!'

'Come off it. You know that's not what I mean.' Judy softened her tone. 'Whoever he is, he's not worth isolating yourself for. He's not worth changing for.'

'Bloody hell, one minute you're saying I need to drink less and get my life sorted, next minute you're on at me for changing? I can't do anything right!'

'That's not what I'm saying. I just mean … it doesn't have to be all or nothing. You don't have to stay in every night for months on end pretending to read *Anna Karenina*. Why don't you have some beers with your workmate at that new surfer bar?'

'I don't wanna go to Wetties with Flick. She's a dumbarse.' Paulina examined the pink mark on her hand. 'And I like staying in with Ric. I feel sad when we're apart … like I'm not me.'

'You're you. You're more you than anyone I know.'

'What do you know? Stupid receptionist.'

'I've been there, Paulina. I *know*.'

'I'm not *you*.'

'I know. You're brighter, and bubblier, and funnier. Which is why I hate the thought of you changing for a man.'

'He's not just any man. I love him.'

'Love isn't everything.' Judy sighed again. 'Gawd help you, Paulina. If this is the man you marry. If you're not bored yet, you will be. You'll cheat. It's in your nature.'

'Bitch!' Paulina's voice cracked. 'Have some faith in me!'

'I have faith in you, darling ... I just don't have faith that he's enough.'

'Fuck you! Get a life! Goodnight!'

Paulina slammed down the phone, huddled up in a brittle ball of tears. When she looked up, Rabbit was wide awake. 'Another fight with your mother?'

Nodding, Paulina sprung from her chair and curled up in his lap.

'She wants me to go back to the *mainland* for Christmas.'

Rabbit parted her fringe, planted a dry kiss on her forehead.

'That's not such a bad idea. It might do you good to get off the rock for a bit.'

'Are you sure you don't want anything from the mainland, Bun?' Paulina burbled from the suicide-seat. 'Maybe I can buy you a sense of fashion while I'm there.'

'Maybe you can buy Dad a less annoying girlfriend.'

'Bunny!' Rabbit warned.

'Nah, he likes them annoying.' Paulina caressed Rabbit's leg. 'Howabout I buy you a diary that actually locks?'

'Daaad. You said you'd tell her to stop—'

'Lina,' Rabbit chastised her mildly. 'Have you been reading Bunny's diary again?'

'Course not! I'm just teasing.'

Paulina smiled at him and he smiled back, squeezed her thigh, and turned into the airport carpark. 'I'll get your bag, gorgeous.'

'Thanks, babe!' Paulina sang. She waited until he'd closed the door behind him before leaning over the back of her seat and smirking at Bunny. '*Dear Diary: Hayden didn't say 'hi' to me today. Why doesn't he like me?*'

'*Dear Diary,*' Bunny retorted. '*I only ate salad today. Why am I so fat?*'

'*Dear Diary! Maybe Hayden doesn't like me cos I'm a brace-faced little cow!*'

'*Dear Diary! Maybe Ric doesn't wanna marry me cos I'm an anorexic bitch!*'

'The plane's refuelling.' Rabbit opened her door. He had her suitcase on his shoulder. 'Looks like we've got time for a coffee!'

'You know that suitcase has wheels?' Paulina chirped, getting out of the car.

'I've got it.' Rabbit hoisted it further up his shoulder. 'Bunny, are you coming out?'

Paulina giggled. 'Crack a window, she'll be right!'

Bunny got out and trailed after them toward the terminal. 'Can I get a Coke, Dad?'

'I suppose so.' Rabbit fished for his wallet. 'Get me a long black. And something for Lina.'

'Diet Coke!'

There was hardly any line for check-in. Paulina clung to Rabbit while she waited, announcing between kisses, 'I'm gonna miss you soooo much, babe!'

'I'll miss you too.' Rabbit looked around self-consciously. 'But it's only a week.'

'A week without *this.*'

She slipped her hands in his back pockets, kissed his neck. The bloke ahead of them in line turned around, eyebrows raised.

'Yorana, Car.' Rabbit greeted him awkwardly. 'You good?'

Car King winked. 'Nay good as you.'

The line moved along. Car dumped his bags, then skulked off to the kiosk, where Bunny was already sitting outside with two Cokes and a coffee.

'I said "Diet"!' Paulina told her off. 'Gawd!'

Bunny smirked. 'Dad, can I have Paulina's Coke, too?'

'No, Bunny.' Rabbit frowned. 'That's how diabetes happens.'

Paulina let the Coke sweat on the table; spent the next twenty minutes canoodling with Rabbit and loudly telling him how much she'd miss him. She bawled at boarding-time.

'It's only a week, Lina,' Rabbit repeated, mystified. 'You can call me every night.'

She stopped bawling on the plane; she had a whole row to herself. 'I thought you nay like old men,' Car King jeered from the row diagonal to her.

'I don't like *fat* old men,' Paulina rejoined; then remembered. '... Sorry about your daughter, by the way. Tiffany?'

'Stepdaughter.' His eyes glossed over. 'She was an angel. Taken too soon.'

Paulina looked out the window at the tarmac, where Rabbit was waiting to watch the plane take off. During the safety demonstration, Car showed her a baby picture in his wallet.

'My new niece, Leilani. Meeting her for the first time.'

'Aw, gorgeous. In Sydney?'

'Perth.'

'No shit?' Paulina handed the picture back. 'My sister's in Perth.'

Car smiled. 'We're together for the long haul, then.'

'Not today.' She folded her arms. 'Just till Sydney.'

Paulina felt Car's eyes on her as the plane lifted into the air. She looked out the window until Rabbit was just a speck on the tarmac, the island a speck in the Pacific. Bar service started.

'From the gentleman,' the flight attendant said, bringing her a plastic cup with an inch of fragrant amber at the bottom.

Paulina looked across at Car. He raised his drink, winked.

'No, thanks.' Paulina was surprised by how little she was tempted. 'Just a Diet Coke.'

She took out *Anna Karenina*, read almost twenty pages before she got sleepy.

She slept so easy, these days.

'Look how fat I am!' Paulina griped, the moment she got through immigration and saw her mum, looking so cute in her sandals and summer dress with her fine, light hair around her shoulders. 'Look: I've even gained weight on my boobs!'

Judy scrutinised Paulina.

'Darling,' she said in a stilted voice. 'When was your last period?'

—

After stopping at the Cherry Hill Plaza chemist, Paulina insisted on going to Video Ezy.

'Oi, do you have that BBC one that's like *Pride and Prejudice*, but not?' Paulina asked the teenage boy at the counter. 'It stars Ric White!'

'He doesn't *star*,' Judy muttered. 'It's a bit-part, at best.'

'Umm.' The boy looked around. 'We have some period dramas over there.'

Paulina rushed to the shelf, picked up a DVD. 'This one's BBC! Oh … It's from the eighties. That's too recent.'

'It would be helpful if you remembered the title.' Judy sighed. 'Can't you just ring him and ask?'

'He'll be offended that I forgot.' Paulina picked up another DVD. 'Is *this* it?'

'Why are you asking me!'

'I reckon this is it,' Paulina said uncertainly. 'Yeah.'

'Oh, for chrissakes, Paulina … I bet it's not even a bit-part. He's probably just an extra.'

'I'm getting it.' She flounced to the counter. 'Ooo, can we get *Girl, Interrupted* too?'

'Yes! Just *hurry up*.'

As Paulina put the DVDs on the counter, Judy handed over her card, then clutched her temples. 'Gawd, Paulina. You've known him *four months*.'

On their way out, they bumped into Adrianna Portelli, who'd been a bridesmaid with her at Carli's wedding. 'Hel-*lo* gorgeous!' Paulina trilled.

'Paulina?' Adrianna did a double take. 'You look amazing!'

'Yeah, island life's really agreeing with me, hey.'

'I'm going to go buy some things for dinner,' Judy said sceptically.

Ignoring her mum, Paulina gave it to Adrianna good.

'It's *paradise*. Every day I wake up and can't believe how *beautiful* my island home is. My boyfriend's got a *hammock* on his porch. We watch the sunset *every day*. There's no traffic and no crime *at all*. Everybody just leaves their doors unlocked! Oh, and the beaches? Palm Beach is *shithouse* compared. Gawd, Sydney's such a shithole — I dunno how you live here, no offence! My boyfriend wanted to come too, but he works for the island government so he's *really* busy and important. He's a bit older, but he's got Polynesian blood so you can't even tell. He's *such* a looker. Used to be an actor. Anyways, howabout you?' '

'Oh. Same old, same old.' Adrianna gritted a smile. 'We should totally catch up for drinks — all the girls!'

'Totally!'

Judy was already waiting inside the car. 'Did you have a nice catch-up with your friend? I don't think I know that one.'

'Pfft! She invited me to some party at the casino for New Year's Eve. I said, "yeah, maybe!" but I really meant, "fuck, no!"'

'That's some nice passive-aggression, Paulina,' Judy congratulated her. 'Very nice.'

Then she burst into tears.

'Mum!' Paulina yelped. 'What's your problem?'

'Nothing.' Judy wiped her eyes. 'You just seem very grown up, all of a sudden.'

Judy kept wanting to talk about the test results. Paulina kept fast-forwarding through the DVD, looking for Rabbit.

'Oh gawd.' Judy took a glug of white wine. 'He's going to be sixty-six when it's ten!'

'Sixty-seven,' Paulina corrected. 'His birthday's next month.'

'Sixty-seven! And that's if he doesn't die of prostate cancer first.'

Paulina bit her lip and fast-forwarded some more. 'Where are the soldiers? He plays a soldier in a red coat.'

'The father of my grandchild played a redcoat … he played a redcoat for the BBC in 1971 …' Judy pressed her glass to her forehead. 'Do you remember 1971, darling?'

'Do *you*, you fucking hippie?'

'You don't remember 1971 … You weren't even *born* in 1971.'

'Geez, you're so smart, you should be a receptionist.' Paulina looked at Judy in disgust. 'This kid better get Ric's brains. You're a dead-end, hey.'

'His name's "Rabbit" and he's having sex with a twenty-eight-year-old!' Judy cried. 'How smart can he be?'

'Really smart. BBC smart.' Paulina sighed as the episode came to an end. 'Anyways, it's not his fault. Everyone knows the pill's not a hundred per cent … and we've been fucking like rabbits.'

Judy wept into her glass. 'Oh Paulina!'

The next episode started, with a whimsical chiming of piano keys, floral wallpaper.

'For fucksake, how many scenes of people sitting in stuffy rooms can there be? I know it's England, but bloody hell!'

'Paulina ... Paulina ... *Paulina.*'

'Mother, mother, mother?' Paulina swiped a stray tear from her own eye. 'What?'

'Look: if you're really keeping it—'

'I'm keeping it! I already said!'

'I know, and I'm overjoyed. But, look: if you're keeping it, the smart thing to do—'

'I'm *not* coming home!'

'Think about it, Paulina. Are the obstetric services on that island really—'

'People have kids on Fairfolk! They've been doing it for like two hundred years! My friend Kymba's having her third kid really soon, and she's not going to the mainland!'

'Yes, but,' Judy said tersely. 'That's different.'

'How's it different? My kid's gonna be a Fairfolk Islander. She's gonna have a mutineer surname, and she's gonna grow up climbing trees and eating fruit from the trees and playing with cows, and every Mutiny Day she'll get to wear a pretty costume.'

'"She"?' Judy noted.

'Yeah. I want a girl. So what?' Paulina probed her belly button. 'Anyways, it's nothing yet. It's probably nothing. There's no point getting stressed or excited or ... anything.'

'Oh, Paulina,' Judy whispered. 'Just because I—'

'I got all your shit qualities!'

'Even so. Modern medicine ...'

'I just wanna take it easy. I wanna be near nature and the man I love and breathing fresh air every day. The air smells so good there.'

'And you call *me* a hippie.'

'Yeah. I guess I got that from you, too. Fuck!' Paulina picked up the remote and fast-forwarded through a scene of ladies rambling through a rose garden. 'You stress me out, no offence. I can't afford to be stressed.'

Judy took a sip of wine. 'I'll shut up then.'

She was still crying, though, and looking at Paulina from the corners of her wet eyes. She was so annoying.

'Stop crying, Mum,' Paulina complained as big, slow tears slid down her own cheeks. 'You're making *me* cry.'

'Can I see it again?' Judy asked. 'Can I feel it?'

'Ugh!'

Paulina tried not to puke as her mum placed her hot, drunk hands on her tummy and cooed, 'Baby! My baby's having a baby!'

Then the redcoats appeared.

'That's him! That's Ric! Look! Gawd … he's good-looking.'

Judy squinted at the TV. 'That one with the mutton-chops?'

'Nah, further back,' Paulina paused it, crawled up to the TV to point him out. 'There! Gawd, he has great genes. He has *such* great genes, don't ya think?'

'Um.' Judy squinted some more. 'They're alright, I s'pose.'

Paulina let the scene play out. Rabbit had one line: *rather*. She rewound it and made him say it again, over and over.

'"Rather!"' she imitated his toff accent. '"Rather"! Isn't he talented?'

Judy had already dozed off on the couch.

They had Christmas at her rich Aunt Caro's place in Mercy Cove, like always. Like always, her mum did the salads and dessert, and Uncle Tim did the meat, and Caro handed out envelopes stuffed with fifties and made sure everyone was drinking as much as she was. Paulina emptied her first glass of champers into the pool when nobody was watching; her second glass into the azalea bush. At the table, she sat next to Judy, who dutifully drank from both their glasses. She made sure to act extra-pissed.

'MAYHEM!' she yelled at her cousin Bronson, who was wearing a T-shirt of the black-metal band, Mayhem. 'Watch out, here's MAYHEM! Oh no! Not MAYHEM!'

Aunt Caro thought it was hilarious and joined in. 'MAYHEM!'

'Mayhem!' Judy giggled, when she was drunk enough. 'Mayhem!'

They yelled it whenever Bronson got up or sat down or said anything. 'It's just a band,' he kept explaining, ears getting pinker.

'Got any New Year's Eve plans, Mayhem?' Paulina asked conversationally. 'Gonna burn down some churches? Sacrifice some bunnies to your dark lord and saviour?'

For presents, she gave everyone Fairfolk Pine-scented air-fresheners. Everyone pretended they were wonderful, till Wyatt accidentally chucked them out with the Christmas cracker rubbish and said in his brand-new American accent, 'Sorry, I thought they were trash.' Wyatt's American girlfriend, Monica, accidentally broke a glass.

'TAXI!' Paulina and Judy and Caro screamed in unison.

Monica looked scared shitless. 'You'll get used to them,' Uncle Tim told her, then went inside for the dustpan and broom.

Caro went inside to change her top. Judy went in to dress the pavlova. Paulina, who didn't trust the olds to be alone together, refilled her glass and announced, 'Gotta piss!'

She bumped into Tim on her way in.

'I'm cutting you off!' he boomed, confiscating her glass. Then he drained it and tapped his nose conspiratorially. 'No need to waste my Veuve Clicquot. I'm onto you.'

'Mum told you?!'

'I give it five minutes before she tells Caro.' Tim hugged her swiftly. 'Want me to keep her distracted while you give your sister a call?'

'Cheers.'

She strolled past the kitchen, where her mum was innocently arranging sliced strawberries on top of the pavlova. 'Where are you going?'

'I'm going for a piss,' Paulina mumbled. 'Geez!'

'Oh, yes. You'll need to wee a lot more often!' Judy said gleefully.

Paulina stomped upstairs; found her Aunt Caro in her bra and open blouse, sneaking a ciggie on the balcony. She offered a drag to Paulina.

'Nah, thanks. I quit.'

'Traitor!' Caro scowled. 'I'll quit on New Year's Day, no sooner.'

'Can I use your phone to call Milly? It's quieter here.'

'Of course, darling.' Caro stubbed out her ciggie in the pot plant, buried the butt, then looked Paulina up and down. 'Is that one of Jude's old dresses?'

'Ew! No.'

'You can pull off anything. But I wouldn't waste my youth dressing like a kindergarten teacher.'

As Caro breezed past, Paulina plucked at her long skirt, frowning.

Inside, perched on the bed, Paulina found her aunt's address book, dialled Milica's number, and shrank into a younger, shyer version of herself.

'Hey, sis ... Merry Christmas. Yeah, I'm good. *Really* good ... Yep, home with Mum for Chrissy ... She's pretty annoying; how's yours? Ha, that's the way ... Yeah, miss ya heaps ... Wish I was there ... I've got some big news — *maybe*. I dunno, it's early days ...'

By the time Paulina crept downstairs, everyone had finished their pavlova.

'Too much booze,' she apologised, yawning. 'Needed a nap.'

The olds smiled at her all misty-eyed.

Next morning, Judy caught her reading *Anna Karenina* in bed and got all weepy again.

'What?' Paulina whinged. 'I just wanna get to the bit where she jumps in front of the train!'

'It's nothing.' Judy wiped her eyes. 'You're just growing up so fast!'

Paulina threw the book on the floor. 'When are we going to Westfield? I wanna spend my Christmas money.'

On the way to Westfield, Paulina complained loudly and at length about the traffic. Then she complained about how hard it was finding parking, then about the crowds.

'Yes, I get it,' Judy sighed. 'We all get it. Your island home is so much nicer than this shithole. Just don't forget your roots!'

Paulina bought a bunch of boob-tubes and halter-tops 'for Bunny', but two sizes smaller than Bunny could fit. 'What about this?' her mum suggested when they encountered a peasant skirt with an elastic waistband. 'It has a lot of stretch.'

'It looks like Jefferson Airplane threw up on it.'

Judy bought it anyway, 'for herself'. Paulina spent a hundred dollars on g-strings. After, they passed the makeup counters. 'Why don't we get our faces done?' Judy suggested.

'Ric likes me better without makeup.'

Judy rolled her eyes heavenward.

Browsing CDs at SANITY, Paulina held up the new Placebo album. 'Look, Mum! There's a song called "Passive Aggressive". Reckon it's about you?'

'Look! *Golden Oldies!*' Judy rejoined. 'Why don't you get it for your boyfriend!'

'I'm getting this for my friend Jesse.' Paulina ignored her mum. 'He likes Placebo … and he's passive-aggressive like you.'

'Aren't you already getting him the PJ Harvey?'

'So? We have the same taste. And this way I get to borrow them both and still get brownie points for generosity.'

Judy kept browsing the oldies. '"Ric" doesn't mind you being friends with a boy?'

'He *hates* it!' Paulina cackled. 'He doesn't think boys and girls can be friends. Lucky Jess comes into Foodfolk every day, otherwise I'd never see him. Ric gets soooo jealous! One time at the Fairfolk Bowmen's Club he almost decked this guy who was showing me how to hold the bow, ha-ha-ha.'

'That's not funny, Paulina.' Judy frowned. 'I don't like that.'

'Good thing he's not *your* boyfriend, then,' Paulina jeered, turning her back on Judy.

Later, they walked past a shop selling kids' stuff. Judy looked at Paulina and she shook her head firmly. Judy didn't push it.

In the car home from Westfield, Paulina slept like a baby.

They stayed in on New Year's Eve, eating watermelon and drinking non-alcoholic champagne and watching *Mutiny on the Fortuna*, starring Daniel Day-Lewis as Gideon King. Around eleven o'clock, the phone rang.

'Oh, hel-*lo*, Ric!' Judy chirped, in full receptionist mode. 'Yes, she's here. Before I pass you along, I just wanted to say: I think it's time you and I had a good talk about your relationship with my daughter, don't you? Wonderful! I'm glad we're on the same page. Speak soon. Happy New Year!'

Judy held the phone out to Paulina like it was contagious. Paulina snatched it up.

'Sorry about that!' She took the phone outside. 'Wow, is it 2001 on the rock already? Gawd, I wish I was there to kiss you at midnight!'

After about twenty minutes of talking Rabbit's ear off, Paulina came back inside, kicked her mum awake. 'Did you give him the good news?' Judy asked dozily.

'Nah. I wanna see his face.' Paulina unpaused the movie. 'Ric says the film from the thirties is the best version; this one's way inferior.'

'*Thirties?* Are you sure he's only fifty-six?'

'Thanks for only being a passive-aggressive bitch.'

Judy yawned. 'I'll give him hell if I need to.'

The next day, Judy drove her to the airport. They both cried at boarding time, but Paulina stopped on the plane; she was seated next to a bronze-haired chick her own age.

'Was that your mum?' the chick asked in a pommy accent. 'She's cute!'

Paulina laughed. 'She gets really emotional every time I come and go.'

'My mum's the same.' The chick swept her eyes across the sea of grey heads around them. 'Can I ask you something?'

'Yep!' Paulina clapped her hands. 'Fairfolk's full of geriatrics! And everything's way overpriced and there's nothing to do but watch cows and boats and get drunk. You'll be so bored! Did Merlinda recruit you?'

The chick nodded. 'I'm doing three months of farm work. Do you know what an "apiary" is?'

'Fucked if I know!' Paulina turned serious. 'I was like you, once. They'll call you a "mainie" even if you're not a mainland Australian; it sort of means "newcomer" but sometimes like "slut" or "dickhead", too. You'll get used to it. You'll get used to lots of things. It's the prettiest place on earth.'

'I'm Brooke.' The chick held out a hand covered in henna tattoos and chunky silver rings. There was a faded nightclub stamp on her wrist. 'I'm *so* glad I'm sat next to you.'

They were best mates by the time they landed. Rabbit was waiting on the tarmac.

'That's my boyfriend!' Paulina pointed him out to Brooke as they disembarked. 'He's really old, hey?'

'I wasn't going to say anything,' Brooke said diplomatically. 'Is he rich?'

'Yeah, sorta. But that's not why I'm with him.' Beaming, Paulina bounded over to Rabbit. 'I missed you, babe!'

'I missed you too, gorgeous.' He clutched her waist. 'The house has been very quiet without you.'

'Nice meeting you!' Brooke called out. 'We should grab a bevvy sometime!'

'Yeah — call me!' Paulina replied, then kissed Rabbit. 'Babe: I *really* missed you.'

Two days later, Paulina started bleeding while restocking the drinks fridge at Foodfolk. She paid an hour's wages for a box of maxi-pads and told no one how much pain she was in.

PERSONS OF INTEREST

Judy didn't know when she started noticing them. But suddenly, they were all she could see.

'I saw another one today,' she told her therapist, Agnes Tran. 'Just a little one.'

'How little?'

'Three, four?' Judy shook her head. 'She was just a tiny thing. She was hanging off the bike rack outside Woolies like it was monkey bars. Then her mum told her off and tried to move her and she had a tantrum and I … just watched.'

Agnes nodded.

'Paulina had so many tantrums.' Judy tried to laugh, but like always, sounded like a small animal being trampled. 'And this one, she had hair just like hers? All dark and wavy and soft … I didn't *touch* it. But it looked so soft.'

Judy gave in to the weeping. It was better, doing it in here than out there.

'I just wanted to grab her and hug her tight and take her home. I want to grab them all; it doesn't matter if they're three or thirty. Gawd, I sound like a kidnapper.'

'You sound like a grieving mother.'

'Nobody tells you it feels like this.' Judy's face flushed. 'Every time I see one of them, I get hot all over, my heart starts racing, I can't think straight, I just want to touch them and smell them and — I don't know. Is that wrong?'

'There's no right or wrong way to grieve,' Agnes said. Agnes said this a lot, but Judy didn't mind; by now, she knew her life was a broken record.

'I know it's wrong,' Judy said. 'They're not her. They're only her in my head and if I got close, they'd stop being her in a second. There's nobody like her. Just … I'm so scared.'

She reached for the tissues.

'What are you scared of, Judy?'

'She's losing her edges.' Judy wiped her nose. 'I used to be able to look at that photo, the one in Croatia? Then it was all over the news, and now … it doesn't even look like her. It doesn't make sense when I see it. You know the one?'

Agnes nodded.

'It's a beautiful picture. But it doesn't look like her anymore.' Judy dabbed her eyes. 'It's happening with other pictures, too. It happened with her answering machine message; I used to listen to that, and it was like she was in the room. Now — nothing.'

'You're still in shock. You won't feel this way forever.'

'What if I do, though?' Judy looked at Agnes helplessly. 'What if this is the only way I can live with it?'

She broke down again.

'You won't forget her,' Agnes reassured her. 'I promise. You *won't*.'

Tears streamed down Judy's cheeks. 'It's happening already. I'm forgetting how *nasty* she was.'

'Do you still have your journal?' Agnes asked this every time, as if she believed Judy would someday just chuck it out with the weekly rubbish.

'Yes.' Judy stared into her lap. 'I'm such a terrible writer, though.'

'You're a fine writer. I want you to write something this week about something nasty she said or did. The nastiest thing you can think of. You'll read it to me next week. Okay?'

Judy nodded; glanced at the clock on the table, its face turned away from her.

'We still have a few minutes.' Agnes said. 'Are you ready for bin day tomorrow?'

'I s'pose.' Judy tugged at her sleeves. 'I was planning to get home early so I won't have to deal with them in the dark. It's harder in winter. It gets dark so early.'

'It'll get better. We're past the solstice. You're still using the yellow bin liners?'

Judy nodded. 'They're better than the black ones. It's just other people's rubbish I still have to see? And sometimes I'll just be driving, any day of the week, and see someone's rubbish by the road. That's worse. I don't know how to prepare for that.'

'She wasn't rubbish, Judy. You know the way she was found wasn't who she was.'

'I *know*.' Judy's chin trembled. 'Just, it takes me back … I see the black plastic then I see her poor ankle, and I can't do anything. She's so hurt, and I can't do anything.'

'You can keep breathing; that's what she'd want.' Agnes took a deep breath. 'Can you breathe with me, Judy? Show me how you'll breathe.'

They spent the last minutes of the session breathing like it was a yoga class.

'It'll get better,' Agnes repeated, rising. 'Some days will be harder than others, but you won't be scared of bin day your whole life. You won't kidnap anyone. You're still Paulina's mum, and she's still Paulina. Death can't change that.'

'Thank you.' Judy stood, smiling politely.

Agnes walked her to reception. 'See you next Wednesday.'

At reception, Judy handed her card over to Jo. Jo's hair was the wrong colour, but she wore it in a ponytail and her wrists were skinny. Judy watched Jo's wrists, her swishing ponytail. When Jo asked Judy if she'd like a receipt, she said, 'Yes.'

She always said yes.

She always got take-away after therapy from the Happy Dragon Kitchen in Cherry Hill Plaza. She always got lemon chicken to eat that night and beef lo mein for the next night. She always bristled if anybody bumped into her, or if she had to repeat herself — her voice was chronically soft these days — or if the food took especially long. *How dare you make me wait! Don't you know my daughter was murdered? Don't you know my life is hell?*

She always ate in front of the TV. She ate the way Paulina would: begrudgingly, with tiny bites, taking an eternity to chew the candied skin and gluey white flesh. She kept the volume low, unless she saw a girl who resembled Paulina. Then she focused intently.

She did her homework for Agnes in front of the TV. It was hard.

Not emotionally, but mentally. Grief had fogged her brain so thick, she knew it was permanently damaged.

When Paulina was eight, I cut her fringe. She hated it and threw the hair clippings at me.

When Paulina was fifteen, she had her friends over for a sleepover. I bought them lots of lollies and ice cream. She called me an embarrassment, told me to get a life.

When Paulina lost her baby, she blamed me. Said she hated my genes, she'd rather kill herself than be like me.

After finishing her homework, Judy closed her journal and turned off the TV. She climbed upstairs and brushed her teeth, applied night creams, examined her roots, examined her collection of lipsticks, went to her bedroom to lay out tomorrow's clothes.

It was drafty in her room. 'There's a draft,' she said, because that was something Marko would say — as if they'd all catch their deaths from a bit of cold air — and it had comforted Paulina when Judy kept saying it after he was gone. 'Better put some socks on.'

She started crying softly.

Once Judy'd finished her ironing, she went to Paulina's room and changed into the Bauhaus T-shirt. It no longer smelled much like Paulina, but there was still comfort in the fact that Paulina had loved it, and that it had touched Paulina's skin as it now touched Judy's.

Wearing the T-shirt, Judy slipped under the sun-and-moon bedclothes, inserted one of Paulina's CDs into the player, and let the music and her weeping lull her asleep.

She was prepared to pass the rest of her life like this.

Caro insisted on Friday night dinners, though. She'd gotten the idea from a TV show called *Gilmore Girls*, where there was a rich grandmother who blackmailed her daughter into dining with her every Friday night. Caro claimed the show was popular with her Year 10s.

'How was bin day?' she asked, ushering Judy into her overheated Mercy Cove mansion. 'Are you still using the yellow bin liners?'

Caro's cheeks were blotchy. It was hard to tell if this was because of the heat or the glass of red in her hand or simply the pressure of being Caro.

'Yes, I'm still using the yellow bin liners,' Judy recited like a pre-schooler.

'Whatever you have to do to make life easier, Jude.' Caro kissed Judy's cheek and dragged her into the hallway. 'You look nice. New lipstick?'

Judy nodded, placed her handbag on the counter, and unspooled her scarf from her neck. Tim turned around from the stove where he was stirring a risotto and gave her a wink. 'We just opened a very fine Nebbiolo.'

Caro got her a glass and sploshed in a generous amount of liquid.

'Not too much,' Judy said. 'I'm driving.'

'You're not driving! You're sleeping over!' Caro always said this.

'I can't. I have to … water the plants.'

'Oh, *the plants!*' Caro mocked her. 'Not *the plants!* Oh, what'll we ever do about those poor, thirsty plants—'

'Caro,' Tim warned.

'Well, anyway! You're going to want to stay once you hear this.' Caro splashed a little more wine into Judy's glass, then topped up her own. 'Get this: that white Land Cruiser that was seen on Klee Welkin Road just after eleven? With the arguing couple inside? Someone reported a man cleaning it *very vigorously* around two o'clock. Blasting it with his hose, vacuuming the boot, the whole hog!'

Judy took a sip of wine. 'The same Land Cruiser?'

'How many can there be on that island? And, look, I *know* what you're going to say: they didn't get a good enough look to see if the woman was Paulina, but look at the timing!'

Tim came up behind Caro, massaged her shoulders.

'Personally, I always sing and whistle when I clean the BMW.' He looked at Judy. 'I know it's not much, but it's something.'

Judy shrugged. 'I guess so.'

'Anyway, Wozzy said he'd get back to us when he's done questioning the bloke.' Caro was calling Detective Wozniak 'Wozzy', these days. 'And he's taking a long time. That could mean a cross-examination. Why don't you just stay over?'

Judy sipped. 'I don't know, Caro. Who is this car-washing bloke?'

'Wozzy won't say.' Caro shrugged off Tim's hands, strode to the fridge and cooled herself in front of it. 'But he's a definite person of interest. And if he *is* the one, his clean car won't save him. We've got prints. We've got witnesses.'

'I don't know, Caro,' Judy repeated. 'I wish I could be as optimistic as you.'

Tim went back to the risotto.

'Cases have been solved on less, Jude.' Caro slugged her wine. 'Look, I *know*. I wish we had an obvious motive. That dirty old rabbit man, he had motive. That perv who vandalised King's Lookout; he did, too. But motive means nothing without evidence.'

Tim shuffled over to the intercom. 'Bronson: come set the table.'

As Caro harped on about the possibility of DNA evidence in the boot of the Land Cruiser, Bronson crept downstairs. 'How are you, Bronson?' Judy asked. 'How's work?'

Bronson shrugged. 'Pays the bills.'

'Not *our* bills.' Tim set a steaming bowl in front of Judy, then Caro. 'Darling wife: no forensics at the dinner table, okay?'

'Darling husband: can we talk about the wine situation?' Caro distributed the last of the bottle between their glasses. 'Let's try the Barolo?'

Despite steering clear of forensics, Caro's dinner conversation wasn't much better. 'How's that Vietnamese girl working out for you? Are you making progress?'

'That's private,' Judy rebuffed her. 'And Agnes isn't a girl. She's forty-three.'

'Milly's age,' Caro remarked slyly. 'Have you thought about calling Milly?'

Judy forked a tiny bite of risotto into her mouth. 'It's very good, Tim.'

'I'll give you a container to take home,' he said.

'That's a wonderful idea!' Caro exclaimed, as if he'd just thought of a cure for cancer. 'Jude, you look like you've lost more weight. Are you eating enough?'

'Are *you*?' Even with the weight Judy had lost, Caro was a stick by comparison.

'This guy makes sure of it.' Caro absently patted Tim's hand. 'He can make sure *you* do, too. Come on, Jude. Cut the crap. You need to stop rattling around in that haunted house of yours. It's positively Gothic!'

'It's not Gothic.' They'd been through this. 'It's my home. It's my family's home.'

'*We're* family,' Caro urged. 'Look: I'm not saying *forever*. And I'm not saying sell the place. But why *live* there? God! You would've killed to live in Mercy Cove when we were young. Remember how Dad used to drive us past all the mansions in his taxi?'

Mercifully, the phone started ringing. Caro jumped to her feet.

'Wozzy! No, it's not too late. Perfect timing, actually! The whole family's here. Oh.' Caro's tone shifted. 'Are you *sure*? Six witnesses? But how can you be *sure*? Oh. And he's given his fingerprints? Well. Thanks for getting back to us. Onward!'

Caro hung up the phone, threw a smile in the direction of the dinner table.

'Well, Land Cruiser guy was surfing till midday, at least. A bunch of people saw him. Then he came home and ate lunch with his wife and kid *and* the wife's friend. Well!' Caro refilled her wine glass. 'One less bastard out of two thousand for us to worry about.'

Caro trotted upstairs. Bronson shovelled the rest of his risotto into his mouth. 'Can I go play *GTA*?'

Tim nodded grimly.

'You know, she's actually *better* when you're around,' he told Judy. 'She puts on a brave face. We'd love to have you here. All of us.'

'She'll give me the shits. Sorry.' Judy smiled weakly. 'How is she, really?'

'Angry all the time. She wakes up angry. She goes to sleep angry ... if she sleeps at all.' Tim sighed. 'I'm worried her heart'll give out before we get any answers.'

Judy reached for Tim's hand, squeezed it.

Tim drew his hand away. 'I'll get you a container.'

Face flushed, Judy went upstairs to check on Caro.

Caro stayed a long time in the ensuite bathroom; so long, Judy had time to apply her expensive hand cream, and wait for it to dry, and snoop inside the bedside drawer.

'Oh.' Caro's face looked uncharacteristically pale when she emerged.

'What are you doing with that thing?'

'"Ulvini Songs".' Judy grimaced. 'Gawd. I completely forget about this.'

'I haven't listened to it. Tim has.'

Judy looked at the hand-drawn album art: Paulina, driving a tour-bus full of old people. 'That boy captured her well … her face.'

'Keep it.' Caro shrugged. 'What the hell. He's not a person of interest anymore.'

Judy rose from the bed. 'I used some of your hand cream.'

'You fucking bitch.' Caro smiled dryly. 'Are you sure you don't want to sleep over? We can take a walk on the beach in the morning. Tim can make us pancakes.'

'I can't.'

'Well!' Caro embraced her swiftly. 'I'm going out for some fresh air.'

Judy watched as her sister slipped onto the balcony and moved the pot plant. A moment later, she was cupping a flame, inhaling.

Downstairs, Judy gathered up her scarf and handbag. 'I'm heading off.'

'Already?' Tim looked apologetic. 'I'm sorry this Land Cruiser guy wasn't the one. Even I got hopeful. Other fish in the sea, huh?'

Judy shrugged and accepted the container of leftovers. 'Take care, Tim.'

They didn't hug.

Driving through Macquarie Park, Judy passed a building site: black tarpaulins rippling in the moonlight. She tried to breathe the way Agnes had taught her.

Someday, Judy would run out of department stores. Someday, she'd have to start retracing her steps, hoping there'd be different girls; or, if they were the same girls, that they wouldn't remember her. Most likely, they wouldn't. Fifty-two-year-old women aren't memorable. But the thought that they *might* was so shameful, she chose to drive further out.

Today, she drove all the way past the airport.

'Can I help you?' a plump girl in a smock with the name tag 'Charly' asked brightly.

'No.' Judy blinked quickly. 'Thank you.'

Judy walked past the Yves Saint Laurent counter three times, just to make sure. This one was very good: skinny, dark hair bundled atop of her head, laughing and chatting in a twangy voice as she applied shadow to another customer's lids. When she was done with that, she walked straight up to Judy in that bold way Paulina had with strangers.

'Wanna try that pink lippie?'

'Oh …' Judy faltered. 'It's probably too bright for me.'

'Never know till ya try.'

Judy's eyes drifted to the girl's name tag: *Bella*.

'Oh, well.' She smiled shyly. 'Why not.'

Bella sat Judy in a high chair before a movie-star mirror smudged with fingerprints. Judy avoided looking at her reflection. When Bella came close, uncapping the lippie, her senses sharpened.

'You're lucky, you've got that English rose complexion.' Bella tickled Judy's lips with a tiny brush. 'Pinks always look so pretty.'

Judy laughed. 'You think so?'

'Yeah! For sure!' Bella smacked her lips together. 'Smooch!'

Judy smooched her thin upper lip against her thin bottom lip.

'Gorgeous!' Bella moved out of the way so Judy could see.

'Oh, maybe twenty years ago.' Judy averted her eyes. 'If I was young and pretty like you. You young girls can wear anything.'

'You should see me in green eyeshadow. I look like Kermit the Frog.' Bella surveyed Judy with interest. 'You know what'd suit you? Coral!'

Judy's breath caught in her chest. 'Oh? Why not.'

As Bella went to fetch and sterilise the coral, Judy breathed deeply, tried to calm her nerves. Even so, Bella noticed.

'You're just like me.' She touched Judy's goose-bumped arm. 'I get so cold in here, too. It's like Antarctica.'

When Judy got home that evening, she put her new lipstick in the drawer with all the rest of them.

CLIFFTOP

It took Paulina two hours to get dressed for her job interview at Mutineers' Lodge. The bloke interviewing her wasn't even wearing shoes.

'Can you clean?' asked Bazel Stevens, crossing his smooth brown legs.

'Yeah.' Paulina crossed her own legs. 'My ex was a surfer. If I wanted clean sheets, I had to change them myself.'

'I can see why he's an ex.' Baz skimmed her resume. 'Sydney, eh?'

'Yeah. Northern suburbs.'

'My partner's got a property in Mosman.'

'We're not that swish. We're way up in the hills.' Paulina laughed. 'My aunt's in Mercy Cove, though. I always begged Mum to buy lotto tickets so we could win big and move there.'

'I've tried. I always end up back on the rock.' Bazel set aside her resume with a flourish. 'Foodfolk. How'd you like working with Rita?'

Paulina faked a smile. 'She's a lovely lady!'

'She's changed since she was "Mrs Tarita Stevens", then.'

'You were *married* to her?'

'God, no!' Baz shuddered. 'My brother, Sam. Rest his soul.'

'Sorry to hear that. The Rita part, and the other part.'

Baz sat back. 'Is there a reason you're leaving Foodfolk? Besides Rita?'

Paulina shrugged. 'I had a miscarriage while I was stacking shelves last month. Can't stand the place.'

'Sorry to hear that.' He glanced at her left hand. 'You're not married.'

'It wasn't planned.' She smiled wanly. 'Never again. Kids are overrated.'

'Tell me about it. I'm the youngest of nine.'

'Bloody hell! Are your folks Catholic?'

'Just dutiful Fairfolk Islanders, keeping the Stevens name alive.' Baz lifted his chin, gold earring flashing. 'Listen: this isn't Westpac. I can pay you five dollars for every cabin you clean. There're twelve cabins, but we're lucky to fill half of them in down season. Do the maths.'

Paulina winced. 'It's not Westpac.'

'My sister Gayle manages the bistro. That's Gayle with a G-A-Y ... as in "happy".' He smirked. 'On a good week, we do breakfast and early-bird specials: seven to ten, five to eight, seven days a week. Bad weeks ...'

Paulina swallowed.

'I usually winter on the mainland.' Baz re-crossed his legs. 'We're closing for renovations, May to June. I'd recommend getting a side gig. You got anything on the side?'

'Just a boyfriend.' Paulina reddened. 'He takes care of me.'

'He taking you out for Valentine's tonight?'

'We're having dinner at The Clifftop.'

'Let him pay.'

'He always pays.' She toyed with the paua-shell bangle Rabbit had given her that morning. 'I just need something to keep me occupied. Something that isn't Foodfolk.'

'I wouldn't hold it against you if you told me to shove this job and caught the first flight back to Sydney. I'd call that pretty sensible, actually.'

'You sound like my mum.' Paulina grimaced. 'She thinks I'm wasting my life here.'

'What do you think?'

'It's my life to waste.'

'Guess what?' She set her handbag on the counter at Camilleri's. 'I'm moving up in the world!'

Jesse looked up from the chops he was pricing. 'You mean I can finally buy choc-milk in peace?'

'Choc-milk, Camels, not my problem.' Paulina stole a glance at his tattooed forearms. 'Oi, wanna get drunk tonight? Celebrate my new career in hospitality?'

'The old man's not putting the moves on you for Valentine's?'

'Ugh.' Paulina palmed her face. 'We're having dinner at The Clifftop.'

Jesse wiped his gloves on his apron. 'Fancy.'

'As if I'm not fat enough already, I have to sit through a three-course meal.'

'Most chicks go crazy for The Clifftop.'

'Why don't you take Brooke, then? Double-date?'

'Nay. I don't celebrate Valentine's.' He smiled. 'I'm too busy celebrating the anniversary of Captain Cook getting stabbed to death.'

'What, you can't celebrate in style? Cheapskate.'

'Did Brooke say I'm cheap?'

'Mate, she's from *London*. As if she's gonna stick around for steak on the porch every night.' Paulina swanned around to his side of the counter. 'Where's your phone book?'

'Hey.' Jesse grabbed her. 'You can't be back here without a hairnet.'

'Don't put your bloody hands on *me*!'

The door dinged and in walked Rita. Jesse dropped Paulina's arm and ruefully approached the counter.

'Yorana. You here for those orders?'

'Aye.' Rita's eyes drifted to Paulina, who was dabbing a bit of meat-juice off her arm with a tissue. 'If you're nay too busy.'

Jesse ducked into the cool room.

Paulina got out the phone directory and dialled The Clifftop.

'Hey, can I get a table for two tonight, seven pm? Nah, not for Valentine's. Killing Captain Cook.' She caught Rita staring. 'Nice one. The name's Jesse Camilleri. Cheers, babe!'

Hanging up, she turned her back on Rita and examined her reflection in the metal sheen of the slicer.

Jesse bore a box out of the cool room. 'Need help carrying it to Foodfolk?'

'Nay.' Smirking, Rita accepted the load. 'Looks like you've got your hands full, already.'

———

After Camilleri's, Paulina took a gulp of the vodka in her glovebox and drove to Fergal Wotherspoon's honey farm, where Brooke was in her protective gear, helping Fergal smoke and lift the bee frames. Paulina squatted under a pine tree and drank from her flask till it was time for Brooke's smoke break.

'You look nice, luv!' Brooke exclaimed. 'New skirt?'

'Nah.' Paulina stroked the flowery fabric. 'I just haul it out for job interviews.'

'Mutes'?'

'Yeah! They loved me. Starting next week.'

Paulina offered up her flask.

'I wish! I'll probably knock over a hive and get stung to bits!' Brooke sniffed the cap. 'Vodka? You're starting early!'

'Celebrating.'

'Is Ric taking you out tonight?'

'We've got a dinner-date at The Clifftop.' Paulina swigged and cringed. 'And we're not the only ones.'

'God, he's not bringing that spoiled little brat, is he?'

'Nah! I mean *you*, babe. Camel's upping his game.'

'Jesse's taking me out?' Brooke got a dopey look on her face. 'Cute!'

'Act surprised, okay?'

'How's this?' Brooke rounded her eyes and gasped.

'Pfft! Is that your O-face? Save it for later!'

They laughed. Brooke got out her smokes, tossed her long bronze hair. 'I'm so sweaty and disgusting. I wish he'd given me some warning.'

'Yeah-hh, that's why *I'm* here.' Paulina rolled her eyes. 'Wanna borrow an outfit?'

'Oh, I'll just wear my white halter. He's mad for my shoulders.' Brooke caught sight of her new bangle. 'Pretty! From Ric?'

'Yep.' Paulina spun it on her wrist. 'Earning my keep.'

'You giving him anything?' Brooke blew smoke sideways.

'Blow-job, probably.'

'Classic. Want some honey to kink it up?'

'Blergh. Too many calories.' Paulina lifted her shirt. 'I'm getting a gut.'

'Bollocks.'

'I can't get rid of this weight I gained over Christmas.' Paulina lay back on the grass and shielded her eyes so Brooke wouldn't see them watering. 'I wish I was your age.'

'God! You're not that much older.' Brooke stubbed out her ciggie and buried it. 'Try wearing one of these bee-suits all day. It sweats everything out.'

'Maybe I'll join the gym. Wanna be gym buddies?'

'Honestly, I don't have the *energy*!' Brooke stood and stretched. 'They work me so hard … most days all I want to do is curl up with Jess and have a bevvy on the porch.'

'Fair enough.' Paulina sat up. 'Back to the hives?'

'Ciao, bella!' Brooke air-kissed her. 'Give me a bell if you change your mind about the honey. It's an aphrodisiac!'

Paulina laughed. 'Later, babe!'

Watching her friend sashaying back to the hives, somehow looking sexy in her white overalls, Paulina drained her flask and muttered, 'Stuck-up pommy bitch.'

It was school pick-up hour. She had to pass the school to get from Fergal's to Rabbit's, and the little kids just reminded her. Reminded her of things she hadn't known she wanted, like chatter in the backseat, and cutting the crusts off sandwiches, and helping with homework, and most of all being a different kind of woman; the kind who wasn't pissed on glovebox vodka at three in the arvo. And then it hit her: she was *really* pissed.

So pissed. The sun suddenly seemed too strong, the roadside pines all wonky, and their shadows on the road — bloody hell, those shadows — like nets she could trip over. Then she looked up, and the blue Subaru that once seemed no more than a wandering cloud on the horizon was *right there*, and, 'Shit!', she'd rear-ended him.

Paulina blinked. A long blink, like a glitch in time.

When she opened her eyes, a red-faced bloke was banging on the window.

'Sorry.' She rolled it down. 'I'm really sorry, hey.'

His mouth was working, spit flying, saying things: *mainie bitch, watch where you're going, how didn't you see?!*

'Sorry,' Paulina repeated, head in agony. 'I'm r-really … reallllly sorry.'

There was smoke furling from the hood of her Corolla. She started crying.

'Sorry, sir. Gawd, I'm sorry!' Paulina peered at him blearily: a bloke, just a normal bloke with a beard and a belly and wraparound sunglasses. 'Ssssorry? I'll p-pay? Wannasee … wannasee my wallet?'

Her wallet. She fumbled, dropped it.

'I don't want your wallet — drunk cunt!' the bloke snarled. 'This is a school zone!'

'Um.' Paulina was blinded by tears. 'I'm really sorry. Please? Maybe … we can work something out. You and me.'

She didn't mean for it to sound dirty. But he stopped shouting, and she felt a rush of relief; his eyes on her lips, her legs — she could handle that.

'Don't go anywhere,' he said.

Watching his fat arse wiggling as he trekked back to the Subaru, Paulina wondered if she'd reached an all-time low. A little boy in a school uniform hopped out of the car, ran down the road. The bloke walked back to her, hitched his pants. She fought the urge to spew.

'The cops'll be here in five,' he spat. 'Don't try anything.'

Paulina nodded. Stared at the blue blanket of the sea beyond the cliffs and wished she was under it.

Paulina's vomit was acid-green, like she'd been munching on grass. The sergeant, Hank Turner, was stern and disappointed like a dad.

'I can see you're sorry,' he said. 'But we take this sort of thing very seriously after what happened to Tiffany King. That girl had her whole life ahead of her.'

'Please don't tell Ric. Please? I'm s-sorry.'

A woman with hair like yellow lambswool kept shoving a bucket in Paulina's face, cups of water and Marie biscuits. Paulina couldn't touch them; she could hardly breathe.

'Please don't tell him. Please? I wanna die.'

She threw up one more time, near the lady's shoes. Then she tried to go to sleep on the cot, but the lady kept shaking her awake, making her lie in a less comfortable position.

'Let me die. I wanna die. Don't tell him. Please?'

Later, Paulina became aware of men's voices, grumbling in Fayrf'k. Men shuffling papers, shaking hands. She prayed her heart would just stop.

'He's here.' The lady batted her cheeks. 'Time to go.'

Paulina's face was sticky; her hair stuck to her face. Everything ached.

'Are you angry, babe?' she asked Rabbit, taking his arm but unable to look at his face. 'Please, don't be angry. Please, I'm sorry. Please — are you angry?'

The muscles in his arm were tense. He didn't say anything till they were inside the car, the doors slammed.

'Yes, I'm angry.' His voice was clipped. 'You had a blood alcohol level three times the legal limit. I just paid a three-thousand-dollar fine. You have no idea how angry I am.'

'Ric! I'm so sorry! I didn't mean—'

He struck her; so abruptly she couldn't believe he'd done it — that he'd *meant* to do it and hadn't just caught her face while shooing a fly.

'Put your seatbelt on, Paulina.'

They drove in silence past Tiffany's shrine, the sun setting over Cookies. It was almost dark when he pulled into the driveway. Paulina sat very still. The sky got darker. She started trembling.

'Come on,' he said after a while, pulling the keys from the ignition.

'I love you, babe,' she whimpered. 'I'm sorry.'

Rabbit climbed out of the car, walked around to her side and hauled her out.

'I love you,' she repeated. 'I love you so much.'

'I don't want to hear it, Lina. Not today.'

The house was cold and dark. 'Where's Bunny?' Paulina quavered.

'She's staying at Hine's,' he reminded her. 'This was our night, remember.'

She started crying again; she couldn't help it.

'Stop it,' he commanded. 'Just stop it.'

Paulina missed her mum, badly. When Rabbit tramped upstairs, she followed. In the bedroom, she had trouble standing. She steadied herself against the headboard and began undressing.

'No.' Rabbit averted his eyes. He stalked out of the room; came back with towels and a bathrobe.

'Clean yourself up.'

'I love you,' she pleaded. 'I'm sorry.'

He walked her to the bathroom and repeated, 'Clean yourself up.'

Paulina nodded, shut the door. Then she slid to the floor and bawled like a baby.

After, she crawled to the cabinet, took out her spare shampoo bottle full of Johnny Walker, and guzzled. Her face in the mirror was so swollen from crying, she couldn't tell if he'd left a mark.

Rabbit was frying onions when Paulina came downstairs, all clean and minty-breathed in her terry-towel robe. She sat at the table and watched him cook. He didn't look at her. After a while, a glass of water appeared in front of her. She lowered her eyes and sipped.

A little later, there was an omelette. It had bits of onion and zucchini inside, herbs sprinkled on top.

'It looks good, babe.' She did her best not to slur.

He sat across from her; watched her chop it into tiny pieces and eat a bite.

'It's really nice,' she said. 'It's just what I needed. Thanks, babe.'

Silently, Rabbit took up his own fork and started eating.

'I love you,' Paulina ventured. 'I'm so sorry. Please forgive me.'

Rabbit ate another mouthful.

'I love you too,' he said stonily. 'That's not the problem.'

'I'm sorry, Ric. It won't happen again.'

'I can't do this again, Lina. I went through this once before, with Tatiana.'

'I'm not T-T ...' Paulina's tongue tripped over his ex-wife's name. 'I'm not *her*. I didn't mean to drink so much. I was just happy about my new job, Ric.'

'Your blood alcohol was three times the legal limit.'

'I know, Ric. I forget sometimes how little I am. And it was sunny ... booze always hits me harder when it's sunny.' She took another bite. 'It's really good, babe. Thanks for taking care of me. Nobody takes care of me like you do.'

Rabbit lowered his head, ate in silence.

'It was so sunny.' Paulina reached for his hand. 'Ric, the sun was in my eyes. That's why I crashed, more than anything.'

He looked up from his plate, lip curled. 'Do you think I'm stupid?'
'No, Ric.'

'Do you think you can just do whatever you want behind my back?'
He stood up so fast, she cowered. 'You think I'll believe anything you tell me?'

Paulina's chin trembled. 'No, Ric. You're smart. *I'm* stupid—'

He hit her again. Harder than the first time, but somehow less shocking.

'Bloody hell, Ric.' She cupped her cheek. 'What're you trying to do, break my face?'

'I'm sorry.' He turned away. 'I'm sorry, Lina. Let me …'

As Rabbit skulked to the freezer for an icepack, Paulina stood. She wasn't shaking anymore; her body felt taut, charged. When he tried to ice her cheek, she snapped like a rubber band. 'Don't touch me, arsehole!'

'I'm sorry,' he repeated. 'I shouldn't have done that. Take this. For the swelling …'

Paulina threw the icepack to the ground and screamed her lungs out. Clutching his temples, Rabbit sat back down.

'I'm sorry, Lina,' he whispered. 'It's just … the drinking. It's ugly.'

'*You're* ugly! Bastard!'

'It brings out the worst in us both. Can't you see that, darling? I'm sorry I … lashed out. It just kills me to see you like this.'

'Like what? *Shitfaced*?' She laughed. 'I was shitfaced the first time you brought me home!'

'Yes.' He sighed. 'And you needed my help.'

'Yeah? Why'd you fuck me then?' Paulina's voice crackled like kindling. 'Why'd you bring me home and fuck me if I was so fucking helpless?'

He lowered his eyes.

'Maybe that was a mistake.'

'You reckon?' She laughed again. 'You know best, Ric! I wasn't even *conscious*.'

Rabbit didn't follow her upstairs. It didn't matter, though. She was in tears by the time she reached the bedroom.

She had nowhere else to go.

MERCY COVE

It was one of those days that started so badly, it could only get better. Unless it got worse.

'You're a smart girl, Sara,' Caro lectured the blue-blazered teenager lounging in the cushy chair across from her. 'Too smart for cheating. Too smart to be cheating and bragging about it to our *French exchange students*.'

'Manon told me everyone cheats on their baccs.' Sara smirked. 'Anyway, that was a private conversation outside school hours, Principal McCunty.'

'What did you just call me?'

'Principal McClusky?' Sara widened her eyes. 'Your name, Ms?'

Caro glared and reached for her mug of herbal tea. She knew the girls called her *McCunty*, of course; had heard the name whispered behind her back, seen it scrawled on bathroom walls. Girls will be girls.

'Thank you, Sara. Just call me *Ms*, that's quite alright.' She sipped her tea and grimaced at the blandness. 'Sara: let's be serious. Your parents pay twenty grand a year to send you here. That might not seem like a lot of money to you, but it is for most people. Do you know what they're paying for, Sara?'

Sara shrugged.

'*Reputation*. Mercy Cove Girls' has a reputation people like your parents are willing to fork out twenty grand a year for. It's a reputation that comes at a cost … whether you're wearing that blazer or a boob tube at a party full of Scots boys.'

'So now I'm not allowed to wear boob tubes on the weekend?!'

'That's not what I'm saying.' Caro swept her limp hair from her face; she hadn't had time to blow-dry that morning. 'I'm saying, when you go to a party and brag to everyone there about paying a girl from

Blacktown to write your social studies essay for you, you're still a Mercy Cove Girl. You're sending the message that Mercy Cove is a school for stupid, lazy girls. Is that the kind of reputation your parents are paying for? Is that reputation going to get you into a top university? Did I say something *funny?*'

'No, Ms. You just splashed tea on your blouse.'

'Oh, grow up, Sara!' As Caro snatched a tissue from the box, her receptionist rang through to the desk phone. 'Yes, who is it? Detective Wozniak? Can he call back in five? Ta!'

Sara was staring at her innocently when she put the phone down.

'You should take the call, Ms. What if he found your niece's murderer?'

'Then he'll tell me in five minutes, when I'm done telling you you're expelled.'

'You're *expelling* me?'

'Mercy Cove has a zero-tolerance policy toward cheating.'

'You can't expel me! That Blacktown girl isn't getting expelled and *she's* the one selling illegal services! That's like punishing a person who buys a tab of ecstasy and letting the dealer walk free!'

'That's a very nice analogy, Sara. You should also know that Mercy Cove has a zero-tolerance policy toward drugs. Perhaps they're more tolerant in Blacktown.'

'Cunt.' Sara muttered. 'Cunty McCuntface.'

'We also don't tolerate that kind of language at Mercy Cove.' Caro stood. 'I wish you the best of luck in finding an institution more suited to your attitude, Sara.'

Sara jumped to her feet, cast a contemptuous glance at the family photo on Caro's pristine oak desk, taken the Christmas before last.

'No wonder your niece was murdered. I heard she was a real cunt like you.'

'Get out of my office,' Caro commanded. '*Now.*'

Despite the herbal tea, Caro's heart leapt when the phone rang. She picked it up with trembling hands.

'Wozzy,' she said in the coolest voice she could muster. 'Sorry for the wait. What can I do for you?'

'It's about the fingerprints.' Wozniak inhaled. 'We've found a match.'

He should've sounded happy. He didn't.

———

Caro went straight to spin class after work; went hard. It didn't help. Neither did the forty laps in the pool, or the forty minutes in the sauna, or the long, lukewarm shower, or the litres of water she guzzled. She was dizzy. She was spent. But she still had so much rage in her, she wanted to set the world on fire.

Tim's BMW wasn't in the driveway. But Bronson was home, playing GTA in the games room.

'Can you pause that, darling?' Caro perched delicately on the couch beside him. 'I have some bad news.'

Bronson paused his game.

'It's about the fingerprints,' she continued. 'They ID'd the man they belong to. His name's Saxon King. He's a bricklayer; he uses those black sheets all the time to move around supplies. Sometimes he leaves them out in the open, at building sites.'

She wished she had a drink. Why hadn't she poured herself a drink first?

'He came forward willingly, with the call-out for fingerprints. He was as surprised as anyone to be linked to the scene. He has a strong alibi. He was at a barbecue. There are photos from the day. Timestamped photos.'

'So …'

'So. We're back at square one.' Caro shrugged. 'No, it's not as bad as that. It's progress. We could've wasted god knows how many more months fixated on those prints if this Saxon King hadn't come forward. It's progress.'

'So … There's no DNA?'

'There's no DNA. Not on her body, anyway. There's never been any DNA.'

Bronson reached for her hand. 'Mum—'

'I'm okay.' Caro rapped his knuckles. 'We're okay. This was always a possibility. Nobody's giving up.'

She smiled resolutely. 'Onward and upward. I'm going to take a shower.'

Bronson nodded, unpaused his game. At times like this, Caro was glad she had sons; a daughter would've noticed her damp hair.

She poured herself a glass of Merlot, took it upstairs. On the balcony, she took her cigarettes from their hiding place under the dracaena and chain-smoked two.

It wasn't enough, she knew. It was more like foreplay.

Her black silk jacquard pyjamas. She took them into the ensuite bathroom with her, along with the Merlot. She locked the door. She took out Tim's shaving kit; the one with the straight razor she'd bought him a few birthdays back, knowing he'd never use it.

She sat with it awhile, just sat.

She peeled off her yoga pants. The scars from last time were unsightly, despite the Bio-Oil she'd been applying twice-daily. She would have to wear loose slacks for the next few days. She would have to avoid the gym. Her legs would sting with every step she took, then itch as the wounds scabbed over, itch all day long.

She took a gulp of wine. Sterilised the razor.

The relief when she made her first incision was mind-blowing.

TRAMP STAMP

Paulina was on her hands and knees, singing and scrubbing the toilet of cabin six, when Jesse chucked a wrapped present on the bathmat.

'Unhappy birthday, ulvini.'

'Bloody hell!' Paulina threw the toilet brush at him. 'Don't sneak up on a woman like that! How long have you been here?'

'Long enough to hear you singing "Suicide Is Painless".' Jesse smirked. 'I know chicks get insecure about ageing, but you take it to the next level, eh.'

As Paulina made a grab for her gift, Jesse backed out of the room. She ripped off the paper to reveal the cheesy grin of Tony 'Tunes' Carlyle: *Tony Sings Fairfolk*.

'This isn't a gift — it's a curse! Oi, where're you going? I want a refund!'

Jesse edged back into the room. 'Sorry, but every Fairfolk Islander needs one. You can't be a Fairfolk Islander if you don't have a copy of *Tony Sings Fairfolk*.'

Gleefully, Paulina wrenched open the CD cover, got out the disc. 'I'm gonna smash it and flush it!'

'Hey … don't.' Jesse intercepted her. 'I put a lot of effort into that.'

'Pfft! They sell these for $14.99 at every souvenir shop.'

'Yeah, but. There's good stuff on there. You can flush the rest … don't flush the disc.'

'I bet it's just Tony singing "Fairfolk Beautiful Fairfolk".'

'Nay. It's good stuff. Trust me.'

'Like I'd trust *you*.'

'Fine.' Jesse folded his arms. 'Your loss.'

Smiling into her uniform collar, Paulina returned the CD to its packaging. 'Nah. I'll switch it with one of yours when you're not looking. You'll live in fear.'

Jesse handed back the toilet brush. 'Worth it.'

'Oi, how come you're not at Camilleri's, slack-arse? No fair I have to work on my birthday, and you don't.'

'Baz wanted to see me.'

'Ooooooo. Bazel and Jesse sitting in a tree! K-I-S-S-I-N-G—'

'It's about the renos they're doing in down season.' Jesse rolled his eyes. 'He's hiring me to paint a mural. Mutineers and Polynesian babes with big tits and all that.'

'Geez, *that's* original.'

Jesse shrugged. 'It's not every day I get paid for my art.'

Paulina stopped scrubbing. 'I'll pay you! I want my tramp stamp.'

'Yeah, nay. I don't have a death wish.'

'Pretty-please, Jesse-Camel?'

'Sorry, but Rabbit'll kill me for slapping a bumper sticker on his Ferrari.'

'Pfft. I'm not a Ferrari. I'm like a Mazda Astina, at best.'

'Yeah, well. Even if you're that totalled Corolla of yours, he'll still kill me.'

'Not if he never sees it.' She stood up and flushed. 'Doggy-style's pretty hard work for a man his age.'

'Thanks. That's a picture I needed.'

'Oi, help me clean the rest of these cabins?' Paulina slipped a fresh roll of toilet paper onto the holder, folded the edge into an inviting triangle. 'Baz says I can knock off once I get them done. Beach day?'

'Are you sure Rabbit won't—'

'I can go to the *beach*.' Paulina crossed her arms. 'If you don't wanna be seen with me, fine. I'll hitchhike.'

'Nay. It's fine.' Jesse looked uncertain. 'I'll drive you.'

'You'll drive me in your Camel-mobile?'

'Yeah. Just don't call it that.'

'Can I smell your air-freshener?'

'Fine. It's your birthday.'

'Do you know what *else* is today?'

'Yeah, yeah.' Jesse cracked a smile. 'It's the one-year anniversary of that time some crazy mainie called me fat at the supermarket. How could I forget.'

———

Paulina made Jesse wait at Cookies, just in case Rabbit was home. He wasn't; just a note saying he was at the Fairfolk Bowmen's Club, along with a bouquet. She plucked a hibiscus from the bunch and put it behind her ear, changed into her beach gear quick as she could, and scratched a note saying: *Gone to the beach! Xxx.*

'This's like an affair, without any fun,' Jesse complained, rolling the car out of Cookies.

'I'm fun!'

'Mind if we go past Fergal's? Maybe Brooke can knock off early, too.'

Paulina pulled down the mirror. 'Like my flower? Ric gave me a bunch.'

She waited in the Commodore while Jesse talked to Brooke. He returned, grinning. 'She'll come in an hour.'

'Awesome.'

At Tombstone Beach, Paulina stripped down to her bikini, got out her sunscreen. 'Oi, can you do my back?'

Begrudgingly, Jesse splatted some sunscreen onto his palm. 'You're such a mainie.'

Paulina laughed. 'You're a fuckwit.'

'Only mainies get skin cancer.'

'I swear, you're dumber than Pellet sometimes. Even Pellet believes in sunscreen.'

'Fairfolk sun isn't dangerous. Our ozone layer's thicker. Nay pollution.'

'You're such a fuckwit.' Paulina kept giggling as Jesse rubbed her back. 'Make sure you do it even.'

'Yeah, yeah.'

'Don't forget the sides of my boobs.'

'What boobs? You're so miggy.'

'Don't forget my lower back.' Paulina giggled some more. 'I gotta keep the skin nice for my tramp stamp.'

'Yeah, yeah.'

'Show me where you're gonna put it.' Paulina arched her back. 'Show me, Jess.'

'You just told me.'

'I want you to *show* me.'

Jesse sighed and traced a circle just above her butt. 'There.' He drew his hand away. 'It's not happening, but. Even if it wasn't for Rabbit, you're scared of the pain.'

'I won't wimp out, Jess.' Paulina turned around. 'I'm ready, whenever you are.'

'Yeah, but.' He got to his feet. 'I don't believe you.'

'Wait! I'll do your back.'

'I'm not a mainie.'

Laughing, Paulina watched him lope to the water and plunge in. Then she reached for his ciggies, got out her Discman, and kept perving till he emerged from the sea.

He sprawled beside her, nicked one of her earbuds. 'Tony Tunes?'

'Yeah.' Paulina smiled. 'You did good.'

They lay like that, listening to her birthday mix, till Brooke showed up.

'Hullo, luvvies!' She smooched Jesse, then Paulina. 'Happy birthday, bella!'

'Don't remind her,' Jesse said. 'She'll start singing "Suicide Is Painless" again.'

Brooke slipped her elephant-print hemp beach-bag off her shoulder and dug inside it. 'I've got something to cheer you up, bella.'

'Geez, thanks,' Paulina mumbled as she accepted a jar of Fergal's Farm honey with a bow around it. 'Must've really gone out of your way to get this.'

'Open it, you ingrate!' Brooke laughed. 'Smell it!'

Paulina unscrewed the cap. 'Whisky? You legend!'

'Jess, can you do my back?' Brooke shed her sack-like sundress.

'Um. Yeah.' Jesse grabbed the sunscreen. 'Hold up your hair.'

Paulina flipped onto her tummy. 'Fuck, I'm old.'

'At least you're not thirty yet!' Brooke said cheerily. 'That'll be much worse!'

She giggled as Jesse smoothed his hands over her curves. Paulina rolled her eyes and picked up her honey jar. 'Be right back. I'm gonna go ask a shark to eat me.'

Squatting in the shallows, she drank. When she looked over her shoulder, Jesse and Brooke were pashing. '*Fuck*,' she muttered, chucked her hibiscus in the water, and swam out further.

'No luck?' Jesse asked when she staggered back to the towels.

Paulina plonked between him and Brooke. 'Even sharks have standards.'

Brooke offered her a joint.

'Nah. That shit messes with your head.'

'And that doesn't?' Jesse pointed at her whisky.

'Respect your elders, Camel-shit.'

'Don't look now, grandma.' Brooke jabbed her in the ribs. 'There's your ex.'

Paulina looked: Laurent was strolling down the beach in his shirtless glory with his new girlfriend, Oliana, and her four-year-old son. 'Fuck!' She hid her face.

'Pretty ironic, eh?' Jesse took up the joint. 'He dumps you cos he's not ready for fatherhood … then straightaway he hooks up with the hottest single mum on Fairfolk.'

'Thanks, Camel. I never would've made that connection. Fuck! He's coming over?'

'Hello,' Laurent said.

'Hi,' they chorused.

Laurent looked from Jesse to Paulina to Brooke, to the joint in Jesse's hand.

'Wanna toke?' Jesse offered.

He looked back at Oliana and her kid, toddling to the shore. 'Yeah, bro.'

Crouching, he took a toke.

Jesse pointed at Paulina. 'It's her birthday.'

Laurent looked at her solemnly. 'Happy birthday.'

'Yeah, you too,' Paulina replied.

Brooke got the giggles. Jesse deadpanned. 'Did you and Oliana do the coastal walk?'

'Yeah, bro.' Laurent inhaled. 'Beautiful views and ocean wind.'

'You should try it at sunset.'

'Yeah, bro. Awesome sunsets.'

Paulina snorted. Laurent looked at her contemptuously. 'You're drinking … *honey?*'

'Yep!' She nodded. 'Fergal's Farm. Want some?'

Sneering, Laurent returned the joint. 'Thanks, bro.'

'There's more where that came from.'

Laurent grinned. 'Mate's rates?'

'Yeah, brudda.' Jesse stood. 'Step into my office.'

As Laurent and Jesse wandered up the path to the cemetery, beyond which the Commodore was parked, Brooke cracked up. '"*Happy birthday! You too!*" Classic!'

'What can I say? I was dazzled by his abs.'

'At least you can say you've been there. That's quite an achievement!'

'Pretty much the only thing I've achieved in twenty-nine years.'

'No words of wisdom, then?'

'Ummm. Stay hydrated!' Paulina sipped. 'Don't fuck rabbits. Join the twenty-seven club while you still have the chance.'

Brooke clapped gleefully. 'Classic!'

Paulina took another sip, watched Oliana and her little boy frolicking in the shallows.

'If you ever cheat on a guy, don't tell him,' she added, after a while. 'Doesn't matter the circumstances. They don't forgive it, hey.'

Brooke turned onto her side. 'Yeah?'

'Yeah. I'd be married now, if I didn't tell. I'd have my life sorted. We were gonna live in Adelaide while Vinnie did his Air Force cadetship. We were looking at home loans.'

'Air Force? Sounds like a stiff.'

'I really loved him. I was really sorry.' Paulina shrugged. 'It didn't matter how many times I said it, but. One fuck-up and you're a slut who can't be trusted.'

'How'd it happen?'

'Some guy from the Melbourne office. I was trying to impress the big bosses and he didn't even have to try; they just liked him better. Then all the bigwigs left, and we went to this club and he bought me all these shots and ...' Paulina shrugged again. 'I woke up next morning in his hotel.'

'God!' Brooke said. 'Did he roofie you?'

'I drank too much. I fucked up.'

'Well. Would you *want* to be married to a guy who couldn't forgive you?' Brooke offered. 'Sounds like you dodged a bullet there.'

'Dodged a bullet, walked into a minefield.' Paulina sighed. 'I *really* loved him. He was perfect. He was serious. Guys like that don't go for me anymore.'

'What about Ric?'

'He knows better than to trust me.' Paulina narrowed her eyes. 'He'll never marry me.'

Jesse and Laurent walked down from the cemetery, went their separate ways. 'You didn't swim yet?' Jesse shifted Brooke's hair from her shoulder and kissed it.

Brooke winked. 'Just girl-talk.'

'Good day for business?' Paulina rolled over.

Jesse turned to Brooke. 'Oh, yeah. Good news: Baz commissioned me to paint a mural for Mutes' this June. Two grand. Nice, eh?'

'Jess!' Brooke smacked his arm. 'We'll be in New Zealand!'

Paulina's guts froze over. 'New Zealand?'

'Well, you know, I was *planning* to go backpacking again right after my work placement … but this fella's made it hard for me.'

Jesse avoided Paulina's eyes. 'I meant to tell you. Just, we haven't booked flights yet.'

'Whose fault is that?' Brooke laughed. 'I'll be gone by May — with or without you, Camilleri!'

'Geez,' Paulina mumbled. 'That's … exciting.'

'Tell me about it! *Civilisation!*' Brooke rolled her eyes. 'Although, we'll be camping out a bit, too. How could we not? Have you been?'

'Nah.' Paulina glanced at Jesse. 'I've heard it's really pretty, but.'

'Yeah.' Jesse avoided her eye. 'Lots of extreme sports, too.'

'Bungy-jumping.' Brooke leaned against him. 'Snowboarding.'

'How long are you going for?' Paulina tried to sound casual.

'Oh, we're playing it by ear! We'll fly to Auckland first, then down to the South Island, then who knows? Maybe back to Australia, even.'

'But … you hate the mainland.' Paulina searched Jesse's face. 'You always say it's full of racists.'

'It is.' Shrugging, he met her gaze. 'But they don't own the place. And I've grown up a lot since last time I was there.'

'Grown up?' Paulina scoffed. 'You're twenty-five.'

'Yeah, yeah. Ulvini.'

'I'd *love* to meet some of Jess's mob over in Brisbane, if he lets me!' Brooke swished her hair. 'You know, in all the time I was in Sydney, I never saw *any* Aborigines? Who would've thought I'd find this guy on *Fairfolk*. That's the beauty of travelling. You never know what's around the corner.'

'Ha, yep.' Paulina drained her honey jar. 'Just watch out your body doesn't wind up in Belanglo.'

'Honestly, better that than dying of boredom on this rock.' Brooke cast a contemptuous glance up the beach. 'I've forgotten how it feels to wear a bikini without being gawked at by inbreds.'

Paulina noticed the pervert in golf gear, lurking. 'Oh. Him.'

'That's just Yooey Turner,' Jesse said. 'He's harmless. He just likes looking at chicks.'

Brooke rolled her eyes. 'Mm-hm. Until someday looking isn't enough.'

'Want me to say something to him?'

'Um, yes please!'

Puffing up his chest, Jesse marched down the beach toward Yooey.

'You'd think he was going to war for me!' Brooke looked askance at Paulina. 'He *would*, you know.'

'Oh, yeah,' Paulina agreed. 'Totally.'

Brooke stood. 'Coming for a dip?'

'Nah. I'm good.'

Once Brooke was in the water, Paulina turned onto her tummy and screamed into the sand. She didn't stop until she saw Jesse's feet. She sat up, glaring.

'What're you looking at, arsehole?'

'Nothing.' Jesse got out his Camels. 'Nothing at all.'

Paulina snatched one, stuck it between her lips.

'You're not going anywhere till I get my tramp stamp.'

The sky was the colour of nectar when Rabbit dropped her off at the Mutineers' Lodge bistro. 'Call me when you're done, gorgeous.'

'Don't worry about it, babe,' she demurred. 'I'll get a lift.'

Rabbit squeezed her hand. 'You know I can't sleep without you.'

'Get some rest, babe.' She stroked his face. 'You work so hard.'

Five minutes later, she was at the bar, watching for Jesse's car. When she saw it, she drained her glass and winked at Gayle, the bistro manager. 'Thanks for the alibi!'

Jesse smelled the alcohol on her as soon as she slipped into the passenger seat. 'You know it thins your blood.'

'Gawd, I haven't been out after dark without Ric in soooo long! Let's go to Wetties?'

Jesse sighed. 'He keeps a tight leash on you, eh.'

'He's from a different generation.' Paulina checked her lip gloss. 'He doesn't think boys and girls can be friends.'

At Jesse's cottage, Paulina had an urge to cry. 'Gawd, I haven't been here in ages,' her voice caught in her throat. 'Tiny, isn't it?'

'Yeah, yeah, you live in a palace.' He began laying out his tools. 'You know the drill.'

In the bathroom, Paulina stripped down and jumped in the shower. When she emerged in her laciest bra and g-string, hair dripping, Jesse did a double-take. 'Jesus!'

'What?' She squeezed her hair dry. 'Don't you want me using your towel?'

'It's fine,' Jesse mumbled, looking away.

Paulina strutted to the kitchen, got the Jim Beam down from the shelf, and poured herself a mug. 'Hope you don't mind.' She crept back to the lounge. 'I made coffee.'

'*Paulina*. I can smell that from here. You really don't care about bleeding, do you?'

'I bleed every month.' Sipping, she watched his thick eyelashes. 'Music?'

'Yeah.' He didn't look up. 'Good idea.'

She tiptoed to the CD rack, bum out and tummy in. Knelt on the carpet and browsed till she felt Jesse's eyes stray to her.

'Hey.' She held up an album. 'What do you think?'

He nodded, averted his eyes. 'Nice.'

Paulina crawled to the CD player, slipped in the disc, caught Jesse looking again, and approached him with the Jim Beam. 'Want some?'

'No. Jesus. I'm working.'

'I'm getting a gut.' Paulina snapped the band of her g-string. 'These never used to fit so tight.'

'Can you get out of my face? It's really distracting.'

She lay on the couch. 'Better?'

Jesse nodded. Paulina stared up at the ceiling, playing with her belly button and singing under her breath, till he approached in his gloves. 'Flip over.'

'Do you think I'd look cute with a belly-button ring?'

'Do you want a tramp stamp or not?'

'I dunno.' She fingered her hipbone. 'Could be cute here.'

'Too bony. You'll pass out from the pain. Flip over.'

Paulina sat up, reached for her mug and drank deep. Then she got on her hands and knees, peeked over her shoulder. 'Better?'

'Lie on your tummy. Lie flat and, like … stay *still*.'

Paulina obeyed. But as soon as he touched her with his cold gloves, she jolted.

'Jesus!'

'It's cold!'

'Want a blanket?'

'… No.'

He tried again. Again, she flinched. 'Jesus! Calm down.'

'I'm cold.' She took up her whisky. '*Sorry* for feeling cold.'

Jesse watched her swallow. 'Alright? Or want a blanket?'

'Alright.'

'You want a blanket?'

'Yeah … nah.' She giggled. 'You're so talented, Jess!'

'I haven't even done anything yet.'

'Do it, Jess. I'm waiting.'

'I'm *trying*. Shut up and lie still.'

'*You* shut up.' She sat up and pulled him close, pressed her lips to his.

'Jesus!' Jesse wiped his mouth. 'What the fuck, Paulina.'

'Let's have an affair!' Paulina looped her arms around his neck.

Jesse recoiled. 'If you're scared of the pain, just say so. Don't play mind games.'

'I'm not scared!' Paulina burst into tears. 'I'm not playing!'

'Nup. Not today.' Jesse peeled off his gloves. 'I don't care how much you pay me.'

He stormed out. Paulina kept bawling until she got tired — he was gone a bloody long time. When he came back, he had wet hair and a fresh T-shirt.

'Get dressed.' He chucked her uniform at her. 'We're going to Wetties.'

———

'The thing about Brooke is, what you see is what you get,' Jesse told her, four pints in. 'She doesn't play games.'

Paulina sneered. 'If you hate games so much, why're you always playing PlayStation?'

'And she's *beautiful*. Not just hot, but, like, naturally beautiful. She doesn't even need makeup. First thing in the morning, she's gorgeous. Those little freckles on her nose—'

'Ric looks good first thing in the morning, too,' Paulina countered. 'All those little wrinkles all over his face? Gorgeous!'

Jesse watched a waitress delivering chips to another table.

'Ugh! You already had chips. You're gonna end up like your dad.'

'Yeah. Well.' Jesse sipped his beer. 'You're gonna end up like … your mum.'

'So? My mum's beautiful!' Paulina stood. 'I'm getting another round.'

Jesse shook his head at his near-empty glass. 'I'm driving, remember.'

'You're boring as fuck.'

At the bar, the first guy she'd hooked up with on Fairfolk was drinking alone. 'Hey, Eddy.' She smiled coyly. 'How are you?'

'Good.' He looked her up and down. 'You?'

She leaned a little closer. '*Good*.'

'What're you drinking?' Eddy pulled out his wallet.

Paulina turned to the barmaid. 'Another round. Don't forget to chuck a shot in Camel's Pine Brew, okay?'

Eddy put his wallet away. 'You and Camilleri, eh?'

'He's going through a break-up.' Paulina winked. 'He just doesn't know it yet.'

'Eddy's married, you know.' Jesse frowned as she set down the fresh round of drinks.

'And I'm with Ric. So? I'm not allowed to flirt?' She simpered. 'Or am I only allowed to flirt with *you*?'

Jesse shrugged. 'Do what you want.'

Paulina looked back at Eddy. 'He's pretty sexy. He's got those Polynesian eyes. Nice and dark.'

'Racist.'

'I like dark eyes.' Paulina shifted her gaze to Jesse. 'Dark everything.'

'Um.' Jesse looked at his beer. 'I don't want this.'

'You're not a mainie. No one cares if you drive drunk.'

Jesse took a reluctant sip. 'This's my last one, okay? I'm feeling it.'

'Piss-weak!'

'Alcoholic.'

Paulina stiffened. Jesse got out his Camels, got up.

'I'm going for a smoke,' he said. 'Then I'm going home.'

'Whatever!' Paulina knocked back her rum. '*I'm* going for a piss.'

In the loo, the walls spun around her. But her reflection was steady in the mirror, applying lip gloss. The waitress came out of the adjoining cubicle to wash her hands.

'How do I look?' Paulina interrogated her. 'Do I look nice?'

'Yeah,' the waitress reassured her. 'You look nice.'

'Did you see that guy I'm with? I love him!' Paulina confided. 'Tonight's the night. I'm gonna fuck him tonight.'

Out in the beer garden, Jesse was smoking with a pale-skinned guy in check pants. 'What's with the pants?' Paulina asked the guy.

'I'm a chef at The Pacifica.' He shrugged. 'The checks hide the stains.'

'Yeah?' Paulina snatched his ciggie. 'All stains?'

He looked at her lips, sucking in smoke. 'Most stains.'

'Come on.' Jesse put out his ciggie in his beer. 'Let's go.'

'Thanks for the ciggie!' Paulina waved, linked her arm with Jesse's. 'Aw, did you make a friend?'

'Why, are you interested?'

'Why, are you jealous?'

'He was just some junkie, trying to score.' Jesse hesitated outside the Commodore. 'Listen: can we just walk back to Mutes'? I'm too drunk to drive Cook's Falls Road.'

'Don't bother, then.' Paulina crossed her arms. 'I'll hitch.'

'Don't hitchhike. Jesus.'

'I'll ask that junkie for a ride.' Paulina blew smoke over her shoulder. '*He* won't mind driving me to Cookies.'

'Forget it.' Jesse fumbled with his keys. 'I'll drive you.'

With painful slowness, Jesse drove out of town. At Cookies, Paulina

unclipped her seatbelt. 'Thanks for tonight. It was nice hanging out …
just us.'

'Yeah.' Jesse wiped his forehead. 'I'll feel it tomorrow, but.'

'Don't think about tomorrow.' Paulina leaned in. 'It's just us, now.'

'Paulina.' He shook his head. 'Come on.'

'*Come on.*' She slid onto his lap. 'It's just us, Jess.'

He turned his face away. 'Cut it out, Paulina.'

She kissed his neck, hitched up her skirt. 'I'm so wet, Jess. I want
you so much.'

'Come on. Don't.' He stayed her hands. 'You're just drunk. Okay?'

'I want you … you want me.' She breathed on his mouth. 'Babe:
you're so hard right now.'

Jesse groaned as she rubbed his dick. 'Paulina …'

'You're so hard, babe.' She ran her tongue over his lips. 'You're so
good. Put that hard dick inside me, babe.'

'What the fuck, Paulina.' Jesse shoved her off his lap. 'Just … *don't.*'

'Please?' Eyes misting up, Paulina kissed his knees. 'I want you so
much. I want you in my mouth. Please?'

Jesse groaned again; pushed her head away as she nuzzled his lap.

'Jesse-babe.' She peeled off her shirt, unhooked her bra. 'See how
much I want you?'

She dragged his hand to her hot breasts; her nipples, hard as
weapons.

'Jesus, Paulina.' Jesse's voice went high. 'Cut it out. Please.'

'Please?' She lifted his T-shirt, kissed the hair on his belly, licked it.
'Let me do this for you, babe. Please?'

Jesse's abs tightened. She licked the soft, downy place right above
where his belt-buckle started, then below it.

'Oh, yeah,' he whispered, finally. 'Oh. Jesus.'

'You're beautiful, Jess!' Paulina congratulated him. 'Can I suck your
dick? Please?'

'Jesus … Yeah.' Jesse covered his face with his hands. 'Before I come
in my pants. Please. Yeah.'

She grappled with his belt-buckle. He helped her.

'Oh, Jess.' She gazed up at him through the curtain of her fringe.
'You're *beautiful.*'

'Yeah. Jesus, you too.'

She took him in her mouth, worked him up and down.

'Oh, yeah,' he whimpered. 'Please. Yeah.'

'Can you come in my mouth?' Paulina raised her head. 'Please?'

'Uh, yeah. Jesus, yes, please.'

Her eyes leaked as she took him deeper. He clutched the roots of her hair.

'Say it again?' she asked. 'Before you come in my mouth? Say "please".'

'Oh, please. Yes, please.'

'Say I'm beautiful? Say it.'

'Beautiful. Beautiful, Paulina. *Please ...*'

It flooded her mouth: creamy, salty, bliss. She swallowed and laughed at the look on his face, like all his dreams had come true. Also, another thing — Rabbit was crossing the reserve with a flashlight, rapping on the car window.

'Do you think I'm stupid?' His lips were white. 'You think I don't know you're down here?'

'Jesus.' Jesse buckled up his pants. 'I'm sorry.'

Rabbit tore his gaze from Paulina to Jesse: 'I need her gone tonight.'

'Fine with me!' Paulina jeered. 'Like I wanna spend another night with *you.*'

'Fuck!' Jesse cried into his hands. 'Fuck!'

'I don't care what you do with her,' Rabbit continued calmly. 'I just need her gone.'

'She's not going with me!' Jesse pleaded. 'I don't want her! Please, Rabbit—'

'She's not my problem anymore.'

'Rabbit, brudda, please. She's yours—'

'You're the one with your plana in her mouth. She's your problem.' Rabbit glanced at Paulina's bare chest. 'One word of advice? Don't get her pregnant.'

At that, he stalked off. Paulina broke down.

'I'm sorry, Jess! He's a bastard. Please, let's go—'

'Don't touch me!' Jesse's voice cracked. 'You fucking bitch! Get away from me!'

'Please,' Paulina bleated. 'Please? I love you so much.'

'Get away from me! Go sit in the backseat!'

'Can you sit there with me?'

'Fuck! No!' Jesse was shaking. 'It's so you don't touch me. If you touch me again, I swear … You make me so fucking angry.'

'Jess?' Paulina cried harder. 'Don't cry. I love you.'

'If you love me, get the fuck away from me,' he said in a stiff, quiet voice. 'Now.'

She stopped crying and grabbed her clothes; scrambled into them in the backseat.

'I'm going out for some air,' Jesse said, after a while. 'Don't follow me.'

While he was gone, Paulina wept herself into a catatonic state. It was an eternity before Jesse returned, with bleeding knuckles.

'Did you and Ric have a punch-up?' she asked, awed.

'No. Fuck.' Jesse started the car. 'I punched a pine tree.'

Paulina made every effort not to laugh.

'I'm sorry,' she apologised as he drove out of Cookies. 'I love you.'

'Stop saying that. You don't.'

'I do! I love you so much.'

'Whatever that was back there, it wasn't love. You don't know what love is.'

'I'm sorry.' Tears burned her cheeks. 'I wish I was dead. I'm so sorry—'

'Shut the fuck up. You're not the victim here. Stop playing the fucking victim.'

Paulina closed her eyes and wished he'd drive her somewhere cold and put her out of her misery. Instead, he drove to Mutes'. 'You have keys, right? You can sleep in a cabin?'

'Yeah,' Paulina mumbled. 'I'll clean it in the morning.'

She got out of the car. Lowered her eyes and said it one last time.

'I know you're sorry.' Jesse sighed. 'But I don't think I can forgive you. Okay?'

It wasn't okay. Nothing would ever be okay again.

8:30 UNSOLVED

Once upon a time, Judy Novak was just a woman who answered phones for a living. Now, she was a woman with a famously tragic surname who answered phones for a living.

'Student Help Desk, Judy speaking. How can I help you?'

'Hi, Judy,' said the girl on the other end. 'Is this Judy Novak?'

'Yes, that's me,' Judy chirped; then it hit her like a bus. 'Why do you ask?'

'Judy Novak, the mother of Paulina Novak?'

'Yes.' Her voice went as cold as the case was. '*Why* do you ask?'

The girl started talking rapidly. *Nicole*, Judy heard. *Channel something. Something 8:30 pm.* Judy listened as best as she could until the roaring of her blood got too loud.

'I'm hanging up now,' Judy said in a small, vague voice. 'Yes. I'm hanging up.'

She hung up. Lana — a new girl she'd help train up for Summer Enrolment period, their busiest period — smiled at her without meeting her eye. Judy liked the new girls; even if they knew, they pretended not to.

The phone rang again. Judy picked it up; it was her job, after all.

'Student Help Desk, Judy speaking. How can I help you?'

Relief flooded her as a teenage boy's voice squeaked on the other end of the line.

'Of course! I can help you with that. Do you mind if I ask you some questions?'

It was late-afternoon sugar-craving time when 'Nicole' showed up in the flesh. Judy was busy with another student; an international student from Shandong who'd enrolled in the wrong course. But she noticed the girl, lingering politely: young enough to be a student but too well-dressed. When Lana asked if she could help her, she smiled and shook her head. 'I'm here for Judy.'

The cheek of it!

'I should call campus security.' Judy handed back Nicole's business card without looking at it. 'This is my workplace. You people can't just come in here.'

'Please, Judy — can I call you "Judy"?' Nicole slipped her card back into her pocket. 'I won't take much of your time. Can I just buy you coffee? I saw a place around the corner.'

'Keen Bean.' Judy knew all the cafes on campus. 'They're no good.'

She gathered up her handbag, donned her sunglasses, and led the way across campus to Samsara, where the chairs were comfier and the baristas were cuter.

'Have you worked here long?' Nicole asked her.

'Yes,' Judy replied tersely. 'How did you know I work here?'

'A friend of mine teaches Journalism. How many years?'

'Nine.'

'That's impressive!'

'It's not.' Judy scowled. 'It's mostly students who work here. I stick out like a sore thumb. No wonder you found me.'

'You must be very experienced, though.'

'I've been a receptionist for thirty years. Just a receptionist. It's all I've ever done. There's nothing impressive about that.'

Nicole pursed her lips. Judy stole a glance at her; she was very pretty. Pretty, petite, brown-haired — like bait.

'Still. You're very experienced. Where did you work before here?'

'I started out as a medical receptionist. I married a doctor. I couldn't stand medical stuff, after he died.' Judy swept her sunglasses onto her head as they entered. 'Then I worked in schools. My sister got me a job at the school where she taught. But ...'

She shrugged. It was all very unimpressive.

'... Universities are nicer. The students actually want to be here. And there's lots of smart people walking around. I'm not very smart, but I like talking to smart people.'

Nicole found a table. 'I think you're selling yourself short, Judy.'

'I'm not smart.' Judy sat. 'My husband was smart. Paulina was smart. I'm very average. You know, you have to order at the counter, here.'

'I'll go up. What do you want?'

'A flat white.' Judy sighed. 'I might have to do a runner while you're gone.'

Nicole smiled: a wide smile, full of dimples. 'I hope not. I like talking to you, Judy.'

While Nicole ordered, Judy tried to think of something self-righteous to say.

'You know, I think it's very manipulative, what you're doing.' As soon as she said it, she felt bad. 'Well, not *you* personally. But your bosses. It's very manipulative, sending a girl like you to do their dirty work.'

Nicole sank into the chair opposite Judy's.

'It's not dirty work. Can I ask what you mean by "a girl like me"?'

'You know. All young and cute, and with the dark hair. It's very manipulative.'

'I'm sure your daughter and I are very different women. I'd like to know more about your daughter. I'd like our viewers to know more about her, too. In your words.'

Judy crossed her arms. 'It's not happening. Sorry.'

'Anything we do would be pre-recorded. We would compensate you generously for your time. We'd arrange for media training, if you want it. You set the terms.'

A cute barista set down their coffees.

'You're not going to use me to make her look bad,' Judy said. 'I know how people talk about her. I won't be part of it.'

'We're just talking,' Nicole reassured her. 'We're just talking over coffee.'

Judy stared into her mug. 'I feel very manipulated.'

'I'm sorry you feel that way.' Nicole gazed at her. 'You seem like a very intelligent woman, and a very loving mother. I can see how much you love her, just sitting here.'

'So?' Judy took a sip of coffee. 'All mothers love their children.'

'Well, it doesn't always shine through.' Nicole broke her gaze, spooned sugar into her latte. 'I won't name names, but we've had some mothers who've had to go through hours of media training, just to get a ten-second sound bite. I'm not saying they don't love their children. They just can't articulate it, through the pain. You're very articulate.'

'I bet you say that to all the grieving mothers.'

'You're very natural.'

'You don't know me.' Judy shook her head. 'My heart's permanently broken. It's hard enough living day-by-day. I have nothing to give you people.'

'Look: Judy.' Nicole stirred her coffee. 'I hate saying this, but we don't need your permission to tell a story about Paulina. We don't even need you to tell a *good* story — and by that, I mean a juicy story. A story people will watch.'

'So, you'll do it with or without me?'

'Not necessarily. It's TV. Things get axed all the time. We might sign you on and never do anything about it. That's the nature of the industry.'

'Why should I bother, then?'

'To put it simply?' Nicole caught her eye. 'For her. I could give you lots of reasons, but that's the only one that really matters.'

Judy shook her head. 'She'd be mortified.'

'She can't be mortified, though. Can she? She can only be remembered. And your memories of her are more important than anyone else's.'

'They're *my* memories. You can't just take them and spoil them for some trashy TV show.'

'I agree. We can't take them. They can only be given. Shared.'

'I take back what I said. You're very manipulative.' Judy took up her coffee. 'Not just your bosses. You, personally. You're very manipulative.'

'Have you seen the show, Judy?'

Judy waved her hand. 'I don't go in for that stuff. Murder for entertainment.'

'You might be surprised.' Nicole leaned closer. 'It *is* entertainment, don't get me wrong. But we're not just rehashing world-famous serial killers. We're all about unsolved crimes, and we're homegrown in our focus. The Beaumont children. Revelle Balmain. The Wanda Beach murders—'

'I remember that.' Judy grimaced. 'That was my time. That was very close to home.'

'Exactly. Homegrown cases. The sort of thing Bob and Lynn next door might be watching on a Sunday night and think, "oh, yes, I remember that. I know something about that." You never know who's watching, what they've been holding onto.'

'Yes, but. They're all still *unsolved*?'

'We can't claim to have solved anything. But you never know who's watching. Somebody on Fairfolk could be watching. Somebody who thought, "that's none of my business" at the time. They could see you speaking about her, with so much love. That could be the game-changer.'

Judy felt the temptation slithering in her, like a serpent in a garden.

'No. I don't think so.'

'You want the case to be solved, don't you? You want justice for Paulina?'

'I don't believe in justice.'

'You don't believe whoever killed her should pay for it?'

'There's no adequate payment. There's no justice. There's just senselessness, and living with the senselessness. That's what you people don't understand.'

'So, you don't care if her killer gets away with it? Kills again, even?'

'I'm too broken to care. I told you. I have nothing to give.'

'I don't believe you.'

All at once, Judy couldn't stand the girl: her unlined skin; her sanctimonious eyes.

'Excuse me, but you really *don't* know me.' Judy reached for her handbag. 'You don't know anything. Maybe someday you'll lose everything, then you'll know. There's no justice.'

She was about to stand, then realised she wasn't done yet.

'Let me tell you something about my daughter: she was suicidal. Did you know that? Did you know, the first thing I thought that day, when I realised something was wrong — and you know, as a mum; you just *know* — I thought: "oh, gawd, she's finally done it!" Even though she seemed happy the day before. She was like that. Sunshine and stormclouds. I thought: "Baby girl, why now? Why didn't you come to me first?" Because she had, before. She'd call me up saying, "Mum, I want to die." Do you know what it's like hearing your child say that? You have no idea!'

'No,' Nicole said politely. 'I don't.'

'I'm not stupid,' Judy continued. 'I may only be a receptionist, but I know people. I know most people would say, "Oh, it's not so bad, then. She didn't even *want* to live." That's how people are; they make all these assumptions about what her life was worth.'

'I'm sorry to hear that.'

'No you're not! You're loving it!' Judy huffed. 'My point is: she could've killed herself. She *wanted* to. Or, there was something in her brain that made her want to. I don't fully understand. She felt the void very intensely. My therapist said she might've had that disorder—'

'Bipolar?'

'No, not that one. Borderline. Like Winona Ryder in that movie.' Judy waved her hand. 'Anyway, she was who she was. Something inside her wanted her dead, and she resisted it. She put one foot in front of the other every day. I was so proud of her.'

'She sounds like a courageous young woman.'

'She *was*.' Judy snatched up a serviette. 'I know you're just saying that, but she really was. That's the thing, though. It didn't matter. She walked out of the house one morning, and the most senseless thing happened. I *wish* she'd killed herself. It would've hurt like hell, but it would've saved us both a lot of pain. I could've made some sense of it.'

Nicole stared at Judy until she rolled her eyes, wiped them.

'Anyway. You've made me cry. Well done.' She bundled up the serviette and shoved it in her handbag. 'Thanks for the coffee.'

'Thank you for speaking with me, Judy.' Nicole stood up with her. 'I feel very privileged, that you shared that with me. I think the people of Australia would also feel privileged ... but that's another story. Please don't throw my card out straightaway.'

Nicole passed her another business card. This time, Judy read it.

'"Nicole Pancik."' Judy glowered. '*Pancik*. Really? So you're Slavic, too?'

'Serbian. On my dad's side.'

'And that's just a coincidence?'

'No coincidence.' Nicole beamed. 'I'm the best woman for the job, don't you think?'

'I think you're very manipulative.'

'I think you should do it,' Caro said. 'I mean, do what you want. But I'm not going to talk you out of it, if that's what you're worried about.'

Quite the opposite. Judy was hoping her sister *would* talk her out of it.

'But … *me?*' Judy stammered. 'I'll be terrible. I hate public speaking. *You* should do it.'

'Mothers trump aunts. And, honestly? I don't have the face for it.'

'You always say my face is stupid.'

'Oh, it *is*.' Caro smirked. 'It's stupid and soft and tragic. I can't stand it.'

'Caro!' Tim chastised from the kitchen.

'She started it!' Caro topped up her Riesling. 'Trust me, nobody wants a woman who looks like *me*. They'll think I did it.'

'Ha!' said Tim.

'Shush, you! You're here to make pasta, not talk.' Caro gave him the finger. 'What was I saying? Your stupid face: that's right. It's perfect. People want a grieving mother to look sort of dazed and helpless. If you're in control, they get suss.'

'I think what my wife means is: you have a kind face, Judy. Sympathetic.'

'*Stupid face*,' Caro mouthed. '*Stupid!*'

Judy blushed, despite herself. 'You really think so, Tim?'

'You look trustworthy.' He squeezed Caro's shoulders. 'Not like this one.'

'It's why he loves me.' Caro smiled up at her husband. 'He cracks people's spines for a living. He's basically the devil.'

'But …' Judy opened and closed her mouth like a goldfish. 'It's trashy. Isn't it? To put it all out there like that?'

'I haven't seen this particular program.' Caro shrugged. 'They're all a bit trashy. But what have we got to lose?'

'It feels dirty.'

'Your daughter was murdered. It *is* dirty.' Caro registered Judy's brimming eyes and backtracked. 'But it's your call, Jude. Don't do anything you're not comfortable with.'

'I don't know,' Judy said. 'I'll say something stupid. Or they'll drag all my skeletons out of my closet and make me look like a homewrecker. Like mother, like daughter.'

'That's what contracts are for.' Caro fiddled with the stem of her wineglass. 'I can get a referral for an entertainment lawyer. One of my Year 11s does TV. She's in that show about horse girls.'

Judy screwed up her face. 'Horse girls?'

'Yes, horse girls. Having horsey adventures. Fighting animal cruelty and romancing stable boys and so on. God!' Caro threw back her head in exasperation. 'Don't give me that look. I'm not a camera!'

'I can't help it,' Judy said. 'It's just my face.'

'It's a really stupid face.' Caro smirked. 'It'd be even stupider to waste it.'

The contract stipulated no mention of the age difference between Judy and her late husband. No mention of any indiscretions that may have taken place during their seventeen-year union. No mention of his previous marriage or the offspring resulting from this marriage. Marko's country of origin was hereby to be referred to as 'Croatia'. 'Yugoslavia' meant war and communism, the lawyer said. 'Croatia' meant sparkling seas and beauty queens.

'Marko's village was a long way from the sea, though,' Judy protested. 'It was way up in the north. Practically Slovenia.'

They filmed the week before Easter. Judy wished they could've filmed some other time. Easter had all kinds of bad associations, the way black plastic did, cows, the moon on certain cloudless nights.

'Today's the day!' Nicole gushed, meeting her at reception. 'How do you feel? How was the media training?'

Nicole had already asked her about the media training twice, over the phone.

Judy shrugged. 'It's a lot to remember.'

'You'll do great. You're a natural. Is that what you're wearing?'

'Oh. Well.' Judy opened the glossy shopping bag she'd brought along. 'I packed a couple of others. There's this white one. Or this, with the flowers. I figured flowers are nice and, well … *mumsy*.'

'White can be harsh under the studio lights. And patterns are

167

distracting. Sal didn't tell you that?' Nicole ushered her into Hair and Makeup. 'Never mind. The blue's good. It brings out your eyes. See you on the other side!'

'You're not staying?'

'I'll be around. Liz will be doing your hair and makeup. Liz, this is Judy. She's doing a pre-record with Brendan. Judy, you'll be great.'

With a waggle of her fingers, Nicole left her in the hands of 'Liz' — a tall, plain-faced woman with a pragmatic topknot.

'What're you recording?' she asked, examining Judy's hair.

'Oh.' Judy wasn't expecting to have to explain. 'This crime show. *8:30 Unsolved.*'

'Are you a witness?'

'A family member. The mother, actually.'

'We'll keep it soft and natural, then.'

'I hope you have waterproof mascara.'

'We use this.' Liz showed her the tube. 'You can cry rivers without it smudging.'

'Well. Good.'

'Brendan's a pro. He'll make it easy. Hair up or down?'

'I don't know. Down, I guess. If you can just give it some volume?'

As Liz mucked around with hairsprays and hot air, Judy closed her eyes, breathed like Agnes had taught her. Wiping down her face, Liz asked, 'Got much on for Easter?'

'Just mooching around the house, probably.' Her chest tightened. 'You?'

'We're taking the kids up to Coffs Harbour. Six hours of bickering in the backseat. I can already hear it.'

Judy smiled and closed her eyes again.

'I know it seems like a lot, but it's not, under the studio lights,' Liz explained when she was done caking on the makeup. 'This is what "natural" looks like in La-La Land.'

Right on cue, Nicole rapped on the door. 'Lovely, Judy! Come on, I'll take you through to the studio. Don't worry about your bags.'

They passed through a maze of halls, doors, cables, bright screens. A young guy in a black T-shirt sat her on a plump couch and unceremoniously attached a microphone to her breast, asked, 'What did you have for breakfast?'

'Toast.' She blinked in confusion. 'Just toast.'

He gave her the thumbs-up, disappeared behind a screen. Nicole smiled, tight-lipped, and checked her watch. 'I'll see where Brendan is.'

Judy sat alone under the lights until Nicole returned with a vaguely familiar-looking middle-aged man.

'Don't get up,' he told her, when she rose to shake his hand. 'I'll get down.'

Brendan sat in the armchair across from her. When the young guy asked what he'd eaten for breakfast, he purred, 'Wouldn't you like to know!'

Then it was just the two of them, and a whole lot of cameras.

'It's all very simple,' Brendan told her. 'If you muck up, they'll edit it out.'

Judy nodded.

'Ready?'

There was no choice but to nod again. Brendan made a cameras-rolling gesture, winked then steepled his hands.

'Judy, tell me,' he said solemnly. 'Who was Paulina Novak?'

'Well.' Judy's eyes were already wet. 'She was the love of my life.'

It aired in July, on bin night. Judy refused to leave the house, but Caro insisted on coming over with two bottles of wine — and on using the good glasses.

'I can't believe you still have these!' Caro cackled, filling the ornate crystal glasses to the brim. 'You're a monster, Jude.'

'What was I meant to do, smash them? It's not my fault Ljubica turned her nose up at them.'

'I mean, it *is* your fault.'

When Judy glimpsed herself on-screen for the first time, with her blue blouse and watery red eyes, narrating that awful day in words she couldn't remember saying, she hid her face with a cushion. 'Turn it off. I'm *hideous.*'

'Shh,' Caro said. 'I'm listening.'

Judy kept her face covered for the rest of the segment. The ad break came quicker than she expected.

'That was *horrible.*' She lowered the cushion. 'Do I really look like that?'

'More or less.' Caro wiped her eyes. 'Sorry to break it to you.'

'Horrible.' Judy sighed as an ad came on for Olay anti-ageing cream. 'I wonder how many people will be rushing out to buy that stuff, after seeing my face?'

'You were good, Jude.' Caro topped up their wine. 'Better than I expected. Really.'

They drank in silence, until an ad flashed by for the latest Mazda. They caught each other's eyes and cracked up.

'Gawd, that's tacky!'

'You shouldn't've mentioned the make of her car so many times.'

'I said "Mazda"?'

'"Mazda this", "Mazda that". They should send you a freebie.'

As the ads wound down, Judy braced herself for her hideous face again. Instead, a photograph filled the screen: Paulina and her ex-boyfriend, Vinnie, in a place of white-washed walls and sunshine.

'Paulina had problems.' Vinnie's handsome face darkened the screen. 'Serious problems.'

'Vinnie?' Caro muttered disbelievingly. 'They got *Vinnie*?'

Vinnie stared down the camera. 'Trusting her was the worst mistake of my life.'

'That little shit.' Caro shot Judy an apprehensive glance. 'Turn it off?'

Judy's throat clenched. Her fingers gripped the wineglass, cold and white.

'No,' she said quietly. 'I'm listening.'

DOWN SEASON

'You're *really* staying here all through down season?' Kymba pulled down her bathers to nurse baby Ollie. 'With the renovations and everything?'

'I barely hear them anymore.' Sipping her Pine Brew, Paulina listened to the distant whirring of machinery. 'Anyways, Baz asked me to collect the mail.'

Kymba fit her nipple into Ollie's mouth. 'Aren't you scared at night?'

'Scared of what? The ghost of Gilligan King?'

'My cousin Cyndee had a guy walk into her house while her husband was away.'

'What, she didn't lock her door?'

'It's unFairfolk to lock doors. People think you're hiding something.'

'What happened?' Paulina watched Kymba's white lion tattoo happily tolerating the feeding frenzy. 'Did he rape her?'

'No … He just complained about his wife for a while then asked for a sandwich.'

'Gawd, Fairfolk men are fuckwits!' Paulina clapped her pale, goosebumped thigh. 'I'll keep some bread by the bed. I'll be right.'

'Mummy!' Hunter, floaties on his arms, wailed from the water. 'I'm hungry, too!'

'Want a sandwich?' Paulina asked. 'Wanna complain about your wife while I make you a sandwich?'

'I want *boobies*!'

'You're too old, Hunty.' Kymba blushed. 'He gets *so* jealous.'

Paulina patted her chest. 'No boobs, but I can make you a sanga, Hunty. Peanut butter, howabout that?'

'You don't have to.' Kymba rolled her eyes. 'He's just attention-seeking.'

Paulina hoisted herself from the sunchair. 'Not like I've got anything better to do.'

She tiptoed to the gate and lifted the latch with care, shivering in her bikini and board shorts. Eddy and his apprentice, Leki, were toting the old ceiling fan out of cabin two.

In cabin twelve, she made Hunter's sandwich, cut it into triangles and sliced off the crusts. Crammed the crusts into her mouth.

'Here.' Paulina set the sandwich down at the poolside, then lay down in defeat. 'I need to quit beer. I'm getting a gut.'

'I can see your ribs.' Shaking her head, Kymba draped a towel around Hunter's shoulders. 'But you *should* drink less beer. If you're worried.'

'Can't really afford vodka right now. I need a new car.'

'Is your probation period over yet?'

'Ended last week.' She reached for her tobacco and papers. 'I had a look in the *Fairfolk Daily*. Nothing but utes. Maybe I should just go to The Car Kings?'

Grimacing, Kymba burped Ollie. 'Car always overcharges.'

'I'll haggle.'

'Want a lift into town?' Kymba handed Hunter a sandwich-half. 'I have to do some shopping before school pick-up.'

'Sure. Drop me off at the bottle-O.'

Standing in line, Paulina's head buzzed with the sound of her own blood. 'Yorana,' the old man in front of her said, raising his six-pack. Paulina smiled and said, 'Yorana.'

Outside the bottle-O, she stopped to pat his border collie.

'That's Jake,' the old guy said. 'Jakey-boy.'

'Jakey-boy!' Paulina ruffled his ears. 'Good boy!'

She stumbled a little, rising from her crouch; mumbled her thanks and weaved down the street to The Car Kings. The glisten of the new cars in the winter sun stung her eyes.

'Yorana, sweetheart.' Car King sidled up beside her. 'See anything you like?'

'Yeah.' Paulina pointed at a blue car. 'That one.'

'The Mazda Astina? You looking to buy?'

'Yeah. Totalled my Corolla on Valentine's Day.'

'I'll give you a good price. Rabbit's a friend of mine.'

'Pfft!' Paulina said. 'Then you would've heard I dumped him?'

'You lymed him, eh?' Car looked her up and down. 'I'll give you a better price.'

'Yeah? How much?'

'$24,999, drive away.'

'Yeah, nah!' Paulina picked up her six-pack. 'See ya!'

She walked back to Mutineers' Lodge in the lengthening shadows, pausing to watch some cows. She checked the mail, then checked in on Eddy and Leki, installing a new sconce in cabin three. 'Looks good,' she said from the doorway, blowing smoke sideways.

'Aye!' said Leki. Eddy said nothing.

She finished her ciggie on the porch, then wandered through the dust to reception. They'd already laid down new floorboards, were installing a desk shaped like a ship's prow.

'Looks good,' she repeated. 'Must be almost done, yeah?'

'Aye,' said Stripe, named for the scar on his cheek. 'Painter comes Friday.'

'To do the mural?'

'Jus' the base.'

Paulina took the mail back to cabin twelve. Cracked open another beer and fridged the rest, then sat on the porch smoking and watching the guys clear up for the day. The sky was pink and blue like baby clothes when Eddy broke off from the crew, strolled over.

'Hey,' he said, dangling his muscular arms over the porch.

Paulina removed her headphones. 'Hey.'

He had her bent over the kitchen counter within five minutes; was done within the next five. He didn't use a condom, but when the cum leaked down her thighs, he fetched a toilet roll.

'Thanks,' she mumbled, cleaning herself up. 'Wanna stay for a beer?'

'Bes' get home.'

'Do you know anyone selling a car?' She pulled up her shorts. 'Something small?'

'You tried The Car Kings?'

'Was hoping for something second-hand.' She shrugged. 'Thanks for the root. Same time tomorrow?'

'Bes' not, eh. It's Eeva's birthday.'

Paulina smoked another ciggie on the porch after Eddy left, fantasised about slapping his wife next time she saw her. Then she went inside to shower.

After her shower, she watched *Big Brother* and ate some carrot sticks with peanut butter. Her mum rang after *Big Brother*.

'You again?' Paulina groaned. 'Bloody hell, you need to get a life.'

'I'm just calling to see how you are.' Judy inhaled. 'If you're busy, I'll go.'

'Yeah, leave me alone.' Paulina waited for her mum to hang up. 'Did you watch *Big Brother*?'

'Of course I did,' Judy said delicately. 'I have no life.'

'Oi, how much do you reckon a Mazda Astina is worth? Brand-new?'

'Oh, I don't know. You should call up some dealers and compare.'

'Can you do it for me?'

'Paulina, you're *twenty-nine*.'

'Yeah, but. You like talking on the phone; you're a receptionist.'

'I get paid to talk on the phone. That's not the same as liking it.'

'Why do you keep calling me, then?'

Judy sighed. 'Well, I *suppose* I can make some calls. I don't think it's a good investment, though. You don't know how long you're going to stay—'

'Forever! It's my home.'

'Even so. All the salt air. It'll degrade faster. You're better off buying second—'

'I want a *new* car! Bloody hell, can't you let me have something to live for?'

'Well, it's your money. Just, try not to be impulsive.'

'I'm asking your advice, aren't I?' Paulina beat her head against her beer can. 'I'm not stupid. You think I'm gonna accept the first price Car King tells me?'

'The car dealer's name is "*Car*"?'

'It's short for 'Carlyle'. Duh!'

Judy sniggered. 'Gawd! That's like me being named "receptionist".'

'Yeah, and my name's "unemployed". Get over it.'

'You wouldn't have any trouble finding a job in Syd—'

'I'm *not* coming home!'

'Okay, okay,' Judy backtracked. 'Paulina: are you *okay?* I mean, are you eating?'

'Ugh!' Paulina swigged her beer. '*Yes.*'

'I don't mean to baby you. Just, I worry about you, all by yourself out there.'

'How do you know I'm by myself?'

'Oh. You're seeing someone?'

'Yeah,' Paulina bragged. 'I am, actually. One of the guys from the work crew.'

'Well. What's he like?'

'Just a regular guy. He's a sparky.'

'Well. Good for you.'

'He's married.' Paulina listened to her mum drawing in her breath. 'Don't judge me!'

'I'm not. Just … *be careful.*'

'Yeah, yeah. We're just rooting, okay? It's not like he wants anything serious. Guys never wanna be serious with me.'

'Don't take it personally. Men aren't very serious.'

Paulina started crying. 'I'm so shit. Why would anyone wanna be with me?'

'You're not shit.' Judy's tone was stern. 'You're smart and good and beautiful. You just need to have a bit more faith in yourself.'

'I had *one chance.* I had one chance with the most perfect guy, and I fucked it up.'

'Ric?'

'No! Vinnie!' Paulina sobbed. 'He was perfect!'

'He wasn't.' Judy sighed. 'I know you loved him, but he wasn't perfect.'

'He gave me everything and I fucked it up.'

'That guy from the Melbourne office practically raped you, and all Vinnie could think about was his bruised ego. He wasn't perfect.'

'I wasn't *raped.* Gawd!' Paulina took another gulp of beer. 'I was a drunk slut. That's all.'

'Paulina. Baby.' Judy must've meant business, calling her *baby.* 'You're not a slut. Don't let anyone tell you otherwise.'

'You're so annoying.'

'You've been through a lot. These past months, especially. You had a miscarriage, for chrissakes. You're going through a break-up. You're very strong, coping all by yourself.'

Paulina wiped her eyes. 'Stop talking shit.'

'I've been twenty-nine before. It's an awkward age. Don't feel bad about having a few growing pains.'

'You're so lame.'

'You're very strong. You're very independent. You have no idea how proud I am.' Judy took a deep breath. 'So, you're really set on this Mazda, are you?'

'I dunno. I was kinda drunk when I saw it.'

'Well, don't go car-shopping when you're drunk. That's like buying groceries when you're hungry. Do you still want me to call the dealerships tomorrow?'

'Nah.' Paulina sniffled. 'I'll do it.'

'Are you sure?'

'Yeah. Not like I've got anything better to do.'

After hanging up, Paulina finished her beer, brushed her teeth, and went to bed. But partway through the night, she woke dry-mouthed and afraid of the total darkness, the howling of the sea winds through the palms.

She pulled the phone book from her bedside, found his number and dialled.

'Jess? I know you said not to call. I just miss you so much. Please, can you come over? We don't have to talk. I'm just so scared. I don't wanna be alone. Please?'

'Um,' a groggy male voice replied. 'I think you've got the wrong number.'

'You're not Jesse? Where's Jesse? Who are *you*?'

'Sean,' he said. 'Sean Campbell.'

'Hey, Sean. Get fucked!'

Paulina slammed down the phone.

On Sunday morning, she woke to a silence worse than all the drills and hammers in the world. She couldn't remember exactly what she'd done the night before, only that it involved getting kicked out of Wetties, and hitching a ride back to Mutes' with a carload of drunk boys who'd made her feel like a cat among a pack of dogs, and many drunken phone calls. She thought about killing herself, but couldn't decide how, and whether to leave a note. *Such a slut, deserve to die*, she wrote in her diary.

She cried a bit; considered calling her mum. But her mum would tell her to come home, and she didn't want to go home; her island *was* her home!

She hauled herself out of bed, pulled on her exercise clothes, fastened her Discman to her waistband, and put her sunglasses on to face the harsh winter sun.

On her walk, people kept raising their hands off their wheels in greeting, slowing down to offer her a ride into town. It was annoying, but she forgot about killing herself for a while.

She was reminded, though, reaching the cliffs near the national park. She walked on in a panic, all the way to Piney's Point, where she watched the surfers cutting through the waves, slick as aliens in their wetsuits.

She wished she'd brought her smokes. She sat, freezing in her sports bra, until some teenaged boys came by, surfboards under their arms.

'Hey, do you smoke?' Paulina asked hopefully. 'Can I bum a smoke?'

They giggled.

'Yeah, yeah. Do you have any ciggies or not?'

More giggles. Then one of them swaggered forward, offered a pack of Winnies. She took one, let him light it for her.

'Cheers, kid.' Paulina sighed as the smoke swaddled her nerves. 'Careful out there. Those waves look pretty big.'

That got more giggles. Paulina rolled her eyes, waved them away.

She didn't plan to go into town. But that's where she wound up. She bummed another smoke from a bloke outside the Blue Moon Café, then walked on to Rainbow Real Estate, looked at the pictures of houses. Trekked uphill to Camilleri's.

'Hey,' she mumbled, door dinging behind her. 'Um.'

Jesse turned away. Opened the door to the cutting room and yelled, 'Dad!'

Joe Camilleri appeared in his bloody apron, looked from Jesse to Paulina. 'Get this mainie,' Jesse muttered, shouldering past his dad.

'Um.' Paulina felt as though there were splinters of glass in her eyes. 'Just a chicken breast.'

Joe scooped a chicken breast into a bag, weighed it up, wrapped and stickered it.

'Shit.' Tears spilled down her cheeks. 'I'm so sorry. I forgot my—'

Joe held out the package. 'Next time.'

Paulina wiped her face. 'Cheers.'

She was barely two steps out of the shop when she bumped into Eddy's wife, Eeva, and his mum, pushing a pram. 'Watch where you're going, cow,' she snapped.

'Stay away from my son,' Eddy's mum snapped back.

'Not my fault you never taught him to keep it in his pants,' Paulina taunted.

The old bitch slapped her. She slapped back; was ready to do worse, only Eeva was grabbing the pram from her mother-in-law's hands and steering it away.

'By the way!' Paulina jeered at Eeva. 'Eddy *hates* wearing condoms!'

She flounced down the street feeling glorious and savage, like she'd just harpooned a whale. But the sheen wore off as soon as Mutes' came back into view.

Silence stretched out like an ocean all around her.

'Yorana, sweetheart.' Car King smiled at her. His teeth were big and white against his year-round tan; his overbite pronounced. 'Couldn't stay away, eh.'

'You gonna offer me a better deal this time?'

'$24,999, drive away.'

'They charge less on the mainland.'

'Import costs. You have any idea how hard it is to bring one of these babies in from the supply ship?'

'Yeah. I know how youse bring them in.'

'With all due respect, sweetheart, you'll never know. It's a man's job. Us men put our lives on the line every time we go out there.' Car moved his collar aside to show her a bit of scar tissue. 'See that? Did it when I was—'

'$18,000.'

'You trying to insult me, sweetheart?'

'You think I don't know about salt damage?'

'Wash her once a week. I bet you wash your hair more often.'

She tucked her hair behind her ears. 'Maybe I'll just go to a proper dealer in Sydney.'

'Not before taking her for a test-drive on our beautiful ocean roads, eh?'

Paulina followed Car inside, wrote her details in the log book, and handed over her credit card as he got the keys. Car glanced at the log book. 'You living at Mutes'?'

'I work there. I'm staying with friends right now.'

'Wanna write your friend's address?'

'Nah.'

'What's this phone number?'

Paulina rolled her eyes. 'It's made-up, alright? Can I have the keys now?'

Car dangled the keys in her face. When she made a grab for them, he closed his fist.

'Fuck this.' Paulina turned away. 'Give me back my card.'

'I'm just playing, eh.' He handed her the keys. 'Be my guest, sweetheart.'

They walked out to the car. She let herself in, inhaled the clean, warm smell. Car came around to the passenger side, made a big show of putting the seat back. 'Nothing like that new car smell, eh?'

'Better than fat old Car smell.'

He laughed. She slipped the keys in the ignition, placed her hands on the steering wheel. 'Like the feel of that wheel? All leather.'

'Uh huh.'

'Automatic climate control.' He showed her some buttons. 'Radio. CD player, for your music. You like music?'

'Uh huh.'

'I've seen you walking around with those thingies in your ears. Always wondered what you were listening to.'

Paulina rolled the car out of the yard.

'Smooth sailing, eh?' Car pestered her. 'Go on. Throw her some curves.'

Paulina sped up, flew beyond the shopping strip and sleepy resorts, towards the scenic bend of Klee Welkin Road. 'You know what "Klee Welkin" means?' Car asked.

'Duh. "Clear sky."'

'Rabbit teach you Fayrf'k?'

She zoomed up to King's Lookout, that view that felt like dying and looking down from heaven. 'It's not like it's hard.'

'You know, the mainie teachers used to belt us for speaking Fayrf'k, back in the day.'

'Yeah, yeah. Ric told me all his sob stories from the dark ages.'

'He teach you our dirty words?'

Paulina smiled. 'I know "kuka", shit. "Plana", banana — as in, dick. "Kuka plana", shit-dick. That's a good one.'

'You know what "pua" means?'

'Flowers … bananas. Youse make everything sound so innocent.'

'Nature's nature. No shame, eh.' He pointed. 'Mind the tour bus.'

Paulina slowed as the bus passed, probably headed back to King's Lookout. She looped down to King's Pier, up again past the airport, the Fairfolk Bowmen's Club, Piney's Point.

'Look at that.' Car gestured out the window. 'Nay views like that in Sydney, eh?'

'I dunno. Palm Beach is alright.'

'Palm Beach? Pssh. I've been all over the world, sweetheart. Trust me, there's nowhere like Fairfolk.'

Paulina didn't trust him, but she did believe him, on that one.

'Go up to the national park,' Car suggested. 'It's beautiful up there.'

'I dunno.'

'Go on. It's beautiful.'

Slowing, Paulina began the steep, winding climb up to the park. The road changed to dirt, trees on all sides. She stopped at the metal gate where the walking track began.

'Wanna get out? Look around?'

'Nah.' Paulina's heart quickened in the sudden dimness. 'I've walked here loads of times. With Ric.'

Car closed his huge hand over her thigh. 'Walking's not what I had in mind.'

'Nah,' she said brazenly, though she felt tiny under the canopy of pines. 'No way.'

'Look how miggy you are.' He squeezed, stroked upwards. 'I bet you've got the sweetest pua, eh.'

Paulina pushed his hand away. 'I don't like married men.'

'Eddy MacArthur?'

'Don't like him.' Paulina put the car into reverse. 'He can't keep it up for more than five minutes.'

Car folded his arms. 'That's cos he's a MacArthur. You need the royal treatment. I'll make you scream all night long.'

'I'd rather sleep all night, no offence.'

She began the swerving drive downhill, a few points above the speed limit.

'You're the boss, sweetheart.' Car's face was patchy-red. 'Mind the speed, though. We're in a thirty-zone.'

Paulina slowed. Car stared out the window like a gorilla in an enclosure. As town came back into view, she asked, 'Do you crack onto all your customers?'

'Never had a customer as pretty as you before.' Car passed his pale eyes over her. 'I wouldn't be a man if I didn't have a crack.'

'It's a shit sales tactic.'

'You're a handful, eh. Surprised you didn't give Rabbit a heart attack.'

'He's in good shape, that's why. I like men who take care of themselves.'

'Why aren't you in Sydney then, dating one of those kuka planas who wears pink shirts and moisturises his face every day?'

Paulina grimaced. 'Gawd, you're a pig.'

'You know that's what you want, deep in your pua.' Smirking, Car pointed out Tabby's Treasures. 'That's my wife's shop. You ever want a nice piece of jewellery, come see me.'

'What does your wife think about you offering discounts to other women?'

'She thinks what I tell her to think. She wouldn't have a leg to stand on without me.'

Paulina turned back into The Car Kings, pulled the keys from the ignition. 'Thanks for the ride.' She handed them back. 'Shame about the company.'

Car got out, came around to her door and opened it.

'Wanna write down your number?' he asked, back at the counter. 'So I can call you about the car?'

'Nah.'

'Howabout so I can ask you out? I'd love to take you out on my boat sometime.'

'Nah.' Paulina coughed weakly. 'I think I'm coming down with something, hey.'

'Where're you staying? I'll bring you some oranges from my orange tree.'

'Thanks.' Paulina held her hand out for her credit card. 'But no thanks.'

The next morning, Paulina woke with a headache that was more than a hangover. Her throat ached too. Her joints. Everything.

She put on her exercise clothes anyway, tied a hoodie around her waist.

On her walk, she picked wild oranges from a tree near Fergal's Farm, gathered them up in her hoodie. A young guy with muscly white arms pulled up in a white Camry and asked, 'Need a lift?'

'Nah, thanks.'

The walk back felt long, though. She stopped at Foodfolk to pick up some supplies.

'Slim pickings,' she complained to Flick, taking her cans of split-pea soup and tuna in lemon-brine to the counter. 'When's the supply ship due?'

'Day after tomorrow.'

'Can I have a bag for these oranges?'

Flick gave her another bag. 'Heard you slapped Eddy's mum.'

'She started it.' Paulina dumped the oranges in the bag. 'It's her fault that bastard was born in the first place.'

As she was pulling on her hoodie, Rita stormed over. 'Did you pay for those oranges?'

'I came in with them.' Paulina sneered. 'Check the CCTV.'

'The CCTV's down.'

'Go fuck a rabbit.' Paulina gave her the finger. 'See ya, Flick.'

Despite her hoodie, she started shivering inside the bottle-O. She grabbed two casks of goon; was already tired of carrying them by the time she left the store.

She started back to Mutes', then got dizzy. Doubled back to Foodfolk and parked herself on the bench outside, head-in-hands.

'You're loitering,' Rita came out to tell her. 'Move along.'

'Give me a break! I'm dizzy.'

'Drunk at eleven am?' Rita shook her head. 'You're worse than Tatiana.'

Paulina wiped her eyes. 'I'll go in a sec. Just give me a sec.'

Rita sighed, went back inside. Paulina clutched her head again, dried more tears. When a car door slammed nearby, she grimaced in pain.

A dog ran up to the bench, licked her hands.

'Hey, Jake.' She recognised him. 'Jakey-boy.'

The dog's owner nodded, noticed her shopping bags. 'Need a lift?'

'Um. Yeah.' Paulina blushed. 'Cheers.'

'Two minutes.'

It was more like fifteen. She had her eyes closed and her head pressed to Jake's when the old guy came out with his shopping.

'Cheers,' she said again, struggling to lift her bags.

He took them off her. Let her into his jeep. 'Where to?'

'Just up the road. Mutes'.'

'They're renovating, nay?'

Paulina's eyelids drooped. 'I'm just crashing till I find something permanent.'

'You should talk to my missus. She's got a cottage.'

Paulina smiled wanly; she didn't feel like talking to anybody's missus.

'Jake likes you,' the old guy said, midway through the drive. Arriving at Mutes', he repeated, 'You should talk to my missus. Vera MacArthur.'

'Any relation to Eddy?' Paulina reached for her bags.

The old guy shrugged. 'Probably.'

'Thanks for the lift.' Paulina got out of the jeep. 'See ya around.'

She staggered up the driveway to cabin twelve; collapsed on the couch with her shopping as soon as she unlocked the door.

By nightfall, she was coughing up green phlegm.

Paulina didn't leave the cabin at all the next day, except to ask Leki to buy her some Panadol. The day after, the drilling woke her. She took a shower so hot it almost knocked her out; huddled on the tiles in her towel.

After a while, she noticed the drilling had stopped. Shakily, she put on her trakkies, an old jumper of Rabbit's.

'Where're youse going?' she croaked, toddling up the driveway.

'Supply ship's arriving!' Leki grinned. 'Wanna watch?'

'Are youse coming back later?'

'Nay! We're getting pissed!'

Paulina watched the guys drive out, before getting shivery again. She went back inside to her hovel of tissues and blankets, slept away the afternoon.

'I miss Ric,' she told her mum that night. 'He looked after me.'

'That's just the flu talking.'

'I miss Ric,' she repeated, sniffing his jumper. 'He loved me.'

Judy sighed. 'I wish I was there to take care of you.'

'I want Ric.'

After hanging up on her mum, she microwaved some goon with orange slices and called Rabbit's. Bunny answered. 'Can I talk to your dad?' Paulina pleaded.

'No!'

'Can you tell him I miss him?'

'No way!'

'Please, Bun?' She started coughing. 'I feel like I'm dying.'

'Eww!' Bunny giggled and hung up.

She trudged back to bed, tossed and turned. Woke to the rustling of the wind — only, it was more than the wind. It was footsteps, her name being called.

'Paulina!' The steps reached her cabin. 'Open up, sweetheart!'

Rolling out of bed, Paulina turned on the porch light.

'What the fuck, Car?' she cried through the flyscreen. 'Go home!'

Car reached for the doorhandle. 'Why's it locked?'

'Cos I'm not letting you in, dickhead.'

'I'm here about the car.' Car leaned closer; she could smell the liquor on him. 'I'm here … to let you screw me over. Open up, sweetheart.'

'Fuck off or I'll call your wife!'

Car pushed the door with his shoulder. When that didn't work, he fumbled in his pocket; started jimmying the lock.

'Car! You can't do that!'

'Aye.' He grunted with the effort. 'Done it many times.'

The door gave way. Car stumbled inside, steadied himself against her. 'You smell good, sweetheart.'

'No I don't. I stink. I'm sick; I'll infect you.'

'I'll take my chances, eh!' He leaned in for the kill.

'Don't.' Paulina turned her face away. 'I'm sick.'

'Too sick for me to lick your pua?'

'Yeah, Car.' She shoved him away. 'I'm too sick.'

Car squinted as she switched on the lights. Then he lurched into the kitchen and pulled up a chair. 'Make me something to eat, eh?'

'Are you kidding me?' Paulina clutched her aching head. 'Fine, yeah. I'll make you a sandwich, you fat fuck. Then you fuck off home to your wife. Okay?'

'You're the boss, sweetheart.'

As she got out the bread and peanut butter, Car got up. 'What're you dressing like that for?' He lifted the hem of her jumper. 'You've got a nice li'l body under there.'

'I'm *sick*.' She slapped his hand away. 'This's how I dress when I'm sick.'

He took a piece of bread, chewed it. 'Bread's stale, sweetheart.'

'Tough shit.'

'Supply ship arrived today.' He slipped his hand inside her jumper. 'I put my life on the line today, so you can buy bread and butter.'

She elbowed him. He caught her elbows, smooched her neck.

'Don't, Car.' She recoiled. 'Go home to your wife.'

'Nice arse.' He nudged his dick aganst it. 'You're miggy, but that's a sweet arse.'

'Do you want your sandwich or not?'

'Nay!' Car put his hands down her pants and laughed incredulously. 'Nay undies? You knew I was coming tonight, eh!'

Paulina kicked him in the shin, struggled free. 'Don't, Car! I'm calling your wife!'

But the phone was in the bedroom, and the bedroom was just a smaller space for him to take over. As she opened the phone book, scanned the rows and rows of Kings, Car ripped the phone from the wall.

'Car!' she yelped. 'Don't!'

If there was a part of his brain that cared about words, it was out of commission. Car pushed her back onto the bed, hefted himself on top. Unzipped.

'Bastard!' She clawed and bit. 'I don't want you, bastard!'

He lodged his forearm against her throat.

'You knew I was coming.' Yanking down her pants, he spat on his palm. 'You're *wet*.'

'I can't breathe. Bastard.' Paulina sobbed as he slicked her up. Stuck it in. 'You're hurting me. Bastard.'

Car kissed her gritted teeth. 'Nay fight me and you'll nay get hurt.'

Car was gone before the drilling and hammering started, but the reek of him wasn't. After showering, Paulina stripped the bed, gathered up the sheets and walked to reception.

'Oh,' she mumbled, seeing Jesse mixing paints. 'Hi.'

Jesse ignored her. She walked on to the laundry. Chucked the sheets in the wash and got some fresh ones from the linen closet.

'Jess?' The tears spilled as soon as she spoke. 'Please, can we talk? I feel so shit.'

'Not my problem,' Jesse replied tonelessly. 'Tell someone who cares.'

Paulina fled to her cabin. The bread and peanut butter were still on the counter. She chucked them.

She chucked her used tissues, orange peels, emptied and rinsed the mugs that potholed the cabin. She made the bed.

Clipping on her Discman and sunnies, she took the rubbish out and kept walking.

'Yorana, sweetheart,' Car greeted her with his usual swagger, but he looked surprised to see her. Nervous, even. 'What can I do for you then, eh?'

Paulina's eyes wandered to his neck. She'd left scratches, bite-marks.

'I'm here about the car.' She crossed her arms. 'I'm here to screw you over.'

KUKA PLANA

There was a certain kind of Fairfolk guy Jesse Camilleri had always assumed he was better than: the kind who hung out at the airport in high season, trawling for fresh meat. Until the day he was waiting for his sister to disembark her flight from Brisbane and saw Bunny White stepping onto the tarmac, looking fresher than milk-fed veal.

'Whew! New mainie in town,' whistled Grandy Greatorex, who had a wife and three kids at home — not that that ever stopped him.

'Sweet legs,' echoed Kristian King. 'How long you bet till I'm between 'em?'

Jesse wouldn't have recognised her either, looking like a mainie in that bejewelled T-shirt, white denim skirt. Wouldn't have given her a second glance, if it wasn't for her flying into the arms of the same man he'd fantasised, many times, about beating to a pulp.

'That's nay mainie, brudda,' Jesse said. 'That's Rabbit's kid.'

They were all quiet for a moment, watching Bunny's skirt inch up her thighs as she hugged her dad; tightening around her sweet little arse as she kissed Rita.

'She's *grown*,' Kristian marvelled. 'Reckon she's been broken in yet?'

Jesse spotted his sister, Janey, descending the staircase with her two little girls. He finished his beer and took another look at Bunny.

'This one's mine,' he told the guys.

'Saw that TV program,' Janey told him, eating a late dinner of spaghetti and meatballs after putting the girls to bed. 'About your girlfriend.'

Jesse dabbed sauce from his lips. 'She wasn't my girlfriend.'

'Jus' friends,' their dad, Joe, backed him up with a wink.

'You looked like more than friends when I walked in on you two dry-humping on New Year's Eve.'

'Everyone hooks up on New Year's.' Jesse flushed. 'And that was two years ago. Can you leave it alone?'

'Leave it alone, Janey.' Joe flicked him a pitying look. 'It was what it was.'

Janey forked a meatball and sucked off the sauce.

'Why do you have to eat them like that?' Jesse cringed. 'It's verly gross, eh.'

Janey got an evil glint in her eye, kept doing it. Then she stopped and said, 'If you were just friends, why are you still single?'

'Jesus-fuck.' Jesse put down his fork. 'Why do you have to know everything?'

'She deserved better, eh.' Janey frowned. 'After that ex-boyfriend. What was his problem? Slagging off a dead girl on national TV.'

Jesse shrugged. 'She cheated on him.'

'Probably had a good reason. Seemed like a controlling little prick.' Janey sighed. 'Her poor mother. All alone. I can't imagine.'

Jesse shovelled more spaghetti into his mouth. *Her poor mother* didn't cut it. Didn't come close to what he'd felt, seeing Judy Novak's tear-streaked face on TV.

A woman to kill for. That was the feeling.

Janey read his mind. 'Still think it was Rabbit?'

'Aye.' Jesse met her gaze. 'He was obsessed with her.'

'Could say the same about you.'

A few days later, Rita came into Camilleri's to pester him about her Christmas ham. She brought Bunny with her.

'Sorry, Rita,' Jesse apologised. 'Seven kilo's the biggest we've got.'

Bunny was wearing board shorts, a white T-shirt that showed a pale strip of tummy. The way she stood — slouched, one arm across her body to clutch the other — reminded him of Janey at a certain age; old enough to get stared at by men, young enough to have a Care Bears collection.

'We've got forty guests to feed!' Rita griped.

Jesse shrugged. 'Maybe you bes' butcher your own hog.'

As Rita sighed and scrabbled for her wallet, Jesse cast another glance at Bunny. She caught it; smiled and tucked her hair behind her ear.

Like shooting fish in a barrel, he thought, and told himself he wasn't that kind of guy. But on Christmas morning he happened to drive past St Bartholomew's, and there was Bunny on the church steps, and, more importantly, there was Rabbit: bald spot gleaming in the morning sun, grinning like a bastard who'd gotten away with it.

Next time he saw Bunny was after New Year's, when he came into Foodfolk on his morning break to buy a choc-milk. She was working the check-out.

'Yorana.' Bunny smiled at him. A real smile, not a customer service smile. 'You good?'

'Aye.' Jesse's eyes wandered down to her name tag: *Elena.* 'You back on the rock all summer?'

'Till school starts.' She rolled her eyes. 'Boarding school.'

'Brisbane?'

'Outside Brisbane. Toowoomba.'

'Full of racists?'

Bunny laughed, shrugged.

'I did a year of fine arts. The mainland's full of racists, eh.'

'Nobody believes I've got Polynesian blood.' Bunny smiled. 'They say I'm too white.'

'Yeah, well.' Jesse glanced at the pale skin inside her wrist. 'You are.'

Bunny laughed again.

He nodded at the cigarette display. 'Some smokes, too.'

Her smile twitched. 'Camels?'

'Aye.' Jesse leaned on the counter. 'You know me.'

Bunny scurried off for his ciggies. Scanned them with lowered eyes.

'Saw you at the airport,' Jesse ventured. 'Almost didn't recognise you.'

She gave him a million-watt smile. 'I got my braces off.'

'That must be it.' He looked her up and down. 'You gonna be down at the beach this summer? Getting some colour?'

Bunny rolled her eyes again. 'Rita's making me work, like, every day.'

'After work?' He leaned closer. 'Sunset?'

Bunny shrugged, blushed harder.

'Fish and chips at the beach, sunset?'

He picked her up at six, around the corner from Foodfolk; drove two minutes up the road to the Great-O White Shark Grill. She stank of some kind of vanilla body-spray, had glossed her lips and swapped her uniform shirt for a camisole. He hadn't changed.

'You coming in?' he asked her outside Great-O's. 'Or too embarrassed?'

He indicated his stained shirt, stubble.

'I'm nay embarrassed.' Her cheeks pinkened. 'You look good.'

Grandy Greatorex was behind the counter. Jesse ignored his winks and thumbs-up. On the way out, though, he smirked at Grandy and clutched the small of Bunny's back.

He parked at Piney's Point, where the sky was doing wild things in pink and orange.

'Check it out,' he told Bunny, spreading a towel on the grass.

The sky turned indigo as they ate their fish and chips. He asked Bunny questions about school, what she planned to do after, but didn't bother listening to her answers.

When it was pitch-black, he disappeared to the car just long enough to make her nervous; returned with a joint. She coughed as soon as she inhaled.

'Never smoked funny pine before?'

'Nay.'

Circling an arm around her shoulders, he showed her how. Soon, she was giggling.

'It tingles.' She clasped her head. 'Wow.'

He asked if he could kiss her.

He'd forgotten how good kissing could be — just kissing a girl, for minutes at a time. Laying Bunny down on the towel, he knew she'd let him do anything he wanted.

'I bes' take you home.' He touched her hair. 'Before your dad takes my gools.'

'Aye.' Bunny sighed. 'Bes'.'

He dropped her off at Cookies.

———

Three days later, he invited her over to play video games, and made her come three times.

'You never had your pua licked before?' he asked, kissing his way up from her crotch to her frantic heart.

Bunny giggled, shook her head.

He kissed her mouth, stroked the curly hairs down there. 'You should shave your notties for next time. Easy access.'

Blushing, Bunny mumbled, 'Okay.'

At work the next day, Joe said, 'Saw you had a girl over.'

Jesse shrugged. 'So?'

'She got a name?'

'Elena White.' Jesse watched his dad's face. 'Rabbit's girl.'

'How old's she now?'

'Old enough.'

'You sure about that?'

He tried to be gentle, but even so, Bunny bled. A lot.

'Sorry,' she kept apologising, even after she'd dressed. 'Sorry about your sheets.'

'It's fine. Jesus.'

On the drive home, she was so quiet, he felt obliged to make her laugh. 'Remember when they had to replace the street sign?' he asked at Missionary Road. 'Cos of the graffiti?'

Bunny shook her head.

He felt bad all over again. 'I guess you're too young to remember, eh.'

Bunny shrugged, smiled. 'What was the graffiti?'

'Someone wrote "position" under "Missionary".'

'That's funny,' Bunny said, but didn't laugh.

Jesse avoided her for the rest of the week. But on his day off, Janey saddled him with his nieces, and they wanted lollies and chips.

'Yorana!' Bunny beamed at the girls, then him. 'Are you babysitting?'

'What does it look like.' Jesse placed the junk food on the conveyor belt.

Blushing, Bunny looked at the girls. 'They're verly cute, eh.'

'Some smokes, too.'

While Bunny was fetching his Camels, he checked out her arse. But the moment she turned to face him, he pretended she was invisible.

'Is their dad … ?' Her eyes drifted curiously to the girls' dark skin.

'What, Aboriginal?' He intercepted her gaze. 'You can say it.'

'Sorry.' She lowered her eyes, scanned his items. 'I was just wondering.'

'He's in the slammer, too. In case you're wondering.'

Bunny looked at him uncertainly. 'Verly?'

'Verly.' He took out his wallet. 'Sixteen years. Unpaid parking ticket.'

'*Verly?*'

'Nay. Aggravated assault.' He counted out the cash. 'Cop came over to hassle him about this ticket, started fucking shit up near Cleo's crib, "looking for drugs".'

Bunny bagged his shopping. 'Sorry, Jess.'

'What for? My sheets?'

Her blush deepened. 'That, too.'

'Should've bought some stain-remover, eh.'

'Sorry.'

'Come over tonight. Make it up to me.'

Walking to the fridge in his jocks, Jesse asked, 'Want a beer?'

Bunny hugged her naked legs. 'I'm underage.'

'You're old enough for that.' He nodded at their clothes on the floor. 'You can have a beer.'

Bunny laughed meekly. 'Okay, then.'

After her first sip, though, she cringed. 'I bes' be careful. Mum was an alcoholic.'

'Yeah?' He slouched down beside her on the couch. 'Your dad has a type, eh.'

'I guess so.'

Jesse put his arm around her shoulders. 'You won't get addicted. Alcoholics drink cos they have other problems.'

'Paulina … ?'

He'd been waiting for her to mention Paulina's name. Even so, his chest tightened.

'Aye. She had problems.'

Bunny took another sip of beer. 'She was loony.'

'Aye.'

She traced the camel tattoo on his arm. 'Was she your girlfriend?'

'Who told you that? Rita?'

Bunny shrugged. 'Everyone says it.'

'She wasn't my girlfriend.' Jesse watched Bunny's face flush with relief. 'She sucked my dick one time. When she was still with your dad.'

Bunny winced. 'Oh.'

He drank, let her sit with that for a while.

'Just once?' Bunny piped up, eventually.

'Just once. Best blow-job of my life.'

His next day off, he got her to chuck a sickie. She answered the door in her PJs, black-and-white cat twining around her ankles.

'Jesus.' Jesse gaped, stepping into the hallway. 'This place is a palace.'

'Aye.' Bunny picked up the cat. 'Say hello, Anastasia!'

'Jesus.' Jesse absently scratched the cat behind her ears. 'You inheriting all this when your old man dies?'

'Maybe.' Bunny smooched the cat, set her down. 'Where'd you park?'

'Why? Embarrassed?'

'Nay. Jus', if Dad finds out—'

Jesse pushed his tongue into her mouth. 'I won't let that happen, eh.'

He fucked her in her bedroom under Anastasia's impassive gaze. After, he wandered around, looking at the photos on her shelf. 'That your mum?'

'Aye.'

'Looks like you. How long since you saw her?'

'Twelve years. I nay remember her, verly.' Bunny turned onto her side, looking like a grown woman with the sheets draped around her naked curves. 'How long since yours ... ?'

"She died when I was three. Bad heart.'

'Sorry, eh.' Bunny's eyelashes fluttered against her cheek. 'You remember her?'

'She wore big earrings, sometimes.' Jesse put the photo down. 'I remember her screaming at me for pulling on her earring.'

'I remember my mum screaming in Russian.'

'Your dad ever scream?'

'Nay. He just goes quiet when he's angry.'

'He gets angry?'

Bunny looked away. 'Nay with me.'

'With Rita?'

'Nay.'

'Paulina?'

'… Nay.'

'Verly?' Jesse raised his eyebrows. 'She could be pretty annoying, eh.'

'Aye.' Bunny bit her lip. 'Mean, too. Always called me fat.'

'You're nay fat. Your body's perfect.'

'So's yours.' She gazed at him adoringly. 'I could look at you all day.'

He took up a photo of her at an archery competition.

'I was fat, then,' Bunny admitted. 'I was so lame when I was a kid.'

Jesse put the photo down. 'You're still a kid.'

Then he found his Camels, stuck one between his lips.

'Bes' you don't smoke in here, eh,' Bunny fretted. 'Dad'll kill me if he smells it.'

'Like he killed Paulina?'

Bunny's face froze in a tight, nervous grimace. 'That's funny.'

'I'm nay laughing.'

Jesse took his Camels out of the room; roamed around till he found a bigger bedroom, with windows that looked over Cookies.

He opened the window, smoked and stared out at the glistening green hills.

Finishing his ciggie, he flicked the butt on the floor. Nipped to the bathroom and took a steaming piss, left the toilet seat aloft. He didn't flush.

'Jess?' Bunny found him in the hall. 'Did I do something wrong?'

She'd put her pyjama shirt back on, but not her shorts. Seeing her bare legs and fraught face, his cock immediately stirred.

'Nay.' He pulled her into the room. 'You're perfect.'

'Rita knows,' Bunny called him in tears the next night. 'She says I bes' lyme you or she'll tell Dad!'

'Lyme me, then,' Jesse said, and hung up.

The phone rang on and on; he didn't answer. He was drawing with his headphones on when she showed up at his front door, face messy and wet.

'What the fuck.' He let her in. 'How'd you get here?'

She fell into his arms, sobbing. 'Are we broken up?'

'Jesus.' Jesse extricated himself. 'Calm down.'

As he fetched her a beer, she bawled into the couch cushions. 'Please don't make me lyme you, Jess! Please — I love you!'

She'd never said that before.

'Okay, okay.' Jesse passed her the beer. 'You don't have to lyme me, okay?'

She drank greedily and said it again. 'I love you, Jess.'

'Yeah. Okay.'

He kissed her, to shut her up.

'I love you.' Bunny reached for his crotch. 'Can I sleep over?'

Jesse stayed her hands. 'I'm out of condoms.'

'I don't mind.' She nuzzled him. 'You don't have to use one.'

'You think I wanna get a teenager pregnant?' Jesse pushed her away.

She started crying again. Jesse put his headphones back on, went back to his drawing.

After a while, thankfully, she shut up and drank her beer. Jesse snuck a glance at her damp eyelashes, rosy lips. Took off his headphones.

'Can I see your drawings?' Bunny asked meekly.

'Aye.'

She crawled over to him, looked through the sketchpad. 'You're verly talented, eh.'

Jesse shrugged.

'Are they tattoo designs?'

'Could be.'

She leaned against his shoulder. 'I love your tattoos.'

'Want one?'

'Dad'll kill me.'

'Not if he never sees it.' Jesse put his hand inside her shirt, tickled the small of her back.

'That's slutty!'

'It's sexy, eh.' Jesse kept stroking. 'Howabout my initials? "J.C.". You can tell Rita it stands for 'Jesus Christ'.'

'Nay!'

'Nay?' Smiling, Jesse turned a new page of his sketchpad. 'Custom design, then.'

'How's Elena?' Jesse asked when Rita came into Camilleri's to order a bunch of meat for Rabbit's sixtieth birthday barbecue that weekend.

Rita glowered. 'You should be in jail.'

'You've got me confused with your husband. Told him yet?'

She handed over her card. 'I'm nay giving you the satisfaction.'

Jesse swiped it. 'I'm getting plenty of satisfaction, eh.'

When he got home that evening, Bunny was in the yard between his cottage and the main house, hula-hooping with his nieces. 'Yorana!' She smiled at him, swirling her hips.

Jesse stalked inside, slamming the door.

'Sorry.' Bunny's cheeks were pink from exercise, when she followed him in. 'They wanted me to teach them.'

'I don't want you teaching my nieces that shit.'

'Sorry. Want a beer?'

'What do you think.'

As Bunny scurried to the fridge, he turned on the PlayStation, sprawled on the couch. She returned with a can of Pine Brew, sat at his feet and watched the screen intently as the anti-piracy messages flashed across it in English, Spanish, Russian.

'It's not a movie,' Jesse grumbled.

Bunny squeaked a laugh. 'I like seeing all the languages. Want your bong?'

'What do you think.'

She got up again, prepared his bong. Even after inhaling, though, he still felt a skin-crawling irritation, seeing her fidgeting at his feet, scratching the bunny on her back.

'Stop itching. Jesus.'

'Sorry.' She stopped itching. 'It's hard to rub the cream in without help.'

'Bes' get Grandy to help you, then.'

'Grandy?' Bunny laughed incredulously. 'Why Grandy?'

'You think I didn't notice you flirting with him at Great-O's the other day?'

'Jess! I was just asking for extra tartare sauce, like you told me to.' Her eyes watered. 'I would never flirt with another guy. I love *you*.'

'Yeah?' He drank. 'Feeling's nay mutual, eh.'

'Jess. Why—'

'Good question. Why're you here? You think I wanna fuck a dumb kid every night?'

Tears streamed down her face. 'You're verly mean today, Jess!'

'Take a hint, then.' He jerked his head at the door. 'Get lost. You're lymed.'

Bunny gaped at him, lip quivering. Then something broke inside her.

'Kuka plana!' she screamed, unplugging his controller and flinging it at the wall.

She'd never reminded him of Paulina until that moment.

'Any talent?' Jesse joined the guys for a beer after ditching Janey and the girls in the waiting lounge.

Grandy snorted. 'Yeah. Your sister.'

When Bunny arrived with her dad and Rita, she looked straight at him from across the terminal and looked ready to cry again. The guys hooted with laughter.

'What'd you do to her?' Kristian questioned him.

'Lymed her.' Jesse shrugged. 'Young vinis get too attached.'

'Should've told me, eh. I'd go sloppy seconds.'

'You break her in?' Grandy asked.

'Aye. She ruined my sheets.'

That got a big laugh. Then they all watched Bunny approach the check-in counter.

'Sweet arse.' Kristian whistled. 'You break her arse?'

'Better.' Jesse rubbed his tattooed arm. 'I branded her.'

'Bullshit.'

'Tramp stamp. Cute little bunny rabbit.'

The guys sniggered so loud, Bunny flinched. Rita shot them a look. Rabbit's grip was tight on Bunny's suitcase.

'You don't have the gools, Camilleri.'

'You think I'm scared of her old man? I did her in his bed one time. She loved it.'

Bunny looked at him, eyes brimming.

'She's looking, brudda.' Kristian laughed. 'Must've verly given her a taste for it, eh.'

'Aye. She likes the taste.' Jesse sipped his beer. 'Young vinis, though. Nay technique.'

They cracked up, louder than ever. Crumpling, Bunny fled to the bathroom.

Rabbit's face drained of colour.

'You've done it now, brudda.' Grandy nudged him. 'Daddy's on the warpath.'

Rita grabbed Rabbit's arm, held him back. Jesse drained his glass, stood up — only to double over in pain.

'What the hell's wrong with you?' Janey twisted his earlobe. 'She's a kid!'

'Jesus, Janey!' He winced. 'Cut it out!'

Dragging him to the waiting lounge, Janey hissed, 'You're lucky it's jus' your ear.'

Before Jesse could say anything to defend himself, she'd dumped him in the waiting lounge with his nieces and gone after Bunny.

'Sorry,' Jesse stammered as the girls stared at him wide-eyed. 'Let's go see the plane, eh?'

It seemed like a long time before Janey and Bunny emerged from the bathroom. Even longer, keeping his distance from Rabbit as they waited for boarding time.

'Sorry,' he repeated to his sister. 'I'm verly sorry. I'm a fuckwit.'

Janey gave him the silent treatment till the plane was ready. When he kissed her goodbye, her cheek was stiff.

'You think Mum would be proud of you? Eh?'

'Nay,' Jesse mumbled, shamefaced.

'It's not that girl's fault your girlfriend's dead.'

'Nay.'

'Kiss your nieces goodbye.'

Jesse did what she said.

He stuck around on the tarmac for take-off. So did Rabbit. White-knuckled, they pretended not to see each other until the plane was in the air. After, though, Rabbit walked right up to him.

'Camel.'

'Yorana, Rabbit.' Jesse's heart quickened. 'You good?'

Rabbit nodded. His lips were pale. His eyes. His whole face. So pale he looked half-dead. He'd just turned sixty. Old.

Dutifully, Rabbit punched him in the face.

Jesse punched him too, naturally. It was what he wanted, more than he'd ever wanted Bunny; he wanted that old man's blood on his hands. For a few ringing seconds, he was sure he'd beat him to death, or be beaten dead — it didn't really matter what. But the moment passed, and airport security broke it up.

It was the talk of the island for maybe a month: the two leading suspects in Paulina's murder, brawling on the tarmac. But by late March, nobody was talking about it anymore.

They were all talking about the white Camry that'd been towed from the vacant block near Fergal's Farm.

KINGDOM BY THE SEA

'Morning, ladies!' Paulina greeted the first lot of olds, who shambled into the Mutes' bistro at seven on the dot. 'How'd ya sleep?'

'Like the dead!' Rosie sighed contentedly. 'It's so quiet without the hubby snoring.'

'Too right. My boyfriend snores like a pig.' Paulina pulled out their chairs. 'I need a nap already.'

'Not us.' Iris sat. 'We're all booked out: horse-and-buggy ride, then the Fairfolk farmers' tour, then this evening we've got the—'

'Ghost tour!' Rosie supplied.

'Geez, I don't know how youse do it.' Paulina set down their menus. 'Just don't knock yourselves out before Mutiny Day. That's a big one.'

'Tomorrow's my shopping day.' Rosie smiled. 'I've been jealous of Iris's bracelet ever since she bought it.'

Paulina's skin prickled as Iris showed off her paua-and-pearl bracelet. 'This "Tabitha King" designs them all herself — you know her?'

'Yeah.' Paulina faked a smile. 'We go way back.'

After her breakfast shift, Paulina rolled out her cleaning cart and did her rounds of the cabins. After, she drove her shiny blue Mazda back to Tenderloin Road, changed into her exercise clothes, and checked her answering machine.

Hi, darling. It's Mum here. Just seeing how you are. I guess you're busy again … ?

'Ugh!' Paulina deleted the message. 'Get a life.'

She went for her usual walk, down Klee Welkin Road and up to King's Lookout. Traced her fingers over the K-I-N-G on the sign. Then she walked into town, strutted into Tabby's Treasures. Car's wife was busy with another customer, but she tracked Paulina with her light-green eyes as she lingered, breathed on the cabinets.

'Can I help you?' Tabby asked once the customer left.

Paulina picked up a business card. '"Tabby." What are you, a cat?'

'Can I help you?' Tabby repeated.

'Oops.' Paulina let the card fall from her fingers. 'My bad.'

'Can I help you?'

'Ooo, that's *nice*.' She touched the glass. 'So's that. Oi, do you do engagement rings?'

'Occasionally.' Tabby blinked her sooty eyelashes. 'I did a lovely custom design recently, for Rabbit and Rita.'

'Nah, I'd want something nicer.' Paulina smirked. 'See ya.'

Rolling her eyes, Tabby fetched a bottle of bright-blue glass cleaner from under the counter and wiped away Paulina's fingerprints.

'Ohh, yeah.' Car's belly slapped against her arse. 'Take it, mainie.'

'Shit.' She whimpered. 'You piece of shit.'

'Yeahh. Take it.' Car's voice got higher. 'Dirty girl.'

'Bastard. Oh, you bastard.'

Grunting, Car gave her hair a final, listless tug. Crushed his heavy body against hers. Then there was just his breath, the dark sea lapping.

'Ohh, yeah.' He kissed between her shoulder blades. 'You liked that, eh.'

'I dunno.' She felt sore, mortified, and a melty-strangeness deep inside her that was almost sweet. 'Maybe.'

It hurt like a ripped bandage when he peeled his sweaty skin from hers, pulled out. 'Ow,' Paulina winced, tears in her eyes.

He spanked her. 'You're leaking, sweetheart.'

She raised herself gingerly on her elbows. 'Where's the towel?'

Car found it, dropped it over her head, and spanked her again, laughing.

'Arsehole.' Shakily, she sat up, wiped herself off. 'The things I do for you.'

Car rolled onto his back, the weight of him denting the mattress. His chest heaved, labouring for breath.

'Fuck, you're a fat fuck.' She looked at his coarse, flushed skin. 'I'm surprised you don't have a heart attack.'

'I'm Polynesian. I'm all muscle.'

'Yeah, and I'm a D-cup.' She prodded his fat. 'I'm surprised you haven't squashed me to death.'

Car closed his eyes. 'At least you won't die a virgin, eh.'

'Oi, don't sleep.' She prodded him again. 'You're literally a kuka plana right now.'

'Lick me clean.'

'I'm not your wife.' She chucked the towel at his crotch. 'I'm not cleaning up your shitty dick.'

Without opening his eyes, he lazily towelled off his groin. 'Bes' marry you instead.'

'Yeah, alright.' She fumbled past the lube on the bedside for her ciggies. 'So long as you promise to have a heart attack and cark it on our wedding night.'

Car's pale eyes opened. 'Nay smoking below deck.'

'It stinks down here.' Paulina stuck a ciggie between her lips. 'I need to smoke out the smell.'

'My boat, my rules.' He whipped her with the dirty towel. 'Take it upstairs, mainie.'

'Make me.'

Quick as a charging bull, he grabbed her by the ankles, threw her over his shoulder, and bore her kicking and screaming above deck.

'Scream all you want, mainie.' Car set her down with a smack on the bum. 'Nobody's listening.'

'Arsehole.' Shivering, she lit up. 'It's like the *Titanic* out here.'

'Romantic, eh?' Car nodded at the glittery blackness above.

'Would be, if I wasn't freezing my tits off.' She stroked his nautical star tattoo. 'Get me my clothes, babe.'

Car tweaked her nipple. 'Nay. I like your frozen titties.'

'C'mon, babe.' She sucked on her ciggie. 'Pretty please?'

He stole the ciggie from her fingertips. 'I won't let you go cold, sweetheart.'

'Yeah?' Breathing white, Paulina reached down. 'You seem pretty cold yourself.'

Grabbing her arm mid-fondle, Car stubbed out the ciggie in the tender pit of her elbow. The pain zapped like lightning.

'Fucker!' Paulina yelped.

Car flicked the butt into the silvery-dark water. 'Nay so cold now, eh.'

Paulina felt the blood leave her face; the pain's nauseous afterglow. 'That's gonna scar, Car.'

Car lifted her arm to his lips, tongued the burnt skin.

She shoved his head away. 'You're disgusting.'

'Marry me.'

'Fuck no!'

'Marry me.' He held her hand to the star on his heart. 'I'll treat you like a queen.'

'You just burned me!'

'We're hot together, eh?' He kissed her. 'Marry me.'

'You're already married, dickhead.'

'I'll get a divorce, eh.'

'You're so stupid.'

'Marry me.' He kissed her tits, her tummy. 'C'mon.'

'Fuck you.'

He kissed her pussy. 'Marry me.'

'You know what?' Paulina laughed. 'You're the first guy to ever ask me that.'

'Ow!' Kymba cried as they were pouring plastic flutes of champers in the Fairfolk Tours marquee. 'How'd that happen?'

'Oh, *that*.' Paulina rubbed the round red welt on her arm. 'Did it on Car's boat the other night. We were really drunk, ha-ha.'

'You're still seeing Car.'

Paulina glanced at Kymba sidelong. 'He popped the question.'

'He *what*?' Liquid bubbled onto Kymba's plump white hand.

'It was really romantic. He got on his knees and everything!'

'But …' Kymba stammered. 'You said "no", right?'

'I said "maybe".'

'Say "no".' Kymba set down the champagne bottle. 'Look: he's my cousin and all, but … he's married. And he's not a good guy.'

'And I'm not a good girl.' Paulina lowered her voice. 'I finally let him … you know.'

She arched her back. Kymba turned so red, she looked ready to explode.

'That's ... none of my business,' she choked out. 'But, Paulina. You can do better than Car. Much better.'

'Who?' Paulina nodded at Tony Tunes, singing off-key and strumming his acoustic guitar a few feet away. 'Tony?'

'Have you thought about going back to the mainland?'

'Ugh. You sound like my mum.'

'Does *she* know about Car?'

'What are you, her spy?' Paulina took up a plastic flute. '*No*, Mum doesn't know.'

'Don't you think it's weird you haven't told her? If you're seriously thinking of marrying him?'

'She'll just judge me. Like you're doing.' Paulina gulped. 'I thought you'd be happy for me? We'd be family.'

'You can do better.' Kymba pushed her granny glasses up her nose; picked up the bottle and poured. 'I don't know what you see in him.'

'He's a man. Like, a real man. He knows what he wants, and he takes it.'

'And that's a good thing?'

'I'm sick of boys.' Paulina looked around the tent. 'And he's a "King". Our kids'd be Kings. I could be out there in a pretty dress instead of in here like a mainie. No offence.'

'I didn't think you cared about all that.' Kymba pursed her lips. 'Besides. There's more to being a Fairfolk Islander than dressing up on Mutiny Day.'

'I *know*. I fucking live here.' Paulina's eyes stung. 'You have no idea what it's like being single, babe. It's brutal.'

'Do you love him?'

'Yeah,' Paulina hesitated. 'He fills the void, y'know?'

She knocked back the rest of her champers. Sniffed.

'You're crying.'

'So?' Paulina grabbed a serviette. 'Why can't you just be happy for me?'

'Because I know Car.'

'Not like I do.'

'Yes, I do.' Kymba's glasses fogged. 'We ... dated for a while. When I was younger.'

'Dated?' Paulina's jaw dropped. 'He's your *cousin*.'

'I was really young. I didn't know any better. Look: this is hard for me to talk about—'

Cracking up, Paulina refilled her glass. 'Gawd, this place is inbred! Did you root?'

'Forget it.'

'Youse are worse than the royals. No wonder he's so desperate to marry me.' Her nose fizzed as she drank and laughed at the same time. 'Wait: how old were you?'

'Just forget it.'

Kymba picked up a tray of drinks and bore them to a table of tippled retirees. Tony finished his song, basked in the glow of their applause. Paulina slow-clapped him.

'Psst, mainie!' Tony covered the mic. 'Pour me a drink, eh?'

Paulina poured a drink. 'If I give you this, will you shut up?'

'Only one way to shut me up, mainie.'

He made a V with his fingers, waggled his tongue inside it.

'Just you wait till next Mutiny Day.' Paulina handed him the drink. 'You won't be calling me "mainie" then.'

Tony winked. 'You'll be long-gone by then, mainie.'

It rained as they were herding the olds out of the marquee and onboard the fleet of Fairfolk Tours buses. 'Careful, Iris.' Paulina took her arm. 'Don't wanna slip on the wet grass.'

'Careful,' Kymba warned behind her. 'You've had a lot of champagne.'

Paulina flung her a death stare.

'You're going to be such a beautiful bride,' Iris cooed as they mounted the bus stairs. 'Don't forget to send us a picture.'

'Will do, Iris.' Paulina flashed a grin at the bus driver. 'Oi, Woody. Where's the after-party?'

'Wetties.' He smirked. 'Wet T-shirt contest.'

'Ha! Mine's already wet. Where's my prize?'

'Come along. I'll shout you one, love.'

Paulina skipped back to the marquee to finish packing up.

'Wanna come to Wetties?' She forgot she was mad at Kymba. 'Wet T-shirt contest?'

'No thanks. I have to pick up the kids.'

'Aren't they with the rellies?'

'I told Simmo we'd be home before dark.'

'C'mon, get your jugs out! Don't you wanna make the cousins drool?'

'No, not really.' Kymba sighed. 'Need a lift?'

Along the winding, splashy roads, Kymba drove the Fairfolk Tours van to the primary school. They carried the plastic furniture through the downpour into an art room. There were seashell collages on the walls.

'This one's Zoe's,' Kymba pointed one out, her ponytail gemmed with rain.

Paulina admired it. 'She's talented, hey.'

Back in the van, she stripped off her Fairfolk Tours shirt; she had a lacy camisole underneath.

'Gawd, I smell like wet dog!' After spraying herself with Impulse, she glossed her lips and shook out her hair. 'Can you turn on the heater?'

Kymba flicked the switch. Paulina spent the rest of the drive drying her hair.

'How do I look?' she asked, parked outside Wetties. 'Do I look nice?'

'You look nice,' Kymba reassured her. 'You always do.'

Paulina got her bag from under the seat, swung it over her shoulder.

'Just so you know,' Kymba said quietly. 'I was fourteen.'

'Huh?'

'I was fourteen. Car was thirty-three.'

'Oh.' Paulina frowned. 'But. That was, like … a long time ago?'

Kymba stared at the steering wheel. 'I guess so.'

'Thanks for the ride, babe.' Stuck for words, Paulina air-kissed her. 'Sorry — lip gloss!'

Then she scampered through the rain into the warm bar.

Car gave her the eye as soon as she walked in — then ignored her for two hours.

Paulina pretended not to care. Woody shouted her two rum and Diet Cokes, then Tony tried his luck for a while, then Merlinda showed up in her old-timey dress screeching, 'Shots! Tequila shots!'

Finally, Car came up behind her while she was sucking on a lemon wedge.

'I'd like to be that lemon, eh.' He flicked the straps of her cami. 'What's this? Looks like underwear.'

'What's *this*?' Merlinda narrowed her eyes. 'Car, you jumping the fence for this miggy mainie?'

Whatever Car said next, it was in Fayrf'k, and funny enough to make Merlinda hoot.

'You gonna buy me a drink?' Paulina interrupted. 'Rum and Diet Coke?'

'*Diet* Coke!' Merlinda mocked her. 'Miggy, miggy, miggy!'

Car whistled at the barmaid, ordered two tumblers of rum and gave one to Merlinda.

'Where's mine?' Paulina cried.

Car flicked her straps again. 'Looks like underwear.' Then he lurched away.

'Car *King*.' Merlinda winked. 'Careful, there.'

'He's the one who needs to be careful,' Paulina scoffed, then scurried to the loo for a cry.

Laurent's girlfriend, Oliana, was in line for the loo, looking gorgeous in her frilly white dress with a garland atop her tumbling, dark curls.

'Gawd, you're gorgeous.' Paulina touched Oliana's hair. 'Like a mermaid.'

Oliana laughed. 'I usually wear it up. Little kids, you know.'

'You look like a princess. Like Puatea. You're sooo pretty, hey.'

Paulina kept giving Oliana compliments till the cubicle freed up. After, they spent time in the mirrors together, then went to the bar, then back to Oliana's table. The only spare seat was next to Jesse.

'Hey, Pellet.' Paulina took the seat. 'Nice beard.'

Laurent stroked his new beard. 'Thank you.'

'Suits ya. You look like a *fatheur*. How d'you like *fatheurhood*?'

'Good.' He stroked his beard some more. 'Yes.'

Paulina fixed her gaze on Zippy, one of Laurent's surfer mates.

'Bet you can't even grow a beard.' She reached across to touch the glistening blond fuzz on his upper lip. 'What's this? Beer foam?'

Jesse got out his Camels, stuck one between his lips and stood. Paulina stuck out a leg.

Jesse looked at her leg like it was a stump of rotting wood. 'Can I get past?'

'Sorry.' Paulina looked him in the eye and crossed her leg. 'Didn't see you there.'

'Uh huh.'

She watched him go, heart twinging. 'Sensitive bugger, isn't he.'

Nobody said anything. She got out her tobacco and papers.

'Did he tell youse why we're not friends anymore?' she asked the table. 'I gave him a blow-job. That's it.'

'What, did you use your teeth?' Zippy joked, terror in his eyes.

'It was great. He was *begging* for it.' Paulina rolled a ciggie. 'Not my fault he feels bad for cheating on his girlfriend. He's piss-weak. Hypocrite.'

Laurent looked at her soberly. 'I think maybe there is more to the story.'

'Didn't know you were capable of thinking, Pellet.' Sealing her ciggie with her tongue, Paulina turned to Oliana. 'Do you smoke, gorgeous? I bet you don't. Your skin's flawless.'

'Well.' Oliana laughed. 'Not *tobacco*.'

'Bloody hippies.' Paulina swigged her rum and Diet Coke. 'I don't touch marijuana, personally. Mum always said it messes with your head.'

'Yes, but.' Laurent's lips twitched into a smile. 'Your head is already messy.'

'When did you become such a smart-arse?' Paulina laughed and turned back to Oliana. 'Sure you don't wanna smoke, babe?'

Oliana shook her head. Dry-mouthed, Paulina stood, stuck her ciggie behind her ear, and stumbled out to the beer garden. It was crowded, but she couldn't see the only person she wanted.

She pushed back inside. Car was at the bar. So were a bunch of teenagers. Leki from the Mutes' work crew was among them.

'Yorana!' He smiled from ear-to-ear. 'How are you?'

'Thirsty!'

'Can I buy you a drink?'

'Are you still on apprentice wages? Aw, I feel bad!'

'I got some money for my nineteenth.'

'Nineteen!' Paulina pinched his cheek. 'You're a baby!'

'Nay.' He blushed. 'I'll be twenty next year.'

'I'll be *thirty*. How gross is that?'

Leki looked a bit grossed out, for a second. Then his dick got the better of him. 'Really? You look younger, eh! Let me buy you a drink. I've got all this money.'

He showed her his birthday money.

'Do you wanna get robbed?' Laughing, Paulina pushed his wallet away. 'Rum and Diet Coke. But I'll get the next round, okay, birthday boy?'

Leki staggered up to the bar, looking like he'd just been blessed by the angels. Paulina watched him — and also, from the corners of her eyes, Car watching her watching.

'Cheers, babe.' Paulina squeezed Leki's arm when he delivered her drink. 'Geez, it's hot in here, hey?'

'You should enter the wet T-shirt contest.' Leki looked at the smear of sweat on her sternum. 'That'll cool you down.'

'Are you joking?' Paulina clutched her tits. 'I'll lose!'

'I'll cheer for you, eh.'

'Will you give me your shirt?' She batted her eyelashes and toyed with the hem of his loose linen shirt. 'I need a white shirt.'

'Aye.' His blush deepened. 'Take it.'

Giggling, she put her hand under his shirt, felt his warm abs. He squirmed.

'Your hands are cold, eh!'

'You're warm.' She snuggled up to him. 'You're *hot*.'

That was all it took. Car shouldered through the crowd; grabbed Leki by the scruff of his shirt.

'Hands off!' He grunted, throwing Leki to the ground. 'She's mine!'

Girls screamed. Glass smashed.

'Car!' Paulina pulled at his arm. 'Leave him alone!'

He punched Leki's face, split his lip, kicked his ribs. Then some other guys swooped in and there was a clear space around Leki; she could see the damage he'd done.

'Bloody hell, Car!' Paulina cried. 'He's just a kid!'

Car looked down at her like she was a total stranger. Then he smiled and snatched her waist. 'You're mine, mainie.'

Tubs of ice. Serviettes. Barmaids tending Leki's wounds. Car dragged her away from it all. 'Come sit on my lap, sweetheart.'

'Fuck you!'

He sat. Pulled her onto his lap. Flicked her straps. 'Looks like underwear.'

'Fuck you.' Smiling, Paulina looked at his red knuckles. 'Are we getting married, or what?'

The following weekend, Car took her out on his boat. He showed her how to reel in a kingfish, then a yellowfin tuna. Then her arms got tired, so she just drank and heckled him.

'Another kingfish? Is it a *Gideon* King-fish?'

'Aye. Direct descendant.'

'Bah-ha-ha-ha! Oi, don't kill it. Leave some in the ocean, you fat fuck.'

'Plenty more fish in the sea.'

'Pfft! You're so fucking lame, *Carlyle*.'

He killed the fish with a knife to the brain, gutted it and threw it on ice. 'Sad,' Paulina lamented, surveying the dead eyes. 'This's why I'm vegetarian.'

'I'm nay marrying a vegetarian.'

Later, he caught a beautiful reef fish, all the colours of the rainbow. 'Don't kill it!' she pleaded. 'It's so pretty!'

'Nay,' Car agreed, and gave it to her to hold. Happy as a child, Paulina slipped its live, glistening body back into the sea and felt everything in the universe.

Later, as the sky purpled like a bruise, they went below deck and gave each other head. Then they fucked like missionaries, like dogs, then Car lost his stiffy and made her pose with her bum in the air while he wanked himself back to half-mast, lubed up and shoved it up her arse. Then he fucked her arse so hard she worried she'd bleed inside, then he pulled out, then he made her kneel and lick him clean, then, and only then, he beat off till he blew his load in her face — a smallish dribble, considering what a bloody song and dance of it he'd made.

'You like that, mainie?' He shook his dick like it was a sauce bottle that still had a few drops left. 'Eh?'

'Yeah, Car,' she moaned. 'I love it.'

He wiped the cum off her face, then pushed his fingers inside her. 'I'm gonna put a King in you.'

'Yeah, Car.' She writhed against his hand. 'Please, yeah. Oh.'

He dozed off with his arm around her waist. She wriggled out from under him, her bladder straining like a full sack of goon.

Squatting on the loo, she pissed for thirty seconds straight, and it was nirvana.

The moment she flushed, she craved a ciggie.

She found her ciggies, her clothes, dressed and climbed above deck. She smoked and gazed at the fairyland of stars, tried to cling to the bliss — but it was already slipping.

She tied her hair in a ponytail, paced and smoked another ciggie.

Below deck, Car was snoring like a pig. How would she ever tell her mum she was in love with this fucking pig?

She went to the galley for a drink. But her hands were drunker than she realised; the Johnny Walker smashed.

'Whassat?' Car woke. 'What?'

'Dropped a glass. Where's the dustpan?'

'Unner …' Car slurred. 'Unner dere. Somewhere.'

The bed squeaked; his heavy breathing resumed. Paulina picked her way over the broken glass, opened cupboards. Something caught her eye: pale aquamarine.

A box. A *jewellery* box. Too big for a ring, but still.

'Shit!' Paulina dropped the box and covered her mouth.

The photos fanned out on the ground. Crouching, she scrambled to get them back in. But her hands — her dumb, drunk hands. And her eyes, flooding tears.

She couldn't see.

Couldn't see. Couldn't unsee. And then Car was there, tearing the photo from her fingertips.

And then he was grabbing her by the ponytail, and then he was bashing her unconscious.

DRIFTWOOD

'I should be past this stage.' Judy grabbed another tissue. 'Waking up in tears.'

'Remember what we said about the word "should", Judy,' Agnes replied gently. 'Remember what we said about "stages".'

'I know, you don't like that language.' Judy sniffed. 'Just, it's been two years.'

'And you've loved her for thirty-two.'

'I should be past this, though.'

'It's not a straight line. It's not a ladder you can climb until you reach a place where it doesn't hurt. Remember what we said, Judy? How grief is like the ocean?'

'I know. There are calm times and stormy times.'

'What else?'

'It comes and goes in waves.'

'What else?'

'It contains a lot. All the living things. All the treasure. All the garbage. Shipwrecks. Sea monsters.'

'What else?'

'Sometimes it glitters in the sun. Sometimes it kills you with its coldness.'

'Anything else?'

'You can spend your whole life searching the depths and never find the answers.'

'And that's okay. Searching is what humans do.'

'I have to set my alarm early. It's so hard getting out of bed.'

'That's okay. Think of it as your morning prayers.'

'I don't know. That's a nice idea, but that's not how it feels. It's agony.'

'Losing a child is agony. It's okay to make room for that agony in your life. It doesn't mean you're not alive.'

'I just miss her so much.'

Judy cried for a while, until the cell phone Caro had bought her for her fifty-fourth birthday buzzed again in her handbag. 'Gawd!' She wiped her eyes. 'It's like a mosquito in a megaphone.'

'Want to answer it?'

'I answered phones all day.' Judy half-smiled. 'I'm not paying you to watch me answer another one.'

Agnes laughed. Then she looked at Judy a while more. Judy looked at the clock.

'We still have a little time.' Agnes waited. 'Would you like to talk about your parents again? You had a lot to say last time.'

Judy waved her hand. 'They're not important.'

Agnes cocked an eyebrow.

'They weren't bad people.' Judy shrugged. 'They were just old-fashioned.'

'You said something last time about Marko. How he was your way of rebelling.'

'I don't know. It wasn't calculated. I fell for him, hard.'

'But you were disappointed when they approved of him?'

'I mean, if Caro had brought home another woman's husband. And a wog, at that …' Judy blushed. 'That's what we called foreigners, back then. It's not a nice word.'

'That's alright. Go on.'

'If it was Caro, they would've disowned her. No question.' Judy dashed a tear. 'But because it was me, it was all: *a doctor! Well done, Jude! So handsome! So European!*

'How did that make you feel?'

'I don't know.' Judy shrugged again. 'It was worse for Caro.'

'It *was* worse for Caro. But that doesn't mean your feelings aren't valid.'

'Just, I was a *teenager*. I didn't even know myself. I shouldn't of been marrying a forty-year-old … and they shouldn't of been patting me on the back for it.'

Agnes nodded.

'I was *horrified* when Paulina took up with that dirty old rabbit man, and she was almost thirty!' Judy raised her damp eyes. 'Why do men do that? Go after girls half their age?'

'I don't know. They do, though.'

'I guess it goes both ways; I was willing. I was head-over-heels.' Judy's handbag buzzed again. 'Oh, for chrissakes!'

'Do you want to get that?'

'No.' Judy shook her head. 'Thank you, though.'

'You were head-over-heels?'

'Of course. He was a doctor. He came from a country I'd never even heard of. I'd never been further than the Central Coast. It wasn't hard for him, impressing an eighteen-year-old from Seven Hills.'

Agnes watched her take another tissue.

'I don't mean he wasn't a good man. He adored me. He adored Paulina. He gave me Paulina, what's more.' Judy wiped her nose. 'Just, even now, I'm so mixed up when I think of him. I'm so old, but I'm so mixed up. I really miss him, then I get angry that he put me through all that when I was so young; I mean, breaking up another woman's *family*.'

Agnes' eyes strayed, barely perceptibly, to the clock.

'Is it time?' Judy asked.

'I'm afraid so.' Agnes smiled. 'But we can pick up where we left off next week. And you can finally see who that is who keeps calling you.'

Judy stood with Agnes. 'It's probably some telemarketer.'

'See you next week, Judy. And thank you for sharing.'

At reception, after handing over her card, Judy dug her phone from her handbag.

Six missed calls. Three text messages, all from Caro; the latest one a nonsensical scream:

HAIR!!!!!

Judy was still sitting in her car when Agnes came out of her office. Agnes glanced at the windscreen, then noticed Judy; registered shock, courtesy. Embarrassed, Judy returned her smile. Rolled down her window.

'Sorry. I'm not a creepy stalker or anything,' Judy apologised. 'I just got some news. Good news … I think. Now I don't know what to do with myself.'

'Oh?' Agnes's eyebrows went up. 'About the case?'

Judy nodded.

'They found her hair in someone's car. After all this time.'

Agnes's face crumpled strangely.

'Do you need a tissue?' Judy opened her handbag.

'No. Thank you.' Agnes recovered. 'Thanks for telling me, Judy. That makes me so happy.'

'I don't know if I'm happy. Well, I am. I don't know how to feel it, though. I don't know what to do with myself.'

'Have you talked to your sister?'

'She wants to get drunk and have a sleepover.' Judy rolled her eyes. 'I can't be bothered.'

'I'm so happy for you.'

'It was just sitting on someone's land the whole time. The people who own the land didn't realise; they were living in Christchurch. They came back and found this abandoned Camry and now …' Judy laughed. 'Wozniak was telling me all this stuff about the case and I just blurted out: "Can I see it? Can I see the hair?" He must think I'm dotty!'

'You're not dotty. It's a wonderful idea.'

'Just, I always regretted not being the one to ID her.'

'That's understandable.'

'Anyway, Wozniak said he'd try to make it happen next week. I'll have to go to Canberra.' Judy's eyes widened. 'Oh! I might miss therapy.'

Agnes laughed. 'I'll let you off the hook this once.'

'I'll have to go to Canberra … I've never been to Canberra.' Judy remembered. 'Oh, wait, yes I have. We went down there about a month after it happened. I barely remember it; I was so drugged up. Just this big table and all these suits.'

'You'll have a better time, this time. It's quite lovely this time of year, with all the trees. They have some nice galleries.'

'I don't care about galleries. I just want to see her hair.'

'You'll have a lovely time, Judy. Call if you need to cancel.' Agnes pressed her hand. 'I'm so happy for you. You've made my day.'

'Thank you.' Judy smiled. 'See you later.'

She rolled her window back up, sat in the car for a while. Then she drove back to her empty house.

It was like nothing Judy had ever seen before. But she kept trying to say what it looked like.

'It's a bit like a tree branch, isn't it?' Judy lifted her eye from the microscope. 'Like a branch, covered in rain.'

'That's the root,' the lab tech told her. 'That bit that looks like rain.'

Then he did something different with the microscope.

'It looks a bit burnt when you do that!' Judy marvelled. 'Like a burnt match!'

'Want to see it with the dark field?'

Judy nodded.

'Oh, it's so different! It's like something in space!' she babbled. 'Like a wormhole in space. Or the tail of a comet. Or, something?'

Then the lab tech brought the focus closer, and it became like a tree again.

'It's like a fallen tree in the forest.' That made her a bit sad, though. 'Or like driftwood. Washed up from the sea. It's very beautiful.'

'It is beautiful.'

While Judy was wiping her eyes, another lab tech showed her some sheets of paper with stats on them. She didn't understand any of it, but she nodded.

'It's a lot. For something so little. There's a lot in it.'

Later, meeting Wozniak for a coffee, he asked her how she'd liked the lab.

'It was a lot to take in,' Judy repeated. 'I couldn't stop gawking. I reckon they were sick of me, by the end of it. Distracting them from their work like that.'

'They loved meeting you,' Wozniak reassured her. 'They don't often get to put a face to the work they do.'

Then he got down to business.

'I'm sorry I can't tell you more. We have to keep a tight lid on it, for now. But we're working closely with the West Australian police. We're building a case.'

'WA.' Judy shook her head. 'Who would've thought.'

After that, she walked along Lake Burley Griffin, looking at the trees and tree-reflecting water, until it was time to catch her flight home.

Two weeks later, Wozniak gave her the name of the man they'd arrested. She'd never heard it before in her life.

THE WALLS

The first thing Paulina saw was the red light. Then she saw it wasn't a red light; it was a white light with red around the edges. The red was in her eyes.

She tried to wipe the blood from her eyes, then it hit her like fists.

'Mum!' she cried. 'Mum!'

The voices switched from Fayrf'k to English. 'Don't touch!' the woman shouted, swooping down to her level.

'Mum?' Paulina bleated. 'Mum?'

'What're you saying?' The woman squinted. Light-green eyes. Not her mum's eyes. 'Stay still. Don't talk.'

'Mum? I want my mum.'

'What's she saying?' The woman asked the man, and Paulina recognised him — his hulking shape. 'Stay still, girl! Don't move!'

'Muuuuum!'

The green eyes sparked with understanding.

'Car. Out. *Now.*'

Car muttered, threw a pale glance at Paulina, before skulking above deck, blood on his shirt.

'Mum. Please? I want Mum.'

'Not yet.' Tabby sighed. 'Shh. We have to get you cleaned up first. Do you want your mum to see you in this state?'

There was too much light, then there wasn't enough. They were making her climb to a dark place where it stank of dead fish.

'No!' Paulina saw the moon glimmering on the water. 'I wanna go home.'

'Shh,' Tabby hissed. 'You're going home soon. But we have to get you to the car.'

'No Car. Please. No.'

'Not Carlyle. I mean a car that drives on the road. Do you remember what a car is?'

'No!'

'How many wheels does a car have? Tell me how many wheels.'

Paulina struggled. 'Get off me.'

'If you fight, he'll have to pick you up and carry you. Do you want Car to carry you?'

'No!'

'No? Okay, then. Walk with me. Slowly.'

Paulina fell against her shoulder. 'Am I dead?'

'You're not dead. You had an accident. You got drunk and had an accident. Silly girl.'

'Fucking cow.'

'There's no need for that. Mind the step. We're almost there.'

She closed her eyes. Then she was in the backseat of a car that wasn't hers, and Tabby was slapping her cheeks.

'Not my car. Where's mine? Mazda Astina.'

'You drive a Mazda Astina?' Tabby sounded impressed. 'What colour?'

'Blue, bitch!'

'Very good.'

Tabby said something in Fayrf'k. The driver laughed. Paulina recognised him all over again.

'Shh. Don't scream. That's just the taxi driver. Do you know where your house is?'

'Cherry Hill. Mum.'

'Not your mum's house, your house.'

'With Ric?'

Car laughed again. Paulina yelped. 'Muuuum!'

'Don't worry about that taxi driver. He thinks he's smart, but he's not. He can't even clean up his own messes. I'm going to clean you up and then you can see your mum. You want to look nice and clean for your mum, don't you?'

'Nice girl.' Paulina's eyelids fluttered. 'Blue dress. Smashing Pumpkins.'

———

Then there was a house, and a pale-aqua room in the house, and Car was gone. Then sleep. Tabby woke her up with a little flashlight in her eyes, put a thumb to her wrists. 'Fuck you!' Paulina clawed at her.

'There's no need for that. Do you need some water? Have some water.'

Paulina pushed the glass away. 'It *hurts*.'

Tabby dipped her fingers in the water, moistened Paulina's lips.

'I know it hurts. I'll give you some more painkillers soon. Have some water.'

'Thirsty.' Paulina opened her mouth. 'Thirsty, Mum.'

'I'm not your mum. Stop saying that.' Tabby gave her more water. 'Is it nice, the water? Want more?'

'More.'

'Just a little more. We don't want you throwing up again.'

'More, Mum.'

'Please don't call me that. My name's "Tabby". Remember?'

'Cat's name.'

'Yes, like a tabby-cat. "Tabby", not "Mum".' She withdrew her fingers. 'That's enough for now. We don't want you throwing up. Or wetting the bed. Do you need the toilet?'

'No.'

'Go back to sleep, then.' Tabby watched her close her eyes. 'It's not so bad. Really. I've seen worse.'

Paulina wet the bed. She didn't mean to; she was dreaming.

'Sea,' she told Tabby. 'Drowning.'

'That's not the sea.' Tabby huffed. 'That's piss.'

'Car's boat. Accident.'

'Not anymore. You're in bed now. What a mess. I'll have to turn you over. I'll have to get rid of these wet things.'

Tabby moved the blanket to the floor, lifted Paulina's damp nightie. Paulina panicked.

'I'm sorry,' Tabby said. 'You can't lie there in your own filth.'

Paulina closed her eyes obediently. Tabby drew the nightie over her head. When she tried to peel off her knickers, though, Paulina's legs clamped shut.

'Don't, Car. I don't want to.'

'Sorry.' Tabby blinked. 'I'll get you some clean ones.'

She left the room, muttering to herself. Came back with clean knickers and a nightie with a rainbow-striped fish on the front.

'Fish,' Paulina said. 'Fishing?'

'You can put these on soon, but first we have to take those wet ones off. Are you ready?'

Nodding, Paulina squeezed her eyes shut again.

'Cold,' she complained, drawing her knees up. 'Ow!'

'I'm sorry. I'll change the sheets now. I'll have to turn you.' Arms akimbo, Tabby frowned down at Paulina. 'We have to be careful of those ribs.'

'Ribs?'

'It's only a fracture. You're lucky he didn't break anything.' Tabby touched her mouth. 'I mean, you're lucky *you* didn't break anything. It was a bad accident. You're very silly, getting drunk and falling over like that.'

'Not an accident.'

'What do you mean? Yes, it was.' Tabby laughed. 'Sorry, but I'm going to have to turn you on your side. Your right side. It'll hurt a bit, but I'll be quick. I'll be quicker if you work with me. Okay?'

'No.'

'I'll be quick. I'm going to move you by your shoulders, and you're going to roll over to the wall. That blue wall. Okay?'

'I'm scared, Mum.'

'I'm not—' Tabby sighed. 'Come on. Towards the wall, like a good girl. Look at the blue wall. You're going to roll over to the blue wall, on the count of three. Okay?'

Paulina winced, nodded. On the count of three, Tabby placed her hands on Paulina's shoulders, rolled her. Then a pain like sharp rocks in her sides.

'Owwwww!'

'Shhh. I know it hurts. Keep looking at the wall. The blue wall.'

'Mum?'

'Shh. It's "Tabby". I'm here. I'm just changing these sheets. Stay still.'

Paulina stayed very still, staring at the wall.

'You've got goosebumps, poor thing. Be patient. We'll get rid of these wet things, then you can be nice and warm and dry in bed.'

Paulina closed her eyes, waited patiently.

'Good girl. We've got some new sheets now. I just need you to stay still while I do these corners. Very good.'

Soon after, Tabby rolled her onto her back.

'Here's your nightie. I'll put this over your head.'

'Fish?'

'Yes, fish. Very good.'

'Ow!' Paulina yelped as Tabby pulled it over her face.

'I'm sorry. Please don't touch your face. It's very tender.'

'Why, Mum?'

'It's very tender. We got all the glass out, though. You're lucky it didn't get in your eyes. How do your eyes feel?'

'Sore.'

'We'll put a cold compress on them later, when you're nice and warm. Can you see okay? Can you see the colours on the fish?'

'Rainbow.'

'Good girl. Here's your knickers, now.' Tabby lifted her feet one by one, put them through the holes, and pulled them up her legs. 'Can you lift your bum? Good girl.'

'Fishing. On a boat.'

'Not now. When you're well, maybe.' Tabby smiled wanly. 'Isn't that better? Warm and dry.'

'Better.'

'There's a pad in there, just in case, but I don't think you'll need it. You'll tell me next time you need to go, won't you?'

'Yes, Mum.'

Later, Tabby put the light in her eyes again and asked, 'What's your name?'

'P-P …' It was too hard to say. 'Lina.'

'And your surname?'

'N-Novak?'

'Do you remember my name?'

Paulina looked at her. She had light hair, like her mum; she wanted to say 'Mum'. The face was different though, and the green eyes.

'Cat's name,' she said.

'Cat's name. It starts with "T".'

'T-T …' Paulina closed her eyes. 'I don't give a fuck.'

'There's no need for that. You know, the reason I ask is, I want to make sure you don't have brain damage. You don't want brain damage, do you?'

'Fuck you.'

'Can you tell me your birthday?'

'No.'

'Have a go.'

Paulina shut her eyes tighter.

'How old are you, then. Can you tell me how old you are?'

'Twenty …' Paulina sighed. 'Nine.'

'Twenty-nine. You should be married with kids. Not falling down drunk.'

'He said we would.'

'Excuse me?'

'Car said.'

Tabby flinched.

'That's a load of crap. You're a stupid girl, believing Car's crap.'

Then there was a nice, dreamy feeling, like riding a chariot through the clouds, a clamshell through waves. Riding. Wet pearls and ocean spray.

'Yeah, Car,' she moaned. 'Please, yeah.'

Tabby wrinkled her nose.

'I'm just checking your pad. Do you need the toilet?'

'No.'

'I think I should take you, just in case. It's been a while.'

Paulina sighed, shook her head, and tried to go back to the waves, the riding.

'I'm just thinking what's the best way to do this.' Tabby stood over her. 'I think, if we shift your legs off the bed first, then you can put your arm around my neck and lean on me.'

'Shhh.'

'Come on.' Tabby moved Paulina's legs; her feet touched soft carpet. 'Just a little way. Then you can go back to your ... whatever that was.'

Paulina hugged Tabby's neck, swayed to her feet.

'Ow!'

'Sorry. That's that bruise on your hip. Nasty place for a bruise. Very bony.'

'Why, Mum?'

'Never mind. We're going to the bathroom. Not far, now.'

The carpet changed to floorboards. 'Cold!'

'You'll be back in your nice, warm bed soon.'

Tiles, even colder.

'Cold!' Paulina cried — then she saw a girl in an oversized T-shirt with a fish on the front, legs too skinny for her fat, misshapen head. 'Who ... ?'

'Never mind that.' Tabby led her away from the mirror. 'Good girl. Down on the toilet now. You can go now.'

Paulina tried to go, but her ribs hurt. Her hip. Nothing much came out.

'Sorry, Mum.'

'That's alright. Take your time. Sit.'

Paulina sat. Shivered.

'Sorry, Mum,' she repeated.

'Never mind.' Tabby broke off a few squares of toilet paper, handed them to her. 'Can you wipe?'

Paulina wiped, shivered.

'I'm just thinking, since we're up ...' Tabby scrutinised her. 'It's just, you already missed work. If you miss too much, people will wonder.'

'Sorry, Mum.'

'That's alright. I'm just thinking.'

'Cold, Mum.'

'Just a minute. I'm just thinking.' Tabby petted her hair. 'Darling: do you remember where you work?'

Paulina didn't remember, but when Tabby said the name, *Mutineers' Lodge*, it had a wistful familiarity to it, like songs from kindergarten.

Puff the Magic Dragon. Never Smile At A Crocodile.

'I fell on the stairs,' she told the man on the phone. 'I'm hurt. I can't work.'

'Were you drunk?' Baz asked.

'No. I mean, yeah. But that's not why I fell.' Paulina clutched her head. 'I dropped the glass cos I was drunk, but that's not why I fell.'

'Gayle's been run off her feet. That tour group from Melbourne arrived today.'

'S-Sorry.' Paulina looked at Tabby. 'I fell on the stairs. I can't work.'

'How long do you need?'

Paulina looked at Tabby again. '*Three weeks*,' she mouthed.

'Three weeks, the lady says.'

Baz exhaled.

'If you're not back by the seventeenth, I'll consider this your resignation.'

'Sorry, sir.'

'*Sir?*' Baz's tone switched. 'How many meds have they got you on, Westpac?'

Tabby took the phone from her and hung it up.

'Why did you say that? About not being drunk?'

'Sorry, Mum.'

'I don't know why you said that.' An angry line appeared between Tabby's brows. 'You think they don't know you're a drunk?'

Something started leaking from Paulina's eyes, searing her face like acid.

'Well, don't cry. What's done is done. Come on, let's get you back to bed.'

Paulina let Tabby help her up from the chair. 'The man was annoyed?'

'Don't worry about Baz. He's a faggot.'

Paulina stopped in front of a photo of a girl. Was it her, 'Paulina'? No. 'I know her,' she said.

'Come on. Back to bed.'

Paulina kept looking at the photo. 'I know her. I saw her photo.'

'Oh?' Tabby's voice caught in her throat. 'That's Tiffany, yes. You probably saw her shrine by the road.'

'Tiffany.'

'My daughter.' Tabby guided Paulina back to bed. 'They think it's respectful, but I can't stand driving past it. It's like a knife in my heart, every time.'

'Not that photo.' Paulina closed her eyes. 'The other one.'

Car was arguing with his wife in the hall, but Paulina wasn't afraid; he couldn't see her.

Then Car caught sight of her through the open door. Sidled into the room, bug-eyed.

'Nay, Car!' Tabby slapped his arm. 'She's frayd!'

'She's nay frayd.' Car laughed. 'She looks rubbish, eh?'

'Aye.'

Car edged closed to the bed. 'You look like rubbish, sweetheart.'

Still, Paulina wasn't afraid; he couldn't *really* see her.

'Anybody in there?' Car clicked his fingers in her face. 'Eh?' Then he turned to his wife. 'She brain-dead?'

Tabby shrugged, tugged on his arm until he left the room.

'A man came before,' Paulina told Tabby, when she came in with a tub of yoghurt.

'What man?' Tabby peeled the lid off the tub.

Paulina looked at her for a long moment. 'The one who beat the shit out of me.'

Tabby breathed deep, held a spoon to her mouth. 'Do you remember his name?'

Paulina nodded, swallowed the yoghurt, and licked her lips.

'You're hungry, aren't you?' Tabby fed her another spoonful. 'Is it yummy?'

'Yes, Mum.'

'You don't eat much, do you? You're skin-and-bone.' Tabby murmured indulgently. 'Do you remember why he "beat the shit" out of you? What you did to deserve it?'

Paulina thought for a bit. 'He's married.'

'That's right.' Tabby smiled. 'You shouldn't be hassling married men.'

Paulina ate more yoghurt, continued thinking. 'I didn't deserve it.'

Tabby looked alarmed. Then she took up the yoghurt tub, stood. 'Just so you know, I put some sleeping pills in there for you.'

Paulina needed to piss. She got up on her own, stumbled to the hall before the pain seared up her sides, her knees buckled.

'What are you doing?' Tabby cried, finding her crumpled on the floor like a used tissue. 'You can't walk by yourself!'

'Don't touch me!'

Tabby crossed her arms, watched Paulina lift herself and hobble a few steps further. She was there to catch her the moment she lost her footing.

'Get off, bitch!'

'Not "Mum" anymore?'

'You're not my mum!'

'No, I'm not.' Tabby led her across the cold tiles to the porcelain bowl. 'I'd be ashamed, if I was. You're a nasty piece of work.'

Paulina squatted. 'Stop perving!'

Tabby slipped out of the room.

Paulina pissed. Remembered another time naked, happy, pissing, a man snoring in the next room. A shadow over the memory.

She wiped. Flushed. Staggered to the sink and looked in the mirror.

It took her a while to realise it was her face: cloudy-red eyes; chipped brow and nose; berry-coloured bruises; a blood-spotted, cottony bandage on her cheek. Then she lost it.

'Don't do that!' Tabby threw a towel over the mirror. 'That's a *very silly* thing to do!'

Paulina cried all the way back to bed.

'Shh. You're alright.' Tabby pulled the blankets over her. 'You won't be pretty for a while, but that's alright. Pretty's what got you here in the first place.'

She was staring at the pale-aqua walls, trying to figure them out, when Tabby came in with a bowl of water and a purple cloth. A black-and-white poster on the wall of a lady with upswept dark hair, jewels around her neck. Was it her, 'Paulina'? No. An actress?

'Is that Winona Ryder?'

'No!' Tabby scoffed. 'It's Audrey Hepburn! In *Breakfast at Tiffany's*!'

'Tiffany.' Paulina pondered. 'Like that girl.'

'She loved that movie.' Tabby swished the cloth in the bowl. 'This is a warm compress, for your eyes. We're done with the cold ones. Close your eyes?'

Paulina closed her eyes. Thoughts furled in the blackness.

'Where's her dad?'

'Tiff's dad? Missing in action.' Tabby softly pressed the warm, damp cloth to Paulina's bruises. 'He was a mainie. Doctor at the hospital where I worked.'

Paulina remembered a man's face: craggy, familiar. A man's foreign accent.

'My dad's a doctor.' A thought like a birthday candle. 'Can I see Dad?'

'Not till you're better.'

'He'll fix me.'

'You don't need a doctor.' Tabby pressed her eyes some more. 'They're useless. All they do is swan around in their white coats, thinking they're important.'

'Dad …' Something happened in Paulina's chest; a landslide. 'He died?'

'Oh? Sorry to hear that. Don't cry, though. It'll sting.'

'Sorry.'

'Your long-term memory seems to be coming back; that's good,' Tabby encouraged. 'Don't worry too much about remembering the accident. Long-term is what matters. Do you remember your birthday?'

'March 31, 1972.'

'Good. You couldn't tell me that, before.'

'I was … late. Born late?'

'You were overdue, were you? Better than being premature. Tiffany was a premmie. She had a machine breathing for her. I didn't think she'd make it.'

'I saw her photo.'

'Yes, you said. She was a pretty girl. Smart, too. *She* could've been a doctor.' Tabby withdrew the cloth. 'Do you remember what you do for a job?'

'Financial advisor.'

'That doesn't sound right.' Tabby scowled. 'Here, on Fairfolk

Island. Where do you work?'

'Mutineers' Lodge.'

'And what do you do at Mutes'?'

'Clean the cabins … waitress.'

'Good. Not too complicated, eh? You'll be back on your feet in no time.' Tabby surveyed her proudly. 'Are you hungry?'

'Yes, Mum.'

'You need to stop calling me "Mum".' Tabby shook her head. 'I know you know better. What's your mum's name? Your real mum.'

'Judy.'

'I feel sorry for her. You're a wild thing.'

Paulina didn't mean to smash the glass. She was thirsty; her hands weren't working.

'What happened?' Tabby rushed into the room, pink-cheeked.

'Accident.' Paulina's heart raced. 'Drunk.'

'Stay still. Don't you dare get up.'

Tabby went out; came back in with the dustpan and broom. Paulina watched her crouch among the mess, the deep line of her cleavage, the part of her gold hair.

'I broke the glass.'

'I know.' Tabby harrumphed. 'Don't I know it.'

'I broke the bottle.' Paulina smelled something strong, over-sweet. 'Johnny Walker.'

'No alcohol for you.'

Paulina squeezed shut her eyes. 'I broke it, then he hit me.'

Tabby looked up. 'That's what happened? You broke Car's Johnny Walker and he hit you?'

'Yeah.'

'He loves his Johnny Walker.' Tabby sighed wistfully. 'No alcohol for you.'

'Rum and Diet Coke!'

Tabby swept the last of the glass into the dustpan and stood.

'You're really a drunk, aren't you? No self-control.'

'Bitch!' Paulina thrashed at the air. 'Bring me a rum and Diet Coke!'

Later, Tabby tried to give Paulina some medicine; she wouldn't take it. A bit later, Tabby came back in with a can of drink. 'Here's your rum and Diet Coke.'

Paulina sipped greedily, then pulled a face. 'There's no rum in this.'

'Yes there is.'

'No there's not.'

'Yes there is.'

She took another drink. 'Lying bitch.'

'There's no need for that. You owe me your life. I could've left you for dead.'

Paulina upended the can.

'You nasty thing!' Tabby scolded her. 'I'll have to change the sheets again!'

Paulina swung her legs out of bed.

'Where do you think you're going?' Tabby grabbed her arm.

'Let go or I'll piss the bed!'

Paulina reeled to the door, like she was on a boat on a stormy sea. Tabby followed her to the bathroom like a shadow.

'Don't perv!' Paulina pulled down her knickers, squatted. 'Get out!'

'I don't trust you not to make a mess on purpose. Nasty thing.'

Paulina looked around for something to throw at Tabby.

'Why's that towel on the mirror?'

'To keep out the vampires.'

'Ha!' Paulina cackled. 'The bats have left the belltower, bitch!'

'Yes. Okay, then.'

'Ha-ha!' Paulina's piss sizzled between her legs. 'Undead, undead, undead!'

The phone rang. Then the ringing stopped. Paulina got up, walked to where Tabby was talking, low and harried.

'Aye, she remembers.'

Tabby noticed her in the doorway, glowered.

'She's up. Nay, Car! Stay out.'

She hung up. 'What're you doing up? You need to rest.'

Paulina looked at the sunlight on the floor. A table with a lamp on it, paper, foam, boxes. Outside the arched window, a blaze of ferns and fruit trees.

'Car lives here?'

'He's staying on the boat for now; don't worry.'

Paulina approached the table.

'That's my work. Don't touch.'

Paulina sat, picked up a pale-aqua box. 'Tabby's Treasures.'

'I'm sending some things to the mainland.'

Paulina looked at her. 'Can I go home?'

'Not yet. I wish you could be out of my hair, but you're not ready.'

Looking at the box again, a chill went through her.

'I wanna go home.'

'Later.'

'Mum's worried.'

'I'm sure it's not the first time.'

'Please.'

'Soon.'

'Car …'

'He'll stay away.'

'He raped me.'

'That's a load of crap. Do you know how many people saw you throwing yourself at him on Mutiny Day?'

'He did it to her, too.' In Paulina's hands, the pale-aqua box blurred. 'Tiffany.'

Tabby snatched up the box, her face blotchy.

'Don't talk about my daughter, ever again.'

'Don't!' Paulina thrashed, waking up to Tabby checking her pad. 'Don't touch me!'

'I have to make sure you haven't soiled yourself. You stink.'

'Fuck off!' Paulina squirmed.

'We can give you a bath. How does that sound?'

Paulina imagined hot water, cleansing her skin. But Tabby's hands were still on her, lifting her nightie. 'Don't.'

'I'm just checking. How do your ribs feel?'

'Piss off.'

'There's a lot of them.' Tabby's fingernails brushed the bruises.

'Look at you. Skin-and-bone.'

'Stop perving!'

'I'm not—' Tabby sighed. 'I'll get that bath ready.'

When it was time for her bath, Paulina numbly let Tabby walk her down the hall. Let her lower her into the too-hot water, and soap her up, and pour bowls of water over her. Let her wash her hair, dry her with a fluffy towel. At the end, she said, 'Thank you, Mum.'

'I'm not—' Again, Tabby sighed. 'I don't understand you. One minute it's "bitch", next minute it's "Mum". It's like having a teenager in the house again.'

'He did it in her room.'

'Here's a clean nightie.' Tabby's hands were shaking. 'Put it on.'

'I saw. Photos.'

'What photos?'

'I saw the walls.'

'What walls?'

'She was in her room. Naked.'

'Get dressed.' Tabby forced the nightie over Paulina's head. 'You should be ashamed of yourself.'

'She was scared.'

'I'm not listening to this.' Tabby tugged Paulina's arm. 'Up you get. Back to bed.'

'You knew.'

'You don't know what you're talking about.'

As Tabby pulled her into the hall, Paulina yelped, 'You're hurting me!'

'It's your own fault.'

'Bitch!' Paulina swiped at her. 'You're worse than him!'

Blood flowered on Tabby's cheek.

'Why don't I call him, then, if that's how you feel? I'll call Car to come sort you out.'

Paulina swiped again. 'Let me out!'

Tabby grabbed her wrist, twisted. Paulina spat in her face.

'You little—' Tabby wiped the spit. 'That's it. I'm calling him.'

'Do it!' Paulina rushed to the door; it was unlocked. 'I'm not sleeping in that room anymore!'

Air. The best air she'd ever breathed: sea, fruit, flowers, manure, wood-smoke, pine needles. She lost her balance on the porch; frantically picked herself up.

'Go on!' Tabby called after her. 'Get off my property! See how far you get!'

The yard seemed as vast as an ocean, the grass cool and blue as water in the fading light. A dog barked in the distance. She ran toward it, feet chafing as the grass turned to gravel, concrete, bitumen. She flagged down the first car she saw: a maroon Honda Civic.

'My goodness!' cried the lady in the passenger seat. Kiwi accent. 'What *happened*?'

'I fell,' Paulina recited. 'I fell down some stairs.'

'Do those stairs have a name? You don't have to protect him.'

'Don't pry, Mary,' the man behind the wheel said. 'Where can we take you, love?'

'Tenderloin Road.'

'"Tenderloin Road." Mary, can you find that on the map?'

'Roy, she needs medical attention!'

'Is there a hospital on this island?' The man looked back at Paulina. 'Sorry. We just arrived from Auckland.'

'Tenderloin Road,' Paulina repeated. 'The house with the cow letterbox.'

'Who lives there, dear? Is it safe?'

'Mary, don't pry. She's a grown woman.'

'She's walking around half-naked!'

'I'm from Fairfolk Island,' Paulina slurred. 'This's how we dress here.'

'There you go, Mary. You heard her. Check the map, will you?'

The lady turned around in her seat. 'You don't have to protect him, dear. Whoever he is. Roy's just afraid of missing the Fortuna fish-fry. But we'll take you to the hospital. Or the police. Wherever you need to go.'

Paulina's brain hurt so bad she wanted to stick a knife in it.

'Tenderloin Road. Near Klee Welkin. The house with the cow letterbox.'

The couple dropped her off outside Vera and Rocky's. 'Look at that!' The man chuckled at the letterbox. 'The mail goes right in its bum-crack!'

Mumbling her thanks, Paulina staggered around the side of the house. She felt a surge of love, seeing her blue Mazda parked outside her cottage. A blast of ice-cold wind, letting herself into the flat and knowing someone had been inside it.

A note on the counter, not her handwriting: *Gone drinking.*

Paulina ripped up the note.

She turned the kitchen tap, guzzled water. Pulled the blinds. Stumbled to bed.

In the ringing silence of her bedroom, she saw her answering machine's blink, like a lighthouse in the dark. Clicked 'play'.

Hi, darling. Mum here. I know you're busy, but can you give me a call? I'm going to Aunt Caro's for tea. Give us a call, if you're free!

I'm at Caro's. She says hi (HI!). Talk soon?

Is everything alright? I haven't heard from you all week; I'm getting worried—

I'm really worried, Paulina. Please, call—

'Get a life, bitch,' Paulina whispered, closing her eyes.

A FAIR TRIAL

The first day of the trial, Judy went into Foodfolk with Caro to buy some cigarettes, and, on the way out, bumped into Jesse Camilleri.

'Sorry,' Jesse said, and tried to step out of her way.

Judy had the same idea. 'Sorry!'

'Sorry,' Jesse repeated. It happened again.

Judy blushed. 'Sorry!'

'Oh, bloody hell!' Caro grabbed Judy's arm and moved her aside.

'Um, thanks.' Jesse hovered. 'Um, good luck today. That bastard deserves to be hanged, eh.'

'Thank you,' Judy murmured. 'Yes, we hope so. Not hanged. But, you know.'

'Yeah, right. Um. Good to see you, Mrs Novak. Ms! Sorry.'

He looked so sorry, you'd think he was the one going on trial.

'It's alright.' Judy smiled and patted his arm. 'I was "Mrs Novak", once. It's not the worst thing you could call me.'

Caro shot her a suspicious glance. Then she simpered; offered Jesse a ciggie.

'Oh. Bes' not, eh.' Jesse reddened. 'Um. Good to see you, too, um—'

'Caro.'

'Right. Sorry, I just woke up.' His eyes drifted back to Judy. 'I saw you on TV, a while back. It was good. I mean, it wasn't good. But you were good.'

'Oh, *that*.' Judy rolled her eyes. 'I'd rather forget about that.'

'Sorry. You were good, though, Ms Novak. I—'

'Come on.' Caro tugged on Judy's arm. 'We'll be late.'

'See you around, Jesse,' Judy mumbled, and let Caro lead her away. Outside Foodfolk, Caro cracked up.

'What?' Judy bleated. 'What's so funny?'

'You! Flirting with that kid!'

'I wasn't *flirting*.'

'That little pat on the arm?'

'I just did that because he was awkward! Like, "there, there", you know?'

'There, there.' Caro patted Judy's arm. 'I *know*.'

Huffing, Judy let herself into the rental car. 'Are you going to accuse me of flirting every time someone's awkward around me?'

'Only if he's cute.' Smirking, Caro sidled in beside her. 'Crack a window, will you?'

'Tim knows you smoke. He's not stupid.'

Caro rummaged in her handbag. 'Shit, I forgot my lighter! Let's go back inside.'

Judy paled.

'Jokingggg!' Caro flashed the pine-green lighter. 'The look on your face!'

'What's wrong with you? We're on our way to a murder trial.'

'No shit.' Caro lit up. 'This is probably the only time I'll get a laugh today.'

Judy started the car. 'Just so you know, I wasn't flirting. I would never.'

'Well, maybe *you* weren't.' Caro blew smoke out the window. 'He was, though.'

'You arrived on Fairfolk Island on March 28, 2002. Is that correct, Ms Novak?'

'Yes.' Judy steadied her face. 'That's correct.'

'A little closer to the microphone, please.'

'Sorry.' She leaned closer, eyes stinging. 'Correct.'

'What was the purpose of your visit?'

'I came to see my daughter, Paulina. We planned to celebrate her birthday together.'

'What did you do upon your arrival?'

'Paulina picked me up from the airport.' Judy pretended she was back in front of the mirror at the Hibiscus Hideout serviced apartments, practising. 'It was about two o'clock. She drove me around the island a bit, then took me to get my rental car. We drove separately to Mutineers' Lodge, her workplace. She helped me check in, then after … we had coffee in my cabin before she started her dinner shift.'

'How did your daughter seem?'

'Happy and healthy. She seemed excited to show me her new home.'

'Did you see Paulina again that evening?'

'Yes. I met her after her shift and—'

'A little louder, please.'

'Sorry. I met her after her shift? For dinner. We went to the Great-O White Shark Grill.'

'How did she seem?'

'Happy. Chatty.'

'Was her mood unusually elevated?'

'Sorry?' Judy blinked. 'No. I mean, she was … happy to see me.'

'Did she appear to be under the influence of drugs or alcohol?'

'Paulina didn't do drugs.' Shaking her head, Judy's eyes leaked furiously. 'We shared a bottle of white wine over dinner.'

'How much did your daughter drink?'

'We shared the bottle. About half the bottle.'

'Half each?'

'Well …' Wasn't the prosecutor meant to be on *her* side? 'I only had two small glasses. I was driving.'

'So, she had more than half?'

'I suppose so.' Judy remembered something, yearned to leave it out. 'I just remembered. She had a cocktail, too.'

'What was in the cocktail?'

'I'm not sure. It was something pink. It had … a fun name.' Her face burned. 'Sorry. I can't recall the name.'

'Was it a strong cocktail?'

'I don't think so. It wasn't like a Long Island Iced Tea or anything.'

She sensed Caro smiling at that, and momentarily felt better.

'Was it typical for your daughter to drink that much during a single dinner?'

'I … wouldn't say "typical".' Judy wondered if this was true. 'We hadn't seen each other in over a year. It was a special occasion.'

'Did she seem drunk?'

'Not "drunk". Buzzed, maybe.'

'How long were you at the restaurant?'

'About two hours.'

'Was your daughter a petite woman?'

'Slim. Not short.'

'Still. A cocktail and more than half a bottle of wine in the space of two hours. I would say that's a considerable amount of alcohol for a slim woman, wouldn't you?'

Judy breathed sharply through her nostrils. 'She liked to drink. She ate dinner, too.'

'What did she eat?'

'She had a whole piece of grilled trumpeter and a green salad, all to herself. She even took some chips from my plate.'

'Fish, salad, and a few chips. That's all?'

'She ate it all. All by herself.' Judy crumpled. 'I'm sorry. But it was a big meal for her. She had an eating disorder.'

The courtroom was intensely quiet as Judy tugged some tissues from the box, wiped her running eyes and nose, caught her breath — every snuffle and gasp audible.

'I'm going to hand you a photograph now, Ms Novak. I'd like you to describe it for the jury. Okay?'

Judy stared at her knees. 'Yes. Okay.'

'Into the mic, please.'

'Yes.' The photo appeared under her nose. She stared at it until the words were as solid as marbles in her mouth. 'It's a picture of Paulina and me at Great-O's.'

'Who took the picture?'

'One of the restaurant owners. Paulina called him "Grandy".'

'Is there anyone else in the photo? In the background?'

'Yes.' Her voice wisped. 'There's a man.'

'Can you describe what the man is wearing? A little louder, into the microphone.'

'He's in a chef's uniform. Checked black-and-white pants and a black smock.'

'Do you recognise the man?'

'Yes.' Judy glanced tearfully at the dock, but she couldn't make out his face through the blur. 'It appears to be the defendant. Sean Patrick Campbell.'

'Did you see your daughter interact with the defendant that evening?'

'No.'

'Did she mention him?'

'No.'

'Did she mention any friends or acquaintances working in the kitchen?'

'No.'

'Did she leave the table at any point that evening?'

'She might've gone to the bathroom.'

'Do you recall her going to the bathroom?'

'I don't recall. But she probably did.' Though unsure if it was permitted, Judy added, 'I did.'

'You left the table to go to the bathroom?'

'Yes.'

'How many times?'

'Once or twice.'

'Once? Or twice?'

'I think twice.' Judy reddened. 'Yes. Twice.'

'Were you apart from your daughter at any other point that evening, besides the trips to the bathroom?'

'After dinner.' Judy clutched her used-up tissues. 'She had a smoke outside while I paid the bill.'

'Did your daughter smoke often?'

'All the time.'

'Was there a particular brand of cigarettes that she preferred?'

'She usually rolled her own. To save money. She wasn't picky, though.'

'Did you notice what kind of cigarette she was smoking, when you joined her?'

'No. She stubbed it out as I walked up.'

'What happened after you left the restaurant?'

'I drove her home. Then I drove back to Mutineers' Lodge and went to bed.'

'Did your daughter have any further plans for that evening, to your knowledge?'

'No. She had an early start the next day.'

'When did you next see your daughter?'

'She came into my room and woke me around six-thirty. She was in her uniform.'

'How did she seem?'

'Happy. She teased me.' Judy's mouth quirked downwards. 'She … made me get out of bed. So she could make it for me.'

She took more tissues, balled them up and held them to her mouth. *Breathe. Just breathe.*

'Are you ready to continue, Ms Novak?'

Judy moved closer to the microphone. 'Yes.'

'Did your daughter appear to be under the influence of drugs or alcohol?'

'No. Of course not.'

'Did she seem hungover?'

'No. As I said, she was happy. Chatty. She bragged about being a morning person.'

'How long did she stay?'

'About twenty minutes.' Judy wanted to say more: the smell of her shampoo, the shimmer of her laugh, the brightness of her sneakers in the dim room. 'Not long.'

'What happened next?'

'I went back to sleep. I woke around eight-thirty. Then I showered and went out to the bistro. Paulina was working.'

'Did you speak?'

'Yes. She suggested I eat at the Blue Moon Café, so she could finish earlier.' Judy shrugged. 'We arranged to meet back at my cabin at midday and go to the beach. She wanted to go for a walk by herself after finishing work. I offered to walk with her, but she said I'd just annoy her. She liked walking fast, with her music.'

'She did that frequently?'

'Every day, to my knowledge.'

'What happened next?'

'I drove to the Blue Moon Café for breakfast. After that I went to Piney's Point and watched the surfers. I was back at Mutineers' Lodge by eleven-thirty. I put on my beach things and waited.'

'How long did you wait?'

'Two-and-a-half hours.'

'Can you describe those two-and-a-half hours?'

'Well, at first I thought she'd been held up, or maybe we got the times wrong. Then it had been over an hour, so I called. I kept calling. She didn't answer.'

Hot and painful, the tears slid down.

'I left some messages. Then I went to the front desk and spoke to her manager, Bazel. I told him to let Paulina know I'd gone out, if he saw her.' Judy steeled her voice. 'I tried not to worry. I figured, she's a grown woman, she has better things to do than spend the day with me. I drove to the pier and saw some guys unloading the supply ship. I walked a bit. Then it started to rain. I drove back to town. The shops were closed for Good Friday.'

'What happened next?'

'I saw a lady go into the jewellery shop, "Tabby's Treasures". I asked to use her phone. I left a message for Paulina saying I was coming over. Then I saw this angelfish pendant and bought it — for her birthday. I drove straight over. As soon as I got there ...'

She swallowed.

'Her Mazda was parked with the windows open. The rain had gotten in. It was a new car. She wouldn't of just left it like that. Unless she planned to be home soon.'

'What happened next, Ms Novak?'

'I tried the door of her cottage. It was unlocked. I went in. I looked around a bit. Then, well ... I blow-dried my hair. It was wet from the rain.'

'Did the residence seem disturbed in any way, Ms Novak?'

'It was tidy. Her keys were on the counter. There was a glass of water she hadn't finished. She'd do that, sometimes; pour a glass then leave it.'

'What happened next?'

Judy took a deep breath.

'Paulina's landlady, Vera, came by with some eggs. I told her Paulina was missing. She invited me up to the house and made some calls. Then she said we should call the police, and they told us to come to the station. That's when I learned about the body. We went to Cook's Falls, and Vera ID'd her. They wouldn't let me do it; they said it wasn't something for a mother to see. I kept wanting to see her, though, until someone said about her clothes being off … then I guess I understood she'd been attacked.'

Judy's welling eyes strayed back to Sean Patrick Campbell. He didn't meet them.

'No further questions, Ms Novak.'

It bucketed down, that night. Bronson and Wyatt went out for fish and chips. When they returned to the Hibiscus Hideout with the piping-hot, rain-specked bundles, Judy smelled the salt and a void opened up inside her. She burst into tears.

'Oh, Jude.' Caro put an arm around her. 'Honey.'

'I'm fine.' Judy smiled wanly at her nephews. 'It smells wonderful.'

She got herself under control as Tim and the boys unwrapped the bundles. At the sight of the chips, though, her chin quivered.

'She took the chips right off the plate. Without me even offering.'

'I know.' Caro patted her shoulder. 'It's very impressive.'

'It was so unlike her. It was … beautiful.'

'It's very beautiful.' Caro flashed a look across the table.

'It's incredible,' Tim backed her up.

'It's awesome,' Wyatt said. 'She was really good, doing that.'

'She was *so* good!' Judy nodded feverishly. 'I was so, so proud!'

'You're right to be proud, Auntie Judy,' Bronson enthused. 'I'd never be brave enough to take chips off Mum's plate without asking.'

'Oh, shush, you little shit!' Caro swatted him.

'Do you want a lemonade, Auntie Judy?' Wyatt offered a can. 'It's nice and cold.'

'Thank you, sweetheart.'

'Want some lemon wedges?'

'Thank you, Bron. That's very considerate.'

'We got tartare sauce, too. Here.'

'You're very kind.' Judy sniffed. 'Thank you, boys.'

Everyone watched with bated breath as she reached for a chip, blew on the steam, and bit in.

'Thank you,' she repeated, tears flowing down her cheeks. 'I'm fine. Really.'

———

'Only on Fairfolk,' Tim quipped, stopping for a cluster of cows on the road.

'Oh, come on!' Caro honked the horn. 'Move!'

A speckled heifer looked past their windshield, before lifting its tail and pissing in the morning sunshine. At their rear, another car slowed down. Then another.

'It's a bit of a jam, isn't it?' Judy looked at the driver behind them, recognised Campbell's defence lawyer, and swiftly looked away.

Caro prodded her husband. 'Do something.'

'And get cow piss on my loafers?'

'Show them where the grass is. Hurry up. We're late.'

Sighing, Tim got out of the car, ineffectually clapped and pointed toward the grass by the road. Judy sank deeper into the backseat. So did Bronson and Wyatt.

'Move!' Caro tooted again. 'Moooove!'

More cars gathered. Campbell's lawyer got out, joined Tim in his clapping and pointing. Then a cyclist whizzed by, parked his bike against a pine tree, and got in on the action. Only when the road was clear, and the men were patting each other's backs, did Judy recognise him.

'Dirty old man,' she muttered. 'Look at him.'

Caro looked from her to Rabbit, and understood.

'Talk about a team effort!' Tim slid back into the driver's seat, pleased with himself. 'Oww. Caro, what the hell?'

'*How dare you.*' Caro prodded him again. 'That's the man who hit Paulina.'

It rained so hard on the third day of the trial that the Islanders who'd been laying down picnic rugs outside the media marquee to watch the CCTV stayed home. An officer met Judy and Caro at the car with an umbrella and escorted them into the warm, dry courtroom.

Later, Shirley Campbell and her other son came into court with squelching shoes, clothes plastered to their slumped shoulders. Judy looked away and linked eyes with a male juror, who winked at her — not for the first time.

'Weekend plans?' asked the guy in line behind her at the bottle shop.

Without looking, Judy knew he was a journo. 'Working on my victim impact statement. You?'

'Filing a story.' He shifted his six-pack in his arms and lowered his voice. 'Can I ask you something? Off the record?'

'Well, it is your job.'

The journo peered around the shop, which was crowded with people who were already looking familiar. 'Do you think Campbell can get a fair trial on this island?'

Judy's wine rested comfortably against her hip, as Paulina once had.

'No,' she said softly. 'But life isn't fair.'

As Judy was crossing the carpark, a border collie scampered up to her, its fur stringy with saltwater and sand. Behind it lagged a beetle-browed old man.

'Yorana,' Rocky greeted her.

'Y—' Judy couldn't bring herself to speak their language. 'Hello.'

She smiled tightly and continued to the car. Caro was already waiting inside, with some shopping bags.

'I bought veal,' she bragged. 'From Paulina's boyfriend.'

Judy heaved a sigh.

'What's wrong? Wanna go back and flirt with him?'

'This place is too bloody small.' Judy passed the wine bottle.

The cow letterbox jogged her memory, though the street didn't. Vera met her out front, still in her church clothes.

'Did you want some lunch? Or just coffee?' Vera made as if to hug her but then pulled away at the last moment. 'Milo?'

'Just coffee.' Judy tried to look less stand-offish. 'Milk and sugar. Thank you.'

As Vera made the coffee, Judy looked at the couch, the walls, the mantle, but felt as numb as she would've standing in a display home.

'Did you renovate?' Judy asked when Vera swept in with her tray of mugs and biscuits. 'It looks different.'

Vera laughed gruffly. 'This house hasn't changed since the eighties. *You* look different, but.'

'Do I?'

'Better.'

'I'm not.'

'Better at hiding it, then. How's your sister?'

'Driving me bonkers.' Judy took up her mug. 'How's your — the one whose room I stayed in?'

Vera surveyed her curiously. 'You must be better, to ask that.'

'I'm not.' Judy met her gaze. 'I'm the same, deep down. There's no getting over it.'

'Miti's going through a mid-life crisis,' Vera obliged. 'Talking about moving back here. I told her she's crazy.'

'Yes, she must be.' Judy blew on her coffee . 'It'll be nice for you, though, having …'

'It'll be nice.'

While Judy caught her breath, Vera noticed the newspaper on the coffee table, attempted to sweep it out of sight.

'It's alright.' Judy waved a hand. 'I've read it.'

'Good for toilet paper. Foodfolk's running low.'

'They got my name wrong. "Julie Novak".' Judy shrugged, smiled. 'I hate how they put their photos side-by-side. Like they're a couple. I s'pose it's what sells. I hate it, though.'

'He's not much to look at. Not ugly. Just … not much. I couldn't believe he'd lived here longer than Paulina. I don't know him from Adam.'

'That's what everyone says. I'd rather not talk about him.'

As they sipped through the silence, Miss Katie strolled into the room, sharpened her claws on the couch. Vera hissed at her. Unfazed, the cat jumped up next to Judy, bunted her hand until she reluctantly scratched its ears and murmured, 'Hello, pussycat.'

'Did you want to see … ?' Vera nodded outside. 'It's still there, like I said.'

Of course, this was what Judy had really come for.

'Are those avocadoes?' Judy marvelled, as Vera walked her through the orchard. 'Gawd, they're big here!'

'Take as many as you want.'

'Oh, I don't want to spoil your harvest.'

'They grow wild. Can hardly give them away.' Vera stopped as they neared the cottage. 'I'll leave you to it. Give me a yell if you need anything.'

Judy kept her cool as the older woman ambled back to the house in her Sunday best. As soon as she'd climbed the porch and opened the cottage door, though, her legs weakened.

She knelt and kissed the walls that had once held Paulina.

Judy swallowed her first Valium of the trial's second week soon after the forensic pathologist took the stand. He was describing the worst of the stab wounds: how the knife had been twisted inside her girl's chest, spearing the heart and filling the lungs with blood.

Caro got as far as the broken pelvis, the defence's claim that it could've been caused by a hit-and-run, before crying, 'Lying bastard!' and bolting out of the courtroom.

'Can I have a Valium, Jude?' she asked, returning raw-eyed and stinking of smoke.

Leaving court at sunset, jelly-kneed, Judy bumped into a burly bloke outside the media marquee. He grabbed her shoulder and waved a can of Pine Brew in her face.

'Ma'am! Gimme a minute alone with the mainie bastard. I'll cut off his dick!'

'Yes.' Judy nodded. 'Okay.'

'I'll cut off his dick,' he repeated. 'I'll feed it to the sharks.'

Judy nodded again. 'Good. Okay.'

'That won't be necessary,' Tim intervened, ushering Judy away.

When she got back to her room at the Hibiscus Hideout, Judy ate two crackers with cheese and crawled under the covers. She woke three hours before her alarm to the revving of drink-drivers, needed another Valium to sleep again.

Shirley Campbell usually avoided glancing toward their side of the courtroom, but the day her other son showed up with a bruised jaw, she shot Judy anxious looks, like a dog begging not to be put down.

Sean still wouldn't look her way, though. Not even when the drugs allowed her to stare at him for an hour at a time, longer. Long enough to memorise his unmemorable skull.

Before the jury was sent out to deliberate on Thursday, they viewed Sean Patrick Campbell's retracted confession tape — the one defence claimed had been made under the influence of drugs and duress by the WA Police. It went for an hour. Sean never raised his voice; had to be asked several times to speak up. He sat with his hands between his clenched knees, shoulders rounded, rocking slightly. When asked how Paulina had died, he said, 'My car hit her.' When asked about the stab-wounds, he shrugged. When asked why her clothes were off, he said, 'I'm not a sicko.'

The 'HAPPY BIRTHDAY PAULINA' graffiti had long ago been scrubbed from King's Lookout. Judy spent a long time looking out. Every now and then, a car would swish past and the driver would raise their hand, and she'd raise her hand — as if she had nothing against these cursed people and their cursed land.

From King's Lookout, she drove to the cemetery. Parked and strolled through the dead Kings and Carlyles down to Tombstone Beach. The sea was the same blue-grey as the eyes that greeted her in the mirror every day; eyes that now watered from the salty wind. She dug in her handbag for her journal, perched on a damp rock and read:

I lost my innocence the day I lost Paulina.

The wind whisked up the pages, whisked her hair. Judy shut her journal with a sigh; kicked off her sandals and wandered to the shore.

A bit of sea-rock, pale and porous as tripe. A metallic abalone shell. A blanched sea-urchin, reminiscent of a small animal's skull. She collected them cheerfully, but by the time she was trudging up from the beach, she felt silly and futile. She dumped them among the graves.

I was fifty-two years old and I lost an innocence I didn't know I had.

There was a red Commodore parked beyond the cemetery, the driver idling at the wheel. Judy's eyes connected with his. They widened. He lifted his hand from the wheel. She raised hers. Tentatively approached.

'Ms Novak.' Jesse rolled down his window. 'I … didn't notice you.'

'That's alright. I'm not very noticeable.'

'I didn't mean—' he stammered. 'It's cold for the beach, eh.'

'A bit cold, yes.' Judy hadn't felt it until he mentioned it, but now a shiver went through her. 'Very windy. I was trying to … read. But the pages kept flipping.'

'Anything good?'

'Sorry?'

'What you were reading.'

'Oh, no.' Judy waved her hand. 'Just my victim impact statement.'

'Oh. Right.'

'I'm sure it's fine. It's just one of those things.' She shrugged. 'I've looked at it so many times, I don't know anymore.'

'Yeah, I get that. With my designs sometimes, I'll overthink it.' His eyes were bloodshot, the lashes dark and matted. 'Then it's like I forget how to draw.'

'You're lucky, to be artistic.' Judy smiled. 'I wish I could draw. Or write. Anything.'

'You were good on TV.'

'Oh, come off it.'

'No, really. You made me cry.'

'Oh?' She laughed. 'Sorry!'

He smiled at her sidelong. 'I forgive you, eh.'

Judy laughed again, patted her hair. 'Gawd — this wind! I thought I'd clear my head, coming here, but all I've done is mess up my hair.'

'I can look at it, if you want,' Jesse offered, and Judy's face screwed up. 'The statement. If you need, like, a second opinion.'

'Oh!' Her face smoothed. '*Would* you?'

'Yeah. For sure.'

Eyes prickling, Judy scurried to the passenger side, watched him clear the seat.

'Sorry about the mess.'

'It's fine.' It *was* very messy though — like the cars of the surfer-boys she'd dated in high school. She noticed a scummy bong in the centre console. 'You don't smoke that while *driving*, do you?'

'Oh, nay,' Jesse bluffed. 'Not really.'

'I don't mean to judge. Just, you could have an accident, doing that.'

'Yeah. Sorry.' Jesse swept the bong out of sight. 'It's not like with Campbell, though. He was mixing it with steroids and shit.'

'I know you're nothing like Campbell.' Judy sighed. 'But still.'

'Sorry, Ms Novak.'

Judy toyed with her handbag zipper. 'The hit-and-run story is a load of crap. That doesn't mean it couldn't happen someday, though.'

'Sorry,' Jesse repeated. 'Do you still want me to read that statement?'

Meekly, Judy unzipped her bag and handed over the journal. 'I hope you can read it alright.'

'Yeah.' He gave her that sidelong look again. 'I can read, Ms Novak.'

'Oh, shush!' Judy batted his arm. 'Get on with it, then.'

'Sorry.' Jesse glanced down at the page. 'You have really nice handwriting, eh.'

For some reason, that made Judy blush so hard she had to turn to the window. But it wasn't long before her gaze strayed back to the beautiful eyelashes, pillowy lips. The tattooed, well-muscled arms tensing as he shut the journal.

'Yeah,' Jesse mumbled, giving it back. 'It's good.'

'"Good"?'

'Sorry.' He pinched between his eyes. 'I don't know what else to say. You sort of just ripped my heart right out of my chest.'

'So it's better than good?'

'It's really fucking good, Ms Novak.'

Jesse tried to smile, but his face had gone red, his eyes were brimming.

'Well!' Judy said softly. 'If we're dropping f-bombs, you'd better call me "Judy".'

'Judy.' He took a deep breath, closed his eyes. 'Can I see that again, Judy?'

Bemused, Judy passed him the journal. Instead of rereading the statement, though, he pulled the pen from the spine and wrote down his phone number.

'That's me. If you ever want to talk. It's the same as when she lived with me.'

'Oh,' Judy murmured. 'Thank you.'

'I'm in the Fairfolk phone book too, under "Camilleri".' Jesse swallowed. 'He was right next to me that whole time. "Campbell". All those years of wondering and his name was right next to mine.'

'It's a small world,' Judy mused. 'Especially here.'

He wiped his nose. 'Yeah.'

Judy would've liked to comfort him, mother him. But from the way he'd curled his body toward the window, she knew he wanted to be left alone.

'Anyway, I'm glad it's small enough that I bumped into you again.' Slipping her journal back inside her handbag, she tapped his knee lightly. 'See you around, Jesse.'

'See you, Ms … Judy.'

As it happened, though, they didn't see each other again. The next afternoon, the jury returned their verdict and Sean Patrick Campbell was sentenced to life — with the possibility of parole after eighteen years.

HUNTING AND GATHERING

Paulina's face had never looked older or uglier. She found five grey hairs within forty-eight hours, then kept seeing more whenever she hobbled to the bathroom. Or hallucinating them.

'If you're not sure, don't pluck them,' Judy advised her. 'It could be a trick of the light. You have beautiful hair, Paulina. You don't want to be pulling it out willy-nilly.'

'Fuck you!' Paulina cried — not because it was bad advice, but because her head felt like a speed bump that trucks kept driving over. 'I'll pull it all out! I'll shave it!'

'Now you're being melodramatic.' Judy sighed. 'Trust me, it's just stress. I wasn't even twenty when I found my first greys, after the first miscarriage—'

'Ugh! I hate taking after you.'

'You don't take after me in everything. Your hair's much more beautiful. Please, don't shave it off. I'll cry rivers.'

'Fuckkkkk! Youuuuu!'

'You're still committed to this "cold turkey" thing, then?'

'Yeahhhh! I'm stone-cold sober!'

'Well, I gathered as much. I'm very proud of you, darling. I have faith in you.'

'Why won't you leave me alone, then?'

'Because … I like the sound of your voice. Even when you're cursing a blue streak. I like to know you're still hanging on.'

'I should bloody well kill myself, so I don't have to hear your voice.'

'Don't, Paulina,' Judy said tersely. 'Please, don't.'

It was so quiet, Paulina could hear the ringing in her ears; they were always ringing, since what Car did. 'Let me die, bitch.'

Judy made a faint, wispy sound.

'No. That's not happening. Sorry.'

Paulina exhaled through clenched teeth. 'I'm fine, okay? Just, my head's killing me.'

'Did you take some Panadol?'

'They do shit-all.'

'I'm sorry to hear that.' Judy's voice was soft as tissue-paper, but it may as well have been a steel scourer. 'It's withdrawal. You'll have to grin and bear it. Keep the light low. Put a cool cloth on your head. Make sure you drink plenty of water. And *eat*, Paulina—'

'Fuuuuck! Offffff!'

'Okay.' Judy inhaled sharply. 'Okay.'

'Okay? Fuck off now.'

'Okay. But call me, please. If you need anything. If you have any bad thoughts. Before you do anything … out of the ordinary. Call me?'

Paulina hung up, screaming.

She didn't scream when she saw Car standing over her bed in the night. The scream stuck in her throat. She waited for him to move. He didn't. She squinted, and his shape became her moonlit curtains. But the fear stayed in her; she heard bugs flicking against the windows, the tin roof creaking. Ribs aching, she got up to check the locks, then felt her way to the bathroom and took a frightened dump in the dark.

When she reached for toilet paper, there was none.

Cursing the wood-fired hot water system, she took an icy shower, emerged white-breathed and jittery. She rugged up and chain-smoked on the porch. The stars faded as the sky turned grey-blue, rosy. Feral roosters crowed. When she saw Vera stomping from the main house to the wood pile, she went back indoors.

Vera knocked while Paulina was watching *Jerry Springer* with her sunnies on, volume tuned to that sweet spot that covered the ringing in her ears but didn't hurt too bad.

'Yeah?' Paulina mumbled, dragging herself to the flyscreen.

'The chooks are overdoing it.' Vera brandished a basket. 'Mind if I offload these?'

Hair falling in her face, Paulina opened the flyscreen. 'Cheers.'

'Avocados, too.' Vera nodded toward the orchard. 'Take as many as you want. We've got them coming out of our ears.'

'Cheers.'

'I'm doing a run to the shops later. Save you a trip?'

'S'alright,' Paulina mumbled — then remembered. 'Actually. Toilet paper?'

'Anything else?'

'Um. Panadol?'

'Some bread? Eggs on toast.'

'S'alright.' Paulina's eyes misted behind her sunglasses. 'Yeah. Alright.'

'Write a list, if you think of anything. Stick it on the door. I'll swing by on my way out.'

Mumbling her thanks, Paulina shut herself inside. She was sticking the list to the door when Vera's cat, Katie, snuck past her feet.

Paulina fell asleep with Katie tucked against her sore ribs like a hot water bottle. When she woke, Katie was gone, and the groceries were unpacked; the receipt stuck to the fridge with a starfish magnet.

'I'm fat. I wanna go for my walk.'

'You're not fat. Don't feel bad about skipping your walks for a while. You won't get fat overnight. What did you eat today?'

'Avocado.'

'Just avocado?'

'Leave me alone.'

'Can you please eat something else? Please, for me.'

'I wanna walk.'

'It's too late for walking. And you need energy to walk. Why don't you eat a proper dinner and, who knows, you might be well enough tomorrow.'

'Fuck you!'

'Go make a piece of toast. Go on.'

'Don't tell me what to do!'

'I'd like it if you made some toast, Paulina. I really would.'

'I don't give a fuck!'

'Well, even so. You need carbs. Protein, too. You said your landlady brought you some eggs? Why don't you boil one to have with soldiers?'

'I'm not a baby!'

'Or, fried. Scrambled.'

'Too hard!'

'Well, okay. Just some avo on toast, then. You can have the eggs tomorrow.'

'I'm tired.'

'I'll help you make it. Where do you keep the bread?'

'Fridge.'

'It keeps the mould away, doesn't it? You can always freeze it, too.'

'My head hurts.'

'I'm not surprised; you haven't eaten, and you're still withdrawing. Did you find the bread?'

'Yeah.'

'How brown do you want it?'

'I dunno.' Paulina started to cry. 'I don't know, Mum.'

'That's alright. What setting is it on? Can you see the little numbers?'

'Three.'

'Let's go with three, then. Put it in. Make sure it's plugged in and switched on. Is it?'

'Yeah.'

'Good. Now we wait.'

Paulina cried while she waited. 'It hurts, Mum.'

'Shhh. It's alright.'

'Muuuuum.'

'I'm here.'

'When's it gonna stop?'

'I don't know, darling. I wish I knew. It's a big thing, what you're doing. Your body's so dependent ... not to mention your *brain*. It'll get easier, though.' Judy's voice became muffled, wet. 'Oh, darling. If you'd just come home. You could go to rehab—'

'No!'

'Or if you'd let me come—'

'No!'

'There's no shame in needing help, Paulina. Please—'

'Fuck you! Fuck off!'

Paulina hung up. The toast popped. She stared at it, nostrils flared, heart racing, till the phone rang again.

'Fuck you!' she answered it.

'Is that toast ready?'

'Yeah.'

'Where's that avo?'

Paulina picked an avocado from the bowl on the counter. 'I need to cut it.'

'Careful, now.'

She picked up a knife. 'I wanna cut myself.'

'No, darling. Let's cut that avo instead. Gently, now.'

'I hate you.'

'I know. Gently. Cut it in half. Is it halved?'

'Yeah.' Paulina's stomach turned. 'It looks gross.'

'If there's brown, just skim that off. Do you have something to spread it with?'

'Fork?'

'A fork'll do. Why don't we put the knife away—'

'Have some faith in me!'

'You don't need it anymore. Can you put it in the sink, out of the way?'

Paulina threw the knife in the sink with a clatter. 'You're such a bitch!'

'I know. Now, let's spread the avo on the toast. You're doing well. How's it going?'

'Yeah.'

'The avo's on the toast?'

'Yeah.' Paulina sniffed. 'It looks shit.'

'Looks don't matter. Try it.'

'It's ugly. *I'm* ugly.'

'You're a beautiful girl. You need to eat so you can keep being beautiful. Please, try.'

Paulina bit into the toast. Every bone in her head got sharper. The crunch was loud as gravel in her ears.

'It hurts!'

'I know, darling,' Judy murmured. 'I know it hurts. But it's good for you. You're very brave, very good. Keep trying; I'm right here with you.'

It took half an hour for Paulina to change out of her trakkies and jumper and into her sports bra and shorts, to tie the shoes that went with them, to clip her Discman to her waistband. The shorts cut into her soft flesh like wire. So did the bra. She didn't like how white her skin was or how it folded over the tight clothes. The bruises were black and brown now.

She put her headphones on. They softened the sounds of the world; the wind in the trees, birdsong, someone mowing a lawn. But not the ringing in her ears.

She got as far as Vera and Rocky's back porch before she got goosebumps. She continued uphill. Her armpits moistened. The driveway was covered in brown dust.

She reached the cattle grid. The cow letterbox. No mail for her.

She saw the road, no cars on it. Shadows of trees on the road. Her heart swelled. Then the wind became a hiss; the birds, alarm bells.

Sharply, she turned back.

'I'm scared,' Paulina whimpered. 'Mum. I'm scared.'

'What's wrong?' Judy sounded foggy, faraway. 'What scared you?'

'Mum!'

'Shhh. I'm here.' Her voice got clearer. 'What's wrong? Was it a bad dream?'

'I saw a man.'

'What man? Where?'

'In my curtains.'

'Are you looking at the curtains now?'

'Yeah.'

'Is there a man?'

'No.'

'There's no man. You'd hear, if a man broke in. The dog would bark, wouldn't it?'

'Why doesn't he just kill me in my sleep.'

Judy sighed. 'I know it's scary living alone sometimes. The things that go through your head at night. I get scared, too.'

'No!'

'No? I'm not allowed to be scared?'

'No.'

Judy laughed, unexpectedly. 'You're a funny little thing.'

'Don't patronise me!'

'Scaring me shitless in the middle of the night, then telling me I can't be scared?' She laughed again. 'I *do* get scared. I'm scared when you're scared. Please, don't be scared.'

Paulina started crying. 'I don't know what's real anymore.'

'Shhh. I know, it's confusing sometimes,' Judy whispered. 'I'm real, if that helps. You know I'm real?'

'Yeah.'

'And you know how much I love you?'

'Yeah.'

'There you go. Your mum loves you. That's very real. Okay?'

Paulina couldn't answer; her chest was clogged with grief.

'Don't worry about curtains and men and things. They're all a big joke. As long as you know you're loved. You know that?'

'Yeah.'

'Okay?'

'Okay.'

'Okay. Get some sleep, baby.'

There was a time of day, just before sunset, when things could go one way or another. When the whole world looked like a diorama, the sky a slow-moving painting, and sometimes she felt lucky to be exactly where she was, smoking on her porch, and other times she wanted to take the washing line and knot it around her neck.

Instead, she took the car keys, drove the Mazda. The phone was screaming at her when she got back, close to midnight.

'Paulina! Oh, gawd. Paulina. Where *were* you?'

'Driving.'

'Driving? Where?'

'Everywhere.' Her hands were trembling; her head was cloudy; she was faint with hunger — but ecstatic. 'I drove the whole island.'

'*Why?*'

'I had some things to see.'

'What things?'

'Outside.'

'At night?'

'There's less people.'

'Oh, Paulina. I must've called fifty times.'

'Bloody hell.' Paulina's tummy rumbled. 'Get a life.'

'Paulina: you *are* my life. If anything happened—'

'I was just driving! Fuck!'

'Okay.' Judy breathed out slowly. 'You were gone a long time, that's all.'

'I had things to see!'

'What things?'

'Cliffs and things.'

'Paulina …' Judy quavered. 'When you're gone for hours, and you tell me you were out looking at cliffs, what am I supposed to think?'

'Stop thinking about me!' Paulina spat. 'Get a life!'

'Look: I know you don't want me to, but I think it's best if I come over there ASAP—'

'No!'

'It's not up for discussion. Either you come home or I—'

'I'll kill myself if you come here!'

'Paulina, that's exactly *why*—'

'I'll jump off a cliff! The sharks'll eat me! You'll never find my body!'

'You wouldn't do that to me.'

'Then don't do that to *me*.'

'Darling. Please. I just want to see you.'

'Tough shit. I don't wanna be seen.' Paulina fingered the cigarette burns she'd made inside her arms, earlier that evening. 'Not like this.'

'Baby. I've seen you all sorts of ways. I gave birth to you, for chrissakes—'

'I didn't ask to be born, you fucking bitch!'

Judy began weeping, quiet and hopeless. 'Oh, sweetheart. Please—'

'*Please!*' Paulina screamed. 'Don't come till I say. You can come see me, but only when I say. Okay?'

Judy snuffled and sobbed for a long time before agreeing. 'Okay.'

'I need to eat now.' Solemnly, Paulina opened the pantry. 'Can you help me eat?'

'Kill me,' Paulina said, the next time she woke to Car standing over her bed. 'Just kill me.'

He didn't.

She rolled onto her tummy and put a hand inside her knickers.

Knives. Broken bottles. The sharp lids of cans. The hot tips of cigarettes. Fishing hooks. Cattle prods. Barbed wire. Jagged cliffs. Fists.

She made herself come, imagining all the ways he could suffer. Then her breathing slowed and the ringing in her ears resumed, loud as ever.

At first Paulina was annoyed when all the channels kept showing the same thing, but after a while she found it soothing. First one tower, frilled with smoke and flames, then the other, then the roaring panic that had nothing to do with her under her blankets on her couch on her island. Judy seemed chipper about it, too.

'It makes you think, doesn't it? Things could be worse! Imagine if you'd got a job in New York instead of Fairfolk.'

'I'd rather be in a burning tower than listening to your stupid voice.'

'Well …' Judy gathered her breath. 'If you're sick of my voice, you could always speak to a professional—'

'No!'

'Paulina. Baby. I love you, but I — I'm not that smart. I can't—'

'Stop crying!'

'Sorry, baby. But don't you think a doctor would be better? Someone who knows things? I don't—' Judy choked on her words. 'I just don't know anymore.'

Paulina hung up. Let the phone ring out three times, before she answered again.

'Bitch,' she muttered. 'Don't cry.'

'I'm sorry. That was stupid.' Judy breathed in-out, in-out. 'I won't do it again. But I mean what I said. I'm just a receptionist. Wouldn't you rather a doctor? Someone smart?'

'I'm not paying to talk to some man with glasses.'

'It doesn't have to be a man. And I've said a thousand times, *I'll* pay—'

'It's always a man with glasses or some judgmental old hippie.'

'You're generalising.'

'You're giving me a headache.'

'Just think about it. Okay?'

'My head really hurts.'

'Okay. Let's get dinner on. Do you have any more of that tuna?'

'I gave it to the cat.'

'Paulina! You need protein more than that cat does!'

'She was meowing and stuff.'

'Well, okay. What else do you have?'

'Just … canned shit.'

'Can you be more specific?'

'Peas … corn … soup … Ugh, it's all just shit waiting to happen.'

Judy laughed. 'You're right, you know. Which one looks less shit, though? If you had to choose?'

Paulina sighed. 'It's all shit, Mum.'

Everything seemed jagged. She walked anyway. Past the yard full of palm trees with metal rings around their trunks. A wind-bloated Fairfolk flag. A buzzing electric fence. She turned on her music, but it was so loud, she turned it off right away. It wasn't just her throbbing head; it was not being able to hear every crackle of the world, to respond quick.

She walked to the end of the road, heart thudding. Turned the corner. Climbed uphill. Stepped over a crust of old cow shit. A truck slid past, driven by a man in hi-vis. She didn't know him, but he waved; she waved back. Okay.

She walked a bit more, expecting more cars, tense with expectation. No cars came. Sweat slicked her ribs, the space between her tits. The road ahead curved, dipped.

She'd done it many times before … but not today.

Once safely inside her flat, she inexplicably opened the fridge, fried an egg, and ate it.

The phone rang, soon after. Bazel, Mutineers' Lodge.

'Still good to come back Monday?'

'Yeah,' Paulina bluffed. 'Monday.'

'Not planning on hijacking a plane and flying it into St Bartholomew's this weekend?'

'Huh?'

'Rabbit and Rita.'

'Yeah. Nah. They deserve a long, sexless life together, hey.'

After hanging up, she closed the curtains, took off her exercise clothes, lay on the bed, and thought of the man in hi-vis, stopping his truck; licking her sweat, licking her cunt, fucking her good.

After, she went to the mirror and looked at her bruises. They'd gone yellow.

Then she tried on her Mutes' uniform.

It still fit. Her body looked good in it, if she ignored her pallor, the burns on her arms. Her face, less good — but better than it had been. Makeup would help.

'Okay,' she told herself. 'You're okay.'

Then her face became too ugly to look at.

'I'm gonna die alone.'

'You'd die alone if you married that old man. Trust me, you're better off.'

'Yep. Going grey and can't eat a cup of noodles without my mum's help.'

'I think you can. Wanna give it a go?'

'Nah.'

'Come on.' When Paulina stayed quiet, Judy said decisively, 'Here's the plan: I'll say bye for now, and you'll try your best, then I'll call back in half an hour for a debrief. Okay?'

Paulina tried not to think of worms, decaying white flesh, choking down the noodles. Or piss, drinking the yellowy-brown noodle water. She tried to ignore the freeze-dried bits of carrot, which looked like something already chewed and spewed up. She resisted the urge to spew and sat teary-eyed in front of the TV, sipping water till her mum rang back.

'How'd it go?'

'I ate like two-thirds.'

'Two-thirds! Well done, Paulina!'

'I wanna walk.'

'You should rest. You have a big day tomorrow. Are you feeling up to it?'

'I guess.'

'Did you iron your uniform?'

'Not yet.'

'You should. And set your alarm, nice and early. Give yourself plenty of time.'

'Yeah, yeah.'

'Call me in the morning, if you need help.'

'Yeah, yeah.'

'I'm so proud of you, sweetheart.'

'Yeah, yeah.'

Paulina watched TV for a bit. Then she laid out her clothes, set her alarm for five. Then, haunted by the clot of food in her stomach, she got her keys and drove: past Tiffany's shrine, past Rabbit's, all the way to the dark, empty place where the cliffs met the sea.

She closed her eyes and listened to the ringing in her ears.

'You look … pale and interesting,' Baz commented, when she swung past reception with a cartload of dirty linen.

'Pale and boring, more like. I'm three weeks sober.'

Baz eyed the black sleeves under her uniform. 'And here I was thinking you'd been shooting up.'

'It's cold today.' Paulina tugged her sleeves. 'I get cold easy.'

'Whatever you say, Westpac. Just don't let it happen again. This place hasn't been the same without you.'

Hot-faced, Paulina pushed her cart to the laundry. When she emerged, Baz was handing a business card to a sprightly couple in visors and hiking boots. 'Give The Car Kings a call, if those hills get too much for you. They do all our car rentals.'

'Better off walking!' Paulina jeered. 'Car King *loves* ripping off tourists.'

On her way back from Mutes', Paulina stopped at Jellyfish Fuel to fill her tank. She had her sunnies on, her back to the storefront; between the purr of her engine and the petrol fumes, she didn't stand a chance.

'Yorana, sweetheart.' Car breezed past, sausage roll in hand. 'How's the Mazda?'

Petrol splashed her leg as she jolted away from the fuel tank. Flashing his big teeth, Car sauntered back to his car.

She looked for him again in her curtains after lights-out. He never appeared. Her skin grew scalding-hot; her heart rapid. *Yorana, sweetheart.* She pictured his teeth, his eyes, the petrol pump. Orgasms of fire. His fat, popping and sizzling like bacon.

'I'm fat.'

'We've been through this, darling. You're not.'

'Am so.' Paulina glared at her belly button. 'This's the fattest I've ever been.'

'You've just had dinner. You're full. Someday, you'll learn to like the feeling.'

'Everything's fat.' A tear plopped onto Paulina's chest. 'Even my boobs are fat.'

Judy's breath caught. 'Paulina …'

'Don't.'

'Just … after last time …'

'I'm not a slut!'

'I didn't say you were.' Judy levelled her voice. 'That guy from the work crew? The married one?'

'I dumped him ages ago!'

'And you've been getting your periods?'

'Yeah … no. I dunno.'

'Think. Please.'

Paulina thought so hard, it brought tears to her eyes. 'I dunno, okay? I've had a lot on my mind.'

'I know it's hard keeping track. But, try. Please.'

Paulina thought of Car's fingers, wiping the cum off her face, thrusting inside her.

'I'm such a slut.'

'You're single. No one's judging. But if there's any chance—'

Car's fists, her ribs.

'Nup. No way.'

'No?'

'No,' Paulina repeated. 'No way.'

'You're sure?'

'I'm just fat, okay? You keep force-feeding me. What do you expect.'

'Oh, Paulina.' Judy sighed. 'There's nothing wrong with having food in your stomach. Try not to let it get to you. And try to keep better track, okay?'

After hanging up, Paulina pulled her diary from the drawer and flicked through the pages, racking her brain. *C wants anal. Should I?* asked her three-month-old handwriting, and her heart broke for how innocent the question seemed, now.

'Any nausea?' asked Dr Jimmy Greatorex, who was about as old as her dad would've been if he was still around.

'Yeah. A bit.'

'Vomiting?'

'Nah, but I feel like it sometimes. Around food.'

Dr Jimmy glanced at her wrists. 'You're very thin.'

'Always have been.'

'How's your diet?'

'Vegetarian, mostly.'

He shook his grey head. 'You need red meat at least once a week.'

'I'd feel like a murderer, driving past all those cows every day.'

'I'll prescribe you some iron pills.' He shook his head again and snuck a look at something else — her skin, her hair? 'Multivitamins, too.'

'Cheers.'

'Can you hop on the scales?'

'No offence, but can I just do the test already?'

'It won't take a second.'

It took many seconds; he was so old and slow. Paulina avoided looking at the numbers, but she knew from the way Dr Jimmy was scrutinising them that he wasn't happy.

'How tall did you say you were?'

'160 centimetres.'

'You look taller.'

'It's my shoes. Can I do the test now?'

Frowning, Dr Jimmy passed her a cup and pointed her down the hall. She peed in furious fits and starts till it was full, then went to the mirror and slapped some colour into her cheeks, took down her hair and fluffed it up.

'Three minutes.' Dr Jimmy took the cup and indicated for her to sit again. 'Mind if I listen to your heart?'

'Yeah, alright.'

Paulina shivered as the stethoscope's cool metal roamed her chest. 'It's very fast.'

'I'm nervous.'

'Take a few deep breaths, in and out.'

Paulina breathed.

'It's still fast.' He took off his stethoscope. 'Have you been under any stress lately?'

Paulina rolled her eyes. 'Yeah, you could say that.'

'Are you a smoker?'

'Yeah. I know it's bad, but I feel worse if I don't.'

'Anxious?'

'Yeah.'

'Drinking?'

'Quit a few weeks ago.'

'What prompted that?'

'Just … healthy lifestyle choice.'

'Any withdrawal symptoms?'

'I dunno.'

'Headaches, dizziness, mood swings, sweating, insomnia, fatigue … ?'

'Yeah. All that. Specially the headaches.'

Dr Jimmy looked away as tears filled her eyes. 'Mind if I check your blood pressure?'

'Do what you gotta do, Doc.'

She was embarrassed of her thin arm, how thickly he had to swaddle it in Velcro before pumping. The band tightened, stinging like a mosquito bite.

'Low,' he proclaimed, unsurprised. Then, without warning, he got up and examined the stick in the cup. 'Congratulations.'

'*Congratulations?*'

'It's negative.'

'Fuck.' Paulina wiped her eyes. 'Thank fuck.'

'I'd be surprised if it came out positive, at your weight.' He pursed his lips. 'I'd recommend gaining a stone at least, if you ever plan on conceiving.'

'Stone?'

'Six or seven kilos … at least. Ten would be preferable.'

'Yeah, nah.' She reached for her handbag. 'Thanks, Doc.'

'It'd be beneficial, not only for fertility reasons. You're at risk of developing osteoporosis, heart failure …' He opened a drawer. 'I have some pamphlets.'

'S'alright. I'm right.'

The phone rang. Dr Jimmy gestured for her to wait. 'I'm with a patient,' he said into the receiver, then his brows jumped up; he switched to Fayrf'k.

Paulina inched toward the door.

'Hold on.' Dr Jimmy held up a hand again. 'Ten minutes. Aye.'

He hung up, handed over the pamphlets.

'Emergency?' Paulina asked, stuffing them in her bag.

'They need a coroner at King's Pier.' Dr Jimmy scrawled a prescription. 'One of the blokes had a heart attack while unloading the supply ship. Dead on site.'

'Geez!' Paulina's stomach butterflied. 'Did they say who?'

'Do you know The Car Kings?'

'*The* Car King?'

'That's the one.' Dr Jimmy handed over the prescription. 'Take them with vitamin C, for maximum effectiveness. Don't take them on an empty stomach.'

'Cheers! You're a lifesaver.'

'No saving this one, I'm afraid. Forty-seven, overweight, and doing the work of a man half his age. It was an accident waiting to happen.'

'When your time's up, your time's up!' Paulina bustled to the door, grin spreading like wildfire. 'Carpe diem, Doc!'

She laughed all the way to the bottle-O.

INCEST?

Just when it seemed like life was moving on, her voice came calling from beyond the grave.

'J-Jesse? It's Judy Novak. Paulina's mum.'

Not Paulina. But she sounded like her. *Fuck.*

'Sorry to call out of the blue. Just, I never told you: that CD you made for Paulina's birthday? I very much enjoyed it. Well, maybe "enjoyed" isn't the word. But I listened to it, many times …'

That CD. He'd forgotten all about it. Like he'd forgotten about giving Paulina's mum his number, in a moment of desperation.

'This probably sounds strange, but listening to that CD was the only way I could fall asleep, for a while … Anyway, I stopped that. I started keeping it in my car instead. To listen to after work, if I was having a bad day.'

Why was she telling him all this? In the middle of the night? It was like being dragged out of bed and crucified.

'The thing is — it's just … it was so *silly* of me. It's been such a hot week. I didn't think. It gets so hot in my car, and I left it too long and I guess — it got burned or something?' She gave a small, disbelieving laugh. 'I didn't know that could happen. Did you?'

Jesse realised she was expecting an answer.

'Yeah,' he said. 'I guess that could happen.'

Judy started weeping.

'Sorry. It was so stupid of me. This is so stupid, calling you like this. I just — don't know what to do …'

The more she cried, the more she sounded like Paulina. The more he felt the nails driving in.

'Judy,' he said, gently as he could — which wasn't very gentle. 'What do you want?'

She whimpered like a scolded child.

'I … don't expect you to make me another CD. If you could just help me remember the names of the songs and the order they're in, I'll do the rest.'

Jesse's heart crumpled like a kicked mound of sand. He held the phone to his chest and made a shocked, strangled sound.

'Sorry.' He brought the phone back to his ear. 'Give me a sec.'

On the other end of the line, Judy sobbed. Jesse placed the receiver down quickly, dashed to the bathroom and let it all out.

'Jess?' Areta rapped softly on the bathroom door. 'Are you okay?'

'Yeah.' He splashed his face. 'Just … sick. I threw up.'

Areta was still in the hall when he came out, her eyes sleepy-squinty, hair wild, though it'd been in a tight, lacquered bun coming off the plane in her uniform that afternoon.

'Is it gastro?' she fretted. 'I can't fly if I get gastro.'

'It's fine.' Jesse reached for her waist. 'Go back to bed.'

'I'm going to my hotel,' she said, and elbowed past him to the bathroom.

Forlornly, Jesse crept back to the lounge, picked up the phone. 'Are you still there?'

'Yes,' Judy said bashfully. 'I thought you'd hung up.'

'I would never hang up on you,' Jesse promised. 'You're Paulina's mum.'

One call. In the middle of the night. Then life would move on.

Except, somehow, he knew she wasn't done with him. When he heard her voice two weeks later, he wasn't surprised.

'Sorry, it's Judy again.' She didn't sound sorry, though. 'I wanted to let you know it worked. The CD.'

'Oh,' Jesse mumbled. 'Good.'

'Jesse …' She let his name linger. 'Can I ask you something?'

'Um. Yeah. Go ahead.'

Judy lowered her voice. 'They're all love songs, aren't they? You were in love with her?'

'No,' he said, quick as a flinch. 'I wasn't.'

'Come on, Jesse. It's obvious you loved her.'

'As a friend,' Jesse admitted. 'Yeah.'

'You were more than friends! Anyone can see that. Why can't you just be honest with me? I'm her mum; I have a right to know.'

'I loved her as a friend; that's all I can say.' Jesse sighed. 'No, I'll say something else: she was my best friend. Okay?'

'You were more than friends,' Judy insisted. 'You said yourself, you "hooked up". You had sex, didn't you?'

She was ruthless.

'It was … complicated.' He clutched his head. 'Look: she turned me on. She knew it. But it was always complicated, with us. We were better as friends.'

'So, you're saying she was too complicated for you? She wasn't worth the effort?'

'I didn't say that.'

'You could have sex with her, but you couldn't love her. You just used her, like all the rest of them. Didn't you?'

'No.' His voice cracked. 'That's not how it was.'

'Really? Then tell me. Because it seems to me, either you loved her and couldn't admit it, or you took advantage of her. I'm right, aren't I?'

'You're *not* right.' Jesse's eyes splintered. 'You're way off the mark, actually. You don't know what the fuck you're talking about, Ms Novak.'

'Judy,' she corrected him. 'If you're going to swear at me, call me "Judy", and tell me the truth.'

'What do you want me to tell you, Judy? That she got me drunk and sucked me off?' Jesse lashed out. ''Cos that's what happened. She got me drunk then she put the moves on me. I didn't want it; I had a girlfriend. She kept touching me. She took her clothes off. She was on her knees. I said "no". She wouldn't take "no" for an answer.'

For a moment, all Jesse could hear was the rush of his blood.

'She would've been drunk, too,' Judy reasoned. 'To act like that.'

'Yeah, she was drunk. She was always drunk. She was an alcoholic, Judy.'

Judy was briefly silent. Then the weeping started, soft but constant as a lapping sea.

'Please don't cry,' Jesse said. 'You'll make me cry.'

'I'm sorry.' Judy sniffed. 'But that makes me so sad.'

Jesse sighed. 'Yeah. Me too.'

'She was so confused.'

'I know,' he reassured her. 'She was confused, and she was sorry. That's the thing with Paulina; she'd screw up then she'd be really sorry. She called me up crying so many times, begging to be friends again. I hung up on her. I should've forgiven her sooner.'

'I should've visited sooner.'

'Please don't cry.'

'Don't *you* cry.' Judy laughed weakly. 'I'll hold it together if you do.'

'I really did love her. She was my best friend.'

'I know.' Judy's voice cracked. 'I just wish she could've had it all. She deserved to have it all. She deserved a man who loved her as much as I do.'

'No offence, but I don't think that's possible. You're a hard act to follow, eh.'

Judy gave him her number after that, 'just in case.' Jesse couldn't think of any case where he'd need it, but he thanked her anyway, then forgot all about her. Until a month later, when he found himself single again and on the last beer of a six-pack.

'Jesse. What a surprise.'

He had the horrible thought he'd woken her. 'Sorry. Is it a bad time?'

'Well ...' She laughed sheepishly. 'I fell asleep in front of the telly.'

'I can call another—'

'No, this's fine.' There was a shuffling on the other end. 'This is nice. I never know what to do on Wednesday nights. I used to see my therapist, but she's moved to Katoomba. Now Wednesdays are a big nothing.'

That was so depressing, Jesse didn't know what to say.

'Sorry. I sound like a head-case.' She laughed again. 'It's not that bad. I kept threatening to pull the plug. I was running out of things to say. Four-and-a-half years.'

'Yeah,' he said. 'I guess it has been that long.'

'Gawd knows what I'll do for the five-year anniversary. Slit my wrists, maybe?' She gave a small squeak. 'Sorry. I don't mean that. I'll bring her some flowers. How are *you*, Jess?'

'Yeah, good. Well, not good. I broke up with my girlfriend.'

'Oh, the flight attendant? Sorry to hear that.'

'Yeah. Well. She broke up with me, really.' His throat tightened. 'Not that there was anything to break up. I misread the situation. I'm an idiot.'

'Now, that's not true.'

'She basically called me an idiot, for thinking there was anything there. I was just a layover. Literally.'

'A man in every port? Sounds like a nice life.'

'She had a fiancé back in Auckland the whole time.' Jesse's blood boiled. 'I was talking about coming to visit her; I wanted to spend some real time with her? And she just points to this diamond ring and says, "You know I'm engaged?" Like I was a total fuckwit.'

'You didn't notice she had a diamond on her finger?'

'I dunno. I just thought it was a ring she liked to wear.'

Judy stifled a giggle. 'Sorry. I shouldn't laugh. Men, though. You lot aren't very good with details.'

'Thanks. That's helpful.'

'Sorry.' Judy turned solemn. 'I'm sorry you're going through that, Jess. She should've told you. Even if she had the Hope Diamond on her finger, she should've come right out and said, "I'm engaged. No strings attached, okay?" That would've been the right thing.'

'Yeah. I don't want no-strings, though. I'm so desperate for strings, I'm tying myself in knots. I'm an idiot.'

'No you're not. You're a wonderful boy. You're going to make some girl very happy someday.'

'Yeah, but. This thing she said …' Jesse felt a pressure behind his eyeballs. 'I was so angry. I asked, "what kind of chick screws around when she's getting married in two months?" and she goes, "You're just something I had to get out of my system." *Out of her system.* Like I'm a disease.'

'Take it as a compliment. She chose you for her last hurrah. That's something?'

Jesse choked a laugh. 'Yeah, I'm something. I'm the halfie island boy who works in his dad's meat shop. No wonder they're lining up around the corner.'

'So what? A job's a job.' Thoughtfully, Judy added, 'Besides, you're an artist, too. You're very lucky, to have that.'

'Yeah,' Jesse mumbled. 'Lucky.'

Judy sighed. 'Don't get me wrong, I'm not on her side. But I get where she's coming from, with that "out of her system" thing. I mean … if I could do it all over again. I was a teenager when I married Paulina's dad.'

Jesse settled back against the couch cushion. 'Jesus.'

'It was too young. He was twice my age. I resented him for having this whole other life before me. He had another family. Did Paulina ever tell you that?'

'She mentioned a half-sister, yeah.'

'He was married when we met. He moved his wife and daughter to the other side of the world, then abandoned them for me.' Judy laughed bitterly. 'I felt *very* powerful. It didn't last, though. I had all these miscarriages. I thought God was punishing me.'

'Jesus.'

'Of course, then Paulina came along, and I was smitten. I spent all day with her, every day. Then she started school and suddenly I had hours of just me. I didn't know what to do with myself. I … cheated. Constantly.'

'Yeah?' Jesse said, like it didn't shock him, though it did.

'For about a year, I cheated. I didn't feel bad about it, either. It was like a hobby, seeing what I could get away with.'

'Yeah.' Jesse's head spun. 'Right.'

'It was the seventies. It was a very "me-me-me" time,' she explained. 'I thought I was in control. I never had affairs, only once-offs. I was always waiting at the school gate to pick up Paulina at three o'clock.'

Jesse imagined a Paulina he'd never known, small in her school uniform, chattering to her mum about her day.

'I was reckless,' Judy continued. 'It kills me, to think how reckless I was. I could've gotten a disease. I could've been killed. This one time, I met these two guys at the beach. I went into their van with them and … Anyway, it was stupid, stupid.'

Jesse listened to her breathing, the heartbeat in her breath.

'Why did you stop?'

'Well, I went too far. Caro's husband.'

'Jesus!'

'Yes. Well,' Judy murmured. 'Really, she was better off without him. He was a Phys Ed teacher. Had flings with his students. But, still.'

Jesse's pulse quickened.

'She came crying to me one day. Caro, crying, can you imagine? She was pregnant. She felt very unattractive. She was convinced he was cheating, and I ...' Judy's voice thinned. 'I came out with it. Her face changed right away. She didn't talk to me for years. She moved to Perth to get away from me.'

'Jesus.'

'Yes. It's amazing we're friends now. She's a better person than me.'

There was nothing in the universe but the phone in his hand, the hush of her at the other end. 'You're not a bad person, Judy.'

'No. I know,' she said quietly. 'I was confused, that's all. That's what I mean, with the flight attendant—'

'Areta,' Jesse supplied, though he'd almost forgotten her name.

'Don't take it personally. It's bad that she hurt you like that, but it doesn't reflect badly on you. Any woman would be lucky. You're a wonderful boy.'

'Yeah,' he said, unconvinced.

'You're a wonderful boy, Jess.'

Wednesday became their night. 'I should start paying you by the hour,' Judy joked, but if anything, it was him who owed her. All he did was mumble. She was smart. Really smart.

Like when he saw Bunny was back on the rock for the summer, back at Foodfolk, and felt the guilt like a corkscrew in his gut.

He tried talking to her once while she was stacking shelves. Another time, he saw her at Wetties — she was old enough to drink legally, now — wearing low-slung jeans that showed off her tramp stamp, and tried to approach her, but her lame friend Hine blocked his way. Another time, she was walking alone after dark, the sky inky-blue and spitting, the wind squalling through the pines. He slowed down, offered her a ride. She refused. He offered again — it was raining, Christ, she'd slip. Again, she refused, walked faster, and he saw her trip over a pine frond, carry on regardless, face frigid, arms swift and straight. 'Sorry,' he said, understanding he'd scared her, and drove away.

'I wrote her this letter,' Jesse told Judy, after filling her in. 'I was wondering—'

'Of course, Jess. Go ahead.'

Jesse read the letter aloud, stumbling a bit, translating bits he'd written in Fayrf'k.

'It's good, Jess,' she said, when he was done. 'Very expressive.'

'So, you think it's okay to give to her?'

'Well, not exactly.' Her voice cut him, delicately. 'Jess: why did you write this?'

'To … let her know I'm sorry.'

'But you said "sorry", didn't you?'

'Yeah, but. I didn't get a chance to explain.'

'You used her and now you feel bad about it. Does she need to know the specifics?'

'Yeah. I mean, I need her to know I'm not that guy anymore—'

'Do you want a relationship with this girl?'

'No. Just, I don't want her to think I'm a kuka plana forever, you know?'

'But you were a …"kuka plana"? She may see you that way till the day she dies. You can't take back what you did.'

'But—'

'Jess,' she said, soft as a caress. 'When Paulina was drunk-dialling you, did that make you forgive her any faster?'

'No.'

'What made you forgive her, in the end?'

'I dunno. I missed her. I got sick of seeing her around and not talking.'

'Well. There you go.'

'But …' Jesse trailed off. 'You're really smart, eh.'

Judy chuckled. 'No I'm not.'

'You're smart. Really smart.'

'I'm not smart; I'm just a receptionist.' Judy laughed. 'I certainly won't be saying anything smart, if I stay up much longer.'

'Sorry.'

'Don't apologise. I hope I've helped?'

'Yeah.'

'You could've called sooner, you know. I do exist on other days besides Wednesday.'

'Sorry.'

'Stop apologising!' Judy scolded him gently. 'I'm just saying. I'm happy to talk whenever. And *I* know you're not that guy anymore, just so you know.'

Three nights later, he called her up to wish her a happy new year.

'Oh, thank you, Jess!' she effused, in a voice so warm and inviting he wanted to nestle inside it and stay there forever.

And then he went and dreamed about her. One of *those* dreams.

He didn't remember much. Just a delicious frenzy of movement, pressure, panting. But it was definitely her. There was no mistaking her.

The next time they talked, he was sure she knew. Her voice was so knowing; sexy. He couldn't focus on her words. At some point, she stopped talking, waiting for an answer. He latched onto the only thing that made sense: his name.

'I like it when you call me that.'

'"Jess"?' Judy laughed incredulously. 'It's your name!'

'I like it when you say it, but.'

'Jess.' She giggled. 'Jess?'

'I'm all embarrassed now.'

'Don't be embarrassed, Jess. It's a lovely name. I like saying it.'

'I like hearing you say it. I like your voice.'

'I should hope so. I'd hate for your ears to have been bleeding this whole time.'

'You have a really nice voice.'

'That's my great talent, sounding nicer than I am. Other people get to be talented artists ... I'm just talented at sounding nice on the phone.'

'You are nice.'

'No, not really. After everything that's happened? No.' Judy sighed. 'But talking to you is nice. I almost forget how bitter I am, talking to you. I like *your* voice, Jess.'

'Yeah?'

'Although, you never say my name.'

'Judy.'

'Yes, that's the one.' She laughed again. 'It's so dated, I know.'

'You're talking to a Fairfolk Islander here. We're like thirty years behind.'

'How convenient!'

'I like "Judy".' Jesse couldn't help himself. 'It's … cute. Classic.'

'So we like each other's names,' Judy said solemnly. 'Good to know.'

She *knew*. Did she?

'Judy.'

'Jess?'

'Nothing.' He combed a hand through his hair. 'I just feel like your sister's gonna bust in and tell me off for calling you the wrong thing.'

'Caro doesn't know we talk,' she said wistfully. 'She wouldn't approve.'

'She doesn't like me.'

'It's not that. She'd just think it's weird.' She thought for a moment. 'It *is* weird.'

'Yeah.'

He could feel her straying, overthinking. 'I dreamt about you last night.'

'Oh?' She didn't seem pleased, as he'd hoped she'd be; nor did she seem especially shocked. 'What was the dream?'

'Uh. I dunno,' he bluffed. 'It was a nice dream, though. I heard your voice.'

'Well, that figures. All these late-night phone calls.'

'Yeah.'

'Maybe it's a sign we've been talking too much.'

'No,' he said quickly. 'I like talking.'

'It's late, Jess.'

'Sorry.'

'Why are you apologising?' Her tone was exasperated. 'I don't want you losing any sleep because of me, that's all.'

'Too late for that.'

'I don't want you losing any sleep. I want you to dream of other things.'

If she was trying to discourage him, it wasn't working.

'I'd rather dream about you every night, eh.'

'Jess!' Judy cried. 'What's come over you? You've gone dotty!'

'It was a nice dream.'

'You can't even remember it!'

Jesse remembered, with an agonising squirm, her hands, her mouth. 'I remember … you.'

Judy sighed, and he was sure in that instant that she knew; that she was thinking of a polite way to tell him to get out of her life.

'I think you need some sleep, sweetheart,' she said, hesitating on 'sweetheart' like it was a shade of lipstick she wasn't sure about. 'Just sleep. No dreams, okay?'

'Yeah,' Jesse mumbled. 'Okay.'

As soon as he hung up, he knew what Paulina would say.

What, so you're trying to root my mum now? Mummy issues, much??

Jesse left it to her to call next, though he craved her voice like nicotine. He smoked too much. He thought about her on his smoke-breaks; at work, slicing steaks. The first time he saw her, adrift in the storm of her grief, in bed in his Bauhaus T-shirt. Dressed up for court, touching his arm outside Foodfolk. Walking up from the cemetery, all wind-battered, rumpled. In his car, so close he could smell the tang of her sweat beneath her perfume.

He thought about her so much, he almost took the tip of his finger off, and his dad had to close up shop to take him to Dr Jimmy for stitches and a tetanus shot. Later, looking at his bandages and bloodied T-shirt, Joe frowned and asked if he had rocks for brains.

'Sorry. What a week!' Judy apologised, when she finally rang. 'It's summer enrolment. The phones have been ringing nonstop. I'm worried I'll lose my voice.'

'Don't lose your voice,' Jesse protested. 'Have, like, some tea or something.'

She laughed. 'I'd rather drink this wine, thanks. How are *you*, Jess?'

'Yeah, good. Well, sore. Almost lost a fingertip, eh.'

He told her a version of the story. She wasn't amused.

'*Jess*,' she chastised him. 'You need to be more careful!'

'Yeah, yeah.'

'I mean it. You're working with dangerous equipment. It's not funny.'

'Yeah.' He made his tone as frustratingly flat as hers was fussy. 'Yeah.'

'Don't "yeah, yeah," me. I worry.'

'Yeah, don't. ' He touched his tetanus-shot bruise. 'You don't need to.'

'I do, though.'

'Yeah, but. Don't.You're not my mum, okay?'

'Fine.' She waited. 'If you've had enough, I'll go.'

'No.'

He heard her pick up her glass; the tap of the rim against the receiver.

'Don't go,' he pleaded. 'I'm a fuckwit. I've got rocks for brains.'

'Do you, now?'

'Aye.' He laughed helplessly. 'Live on a rock long enough, your brains turn into rocks.'

'Well … you can always come to the university, if you want to improve your brain.' There was a smile in her voice. 'I can help you enrol!'

She laughed at her own joke, way more than it deserved.

'How much wine have you had, Judy?'

'Oh, shush. I'm not the one slicing off fingers.' She sighed. 'Really. You should study. Finish your fine arts degree. You're wasting your talents on that rock.'

'I'm too old to study.'

'You're what, thirty?'

'Thirty-one.'

'Take it from an almost fifty-seven-year-old. That's *nothing*.'

Jesse hated when she mentioned her age. It made him feel like he was in chains, condemned to a life of hard labour.

'Nay, it's not for me, eh,' he mumbled. 'Fairfolk's my home.'

'Even so. You should see the world. Travel. Find yourself a cute twenty-five-year-old—'

'I don't want a twenty-five-year-old.'

He held his breath, waiting to see if she'd acknowledge the elephant in the room.

'I'm just saying, you don't want to get to my age—'

'You should take some of your own advice, Judy. Travel the world. Find yourself a twenty-five-year-old.'

'Now you're just being cruel.'

'Sorry.' Jesse glanced out at the palms rustling in the clear summer night. 'The thing with Fairfolk ... even if it's boring, it's paradise.'

'You sound like Paulina.'

'We don't have homeless people here. I hated that, on the mainland. All these poor buggers sleeping on the street and people walking right over them.'

'It's a problem, yes.'

'And the rules? One time they wouldn't let me in a pub cos my shoes were wrong.'

'Yes, that happens.'

'All kinds of rules.' It hurt to even talk about. 'Like, one time, on the train? Empty carriage. I was drawing. I had my feet up. I didn't know that's not allowed. Anyway, this guard comes along, only I don't hear him, I've got my headphones on ...'

'Oh, Jess.'

'Then he rips the headphones off and starts calling me "boong", "abo". He throws me off the train. Just for resting my feet? I got thrown off the train.'

'Jess. You poor thing.'

'I got bruises, where he threw me. I got a rip in my jeans; they were my only jeans. I was scared taking the train. I had to take the train to uni. You wonder why I dropped out?'

'Oh, sweetheart.'

'That's the mainland, eh.' He shrugged. 'No one cares what shoes I wear, here. And you can actually see the stars here? I never saw them, in Brisbane. Right now, outside, there's so many stars.'

'Sweetheart,' Judy repeated, her voice like a trail of fingers over his back, a kiss on the brow. 'That reminds me. I dreamt about Fairfolk the other night. You were there.'

'Yeah?' His heart swelled.

'Isn't that funny? You were just saying last time how I was in your dream.'

'Do you remember it?'

'Oh, not much. Just, we were outside somewhere. I think it was your house ... not that I've seen it. We were sitting outside, and I got the feeling it was your house.'

'Yeah? How'd it look?'

'I didn't notice. I was looking at your hands. There were these sunbeams ... they kept going on your hands while you were talking. I don't know what you were saying. I just kept looking at the sun on your hands.' She laughed softly. 'What a thing to dream. I don't even know what your hands look like, really.'

Jesse looked at his bandaged hand. 'They're nothing special, eh.'

'Well, they were nice in my dream. With all the sun on them.'

Jesse sat quietly, too flattered to speak. He heard her inhale and, worried she'd say something to kill the mood, blurted out, 'I remember your hands. That time you touched my arm at Foodfolk.'

'Oh, gawd!'

'What?'

'I wish you didn't remember that.' She laughed. 'Caro gave me hell about that.'

'Why?'

'Oh, she said I was *flirting*. Really, I think she was trying to take my mind off the trial. But she wouldn't shut up about it. I'm embarrassed you remember that.'

'It was nice,' Jesse said earnestly. 'I liked it when you did that.'

Judy got the giggles again.

'What?'

'Nothing. You're a funny little thing, that's all.'

Jesse couldn't bring himself to go inside the travel agency and actually book a one-way ticket. But he noticed himself looking at the prices every time he passed. Like he noticed his chest tightening when the planes to Sydney roared overhead, three times a week.

'I was thinking,' he told her, resigned to his fate. 'About what you said the other week. About leaving the island.'

'You want to travel?' She sounded vaguely crestfallen. 'That's wonderful, Jess.'

'Yeah. It's just a thought. Maybe Sydney's less backward than Brisbane.'

'Oh, that's wonderful!' she said, meaning it this time. 'You'll have to visit me.'

'Yeah. Definitely.'

'I'll cook you dinner.'

'Yeah.' His heart throbbed. 'I dunno. I dunno where I'd stay.'

'Lots of young people like the nightlife in Newtown.' She laughed. 'I'm in the middle of nowhere. There's nothing near me.'

'Yeah, but.' He flushed. '*You're* there.'

'I mean ...' She laughed. 'You're welcome to stay here, until you find your feet. I should've offered.'

'No,' he said quickly. 'Unless. Would you want that?'

'I'd love to have you in my house, Jess.'

'You don't have to say that.'

'I wouldn't say it if it wasn't true.'

'Yeah. Just.' He felt like a deep-sea diver running out of oxygen. 'I dunno.'

'Well, let me know.'

She sounded so calm; he wanted her hot, flustered. 'Where would I sleep?'

'Sorry?'

'If I stayed with you.' It was torture, putting it into words. 'Where would I sleep?'

'Don't worry, there's plenty of room,' she said breezily. 'I won't put you in Paulina's room, if that's what you're worried about. There's a spare room.'

Jesse groaned under his breath. 'Yeah. Maybe.'

'Is everything alright, Jess?'

'Yeah ... nay,' he backtracked. 'I'll probably get pulled over ten minutes down the road from the airport, eh.'

'Well, *I'll* pick you up from the airport. Obviously.'

He imagined being in her car. Went quiet with imagining.

'Jess? Are you still there?'

'Yeah, nay.' He shook his head. 'I dunno anymore.'

He smoked two bongs, for courage. Smashed two cans of Pine Brew. On his third, he dialled her number and, before she'd even asked how he was, let loose.

'Look, I'm coming, okay. I definitely wanna come.'

'Oh?' she said. 'That's ... wonderful. Have you decided on dates?'

'Soon. Next month.'

'Of course. Like I said, you're more than welcome to stay here.'

'Yeah.' He took another swallow of beer. 'Just. Can we talk about where I'd sleep? I think we should decide that, before I come.'

'I thought …' Judy sounded genuinely confused. 'I said there's a spare bedroom, didn't I? It's not much, but I can make it comfy, now I know you're—'

'Is that really where you want me?'

'I mean … I want you to be comfortable. Is there somewhere you'd rather be?'

'You tell me.'

'I …' Judy sighed. 'No, *you* tell me. What are you asking?'

'What do you think I'm asking?'

'No. I'm not doing this. Where do you want to be, Jess?' When he didn't answer, she sighed again. 'Maybe we should just call the whole thing off.'

'No,' he said urgently.

'Jess … I don't know what you want me to say!' Judy's voice cracked. 'You hold all the cards here, not me.'

'I don't. Please, just tell me—'

'No,' she said firmly. 'You started this.'

Face burning, Jesse relented.

'Look: if I'm coming all that way, it's not to sleep in a spare room.'

'… Okay.'

'Okay? Do I have to spell it out?'

'Yes.'

'I want to be where you are. I want to be with you. Okay?'

She was quiet for so long, he worried he'd scared her off.

'Oh, Jess,' she murmured, finally. 'You don't want that.'

'Yes I do.'

'No, sweetheart, you don't. Maybe you've got a little crush—'

'It's not a fucking crush. I love you.'

To Jesse's alarm, she started crying.

'Don't cry,' he told her. 'Please. Tell me to leave you alone and I will. Don't cry.'

'I don't want you to leave me alone.' Judy sobbed. 'Give me a sec. Okay?'

She put the phone down. When she came back, she was hoarse.

'Sorry,' she said. 'I needed a drink.'

'Yeah, fair enough. Cheers.'

'Jess.' She gave a meek, broken laugh. 'Oh gawd, Jess … *why?*

He didn't say anything, just listened to her breathe.

'Look: I feel it, too,' Judy admitted. 'Don't think I don't. But I'm not stupid. I'm old enough to be your mother. You'll change your mind when you see me.'

'I've seen you,' he argued. 'I like how you look.'

'You've seen me three times. You've built me up in your mind. You have no idea.'

He closed his eyes and saw her clear-eyed, cobwebbed beauty; her skin so pale, her hair so fine and light. Her hands. Her mouth.

'I like how you look,' he repeated. 'I like everything about you.'

'Jess …'

'Judy.' He swallowed. 'Take a compliment, will you?'

Judy laughed again.

'I don't know, Jess. I really don't.' Her breath snagged. 'Just come, okay? We'll figure it out. Please, just come.'

He booked his ticket the next day.

For the next couple of weeks, they said 'I love you'. He gathered gifts: guava jam, honey, seashells, pressed hibiscuses. He joked about losing all his fingers to daydreaming.

'Don't,' she protested. 'I want you here in one piece.'

He had a burning sensation in the pit of his stomach, like acid eating through cast-iron. In the few hours he slept, his dreams were frantic and crowded, like dreams after a night of hard drinking. When he fucked her in his dreams, it wasn't like the first time. There were always spectators — guards, suits, men in hi-vis with cans of beer. He struggled to finish.

Packing, Jesse felt ashamed of his clothes, which only seemed suitable for an island.

'I don't care about your clothes,' Judy reassured him. 'I can't wait to get you out of them, actually.'

She made him hard, talking like that. But the pain in his stomach was worse than ever.

The weekend before his departure, Jesse's dad closed up shop to take him fishing.

'You look miggy,' Joe said, noticing Jesse's loose shorts. 'Hair's good, but.'

Jesse had gotten a haircut, hoping to look more city.

Baiting his hook was difficult; his hands trembled so much. Waiting for a bite, he couldn't stop fidgeting. Joe noticed.

'You're gonna scare all the fish.'

'Sorry,' Jesse mumbled.

The sun sparkled on the sea, brought tears to his eyes. He drank beer, hoping it'd settle his tummy, but it only made him queasy. His dad kept looking at him sidelong.

Jesse cleared his throat. 'You know how I said I'm staying with a friend in Sydney?'

'Girlfriend?'

Jesse nodded, wished he could leave it at that. 'She's … ulvini.'

Joe raised his eyebrows.

'Judy Novak,' Jesse said, throat so tight he couldn't breathe.

Joe squinted. 'Paulina's *mother*?'

Nodding, Jesse stared at the sea, tears curdling in his eyes.

'We've been talking. I can't stop thinking about her. I have to see her.'

'She feels the same?'

Again, Jesse nodded. Hot tears fell.

'I'm such a fuck-up,' he heard himself say. 'I don't know what to do.'

'You nay wanna go?'

'I *do*. I want her.' Jesse closed his eyes. 'I don't know what to do, Dad.'

'You want my blessing?'

Jesse covered his face. 'She's so beautiful. I've never met anyone like her.'

'You want my blessing?'

'No.' Jesse crumpled. 'I love her, Dad.'

Joe nodded, as if this was a fact as evident as the blueness of the sea. Then he grabbed the back of Jesse's neck and pulled him into a hug. 'You're still my kid, okay?'

Jesse cried like a motherless child.

—

'I don't understand,' Judy said, her voice small and frayed. 'You let me make all these plans.'

'I know. I'm a fuckwit.'

'You let me ...' she stammered. 'You let me say all these things. You let me make an idiot of myself.'

'You're not. I'm the idiot. It's all me.'

'Don't give me that crap.' She sobbed. 'Just tell me the truth: the thought of being with me disgusts you? You thought you could, but when push comes to shove, you just want some pretty young thing.'

'No. It's not like that.'

'Stop lying. Haven't you lied enough?'

She cried and cried, and he felt powerless, like he was watching a truck back over a tricycle. 'It wasn't lies. I meant it. Please, don't cry. You're making me cry—'

'Good! I hope you cry forever, bastard!'

Christ, she sounded like Paulina.

'Please, Judy—'

'Don't say my name.'

'Please. Look. You're beautiful. You're perfect. It's just—'

'I'm old. Just say it.'

'It's not—' he faltered. 'You're older, yeah. But it's not just that. You're Paulina's *mum*.'

'You wouldn't've looked at me twice if I wasn't her mum!'

'Judy. What would she think?'

'Don't you dare use my dead daughter against me. I live with it every day, that she's gone. Don't talk to me about what she'd think!'

'Sorry, but ... you look like her. It's too weird.'

'I don't. She looked much more like her father.'

'You don't see it. You do.'

'I don't, but so what if I do? It was my face first. I'm the original.'

'Judy—'

'Stop it. Just stop it.'

He was quiet until she started crying again; he couldn't stand her crying.

'I meant it, Judy. I've never felt this way before. It's just, I had this bad feeling. I kept having these bad dreams. I talked to my dad—'

'Why didn't you talk to *me*?'

'Cos when I talk to you there's only you. I can't think straight.'

She stopped crying. Softened her voice to a caress.

'One night? Couldn't we just have one night?' Judy sniffed. 'Just to get it out of our systems? We'll be together, and forget the world, and then we can go our own ways—'

'We can't, Judy.'

She cried harder. 'How could you do this to me? After everything I've lost?'

'I'm sorry—'

'Just one night, Jess?'

'Judy.' He winced. 'I couldn't live myself. Even if it was just once. It's like … incest.'

'*Incest?* She scoffed. 'I didn't give birth to you.'

'Incest, or necrophilia or something. It's not right. I dunno how I'd get over it. Please, this is really hard for me—'

'Fine,' she cut in. 'I'll make it easier.'

'Judy—'

'I hope you have a very nice life,' she said primly. 'I hope you find everything you're looking for.'

Then she slammed down the phone, cutting off her sobs before he could find the words to soothe them.

TOMBSTONE

'Shopping again? Do you have a second job I don't know about, Westpac?'

'I'm almost thirty! Time to start taking some pride in my home.' Paulina waved a catalogue-page in Baz's face. 'What d'ya reckon? Cherry blossoms or damask?'

'Damask. But if you rack up a phone bill from my desk, I'm docking your pay.'

'Ooooo, check out this lamp. That'd be cute for reading in bed. I might finally finish *Anna Karenina*, with a lamp like this.'

'I'm off to St Bartholomew's. Don't forget to answer the phone if it rings.'

'Mate, my *mum's* a receptionist. Answering phones is in my blood. By the way: you look really nice in your suit, boss. You should wear pants more often. Tell me your size and I'll pick some out, no probs—'

Baz drifted out of reception in his funeral attire, shaking his head. Alone, Paulina picked up the phone and dialled.

'Listen: my name's Paulina and I wanna spend some money. Do youse ship to Fairfolk Island? *Fairfolk Island*, not "Finland". Do I sound bloody Finnish to you? Yeah, yeah, I'll hold. Don't keep me waiting, but. I'm a working woman.'

As the hold music rankled her ears, Paulina spun in her chair, watched the mural blur.

'About fucking time!' she bitched when the chick returned. 'I was about to call Ikea, ha-ha. You do ship to Fairfolk? Nice one! Yeah, nah, I never heard of Fairfolk either till I moved here. Are youse based in Sydney? Geez, I feel sorry for you, babe. I live in paradise. Only thing is, we don't have department stores, so if I want the good stuff I have to get it shipped, and the ship only comes like once every six weeks, and it can't even dock here, there's this big reef so all the blokes have to go out in their boats and unload it by hand. It's pretty dangerous! My ex carked it just last week, ha-ha-ha. Nah, don't apologise! He got what he deserved. He raped me. He bashed me. I almost died cos of him. My head's still fucked. My face is fucked. I used to be really cute. Now I'm shithouse without makeup. Oi, can I buy makeup from you, too, or is that like a separate department? Yeah, babe. I'll hold.'

'Paulina! What are you *doing*?'

Paulina was slow to turn. It wasn't just the beer, slowing her reflexes; it was King's Lookout in the dark, so sprawling and swirly with stars, she didn't want to look away.

'Kymbaleeeee!' Giggling, she staggered to the car window. 'I'm walking, duh.'

Kymba was dressed in black. In the passenger seat was Merlinda, red-faced and sticky. In the back, nodding off, was Old Merle.

'Geez! Three generations! You celebrating?'

Kymba flushed and glanced at Merlinda. 'We're just coming back from Car's funeral. Why're you walking in the dark?'

'Was at the Mutes' front desk all day. Only just knocked off. You know me; I get stir-crazy if I don't get my walk.'

Merlinda laughed. 'Like a dog!'

'Don't mind Auntie Merlinda.' Kymba rolled her eyes. 'She's grieving … and drunk.'

Paulina sipped her beer. 'I'm just getting started. Gonna pop a bottle of champers when I get home.'

Merlinda stopped laughing. 'What's that supposed to mean?'

'It means I'm living it up.' Paulina flipped the bird at the K-I-N-G on the sign behind her. 'The King's dead! Fuck the King.'

'That's my nephew you're talking about.' Merlinda's nostrils flared. 'Do you have any idea how hard he worked?'

'Not as hard as he hit me, hey. Not as hard as he choked me when I said I didn't want it. Not as hard as he stuck it in—'

'Lying mainie! Why don't you come here and say that to my face?'

'Auntie Merlinda.' Kymba sighed. '*Please.*'

Paulina yanked the door open, slid into the backseat beside Merle.

'Hey, Merle, how are ya?' She patted his papery hand. 'I was just saying what a bastard Car King was. He's probably burning in hell as we speak, yeah?'

'Don't touch my father!' Merlinda grabbed her hair. 'Mainie bitch, you're all the same. Using and abusing our men!'

'Merlinda!' Kymba cried.

'I didn't use him.' Paulina dug her nails into Merlinda's plump hand. 'He used *me*.'

'How much did you pay for that Mazda Astina, then?'

'I paid!'

'How much did you pay?' Merlinda tugged her hair harder. 'How much?'

'I fucking *paid*.'

Paulina thrashed wildly at Merlinda; caught Merle's cheekbone with her elbow. 'Oh!' the old man bleated, small and startled.

'Shit!' Paulina saw his face go patchy. 'Sorry Merle! Gawd, I'm sorry.'

'You assaulted my father?' Merlinda pulled her hair again. 'You come to our island, you disrespect our men, then you assault one of our elders?'

'It was an accident. Kymba, you saw—'

'Kymbalee!' Merlinda barked.

'Kymba! Tell her.' Paulina pleaded. 'You know what Car was like. Tell her.'

'Kymbalee!'

'Kymba?'

'Just shut up.' Kymba turned around in her seat, eyes crystalline with tears. 'Paulina: it's done. He's gone. Can't you just shut up, for once?'

'But—'

'Go home, Paulina. It's been a long day. Please, just leave my family alone.'

Paulina cast a glance at Merle; he was staring out the window, arms crossed over his scrawny chest. 'Sorry, Merle,' she mumbled, peeling herself from the backseat.

'You should be!' Merlinda honked. 'Go back to the mainland where you belong!'

Behind the wheel, swinging the car around, Kymba's face was white and clenched. Paulina squinted in the headlights, then reeled in the sudden darkness. Slapped a mosquito from her neck.

They sucked her blood all the way home.

'"Closed"! Are you kidding me?'

Paulina banged her palm against the warm glass door of the cop-shop; shielded her eyes and peered inside. There was sun on the carpet; dust motes playing in the sun. A fat blue water cooler. A table full of brochures. Not a soul in sight.

'Try breaking in.'

Flinching, Paulina spun around to look at the young guy smoking a ciggie by the hibiscus bush. 'Bloody hell! Didn't see you there. You waiting too?'

He nodded. 'Need to update my work permit.'

'Wrong place, hey.' Paulina dug in her handbag for her own ciggies. 'There's this office in the historical district. My ex used to work near there. Still does, I guess.'

'Cheers.' He offered his lighter. 'You a mainie, too?'

'How'd you guess?' She laughed, cupped the flame. 'Sydney. You?'

'Perth.'

'Oh, nice. I've got a sister in Perth. She teaches ESL at a school near Freo.'

'I'm way north of the river. Marangaroo.'

Paulina sipped in smoke. 'I dunno where that is.'

'Not worth knowing.' His eyes skimmed her legs; she was wearing her nice-girl skirt, strappy sandals. 'I've seen you walking.'

'Yeah, I walk. Good exercise.'

'I get bored, walking. Prefer the gym.' He flexed his arm a bit. 'I offered you a lift one time. You weren't interested.'

'That'd be right.' She looked at his arms; they were muscly. Cute face. A bit pale, but; the brown hair a tad too long, greasy. 'Anyways, I updated my permit a few months back, when I changed jobs. It's easy.'

'Cheers.' He flicked away the butt of his ciggie; she caught the flash of a wedding band. 'I just got a new job. They want me to get all my shit together by Friday.'

'Where's the job?'

'Great-O's. I was a chef at The Pacifica, before then.'

'Ha, my first job here was s'posed to be at Great-O's … then they burned down. They're my great white whale.'

'Need a lift back into town?'

'Nah, I'm good. I'll wait a bit.'

'I waited ages. I reckon they've closed up shop.'

'Bloody slackers. I'll wait a bit.'

'You sure?'

'Yeah.' She blew smoke toward the street. 'I'll wait. I'll walk.'

'Sure?'

'Yeah, I'm good.' She forced a smile. 'My car's parked at the school, anyways. It's not far. Good luck with the permit, hey. They'll help you out down there. It's really easy.'

'Sure you don't want a lift to your car?'

'Yeah, mate.' Her voice bit like a cornered animal. 'I'm good, alright?'

'Alright.' He ducked his head politely. 'See ya around.'

'See ya.'

Paulina smiled tightly till the guy crossed the road, got into his white Camry, and drove off. Then she stamped on the butt, lit another ciggie, looked into the sunlit station some more, but couldn't find whatever she was looking for.

She was drunk on goon when she dialled the emergency number. A lady answered.

'Where's your emergency?'

'Yeah, nah. It's not an emergency. I just wanted to talk to someone about—'

'You need to call the station during business hours.'

'Yeah, I tried. They weren't open. I—'

'Try again during business hours.'

'Lady, can I just talk to the officer on duty? I wanna report a rape.'

The lady's tone shifted. 'Where're you calling from?'

'I'm home.' Paulina's head twanged. 'But, look. It happened a few months back. The guy's not around anymore—'

'He's left the island?'

'Nah, he's still here. Six feet under.' She laughed wanly, swallowed more goon. 'They buried him a few days ago. Only, I keep seeing his name. I read his obituary; it said all this shit. *King among Kings. Loving Husband, Father.* Didn't say he's a rapist, paedophile, scum of the earth—'

'Darl,' the lady cut in. 'I'm sorry, but this isn't a police matter.'

'Yeah, but. What he did. That's a crime.'

'There's nothing we can do, if he's dead.'

'But! His name? They keep saying his name like it's good, but it's shit. I know it's shit. Can't you do something? It's fucking shit—'

'Darl. I think you need to sleep it off. Tomorrow's another day.'

'But—'

'This isn't a police matter, darl. Try phoning Vy Carlyle; she's a psych—'

'I'm not talking to anybody named "Carlyle", bitch!'

'Sorry.' The voice frayed. 'I can't help you.'

Then the line went dead.

'Bitch!' Paulina ripped the phone from the wall and stared for a long time at the cord on the floor, tempting. She clenched and unclenched her hands, drank more goon. It was ages before she picked herself up and tremulously plugged the phone back in.

She went outside and smoked. Outside was safer. After a while, Vera's cat Katie jangled out of the darkness. 'Hey, puss,' Paulina mumbled. 'What's up?'

Katie dashed inside. She had something in her mouth.

'Oi!' Paulina cried. 'What the fuck!'

Katie dropped the thing in the kitchen. It was a cockroach, still living.

'Oi!' Paulina watched it scuttle away. 'Why'd you drop it?'

Katie pounced like an idiot.

Paulina laughed. 'It's gone, dickhead!'

Even so, Katie kept pouncing, yowling, walking in circles, her pupils big as coins.

'Stupid cat.' Paulina's knees turned to jelly. 'You're so stupid.'

She sat herself down at the kitchen table, clung to it like a raft. The whole room merry-go-rounded. Then she threw up in the sink; guzzled tapwater.

A little while later, her mum rang.

'Not you again,' Paulina slurred. 'Get a life.'

'I'm just calling to see how you are. I won't keep you long.'

'Yeah. I've got enough on my plate, without you hassling me.'

'Did you eat?'

'Ha-ha! Cheese and crackers. It's all down the sink, now.'

'You *threw up*?'

'Not on purpose!'

'That's not a good dinner. Can you please eat something else?'

'Too drunk to cook.'

Judy sighed. 'You know, if you lived in Sydney, you could order a pizza.'

'Crackers!'

'Oh, fine. Eat some crackers. As long as you put something in your stomach.'

Paulina set the phone down, got the box of crackers, and picked the phone back up.

'I'm eating crackers.' She chewed emphatically. 'Happy now?'

'Not really. But it'll do. How are they?'

'Stale.'

'You know, if you lived in Sydney, you could go to Woolworths and buy everything fresh, instead of stale things from a mouldy old ship.'

'What, are you the spokeswoman for Woolworths now?'

'Still a receptionist.' Judy sighed. 'At least put some peanut butter on those crackers.'

'I hate peanut butter.'

'Since when?' When Paulina didn't answer, Judy sighed again. 'Gawd. You get fussier every day. Do you still eat cream cheese?'

'Finished it.'

'Did you? Good girl. Well, buy some more at Foodfolk tomorrow.'

'Foodfolk, the stale food peeeeeople!' Paulina sang and cackled. 'Gotta buy some bug spray, hey. This stupid cat, she brought a cockroach in—'

'Nasty thing!'

'Calm down. It's just a cat, geez.'

'Well, sorry! I don't like them, though.'

'You're so mean. You never let me have pets.'

'I let you have those budgerigars! And goldfish. I offered to get you a bunny, too, like your cousins had—'

'Nah. Bronson would've killed it when he came over to play. Bloody serial killer.'

'Yes, probably.'

'Have they found the bodies yet?'

'Any day now.'

'Ha-ha!' Paulina's eyes stung with tears. 'But, *Mum.*'

'Yes, child?'

'I *lied*, Mum. Bronson didn't kill Lappy.' Paulina covered her face. '*I* killed Lappy.'

'*You* killed Lappy?'

'Yeah — me!' Paulina burst into tears. 'I mean, like, it was an accident, obviously. I played with him too rough. But it was me, all me. Then I said Bronson did it, and youse all believed me, and Aunt Caro read all those books about serial killers and was always checking Bronson's bed to make sure he didn't wet it and — Why're you laughing?'

'Oh, Paulina!' Judy choked out. 'That's *brilliant.*'

'How's that brilliant, psycho?'

'Keeping quiet about that for twenty years? Gawd, no wonder you drink … you've got a guilty conscience!'

'Muuuum!'

'Darling.' Judy laughed. 'Don't ever change, okay? There's no one like you.'

'No wonder. Look at who made me.'

'You know, sometimes I think I've done nothing with my life.' Judy laughed again. 'Then I talk to you and think, "oh, wait, yes I have. Look what I made!"'

'Bloody hell,' Paulina groaned. 'You have the lowest standards ever.'

Paulina's head hurt worse than usual, waiting tables at the Mutes' bistro. So bad, she felt the individual bones of her skull grinding against each other, her vision blurring.

When she dropped a plate of bacon and eggs, she screamed, 'Fuck!' and dropped to her knees, tears streaming.

'It's alright.' Gayle, the bistro manager, crouched beside her. 'Take a break. Wash your face. It's alright.'

After work, she planned to go to Foodfolk. But when she passed Tabby's Treasures and saw that curly blond head behind the counter going about her business, she could've driven her Mazda right into the shopfront, mowed the bitch down.

Instead, she parked.

'Oi, Tabitha!' She pushed inside the store. 'Mourning period's over already?'

Tabby's nose narrowed. 'I have a business to run.'

'Yeah?' Paulina picked up a business card. 'Still going by "Tabitha King"?'

'It's still "King", yes.'

Paulina's eyes roved around the store; latched on a framed photo behind the counter. 'You put up a picture of him?'

'Yes, I put up a picture of Carlyle.'

'You're fucked in the head.'

Tabby looked her up and down. 'You've off the wagon, aren't you?'

'I'm not drunk.'

'You have been, though. You're not doing yourself any favours. That's the worst thing for it.'

'For what?'

'Your head.'

'Your head's more fucked than my head.'

'Cut out the drinking. It'll heal faster. And, if you really want to get better, go back to the mainland. I'm surprised you haven't already.'

'I'm here to stay, bitch.'

Tabby crossed her arms. 'I don't know what you hope to achieve, staying here. Coming into my place of business. You'd be better off going home to your mum.'

'Leave my mum out of this.'

'I heard a lot about your mum, when you were with me. "Mum, Mum, Mum," that's all I heard. Why don't you let her look after you?'

Paulina shredded the business card. 'You'll never get rid of me.'

'What do you want from me? I really don't understand. I looked after you. I could've left you for dead. We could've thrown you in the ocean. We talked about that, you know.'

'Fuck you!' Paulina knocked the pile of business cards off the counter. 'You want me to be grateful you didn't put me out of my misery? Everything hurts, every day!'

'Cut out the drinking. Go back to the mainland. It'll hurt less. It'll all feel like a bad dream, in time.'

'I *need* to drink, after what I saw. Bloody hell, don't you? He raped your daughter in your own house!'

'I don't know what you think you saw, but you were a drunk long before that. It's probably why Car went for you. Just a cheap drunk who'll say yes to anything.'

'I know what I saw!' Paulina banged on the nearest cabinet. 'I know you *know*.'

'If you're going to start destroying property, I'll have to call the police.'

'Do it! I'll tell them everything. I'll tell them how you kept me in her room and drugged me.'

'If that's what you want.' Tabby moved toward the phone, folded her hands over it. 'But, just so you know, Sergeant Turner is an old friend of Car's. Spoke at his funeral.'

Paulina screamed, swung at the cabinet. It shook but didn't shatter.

'You nasty thing.' Tabby came over and steadied the cabinet, her green eyes aglow. 'I'm just trying to get on with my life. Can't you?'

'No!'

'What do you want? Money?'

'No! Fuck.'

'I'll write you a cheque. I'll pay for your flight home, and some. The Car Kings will buy back your Mazda. You'll probably get more than you paid, seeing as Car gave you that discount.'

Paulina screamed again, hit the cabinet harder. This time, her hand went through.

'Look what you've done!' Tabby gasped. 'Who do you think you are?'

She bustled to the shopfront, locked the door and turned the sign to 'CLOSED'. Paulina drew her hand from the glass, marvelling at the red slicking her arm, how little pain she felt.

'Do you feel better now? Tabby cried, getting a broom from behind the counter. 'Do you feel good, now you've made another mess for me to clean up?'

Paulina reached her hand back through the spiky glass, picked up a rack of earrings and flung it.

'Stop that.' Tabby grabbed her arm. 'Look at you. I'm not cleaning you up.'

Paulina laughed. 'You've got blood on your hands. And it's not just mine.'

'What do you want?' Tabby's chin trembled. 'As far as I'm concerned, we're more than even. You're still alive. You've made a mess of my life. If you want money, I'll give you money … but that's more than you deserve.'

'I don't want your money.' Paulina walked around the counter, plucked Car's photo from the wall. 'When was this taken? He's less fat. Still an ugly bastard, but.'

'You're going to break that too?'

'Yeah, alright.' Paulina chucked it across the shop. 'Since you offered.'

'Feel better?'

'No.'

'Go home to your mum. Go on. If you're going to act like a child, you'd be better off home with your mum. I'm not your mum.'

'I know you're not my mum! My mum's *beautiful*.'

'Go home to her, then.'

'Not till you say!'

'I can't tell you what you want to hear; it simply isn't true.'

'He raped her.'

'That never happened.'

'He did. I saw the pictures. He took pictures of her.'

'You have no proof.'

'The proof's all over your face!' Paulina peered at Tabby's tight mouth, flaming cheeks. 'Why're you still lying for him? Did you even love her?'

'Of course I loved her!' Tabby rubbed her face, smearing it with blood. 'I loved that girl more than life itself. She was a wild thing, but I loved her.'

'You're insane.'

'She threw herself at Car. I still loved her. I forgave her.'

'I saw those pictures. She was a kid.'

'She was a Fairfolk girl. Our girls mature faster.'

'She was scared shitless.'

'She was a pretty girl. She knew it. She wouldn't leave him alone. I don't blame her … she never had a father till Car. I forgive her.'

'That's the story you're telling yourself?'

'It's the only story.'

A group of tourists stopped at the shop window, squinted at the 'CLOSED' sign, then at Paulina and Tabby. 'I can't tell you what you want to hear,' Tabby repeated. 'And I don't know why you think I owe you anything. *You* owe *me* your life. He's dead. My daughter's dead. I'm just trying to make the best of what I've got left.'

'What, a jewellery shop he paid for?'

'Yes. My business. My home. My health. My good name.'

'Your name's shit!'

'I'm proud of my name. I'll defend it to the grave.' Tabby raised her chin. 'So will a lot of people around here. Can you say the same for yourself?'

'Who cares!'

'You know what people think, when they hear the name "Novak"? They think you're mainie trash. You're a drunk. You're a slut who can't be trusted.'

'Better than "King".'

'Maybe on the mainland. But you won't find anyone around here, saying that. Go back to the mainland, why don't you. Go home to your mum.'

'Nah, bitch! This's my home, too. I've got blood here!'

Paulina stalked toward the shopfront, smeared her bloody arm across the window.

'See? That's Novak blood. I'm here to stay. Don't ever call me "mainie" again.'

She drove to Tombstone Beach straight after her dinner shift. It was totally black out. Dark came early, still. It was cold, even rugged up in her trakkies and hoodie. Lifting the graveyard's quaint wooden gate, she saw her breath rise up like a ghost.

He was hard to find. There were shitloads of them, going back to the 1800s. Then her torch found a flash of bright-blue tiles among the grey stones.

TIFFANY EMILY KING
1985—2000
A beautiful angel
Briefly among us
Forever in our hearts
We'll miss you every day
Until we meet in heaven, sweetheart
Mum & Dad

There was a dolphin engraved on the plaque. Seashells and starfish glued to the tiles. Blue glass hearts. Like a teenage girl's bedroom in grave form. Paulina didn't know whether to cry or throw up.

She passed her torch over the neighbouring headstone, and there he was. *King Among Kings. Loving Husband, Father.*

She took a swig from her flask. Then she shook up the spray-can.

Something rustled. Her heart stopped. Shit solidified in her guts, though she hadn't eaten since yesterday. She flicked off her torch, tried to silence her body.

Nothing. Probably just the wind, or a feral chicken or something.

As soon as she flicked her torch back on though, there he was: golf shirt, pale lips, pale eyes, creeping among the headstones.

'Oi, Yooey, you perv!' Paulina chucked the spray can at him. 'If you want a date, go to the pub like everyone else, for fuck's sake!'

He bolted.

Terror in her heart, Paulina power-walked in the opposite direction, back to her car. As soon as the doors were locked, she guzzled the contents of her flask.

She found him the next day, right where she expected him to be: waiting for his Hawaiian ham-steak and chips at the Bowls Club.

'Hey, Merle,' she said softly — too soft for him to hear. She tried again, louder, with a little wave. 'Merle?'

Merle started. The look in his eyes was pure alarm. He still had a mark on his cheek.

'Making it up to your boyfriend after your tiff, eh?' Kobby heckled her from the green.

Paulina rolled her eyes. 'Yeah, something like that.'

'You know where to find me, if it doesn't work out.'

'Cheers.' Paulina pulled up a chair and looked at Merle. 'Can I?'

He looked at her for a long time, unreadable as a cat perched on a high fence. Then he said, 'Alright.'

Paulina smoothed her nice-girl skirt as she sat.

'Just wanted to say, I'm really sorry for …' She pointed at his cheek. 'All that. It was an accident. I feel so bad.'

Merle nodded.

'Do you think you can forgive me, someday?'

Merle nodded, smiled. 'It's alright.'

'Geez! That was easy.' Tears spilled from her eyes. 'I got you some presents, too; Fisherman's Friend. I know how you like them.'

Paulina rummaged in her handbag, pulled out a handful of packets and arranged them in front of Merle. He nodded appreciatively. 'Thank you.'

'Also, this.' She brandished a tube of sunscreen. 'I thought you might need it, since summer's coming. The sun gets pretty strong out here.'

Merle pulled a face like she'd fed him something sour. 'I'm not a mainie.'

'Yeah, I know!'

'Keep it,' he told her. 'For yourself.'

Paulina rolled her eyes and stuffed it back inside her bag. 'Fine, but don't blame me if you get skin cancer.'

Merle found that hilarious. When he was done laughing, he said, 'Lunchtime?'

'Yeah.' Paulina glanced at her watch. 'Should be here soon.'

'Salad for you?'

'Oh, nah. Not today.'

Merle looked so heartbroken, Paulina bit her lip, checked her watch again. 'I mean … I guess there's time. They're probably closed for lunch, anyways.'

Merle didn't ask who "they" were, just smiled big.

'Hey,' Paulina greeted Barry, the bartender. 'What salads do you have today?'

'Pine Brew. Lion Red. Steinlager—'

'Yeah, nah. Actual salad.'

'Caesar. Pasta. Niçoise.'

'Ugh … Niçoise, I guess.' She handed over her card. 'I'll get Merle's lunch, too.'

When the salad came, it was just a dank mix of lettuce, pickled vegetables, and canned tuna. She picked up her fork begrudgingly, nibbled an olive.

'Alright?' Merle asked her.

'Yeah,' Paulina bluffed. 'It's alright.'

She ate just enough for it to not seem like an insult.

It was an hour till school pick-up when Paulina left the cop shop, but Kymba's car was already parked outside. Kymba rolled her window down as Paulina was walking to the Mazda.

'There you are. I was wondering why your car was here.'

'Oh, yeah. I was at the station. Yooey was being a pest again. Was hoping they could give him a warning or whatever.'

'He's had so many warnings.' Kymba rolled her eyes. 'He didn't touch you, did he?'

'Nah, just spooked me a bit. It was nighttime. I didn't know he came out at night.'

'He usually doesn't. His mum's in hospital right now. That's probably why.'

'Yeah, that's what they said. Oi, why're you here so early?'

Kymba nodded at Ollie, strapped into his baby chair in the backseat. 'I was driving him around. It helps put him to sleep. Then I figured, the others will be out soon. I may as well enjoy the quiet time while I have it.'

Paulina laughed, glanced at the passenger seat.

'Go ahead.' Kymba smiled. 'It's nice talking to an adult after a day of goo-goo ga-ga.'

Letting herself into the car, Paulina shut the door softly. 'Gawd, he's beautiful. Look at those cheeks.'

'No freckles, yet. Hopefully he won't take after Simmo like the other two.'

'I saw Merle before.'

'Oh? How is he?'

'Yeah, fine. Just wanted to say sorry for the other night.'

Kymba looked blank.

'You know.' Paulina mimed. 'After Car's funeral. When I elbowed him?'

Kymba flushed. 'Oh God! I completely forgot. Can you tell my brain is mush?'

'Ha, kinda.'

'Sorry about that. Merlinda was way out of line.'

'Yeah. I provoked her, but.' Paulina drew up her sleeve to show her bracelet of bandages. 'Tabby, too.'

'Oh my God, Paulina!' Kymba gasped. 'What did you do?'

Paulina shrugged. 'Tried to get her to own up to some shit. She wouldn't.'

'They're all like that, the older ones.' Kymba waved her hand. 'Well, not all of them. But a lot of them. They're so attached to this idea of what it means to be a "King", it's like the law doesn't apply to them. It doesn't, a lot of the time.'

'Yeah?'

'A few years back, when I was pregnant with Hunter ...' Kymba fingered the steering wheel. 'A group of boys ganged up on this one girl. When her parents tried to report it, the boys' mums all said they were home watching TV.'

'Shit.'

'I wanted to leave, then and there. Simmo convinced me to stick it out. He said this place'd never change if we just left it to the dogs. I'll see if he's still saying that when Zoe turns twelve.'

'Bloody hell.'

Kymba shrugged. 'It's not like those things don't happen on the mainland; it's just not someone with your surname, normally. At least I can tell Zoe who to avoid.'

'Hope she listens better than me.'

'Car.' Kymba shook her head. 'I felt so cool, when he took an interest. I didn't stop to think what this big man who'd travelled all around the world was doing buying booze for his kid-cousin.'

'You were cooler than me. I never drank till I was legal. Just stayed home having screaming matches with Mum.'

'Oh, I did that, too. I'm sure I've got some bad karma coming.'

'You'll be right.'

'I'll stay away from the supply ship, just in case.' Kymba smiled at her sidelong. 'I still can't believe that happened, you know. It makes me so happy.'

Paulina laughed. 'I was at the doctor's. I just cracked up. He thought I was mental.'

'Sometimes I start laughing when I'm home with the kids and they're all, "What's so funny, Mummy?" I don't know what to tell them: "Oh, just thinking about how your Uncle Car had to be fished out of the Pacific so the sharks wouldn't eat him"?'

'Ha, maybe when they're older.'

'No,' Kymba said. 'They won't even know they had an Uncle Car, when they're older. His name won't mean anything.'

CASUARINA

'I knew it!' Caro clapped her hands. 'I *knew* it!'

Judy burst into tears. 'You had no idea!'

'I knew it, I knew it, I knew it!' Caro poked her in the ribs. 'I've been suss ever since you asked me about gym memberships!'

'Ouch!' Judy winced. 'It's not the gym. I'm lovesick. I can't eat. I can't sleep.'

'You can *drink*.' Noting Judy's empty glass, Caro went over to the intercom. 'Tim, we're going to need a bottle.'

A minute later, Tim shuffled upstairs, handed Caro a bottle of Merlot, and frowned at Judy's red eyes. 'Should I set up the spare room?'

Caro nodded.

'I invited *him* to stay in the spare room,' Judy lamented, once Tim had made himself scarce. 'I never dreamed of more. He kicked up a big stink about it. "I'm not coming all that way to sleep in a spare room" — he said that.'

Caro refilled their glasses. 'Sneaky little shit.'

'He said I was beautiful. He said he loved me.' Judy drank. 'He lied.'

'A man, lying? Stop the presses.'

'I never would've let it go this far, if he didn't say those things. He said them, then he took them back. He told me being with me would be like necrophilia. Like I'm a corpse.'

Caro dabbed Judy's cheek. 'Corpses don't cry.'

'I'm dying of shame. Just bury me now.'

'Jude.' Sighing, Caro sat cross-legged on the bed. 'I think what he meant is, it'd be like digging up the dead. Disrespectful to Paulina?'

'No. I'm decrepit.' A tear plopped into Judy's glass. 'I really thought he loved me.'

'Jude.'

'He said he'd never felt like this before. He felt it from the first time we met—'

'What, when you were drugged to the eyeballs and could barely dress yourself?'

'We … connected.'

'You were *grieving*.'

'I love him.' Judy hugged her knees to her chest, cried into them. 'It hurts.'

'Oh, honey.' Caro plucked Judy's glass and moved it to the nightstand. 'I know.'

'I love him so much.'

'I know, I know.' Caro petted her hair. 'But, Jude: surely you didn't think you were going to run off into the sunset with your daughter's boyfriend?'

'He wasn't her boyfriend. And, not the sunset, just—'

'A good root?'

Judy rolled her eyes, nodded. Caro cracked up, all over again.

'Please, don't.' Judy grabbed a silky pillow to dry her face on. 'I'm ashamed enough, already.'

'Sorry, but …' Caro stifled a laugh. 'This is *brilliant*.'

'It *isn't*.'

'Jude. When was the last time you seriously thought about rooting anyone?'

Judy shrugged. 'After Marko died, sometimes.'

'Fifteen years? Twenty?'

'Paulina was so angry after the funeral.' She sniffed. 'She was this little ball of rage. I wasn't going to make it worse by bringing some bloke into the house.'

'She *was* angry.' Caro took a swallow of wine. 'Understandably.'

'And I always worried, what if I did and he ends up molesting her or something? You never know.'

'No,' Caro agreed. 'You were right to be cautious.'

'Besides. I was so busy putting dinner on the table and making sure she ate it. The blues we had … any man would've run a mile.'

'I would've helped out more, if you let me.'

'I've never wanted — no man. Not like this.'

'Marko?'

'Not like this.'

'Come on, Jude.'

'Not like this.' She reached for her glass; drank deep. 'No man's ever called me *smart* before.'

Caro laughed in disbelief. 'That's it? Not … his body?'

'Yes, that, too.' Judy sighed. 'But he took me seriously.'

Her sister looked at her sideways. 'You know, all things considered, he's not the worst guy you've gone for.'

'He's perfect.'

'Perfect? No. He's your dead daughter's boyfriend.'

'They were just friends.'

'You don't believe that.'

Judy wiped her eyes. 'No.'

'He would've fathered your grandkids.'

Nodding, Judy's eyes welled with fresh tears. 'How could I do this to her?'

'She's laughing her arse off, wherever she is.'

Judy watched her sister's bony hands, topping up their glasses.

'You remind me of her so much, sometimes.'

'Fuck. So do you.' Caro averted her eyes. 'Sometimes you'll make a face or say something, and it's like she's in the room with us. It gives me the willies.'

'She was more like you.'

'In some ways. The *crying*. That was you.'

'She was like you as a kid.'

'Well, you did a better job than our parents did.' Shiny-eyed, Caro gulped. 'Even with all your screwing around.'

'I haven't changed.'

'Falling for your daughter's boyfriend? Classic Jude.'

'I'm so stupid.'

'*So* stupid. Look at that face.'

'How could I be so stupid?' Judy gestured with her glass. 'To think he'd want a stupid, dried-up receptionist—'

'Stupid receptionist! You spilled wine on my pillow?'

'Oh, it's gone on my shirt, too.'

Caro jumped up and veered over to the walk-in wardrobe. 'Here!'

A pair of silk pyjamas flew into Judy's lap. Bleary-eyed, she rose and blundered to the ensuite bathroom.

In a kinder world, the alcohol in Judy's blood would've made her reflection tolerable. In fact, she'd never looked blotchier. She turned her back on the mirror and struggled into the pyjamas with the wounded pride of a dog that goes under the house to die alone.

When she emerged, Caro was shimmying into an almost identical pair. Judy's eyes went straight to the scars on her thighs.

'I know; they're nasty things.' Caro caught her looking. 'I've slathered them in so many creams and oils, but old habits die hard. Speaking of which.'

Judy followed her out to the balcony. Shook her head when Caro offered up the pack of Marlboros.

'*He* smoked, didn't he?' Caro lit up. 'Camels?'

Judy nodded.

'Just think of all the tar in those kisses.'

Watching the smoke in the darkness, Judy tried to imagine a world where she didn't want to taste him.

'I know you don't like being told what to do.' She frowned at her sister. 'But I wish you *wouldn't*.'

'I know.' Caro dragged. 'Thank you for your concern.'

'Tim, too.'

'I know.'

'He's a good one.'

'I'll leave him to you in my will when I get terminal lung cancer.'

'You're terrible.'

'I know.' Caro stubbed it out, finally. 'I still pinch myself, sometimes.'

'You chose the right chiropractor's office to walk into.'

'Well, he's got friends, you know.'

Judy giggled. 'No he doesn't.'

'I'll get him to make you an appointment with one of them. You can say you threw your back out rooting a thirty-year-old tattoo artist.'

'Actually, can I have one of those?' Judy held out her hand. 'I need a smoke, if we're having this conversation.'

Gleefully, Caro handed over her Marlboros. The glee fled her face as soon as Judy flung them off the balcony.

'Litterbug!' Caro shrieked. 'You can't litter in Mercy Cove!'

'I can do anything I want.' Judy sipped her wine. 'I'm a grieving mother.'

Caro snatched Judy's glass. 'You *can* do anything. That's what I'm saying. Break the dry spell. It doesn't have to be a chiropractor—'

'No.'

'Online dating? Or use up your annual leave and go to Europe, find another wog—'

'No.'

'Go *somewhere*. You're pushing sixty and have never been further than Fairfolk. It's pathetic.'

'No.' Judy snatched back her glass. 'Well. Maybe.'

'Where?'

Judy downed the last of her wine. 'West.'

'West?' Caro's brow creased. 'Perth?'

'What have I got to lose at this point?'

Caro grinned. 'Jude!'

'I said, maybe.'

'Jude!' Caro grabbed her close. 'It's about fucking time.'

Judy wished she didn't notice the young man. Board shorts, sleeveless shirt, tribal tattoos, seemingly immune to the airport's chill. His carry-on luggage was lumped boulder-like on the chair beside him, his legs wide-spread like the world belonged to him. He drank flavoured milk; left the carton on the ground when boarding time was announced.

Onboard, he sat diagonal from her. She watched him for most of the three-hour flight. He didn't notice.

At arrivals, FIFO workers in citrus-coloured uniforms swarmed by, baby-faced and muscular. She approached the rental car counter with just her carry-on and a box marked 'FRAGILE'.

Over the unfamiliar highway, the sun burned strong and gold. No one seemed to know how to merge.

'You're right. It is too little, too late,' Milica said. 'But thanks for the effort.'

Judy tried not to scrutinise Milica's face too closely, though there was a lot in it. Ljubica. Marko, a few years before he got sick. Paulina, at an age she never got to be. And, buried under the crow's feet, the nine-year-old girl whose home Judy had wrecked.

'I don't know what to say.' Judy's eyes strayed to a tied-up Labrador, splashing its tongue into an ice cream tub full of water. 'Except, it wasn't personal.'

'Are you serious?' Milica's face soured. 'Sorry, but, to me it was very personal. You took my dad.'

'I know.'

'And not just that. The fact that it was *you*. To me that was very personal.'

'I was just the receptionist.'

'You weren't *just* the receptionist. You were "Judy".' Milica said 'Judy' in the sunshiny tone that Judy used to answer phones. 'You gave me jelly beans when I came in after school. You read *Women's Weekly* with me. You made me feel like I belonged. Do you know what school was like for me? I barely spoke English. I had no friends. I *looked forward* to seeing you.'

'I'm sorry. I never realised.'

'No. You were just showing off for him. "Look how nice I am to your daughter. Look what a good mother I could be."'

'It's true.' Judy nodded. 'I wanted him to think that.'

'You were very good at it.'

'I was so young. I just wanted to get out of my parents' house; it wasn't—'

'I don't need to hear about your childhood. No offence.' Milica waved her hand. 'Caro told me enough.'

Judy looked some more at the Labrador.

'I don't blame you more then I blame him. I blame you a lot. I blame Mama, too. I blame him the most.'

'We all could've handled it better.'

'Caro was the only one who cared that we were sisters. If it was up to the rest of you, Paulina wouldn't've known I existed.'

'I'm glad she reached out,' Judy said — though she couldn't help but wonder if her sister's intentions had been completely pure.

'I spent so many years wishing he'd ask me to move in with the three of you. I hated my life with Mama. I wanted to be part of your perfect little family.'

'It wasn't perfect, it that helps.'

'To me, it seemed perfect. And *you*.' Milica gave her an appraising look. 'I wanted to look just like you. I thought Mama and I were so ugly. I thought that's why he left. I hated looking like her.'

'No.' Judy shook her head. 'I was very ordinary. You two were much more striking.'

Milica rolled her eyes. 'The grass is always greener.'

Judy looked at the grass, eye-burningly green, littered with pine fronds. The soft white dunes beyond it. 'They're smaller than on Fairfolk,' she murmured, nodding at the pines.

'I've seen pictures.' Milica lifted her coffee to her mouth. 'It looks creepy. Paulina loved it, though.'

'How often did you two … ?' Judy's throat slimed with guilt.

'Talk?' Milica smiled wryly. 'About as I often as I get my power bill.'

'I'm sorry.'

'We weren't sisters, like you and Caro. I was more like … a distant aunt or something.'

'I'm very sorry.'

'She told me about the baby, though. She said she wanted to give it a real Yugo name, like Snežana or Dragana.'

Judy was glad she had her sunglasses on. 'She really wanted a girl.'

'Of course she did.'

Judy lowered her eyes, unsure whether to feel flattered or chastened. 'I offered to visit, after she lost it.' Milica fingered the rim of her paper cup. 'She said don't worry. I guess she didn't need me, when she had you.'

'She didn't want me there, either.'

'Well. She had you, anyway.' Milica shrugged. 'Last time we spoke, she seemed happy. It was right after New Year's. She liked a guy, but was worried she'd screw things up.'

Cheeks burning, Judy changed the subject. 'Do you … have someone?'

'Boyfriend. He's divorced. Three kids. He has them most weekends. We're going to the footy tonight.'

'And what does he do?'

'He's a Phys Ed teacher.' She must've made a face, because Milica laughed. 'Caro had the same reaction. Mama loves him, though.'

Judy's eyes drifted to the 'FRAGILE' box.

'I can call her now, if you like.'

'Oh.' Judy tried to buy some time. 'There's no rush.'

Milica finished her coffee. 'She knows you're coming. She's been cleaning the house. She probably has a meat platter ready for you.'

'Oh gawd.' Judy clutched her head. 'I'm terrified.'

Milica whipped her phone from her handbag, dialled. Within seconds, she was speaking a language Judy hadn't heard in years.

'I'll drop you off; it's not far,' Milica said, after hanging up.

'It's such a beautiful language.'

'Kajkavian,' Milica grimaced. 'I tried to speak it with some of the Yugo kids I taught ESL to. They'd give me these blank stares.'

'It's very beautiful. I wish Paulina had it.'

Milica got up, picking up the pale-aqua jewellery box as she went. 'Thanks again, for the pendant.'

'I have so many of her things.' Judy rose from her white plastic chair. 'You're welcome to them. I almost brought some of her baby things. I … wasn't sure. If you're ever in Sydney, though.'

On their way from the kiosk to the carpark, a dark-skinned boy in a rashie and bucket hat broke loose from his mother's grip and flung himself toward Milica. 'Mrs Novak!'

'Hello, Ali.' Milica smiled from the boy to his mother. 'Hello.'

Judy smiled as well. 'Hello.'

'One of my students,' Milica explained, once they'd passed. 'A lot of them call me "Mrs Novak" by mistake.'

'I get that all the time. It doesn't bother me too much.'

'That's nice to hear,' Milica said briskly. 'I'd hate for you to have gone to all that trouble for a name you don't even want.'

When Ljubica saw what was in the 'FRAGILE' box, she laughed — full-throated, mocking. Then she set the crystal glasses on the counter and said something in Kajkavian.

'Mama, no!' Milica protested.

Ljubica waved her hand, opened the pantry. Again, Milica protested

— a velvety flurry of words Judy didn't understand — then got up on her tiptoes and removed the bottle herself.

'*Rakija*,' Ljubica proclaimed.

Milica rolled her eyes. 'She makes her own.'

They started speaking Kajkavian again, and Judy had to remind herself that they weren't doing it just to show off. Ljubica handed her a glass.

'Thank you,' she mumbled.

Ljubica winced and sat herself down. She was old, truly old.

Milica leaned against the kitchen counter. Took a sip of her *rakija*, pulled a face, and poured the rest back in the bottle. Ljubica scolded her. Rolling her eyes again, Milica slung her handbag. 'I'll leave you to it. Nice seeing you, Judy.'

'Yes, you too.' Judy stepped forward, unsure if they should hug or shake hands or nothing. In the end, they clasped each other's wrists, exchanged dry cheek-kisses.

Then they were two.

'I saw you on TV.' Ljubica raised her glass. 'I thought, my god. She's *aged*.'

'Yes.' Judy tried not to be offended. 'The years really do add up.'

'Until then, you were still very young, to me. Even at Marko's funeral, you were, what, thirty?'

'Thirty-seven.'

'Still young. Then I saw you on TV and I thought, my god, what happened to little blondie who wandered in from the beach to answer phones and steal husbands?'

'Life happened.' Judy crossed her arms. 'Grief happened.'

'Have you tried the *rakija*?'

Judy obediently took a gulp of the liquor. 'It's good.'

'I make it with plums, from my garden.' Ljubica hefted herself from her seat. 'Come, see my garden.'

Judy made an effort to appear unfazed by the slowness of Ljubica's movements. Still, she read her mind. 'You're old now. I'm *very* old.'

'It happens to the best of us.'

'Not Pavlina.'

'No. Not *Paulina*.'

'I prefer "Pavlina".' Ljubica led her into the sun-washed backyard.

'Marko said if ever we had another daughter, we'd call her Pavlina.'

'He suggested it. I didn't want the kids at school calling her "Pavlova".'

Ljubica laughed. 'Like Milly. "Why did you name me after the little gel packets you get with new shoes?" Aussies, they think it rhymes with "silica".'

'You have a beautiful garden.'

'These are my plums. Grapes. Lemon tree. Pomegranate — it doesn't grow much.'

'You do it all yourself?'

'Milly's boyfriend — *very* Aussie — built the trellis. Here, raspberry.'

'No thank you.'

'Take it.' Ljubica forced a raspberry into Judy's hand. 'I remember the sweet tooth. You made Milly fat, giving her all those jelly beans after school.'

It wasn't sweet. 'Very ... fresh,' Judy bluffed.

'Everything is very fresh.' Ljubica pointed. 'There's the veggie patch. Herbs, too.'

My life isn't small, Judy knew she was really saying. *You may have robbed me, but my life isn't smaller than your life.*

'It's very impressive.' Judy knocked back her liquor.

'Why do you drink so fast?' Ljubica smirked. 'This isn't the pub. We're not getting pissed.'

Then she indicated for Judy to go ahead of her. 'Go, sit inside.'

Judy found the lounge room, sat. Her eyes wandered over the blind TV screen, piano, bookshelves. Not a speck of dust in sight.

'More, for the sweet tooth,' Ljubica returned with a plate of cakes and biscuits. 'Coffee's coming.'

'Do you need help?'

Ljubica didn't hear the question, or ignored it. She came back again with coffee. Again, with the *rakija* and a biscuit tin, which Judy eyed warily.

'Photos.' Ljubica plumped on the other end of the couch. 'Try the walnut cake.'

As Ljubica struggled to get the lid off the biscuit tin, Judy took a slice of cake.

'Our wedding.' Ljubica showed her a black-and-white photo of a dour, dark-haired couple. 'We were happier than we look.'

Judy nodded.

'Milly's baby photo.'

Judy nodded again.

'Zagreb in winter.' A picture of a young family in a snow-pixelated square. 'We were real people before you came along. We weren't made of cardboard.'

Judy nodded again.

'Sydney, when we first arrived. I don't have many pictures from then. I tried to take pictures for my family in Zagreb, but it was such a short time ... then everything changed.' She shrugged, passing Judy a pile of photos. 'I was too embarrassed to go back. My parents said Marko was a peasant. I was wrong to marry a peasant.'

'"Peasant",' Judy repeated carefully. 'Really?'

'Peasant, villager. No culture.' Ljubica settled back against the cushions. 'His ancestors were serfs. Everyone in his village was related, somehow.'

'Paulina visited,' Judy said defensively. 'She thought it was beautiful.'

'Yes, beautiful, with the hills. But *inbred*. Like Fairfolk.' Ljubica sipped her *rakija*. 'He was smart to know he should marry outside the village. He met me. Then he met you ... and you were more exotic.'

'I thought *he* was exotic.' Judy laughed, to hide the pain. 'Gawd. I'd never even heard of Yugoslavia.'

'If it wasn't you, it would've been some other stupid receptionist.'

Judy pursed her lips, handed back the photos.

'My second husband, Dom.' Ljubica sorted through another pile. 'Dead since nine years. I met him at the pharmacy. First, I worked in a bakery. Later, they let me work in a pharmacy. I worked in a lab in Zagreb, in the sixties.'

Judy nodded, pursed her lips some more.

'Here she is.' Ljubica smiled. 'Little Princess of Darkness.'

Judy's heart leapt into her mouth.

'First time she visited. Eighteen?' Ljubica handed over the photo. 'When Milly told me she was coming, I thought, "Oh, god, here we go, another blondie, another bimbo." But she was nothing like you.'

'She'd be pleased to hear that.' Judy fingered the picture of Paulina at a strange dinner table, fledgling-frail and unearthly in her Gothic lipstick. 'Oh, she was so cute!'

'Very cute,' Ljubica agreed. 'Very shy.'

'*Shy?*'

'Very shy. Very sweet. Nothing like you.'

'Are we talking about the same girl?' Judy cry-laughed. 'Oh, gawd. Did she *eat?*'

'Not much. No meat.'

'That'd be right.' Judy wiped her eyes. 'I had to force-feed her, practically.'

Ljubica set the photo aside. 'I'll make a copy. Try the *rafioli*.'

Judy stuffed a ravioli-shaped biscuit into her mouth, concentrated on chewing.

'Next time, with the boyfriend.' Ljubica found another photo. 'Very different.'

It was true: gone was the black makeup, black velvet. Her hair was a lighter shade of brown, her face dewy. Vinnie's arm circled her shoulders.

'I didn't like him,' Ljubica said. 'Even before he went on TV.'

'No,' Judy said. 'Neither did I.'

'He was quiet, but every little thing had to be just so. His way or the highway.'

'You hit the nail on the head,' Judy agreed. 'I was happy when they broke up. She never got over it, though.'

'I'll make a copy of that, too. You can use the scissors and cut him out.'

Judy laughed. 'Yes, good idea.'

Ljubica returned the photos to the tin. 'You can ask Milly if she has others. She visited her in Sydney, twice.'

'I had no idea.'

'You were such a bitch at Marko's funeral. Telling us we didn't belong.'

'I know.' Judy sighed. 'There's no excuse.'

Ljubica nibbled at a crisp, ribbonlike biscuit. 'Have you been to Casuarina?'

'To see Campbell? Gawd, no.'

'I did.'

'You visited *Campbell*?' Judy gaped. 'What was it like?'

Ljubica shrugged. 'He didn't say much. We talked about his family, a little bit. His grandma. I told him I was Pavlina's grandma.'

'Why on *earth*?'

'It's better than "I am her father's first wife". I wanted him to explain. He didn't.'

'No surprises there.'

'Maybe you'll have better luck. But I don't think he can explain. All he says is, "I didn't touch her", "I'm not a sicko", "They tricked me". The way he talks; he's "drug-fucked".'

'You *do* think he did it, though?'

Ljubica shrugged. 'People destroy other people for no reason.'

Judy exhaled raggedly. 'She'd be thirty-five now.'

Ljubica crossed herself, poured more *rakija*, and held her glass aloft. Judy downed hers like it was a shot.

'There you go, getting pissed again. Aussies: always getting pissed then drink-driving.'

'Oh, shit.' Judy checked her watch. 'I left my car at the beach. It was a two-hour zone. Oh, I've *definitely* got a ticket, haven't I?'

Ljubica laughed. 'Finally, my revenge.'

It was bushland, out where Sean Patrick Campbell lived. The building was whitish-gold like a sand dune against the spiny-dark vegetation, smudged with bore stains. 'NO ADMITTANCE UNLESS ON OFFICIAL BUSINESS', read the signs. Judy drove around, trying to see what she could through the trees. She parked off road and cried. Then she just sat, watching the last light pulse from the sky until a guard strolled over.

'Visiting hours are over. If you wanna visit, you need to make an appointment.'

'No. Sorry.' Judy shook her head. 'I'm just looking. The man who murdered my daughter is in there. I don't want to see him. I just wanted to see … where he lives.'

'It's not the Ritz-Carlton.'

'No, I figured. I thought I'd be able to see more from here, though.' Judy glanced at the pale, shadowy walls. 'Is it big?'

'680 capacity.'

'That doesn't sound so big,' Judy murmured. 'It's smaller than Fairfolk Island.'

'It's no island.' The guard shrugged. 'It's no Ritz-Carlton.'

'It doesn't really matter. He could be on Pluto. It wouldn't bring her back.'

'What's the bastard's name?' the guard asked. When Judy told him, he shrugged again. 'Never heard of him.'

'Fair enough.' Judy started the car, then stopped and looked at the guard. 'Her name was Paulina.'

'Paulina?'

'That's her name. Don't ever forget it.'

THE GREAT WHITE WHALE

Paulina didn't think anything when she saw him riding his bike along Klee Welkin Road on Saturday morning, at the exact time she was taking her walk. Or when she saw him the next day at the same hour, though he should've been at church with Rita and Bunny. It wasn't till he showed up at the Mutes' bistro half an hour before closing that she realised she'd been seeing more of Rabbit White than usual lately.

'Oh, shit!' Paulina looked up from the table she was wiping. 'Hello.'

'Hello.' Rabbit glanced around the bistro. 'I was hoping to get a bite to eat?'

'Early bird specials finished at six-thirty.'

'Oh.'

'Like, we're open till eight.' Paulina swept her fringe from her eyes. 'I reckon the chef's turned off the deep frier by now, but.'

'That's alright. I just want something light.'

'Like, cheese and crackers?'

'Perfect.' Rabbit pulled up a chair. 'Mind if I sit here?'

'Sit anywhere. It's just those guys left.' Paulina nodded at a table of grey-haired men, even older than Rabbit. 'They're guests. It's mostly only guests who eat here.'

Rabbit blushed. 'I was in the area.'

Paulina smiled through his bullshit, crossed the room to the serving hatch. 'Psst, Toa!' she called into the kitchen. 'Can you get some cheese and crackers, quick? My ex just came in. I wanna get rid of him before closing.'

Toa leaned through the hatch on his big arms. 'That old bloke?'

'I dunno what he's doing here. He's married now.'

'Want me to stay back? Make sure he doesn't try anything?'

'If he doesn't take the hint, yeah.'

She came back with Rabbit's cutlery, wrapped in a napkin. A bottle of tapwater. He sat back and watched her fill his glass. 'A glass of red, too.'

'No worries.' Paulina tried not to look surprised. 'House okay?'

Rabbit nodded. She felt his eyes on her as she walked off to pour his wine; met them when she returned with it on a tray, along with his cheese and crackers.

'Rita know you drink?'

'She's visiting her sister on the Sunshine Coast.'

'Howabout Bun?'

Rabbit sniffed his wine. 'She's at Hine's tonight.'

Paulina checked the clock. 'Well, we close at eight.'

'Plans after work?'

'Yeah. I'm playing PlayStation with Jesse.'

Soon after, the men at the next table paid up. Paulina cleared up, aware of Rabbit's gaze. Ten minutes before closing, she brought over his bill.

'Thank you, Lina,' he said, looking into her eyes.

'What the fuck,' she complained to Toa. 'Go home already.'

At two to eight, Rabbit finally got up, thanked her, and ambled toward the exit.

When she checked the faux-leather bill folder, she found a fifty-dollar tip.

'Poor old bugger.' Toa whistled. 'Must be really horny.'

He showed up again two nights later and ordered the same thing.

'What's the story?' Paulina came right out with it. 'You can eat better at home.'

'Bunny's at Hine's again.'

'You shouldn't let her have so many sleepovers on school nights.'

'I don't mind.' He gazed at her steadily. 'It's a nice change of scene.'

While Rabbit ate, Paulina hid out in the kitchen. One minute before eight, he was still at his table. Toa came out and stood around, arms crossed, till he paid and left.

Again, a fifty-dollar tip.

'Take it.' Paulina offered it to Toa. 'I don't want his money.'

Toa shrugged his bulky shoulders and walked her to her car, same as the night before. Back at her cottage, she opened a box of goon and called Jesse.

'Oi, Camel-shit. Still coming over?'

'Sorry.' Jesse's voice was stuffy. 'I fell asleep.'

'Bloody useless. What's the point of even being friends with you?!'

'Calm down. We hung out yesterday.'

'Yeah, and you fell asleep then, too. Useless.'

'Wetties tomorrow?'

'What, so I can watch you eat chips and stare at tits?'

'You can stare at Pellet. He's coming, too.'

Her head twinged. 'Yeah, nah.'

Paulina hung up. Turned on her stereo and blasted it, in defiance of her aching head. Then she smoked and drank on the porch till Vera came out in her boots and bathrobe and told her, 'Party's over.'

There was a message from her mum on the answering machine, when she got in:

Hi, darling. Not long now! I know you said you wanted a new Discman, but I'm going clothes shopping this weekend so if there's anything else—

Paulina couldn't be fucked listening to the rest of it.

'You're gonna turn into a mouse,' Paulina warned Rabbit, taking his order the next night.

'Have a drink with me,' he said.

She pretended not to hear him.

He said it again when she came back with his cheese and crackers. 'Have a drink with me, Lina.'

'I'm working, if you didn't notice.'

'After.'

'What, here?'

'Or, you could come to the house.'

Paulina looked around. A husband and wife were still plodding through their desserts. 'Yeah, nah,' she said, and walked off.

She nicked off for a smoke. It was quarter to eight when she returned. She fixed the bill for the husband and wife, began clearing their table. Rabbit watched her.

'Need me to give your old man the boot?' Toa peeked his head through the hatch.

'S'alright.' Paulina waved her hand. 'He's harmless. Go home, if you want.'

'Seriously?'

'Yeah. I'll have a drink with him.'

Toa looked at her like she was crazy.

'S'alright. We've got unfinished business.'

The husband and wife got up to leave. Paulina beamed at them. 'See ya next time!'

She brought Rabbit his bill. 'Just so you know, fifteen to twenty per cent is standard.'

He drew out his wallet, laid out a twenty for his wine and cheese, another fifty on top. She shrugged and took the faux-leather folder to the counter, poured herself a glass, and started on the books. Toa emerged from the kitchen, looked from her to Rabbit. 'Alright?'

'Yeah, all good.' She sipped. 'Say hi to Christy and the kids for me.'

Toa gave Rabbit the stink-eye on his way out. The clock ticked past eight. Paulina finished the books, locked up the cash, and sauntered over with her wine.

'Big guy.' Rabbit nodded toward the door as she sat. 'Protective?'

'He's nice. Started in December. His wife works at Jelly's.'

'You with Camilleri now?'

'No.' She looked at him steadily. 'We're just friends.'

'You didn't look like just friends, that night—'

'You hit me, Ric. I felt like a prisoner. What do you expect?'

He looked at his lap. 'I'm sorry.'

'I lost our baby and then you hit me.'

'The drinking …' He trailed off, red-faced. 'I was too controlling, I'm sorry.'

'Yeah.' She swallowed her wine. 'You should be.'

'You're so beautiful.'

Paulina rolled her eyes. 'It's just makeup.'

He reached for her hand. 'I miss you.'

'I miss you too, sometimes.' She looked at his wedding ring. 'It's been a bad year, Ric. Worst year of my life. You have no idea.'

'I have some idea.' He squeezed her hand. 'I've missed you so much, gorgeous.'

'You have no idea. I'm thirty in three weeks. What do I have to show for it?'

'Come home with me.'

'Yeah, nah.' She laughed. 'I'm not rooting you in the bed you share with Rita.'

He drew her hand to his mouth. 'Lina.'

She pulled it away, finished her wine, then his. Stood and cleared the table.

'Lina,' he repeated. 'Gorgeous.'

'Yeah, yeah. Give me a sec.'

She ducked into the kitchen, had a cry while she loaded the dishwasher. Then she came out and crossed her arms.

'I live on Tenderloin Road now, if you wanna drive me home.'

Paulina took her hair down, during the drive, knowing Rabbit liked it like that. Smoked, knowing he didn't like that. The lights were on in the main house. 'Do you know Vera and Rocky?' she asked him.

Rabbit looked sheepish. 'I know everybody.'

There was no question of them not fucking, but she showed him around the cottage first.

'This's my first time living alone. I wanted to make it nice.'

'You could've decorated my house any way you liked.'

'Yeah, but. It was already nice. And it's your house, not mine.'

He took her waist. 'It's very nice.'

'I wanted it kinda beachy, but feminine?' She slipped out of his arms. 'I put these little hooks in the bathroom, for towels. They're shaped like seahorses.'

She snapped on the bathroom light. 'See? Cute, hey?'

Rabbit nodded, took her waist in his hands again, and kissed her. He tasted like wine. Paulina broke the kiss and looked at the two of them in the mirror. They looked wrong together, like they always had.

'Do you like the towels?' she asked. 'Turquoise?'

'I like everything.'

Within five minutes, he had her on her back, was kissing her wet pussy through the thin fabric of her g-string; unhooking the string from around her raised hips, knees, ankles.

'Ric,' she sighed as his tongue turned her on like fairy lights. 'I missed you.'

He spent a long time with his head between her legs, making her quiver and whimper. When she couldn't take it anymore, she tried to guide him up, but he just kept lapping at her like he was lost in the desert and she was the only source of moisture. He wanted her to beg.

'Fuck me, babe,' she pleaded. 'Please, Ric. Fuck me.'

Then he was inside her and his face above hers was tender and grim, familiar and unfamiliar; it had been so long. At one point, the force of his thrusts caused her head to bump against the headboard. He cradled it in his hands, kissed her brow, and kept thrusting till, with a startled groan, he pulled out and came on her thighs.

'Oh, babe.' Paulina kissed him. 'You're so good.'

She reached for the tissues, mopped up his spill, but didn't want to stop kissing, touching. He didn't seem to mind. With a mildly amused expression, he pinched her nipples, traced her waist, stroked her pussy as he might stroke a flower in a vase at a restaurant.

She came, again and again. So readily, it felt a bit melodramatic.

'Babe.' She fondled his dick; it'd gone soft. 'I want you so much.'

He shrunk away. 'I bes' go.'

'Stay, babe.' She pushed her tongue into his mouth, clenched her thighs around his wrist. 'We can do other things.'

He withdrew his hand from her thighs; they were totally slick. 'You bes' find another customer.'

Paulina stiffened. 'What's that s'posed to mean?'

Rabbit sat up, sniffed his fingers, and wiped them on the sheets. 'Do you think I'm stupid?'

'Oh, bloody hell!' She switched on the lamp. 'This again?'

Rabbit was already pulling on his pants. 'I'm not making the same mistake twice.'

'Yeah?' Paulina found her ciggies. 'What mistake's that, Ric?'

'Waking up next to a whore.' He took out his wallet. 'I pay by the hour now.'

'Har-har. I bet you spent ages thinking that one up.'

He chucked three fifties on the bed. 'That should do it.'

'You know what, Ric?' She lit up. 'I *do* think you're stupid. Always have. I've met some dumb pricks in my time, but you take the cake, hey.'

Rabbit found his shirt, started buttoning up, his lips pale and tight.

'What's wrong, babe?' Paulina wheedled. 'Run out of smart things to say?'

He caught sight of *Anna Karenina* on her bedside table. 'Still not done with that?'

'Nah. I'm a slow reader. I get headaches if I read too long. Is that the best you can do, Ric?'

Smirking, he shook his head, tucked in his shirt.

'Gawd, you're a miserable old prick.' Paulina blew smoke at him. 'No wonder Tatiana walked out on you.'

His jaw clenched, shoulders tensed.

'I feel sorry for Bunny,' she continued. 'She's a smart girl. Someday she'll grow up and see what a miserable prick you are. You'll be lucky if she talks to you once a year.'

His fists tightened.

'Whatsamatter? Wanna hit me again?'

He turned his back, mumbled, 'You're nay worth it,' and stalked out of the cottage.

Paulina saved her tears till his car had gone. There weren't many. Then she hunted around for her g-string, but it was nowhere to be found. 'Sick fuck,' she muttered, lit another ciggie, and scrawled in her diary:

R over for a root after Mutes', called me a whore. Made off with my undies. Wanker!!!

Then she called her mum and told her all the things she wanted from the mainland.

'No wonder he was grumpy.' Jesse played it cool, when she told him. 'You kept him up past his bedtime.'

'Har-har.' Paulina snaked her tongue along her ciggie to seal it. 'What's your excuse?'

'I'm not grumpy.'

'Are so. What's wrong? Jealous?'

'Of Rabbit?'

'Of my multiple orgasms.' She crossed her legs. 'He's good with his tongue. When he's not using it for talking.'

'Maybe you should change lanes, eh,' Jesse suggested, nodding across the beer garden at Oliana, who was wandering around with two pints, looking lost.

Paulina waved. 'Oi, babe. You lost?'

Oliana crept over to their table, green eyes damp and red-rimmed. 'Hi.'

'Geez, how stoned are ya?' Paulina interrogated her. 'Looks like you've been crying.'

Oliana sat down and burst into tears.

'Jesus!' Jesse looked deeply uncomfortable.

'Whatsamatter, babe?' Paulina's eyes flashed. 'Pellet break up with you?'

Oliana shook her head, kept weeping. Laurent emerged from the bar, looking pallid and shellshocked. His eyes were as red as Oliana's.

'Oi, Pellet,' Paulina beckoned him over. 'What the fuck.'

Laurent crossed the beer garden. Slumped beside Jesse. 'I'm going back to Montréal.'

'You getting deported?'

He shook his head. 'It is ... canceur. Testiculeur.'

Paulina gawked. Then she burst into tears, too.

'Please.' Laurent reached for his beer. 'You're not helping.'

'But ...' Paulina tried to light her ciggie. 'You're so good-looking?'

Laurent shrugged.

'But!' She sobbed. 'You can't lose your balls. You need to pass on your good-looking genes!'

Jesse kicked her under the table.

'Just one ball.' Laurent drank. 'There is a chance of infertility ... if I live.'

Paulina looked at Oliana, who nodded tremulously. They flung their arms around each other and sobbed.

'Jesus, brudda.' Jesse patted Laurent's shoulder. 'That's ... rough.'

'Yes.' Laurent nodded. 'Very rough.'

Paulina stopped crying, whispered in Oliana's ear. Oliana stopped, too. They stared at each other, whispered some more, before linking hands and rising.

'Scuse us.' Paulina sniffed. 'We need the loo.'

Nodding, the guys stared into their drinks. They were in exactly the same position when Paulina and Oliana returned, cheeks aglow, still holding hands.

'Loh-rent?' Paulina smiled bravely. 'You know Oliana loves you, right?'

Laurent nodded glumly.

'And you know I love you. As a friend, and an ex-girlfriend.'

He shrugged.

Oliana took his hand, without letting go of Paulina's. 'We both love you.'

'Oh, shit.' Jesse laughed. 'Is this what I think it is?'

'Threesome.' Paulina took Laurent's other hand. 'To show how much we care.'

Laurent stopped looking glum. 'Err?'

'We love you!' Paulina and Oliana chorused. 'So, so much!'

They kissed, to show him.

'Wow,' Jesse marvelled. 'Just, wow.'

But Laurent was unconvinced. 'No, thank you.'

Paulina and Oliana broke down, again.

'Take the threesome, brudda.' Jesse nudged his friend. 'How can you say no to those faces?'

Paulina wiped her eyes. 'You're invited, too, Jess.'

'Nay.' He reddened. 'Four's a crowd, eh.'

'Seurry.' Slipping his hand free of Paulina's, Laurent looked at Oliana, only Oliana. 'She is enough for me.'

Paulina sighed, picked up her ciggie. 'Well, just so you know. My door's always open.'

'Thank you.' Laurent finally cracked a smile. 'You're very generous.'

Jesse lit her ciggie. 'She's a psychopath. She's using your cancer as an excuse to get laid.'

'Sex and death, babe.' Paulina blew smoke at him. 'I didn't make the rules.'

———

She almost proved her point in a dark corner of the beer garden, later. But when Jesse's tongue tickled the roof of her mouth, the beer swelled up in her, the three shots of rum she'd snuck behind his back. She pulled away and spewed under the nearest kentia palm.

'Jesus.' Jesse held hair, her shaking shoulders as she cried. 'Not again.'

'I'm such a fuck-up. I fuck everything up.'

'Yeah, yeah.' He stroked her hair. 'Nobody's perfect.'

Inside, he made her drink water. They left Wetties together, his arm around her waist so she wouldn't fall.

She tried to kiss him again, up against the Mazda.

'Sorry.' Jesse turned his face away. 'Your breath.'

'Tic Tacs!' Paulina tumbled into the passenger seat, opened the glovebox, poured the whole cannister of mints into her hands and tried to swallow them like pills.

'Jesus, that's a choking hazard.' Jesse saw her reach for her flask. 'Oh, come on. Don't.'

'Fuck you!' Paulina washed the Tic Tacs down with vodka. 'My head hurts!'

Then she scrambled over to the driver's side, tried to start the car.

'Not happening.' Jesse jangled her keys. 'We're walking.'

'I already went for my walk today!'

'This's tomorrow's walk. It's Saturday morning, fuckwit.'

Coming around to her side of the car, he hauled her out.

'You're so strong!' Paulina giggled. 'Carry me!'

Jesse picked her up, carried her as far as the public toilet block with its mosaic of flowers. There, she grabbed his face and kissed him.

'You taste like Tic Tac vodka,' he sighed, putting her down.

Paulina slipped him her tongue. 'Like it?'

'Aye.'

They clung to each other, sucking faces, pressing hips. When she tried to lead him into the toilets, though, he sighed again and shook his head.

'I'm such a fuck-up.' Paulina's eyes overflowed. 'My whole life's a fuck-up.'

'You're alright. Come on.'

Hand in hand, they stumbled up the road.

'I'm gonna die alone! I'm so fucking old!'

'Calm down, ulvini. At least you don't have cancer.'

'Pellet!'

'Yeah. Poor dude.'

'If you get cancer of the balls, we'll fuck, okay? You'll let me have your babies?'

'Yeah, fine.'

'You have such beautiful lips! And eyelashes. And skin. I want our babies to have all your things, none of my shit.'

'Um. Okay.'

'I'm so shit. I'm gonna die alone, Jess!'

'Can you shut up? You're bumming me out. Look: there's your place.'

He pointed at the Great-O White Shark Grill, further up the road.

'Ohh, Great-O's!' Paulina dropped his hand. 'My great white whale!'

'Great white shark,' he corrected her. 'Shark.'

'My great white whale.' She stood on her tippy toes, stretched her hands up to the shark's wide-open jaws. 'I love, love, love it!'

Without her having to ask, Jesse lifted her up so she could touch the jagged teeth, trace her fingers over the glassy eyes.

'I love it so much, Jess! I really love it. You don't know how much I love it.'

'I do, but.' Smiling, he lowered her. 'You tell me every time.'

She blew kisses at the shark till they turned the corner, started uphill toward Jesse's. 'I'm tired,' she whinged. 'Camel-ride?'

After a while riding on his back, she complained again.

'Don't walk so hard! My head hurts!'

'Cos you drank too much.'

'I'm gonna spew.'

She didn't, though. Only coughed over the grass then lay down and closed her eyes.

'Don't, Paulina. You're getting cow shit in your hair.'

'Leave me alone.'

'Come on.' He patted her cheek. 'This's where cows sleep. You're not a cow.'

'Am so. Fat cow.'

'You're so miggy, I'm surprised you're not dead yet.' A note of annoyance crept into his voice. 'Fucking hell, Paulina. Beer isn't food.'

'You're not my mum.' She grabbed his crotch. 'Will you meet my mum?'

Jesse pushed her hand away.

'Yeah, I said I would. As a friend, though. Just friends, okay?'

'Sex friends?'

'We've talked about this, remember?' Sighing, he took out his Camels. 'Not when you're like this. If it happens, I want you to be able to remember it.'

'But I'm always like this, Jess. I'll never remember.'

'Yeah.' He crouched down, lit a ciggie and placed it between her lips. 'It's a shame.'

When Paulina woke in Jesse's bed in just her g-string and his Bauhaus T-shirt, she couldn't remember how she got there. But her skin was sticky-hot. Her heart scrabbled in her chest like a rat in a burning cage. She had a bad taste in her mouth, a thirst greater than the Pacific.

His arm was around her, warm and tattooed and tanned and hard.

She looked at his cute full-lipped face, his sleeping eyelashes, and the love was so strong, so at odds with the trash-heap of her body, it instantly flickered to fear. Fight-or-flight.

'Arsehole!' She kicked him. 'Why am I here?'

'Huh?'

'Why'd you make me sleep here!'

'Drunk.'

'Arsehole!' She kicked him again. 'I've got work.'

'Later.'

Jesse curled his arm back around her, as if he couldn't smell the garbage.

'Fuck you!' She rolled out of bed, found her skirt. 'I'm gonna get fired.'

'Sick day.'

'We don't all work for our dads, Camel-shit.'

'Shhh. Sleeping.'

'Don't shhh me!' She zipped up her skirt, fanned his T-shirt over it. 'I'm stealing this!'

'Mmmm.' He rolled over. 'Shh, now.'

Paulina spied his jeans slung over a chair, his Camels peeking out of the back pocket. She nicked them. 'These, too.'

Jesse covered his head with a pillow. 'Sleep, now.'

'Fuck you.' Paulina paused in the doorway for one last perv. 'You're beautiful, Jess.'

In the bathroom, she scrutinised the stains on her knickers, the nicks and bruises on her arms and legs. Her piss was dark and foamy. She drank straight from the tap, splashed her face. It looked older than almost-thirty.

She found her shoes by the front door.

'Fucksake,' she grumbled, leaving the cottage and seeing no car in the drive.

It came back to her, step by step. A pine he'd stopped to piss under. A cigarette butt with a tiny camel on it. A barbed-wire fence she'd grabbed. In the pre-dawn air, her sweat cooled and reeked, ripe and beery. She tried to breathe only dew, grass, ocean.

As the world throbbed with new light, she stopped to stare at the valley below, the pines turning from black to green.

Her hands shook, drawing a ciggie from the pack. But, for once, her head didn't hurt.

She walked a bit more. Stopped. Sat on the hill among the cow shit and, for no other reason than just being there, cried her eyes out.

She was still crying when a lady drove up, a little later. She was about her mum's age, wanted to know if everything was okay.

'Yeah.' Wiping her face, Paulina waved at the valley, the blue sea beyond. 'It's just this place. It's so pretty. I can't believe I live here, sometimes.'

AULULARIA

Judy took him for a professor, the bloke the next table over with the off-white hair. Then she saw the dictionary he kept checking, his book so heavily annotated it looked like it was bleeding. When she saw the title, she laughed.

'Sorry.' Judy blushed when he looked over. 'Just, that's the unfinished one, isn't it? *The Pot of Gold?*'

His face fell. 'You're telling me I've spent hours translating this play and I don't even get to find out the ending?'

'Your tutor didn't tell you? I s'pose she wanted to motivate you to finish it.'

The bloke set down his book. 'There goes my motivation.'

'Oh, don't stop reading because of me! You'll fail your class.'

'You don't have much faith in me, do you?'

'Sorry.' Judy steadied her face. 'What's it about, then?'

'There's this old man. Euclio. He's a tight-arse.'

'That's what it says in the dictionary? "Tight-arse"?'

'That's a John Quinlan translation.' His eyes were very blue, all of a sudden. 'I'm John.'

Judy knew she should probably introduce herself, but instead she just tapped her name tag. 'I better get back to the Student Help Desk.'

'Help Desk?' His eyes followed her as she stood. 'I thought you were a professor.'

'You're joking.'

'I was considering dropping Latin and signing up for your class.'

'Sorry to disappoint.' Hot-faced, she slung her handbag. 'But if you ever need to change classes, come see us. We'll sort you out.'

'You'll sort me out?'

She mustered a smile. 'I don't think you should drop Latin, though.

After all that hard work.'

'Alright.' He winked. 'I like to finish what I start.'

Judy's cheeks were aglow, walking briskly across campus. By the time she was back at her desk, she'd pushed the reason for their glow out of her mind. By mid-afternoon, she'd forgotten what he looked like. She remembered, though, once he was standing before her.

'Oh, hello,' she stammered. 'You've got an enquiry?'

'I've got an enquiry, yes.' He sat. 'Can I take you out to dinner?'

Judy forgot what he looked like again, in the time between when he asked her out and when they met, two nights later, outside the library. 'There you are!' He appeared out of the shadows, grinning like a ghoul, taller than she remembered, hair yellowish and semi-transparent in the streetlights.

'John.' She flinched. 'Sorry. I forgot what you looked like.'

'That explains the look of horror.'

'No! I just mean … nice jacket?'

John dusted off his sleeves. 'Covered in cat hair.'

'You have a cat?'

'Three.' Her face must've done something. 'Not a cat person?'

'Well.' She laughed weakly. 'Three's better than thirty.'

They started across the dark campus, pace slow, height difference awkward.

'I thought, this Italian place—'

'You told me.' He smiled. 'I made a booking.'

'Oh? Lovely.'

'How was your thing?'

'Sorry?'

'Wednesday. You said you had a thing.'

'Oh, yes. Volunteer work.'

'Really? Where?'

'A suicide prevention hotline.'

'Really?' John looked impressed. 'Must be hard work.'

'I seem to have a knack for it.' Judy picked up her pace. 'My daughter, Paulina. She … had trouble.'

'I'm sorry.'

'Me too.'

Judy kept her eyes down, hoping he'd get gastro or remember he had to feed his cats or something.

'I've got four,' John piped up. 'Daughters.'

'Four daughters,' Judy repeated. 'Three cats.'

'No sons. No dogs.'

'Wives?'

'Two exes.'

'Do they hate you?'

John laughed. 'You don't pull any punches.'

'Sorry,' Judy mumbled. 'I don't know why I said that.'

'They tolerate me.'

'You're tolerable, then?'

'You'll have to let me know later tonight.'

It was too warm and bright inside the restaurant, the air bready and fragrant with tomato and basil. Judy felt like a scientific specimen, unwinding her scarf from her neck.

'You look stunning,' John said. 'I meant to tell you.'

Judy waved her hand, pretended to peruse the wine list, though she couldn't read a word without her specs. John took a pair from his pocket; they aged him another five years.

'Should we get a bottle?'

'Good idea.'

'Barolo? Nebbiolo?'

'I don't mind.'

'Sangiovese?'

'Really, I have no idea.'

'Neither do I.' He looked sheepish. 'I hoped you did.'

The waiter who brought their bottle was distractingly handsome, with pants so tight Judy didn't know where to look. He stood very close as she sampled the wine.

'Yes.' Judy swallowed. 'Good.'

When he tried to pour John's sample, he held up a hand. 'I'll take her word for it.'

'Have you been?' John asked, as she stared after the gorgeous waiter. 'Italy?'

'Gawd, no. I've never been anywhere, except—' she faltered. 'I've never travelled.'

'Never wanted to?'

'Not really.' She laughed. 'I sound like a rube, don't I?'

'Don't ask me. I'm a cultural wasteland, according to my daughters.'

'That's why you're learning Latin? To get some culture?'

'That.' He shrugged. 'And coming to terms with my shitty Catholic childhood.'

'Oh, I had one of those.'

'Come to terms with it yet?'

Before she could answer, the waiter returned with his notepad. 'Um,' Judy hazarded a guess. 'I'll take the gnocchi?'

John frowned at the menu, glasses perched on the dry, reddish tip of his nose.

'Rigatoni, please.' Once the waiter was gone, John removed his glasses. 'You could've borrowed mine, you know.'

'Sorry?'

'My specs. Or I could've read the menu to you.'

Judy took a deep swallow of wine. 'There wasn't much to come to terms with, really. I had an easy time. I was the baby.'

'I was smack in the middle: two brothers, two sisters.'

'Sounds crowded.'

'Not always. We had a dairy farm outside Ballarat. Lots of fresh air, cows—'

'I hate cows,' Judy let slip.

'You hate *cows*? Why?'

'I just do.'

'There must be a reason.'

'I hate how they look. I hate the noises they make. Everything about them.'

'Wow.' John sat back. 'Okay.'

'Don't look at me like that.'

John smirked like a schoolboy. 'They're sacred in some parts of the world, you know.'

'Oh, come off it.' Judy rolled her eyes. 'Some people hate snakes. I hate cows.'

'Alright.' John swished his wine. 'How do you feel about steak?'

She smiled. 'You're not funny.'

'Siblings?'

'Just my sister, Caroline. Three years older.'

'And your folks called themselves Catholic?'

'They were pretty pick-and-choose with it.' Judy toyed with her bracelets. 'My husband was married when we met. They turned a blind eye. He was a doctor.'

'Good catch?'

'Dad was a taxi driver. Mum wanted better for me. I was the pretty one, supposedly.'

'I believe that.'

'It was different for my sister. Remember what they used to say, "seen, not heard"?'

'I remember.'

'I was good at that.' Judy sipped. 'Caro wasn't. She was always sticking her nose in everything.'

'Sounds like my brother, Matt. He probably ran away ten times before he hit puberty.'

'Caro ran away, too.' Judy hesitated. 'She sort of went off the rails after … well, something happened to her.'

'Priest?'

'Dad's friend.' She shrugged. 'I was too young to understand. All I knew was he stopped coming over and Caro started cutting her legs.'

'My sister, Bridget, used to pour hot candle-wax on her legs.' John laughed uneasily. 'She'd try to make shapes with the burns. Smiley faces and stuff.'

Judy palmed her face. 'We're butchering this first-date conversation, aren't we?'

'I'm glad we're calling it a date.'

'I talk to suicidal people twice a week. What's your excuse?'

'Small talk's overrated.' John drained his glass, got up. ''Scuse me.'

Watching his tall body slouch off to the men's room, Judy considered doing a runner. Instead, she topped up her wine, drank as much as she could in his absence.

'You didn't do a runner,' John noted, sitting back down.

'Neither did you.'

'Not on an empty stomach.' He picked up the wine. 'You've been busy.'

'Lucky you. I'll be laughing at all your bad jokes, now.'

'I should get the kitchen to leak some gas … then I'll really have you in stitches.'

'Or just frown over your textbooks? That worked the first time.'

Frowning deeply, John filled her glass to the brim. His frown dissolved when she giggled. 'You have a pretty laugh.'

'Gawd.' Judy clutched her warm cheeks. 'I haven't done this in so long.'

'Try five years.'

'Is that supposed to impress me?'

'I reckon it's more depressing than impressive.' He filled his glass. 'You?'

Judy grimaced. 'More than five years.'

'Well, you know what they say …' His blue eyes caught hers. 'It's like riding a bike.'

'I never learned.'

'You're kidding?'

'I always thought it was unladylike.' Judy fiddled with the stem of her glass. 'Caro's tried getting me to join her spin class. She's fighting a losing battle.'

'You're close?'

'She's my best friend.' Judy smiled. 'She's tough-as-nails. Her heart's as big as a house. A mansion, really. You should see this house she lives in. That's how big her heart is.'

'And your house?'

'Tiny. Like my heart.'

Even so, Judy invited him over for a nightcap. Easier that than finding a bar where they could hear themselves over the music. At the bottle shop, John insisted on buying wine with a cork instead of a screw-top. Leaving the shop, she shivered. He looked at her. 'Want my jacket?'

'With all that cat hair? No thanks.'

He reached for her hand. 'How's this, then?'

They held hands for the two blocks to her building, eleven floors in the elevator.

'This is it.' Judy let him in. 'It isn't much.'

'It's enough.' John looked towards the balcony. 'Great location.'

'I was in Cherry Hill before. Almost forty years in the same house.'

'Miss it?'

'I do.' Judy folded up her scarf. 'But this makes more sense. I'm close to work. I'm closer to Caro's. And Field of Mars.'

'Field of Mars?'

'That's where Paulina's buried. And her dad.' She nipped into the kitchen for glasses. 'I visit on weekends. It's a bit like a divorce, if the king of the underworld got sole custody.'

John turned toward the fridge, picked up the photo she'd stuck there. 'Where's this?'

'Oh ... just the ocean. I don't remember when I took it.'

John turned the photo around.

'"All the living things. All the treasure. All the garbage. Shipwrecks. Sea monsters",' he read aloud. 'Is that a poem or something?'

'I heard it somewhere.' She opened the cutlery drawer quickly. 'Where's that bloody corkscrew made off to?'

John came up behind her. 'Is this it?'

'That's a potato peeler.'

'Is this it?'

'That's for crushing garlic!' Judy sighed. 'I told you we should just get a screw-top.'

'Sorry for trying to treat my woman.' John fished inside his pocket. 'I've got an idea.'

'*Keys?*'

'Give me that.' He took up the bottle. 'I've got it.'

'Keys, John? That can't be hygienic!'

'I'm not dipping them in the stuff. I just need to loosen the thing.'

'Oh, gawd.' Watching him struggle, Judy got the giggles. 'That's *not* working.'

'Have some faith in me, woman. Christ.' His face reddened. 'Do you have a knife?'

'I'm not letting you near my knives!'

'Hold on.' He struggled some more. 'It's working.'

'It's not, though.'

'It just needs some elbow grease.'

'Oh, is that what we're calling it?' She noticed a glimmer of sweat on his brow, mopped it. 'You're cool as a cucumber.'

'Hold on.'

She laughed against his shoulder. 'Shall I go back to the shops? That'll be faster.'

'Woman, I told you. I always finish what I start.'

'Oh, gawd! Don't hurt yourself.'

'It's in there … It's in … Oh, *shit.*'

'John! It's fallen in!'

'It's fine.' He pursed his lips. 'If you don't mind a bit of cork in your wine.'

Smothering her laughter, Judy peered at the broken cork floating in the dark liquid. 'Is this a sign of things to come?'

'I got the job done, didn't I?'

She touched the lapel of his jacket. 'You're right, it's covered in cat hair. It's like an extra layer. No wonder you're overheating.'

He shrugged off his jacket, threw it on the counter. 'Better?'

'Better.' Judy hugged his waist. 'Let's see those keys.'

John handed over his keys. 'I think it's bent. I won't be able to get in my front door.'

'I think you're right.' She slipped the keys back into his pocket. 'You'll have to find someplace else to sleep tonight.'

'Any ideas?'

'You tell me.'

'You said this is a one-bedroom apartment?'

'One bedroom. My bedroom.'

'Well. There you go.'

'There I go?'

'It's an idea.'

'You're a real ideas man tonight, aren't you?'

'Am I?'

'Are you?'

'You tell me.'

'I have no idea what kind of man you are.' She lifted her face to his. 'You'll have to show me.'

'He's adorable, Jude,' Caro effused, sequestered on the terrace in front of the brazier twelve Fridays later. 'Why'd you keep him hidden away for so long?'

Shrugging, Judy glanced through the glass into the spacious living room, where John was frothing over Tim's record collection. 'He's such a dag.'

'So?'

'He's a mature-age student. All the young people make fun of them.'

'You think they don't they make fun of the ancient receptionist?'

'He's too tall.'

'Tall is good!'

'He's not the good kind of tall. He stoops.'

'Anything else?'

'He's got a weak chin.'

'Oh, come on.'

'And blue eyes. I like dark eyes; you know that.'

'Who cares what colour they are? It's the look in them that counts.'

'He's too white. He gets rosacea when he drinks.'

'Please don't tell me you're still hung up on that boy.'

'No. Of course not.'

'He hasn't been emailing you again, has he?'

'No.' Judy folded her arms. 'Of course not.'

'Well, don't go comparing him to a thirty-year-old. That's not fair.' Caro threw a glance through the window. 'Besides, you can tell he was a looker when he was young. Have you seen pictures?'

'Why would I?'

'I *love* looking at pictures of Tim in his glory days. You should ask for pictures.'

'What, from his first wedding?'

'You can't seriously be complaining about a man in his sixties being *divorced.*'

'Twice divorced.'

'Better five divorces than fifty years in a loveless marriage.'

'He cheated on the first one.'

'Throwing stones, glass houses, Jude.'

Judy lifted her glass to her lips. 'He's probably a deadbeat dad. His daughters never return his calls.'

'Meet them.'

Judy shook her head.

'Why not?'

'They're just somebody else's daughters.'

'Jude. No one's talking about replacing her.' Caro scrutinised her. 'You haven't told him yet, have you?'

'He knows enough.'

'What, you're think he'll drop you, if he knows your daughter was murdered?'

'He won't be able to drop me. He'll *pity* me.' Judy covered her face. 'Gawd, I'm pathetic. After everything that's happened, I'd probably go for any man who showed an interest.'

'Bullshit. You're very picky.'

'He's nothing compared to her, Caro. I'll never love him a fraction as much.'

'You're using that word already?'

'No.' Judy set her jaw. 'He's *nothing*.'

Caro drew up her legs. 'Well, if that's true, you'd better break it off before you really hurt the guy.'

'Yes.' Judy touched her lips. 'Maybe.'

'Don't you dare! I'll start smoking again.'

'That's emotional blackmail.'

'Keep him, please,' Caro begged. 'Keep him so Tim can have a friend, at least. Look how cute they are.'

Judy looked. They did look cute, sitting on the floor with their shiny faces and rolled-up sleeves.

'He has cats,' Judy protested weakly. 'They leave hair everywhere.'

'Buy him a lint-roller.'

'What if he wants to move in? I've gone to all this trouble downsizing and now this guy comes along with his cats and his long legs. They'll take up so much space—'

'Steady on, Jude. You've only known him three months.'

'I know. But it feels like longer.'

'Then don't wait another day. Give him all the bloody details.' Caro smirked. 'Except for the boy. Let's keep that between us.'

Lining up to board the Fairfolk Tours bus, Judy rolled her eyes at John. 'I told you. Nothing but nearly-deads.'

He winked. 'And newlyweds.'

'I think the honeymoon's over.'

She didn't recognise the bus driver, nor did he seem to recognise her. Even so, they sat toward the back.

'My wife came here with her first husband,' John boasted to the couple across the aisle. 'I promised I'd show her a better time than he did.'

As the bus rolled through town, Judy stared out at the faded shopfronts. Tabby's Treasures was gone, a Chinese restaurant in its place. 'FOR SALE' signs screamed out of every other window. Fairfolk flags flew high. Around the corner from Rainbow Real Estate, she saw a slash of graffiti: 'MAINIE PIGS STAY OUT'.

'Isn't that where Paulina's boyfriend worked?' John pointed out Camilleri's.

Judy blushed. 'I'm sure he's moved on.'

The bus stopped at King's Lookout. While the other couples oohed and aahed and took photos, Judy clung to her husband. 'She loved this view.'

'I can see why.'

'She walked here every day. No matter what sort of day she was having, she walked here and looked at the sea.'

They looked at the sea until it was time to re-board the bus.

Back onboard, another passenger asked, 'Didn't a girl get murdered around here?'

'Aye. Sydney girl.' The driver whistled low. 'Wild thing. Big drinker.'

Judy glanced out at the pointy heads of the pine trees in the valley below. John squeezed her hand tighter.

'Did they catch the killer?'

'Good-looking guy from Perth.' The driver chuckled. 'He was married … she wasn't. It got messy.'

John let go of Judy's hand. 'Nice of you to blame the victim, mate.'

'What's that?' The driver's eyes sought John's in the rear-view.

'I said, nice of you to blame the victim,' John raised his voice. '*Mate.*'

The other passengers turned to look. Judy hid her face against the window, mortified.

'She was just going for her walk,' John continued. 'She was minding her own business. You could learn something from her, mate.'

'Brudda,' the driver matched John's tone. 'I've lived here sixty-nine years—'

'Yeah? Then you're old enough to know better. That girl deserves some respect and so does her mother.'

Judy kept her face pressed to the window, caught somewhere between laughter and tears, until the bus reached King's Pier. Getting off, she avoided the driver's eyes, but even so, he put it together. 'Sorry, ma'am. No disrespect.'

'We're getting off here.' John frowned. 'And we're leaving you a one-star review.'

The tears and laughter came, together.

'Oh, gawd, John!' Judy pulled him away from the crowd of curious co-passengers. 'You're a dickhead.'

'Me? He's the dickhead. Where the hell does he get off—'

'You're *not* leaving a one-star review. The tour came free with the hotel.'

'So? People deserve to know the driver's a dick—'

'You're the one who said "yes" to the tour in the first place. I didn't want the thing. I know this island like the back of my hand.'

'Sorry.' He bowed his head. 'I thought it'd be fun.'

'You dickhead.' Judy laughed against his shoulder. 'Where're we going now?'

'You tell me.' He kissed the back of her hand. 'I don't know this place like I know these.'

She took him to the cemetery. They hadn't been walking long before they came upon a fresh grave marked 'MERLE ALFRED CARLYLE'.

'Oh.' Judy's hand flew to her mouth. 'She used to take care of this old man.'

'1919? He had a pretty good run.'

A little further in, they found a teenaged girl's grave, eye-catching with its blue tiles and glued-on seashells. 'Fifteen,' Judy murmured. 'Poor little thing.'

The mutineers were on the far side of the yard, a stone's throw from the beach. John paused in front of Gideon King. 'Here's that bugger who put his name on everything.'

Then they pushed through the cemetery gate to Tombstone Beach, slipped off their shoes. The sand was soft as silk, dark rocks jutting through it like bones.

'Careful,' Judy warned, when John's knobbly, thin-skinned feet ventured too close to the rocks. 'Don't cut yourself.'

He'll die before me, she didn't say, but thought. *I'll die alone, yet.*

After a while, tired of walking, they just sat. Watching the wild water, its variegated blues and veins of white, Judy cried; first softly, then hard, very hard.

'Ten years, John.'

'I know.'

'You don't know.'

'I know. But I know.'

'It's too long.'

'I know.'

'How can I live like this?'

'I don't know. Keep at it, though.'

'How am I alive? It hurts so much.'

'You're very brave.'

'She's everything.'

'I know.'

'You *don't* know.' Drying her eyes on John's collar, Judy gave him the highest compliment known to mankind. 'She would've loved you.'

There were three 'Camilleris' in the Fairfolk Island phone book, but he was the first one. He answered after three rings, his voice low and lovely and familiar as blood.

'J-Jesse?' Judy stammered. 'Sorry. It's Judy. Novak.'

'Judy. Yeah. Of course.'

'Sorry to call out of the blue, just—'

'You're back on the rock, eh.'

'Yes.' She laughed. 'News travels fast?'

Jesse paused just long enough for her to get goosebumps. 'That. And I drove past you. I think it was you. You were with a man.'

'My husband.'

'Yeah, I figured.' He went quiet again, and Judy felt herself sliding back in time, drowning in his silences. 'I'm married, too.'

'Oh? Congratulations.'

'Sorry. I don't know why I said that.'

Judy laughed again. 'Why not? It's good to know.'

'Yeah. Um. I met her in Brisbane.'

'What's her name?'

'You'll laugh, eh.'

Judy glanced at the phone book in her lap. 'It's not "Jessica", is it?'

'Yeah.' He laughed. 'I told you you'd laugh.'

'Well, we can't help who we fall for.'

'True.'

Judy breathed deep before the next question. 'Kids?'

'Just one. Grace. She's three.'

'Oh. You named her after your mum?'

'Yeah.'

'Lovely.'

'Yeah. She is.'

'Anyway … I just wanted you to know.' Judy toyed with the phone cord. 'We're just here for a few days.'

'Her birthday.'

'Yes.'

'It's good you came.'

'I don't know. It's very weird.'

'I …' Jesse faltered. 'I mean, if it's not too weird. I've got the day off tomorrow.'

'Oh?'

'Yeah. I mean, bring your husband, too. If you want. I'll be around all day.' He started talking faster. 'Jess'll be around, too. Come any time. If you want. If it's not too weird.'

'Honestly, Jess!' Judy laughed. 'I think the weirdness peaked about five years ago.'

'Yeah. Sorry,' he mumbled. 'Um. Sorry about the emails.'

'Oh.' She was glad John wasn't around to see her red cheeks. '*Those*.'

'Yeah. Sorry. I was confused.'

'I gathered as much.'

'Sorry. Yeah.'

'Stop apologising, will you?'

'Sorry.' He caught himself. 'Fuck. I'm still confused, eh. It's weird, hearing your voice.'

'Well, if it's too weird, I won't—'

'No. Jesus. Come any time, okay? You've come all this way.'

'I didn't come here for you, Jesse.'

'Yeah, I know! Jesus. But it'd be weird not to see you. You're ... Paulina's mum.'

'That's true.'

'Come any time. Tomorrow, or any day. Any time.'

'I can't come *any* time. Give me a time.'

'Any time.'

'Give me a time.'

'Any time.' She could hear him smiling, sidelong. 'You hold the cards here, Judy.'

'Oh, fine! Two o'clock?'

'Any time.'

'Fine! See you at two.' Judy hung up, feeling pretty pleased with herself, before realising she'd forgotten something. Sheepishly, she rang back. 'Sorry. What's your address?'

'It's pretty small, by Fairfolk standards.' Barefoot, Jesse walked them from their rental car to the house. 'The cottage is even smaller. Dad's there now. He always said he'd give me the house when I had a family. I don't think he ever believed it'd happen, but.'

He'd gained weight and was shorter than Judy remembered — especially next to John. She hated to think how far she'd fallen from whatever pedestal he'd put her on.

'Well, it's big by Sydney standards,' she piped up. 'We live in a townhouse.'

'She was in this shoebox apartment when we met,' John supplied. 'I felt like a giant every time I came over.'

'You sold the place in Cherry Hill?'

'No.' Judy looked down. 'I can't bring myself to sell it.'

'She rents it out to uni students. She should raise the rent. They move in and make a mess and every year she's back there, cleaning and gardening for days.'

Judy smiled. 'It's sort of my yearly pilgrimage.'

Jesse led them around to the backyard, where a stout brunette was raking compost. 'Jess!' Jesse called to her, and she looked up, swept her hair from her ruddy brow.

'Hey.' Smiling, Jessica strolled over. 'Judy, right?'

'Yes.' Judy tried not to let her disappointment show; she looked nothing like Paulina — or like her younger self, for that matter. 'That's me.'

'And you're …' Jessica shrugged at John. 'Sorry. No idea.'

'John.'

'John?' Laughing, she counted. 'Triple-J.'

'Gracie!' Jesse called out, and a grubby, half-naked child looked up from the pile of leaves she was playing with. 'Hey, Gracie! Here, girl.'

'She's not a dog, Jess.'

'Hey, Gracie.' Jesse clicked his fingers and, when that didn't work, wandered over and scooped his daughter up in his big, tattooed arms. 'Here's a lady I want you to meet.'

Judy took a sharp breath, kept her smile in place.

'Gracie, this is Judy.' Jesse combed the girl's tumbling, dark hair from her eyes. 'She's my friend from before you were born. Can you say "hi"?'

Grace stared at Judy, then hid her face.

'Sorry.' Jesse grimaced. 'She's shy.'

'Raised by camels.' Jessica licked her finger, wiped a bit of grime from Grace's twiggy, brown arm. 'She needs a bath.'

'I'll give her one later.'

'Can you?'

'Yeah, later. Before dinner.'

'I'm not cooking. I'm working at the shelter tonight, remember?'

'Yeah, I know. Dad's cooking. Remember?'

'*Remember?*' Jessica sing-songed, poking him in the side; then caught Judy's eye. 'He thinks I've got amnesia.'

'Yeah, cos you do.' Jesse sniffed his daughter's hair. 'Jesus. Has she been rolling in cow shit?'

'Probably.'

'Sorry.' Jesse smiled apologetically. 'Comes with the territory, eh.'

'Doesn't bother me.' Sensing Judy's glistening eyes, John wrapped an arm around her shoulders. 'I grew up on a dairy farm.'

'No shit?' Jessica's face lit up. 'Where?'

'Ballarat. Country Victoria.'

'No shit? I'm from Ararat.'

'I thought you were a Queenslander.'

'Don't insult me.' Jessica laughed. 'I moved up there with my ex. Moved away the first chance I got.'

Jesse grimaced. 'Aye. I couldn't hack the mainland, eh. White man's world.'

Grace squirmed. Jesse set her down and she scampered off, dark curls flying.

'She's beautiful, Jesse.' Judy's nose stung. 'She looks just like you.'

He shrugged. 'I should hope so, eh.'

'*Excuse me?*' Jessica flashed him a death-stare.

'I didn't mean it like that.' Smirking, he raked a hand through his thick, dark hair. 'She takes after you, too. You both … smell like cow shit.'

John laughed. Judy smiled weakly, eyes burning.

'Sorry.' She looked toward the house. 'Mind if I … ?'

'Bathroom?' Jessica caught her drift. 'Need me to show you the way?'

'S'alright. I'll find it.'

Like a homing pigeon, Judy flew inside the house, navigated through the young-family clutter to the bathroom. They hadn't cleaned for her visit. Toothpaste scummed the sink. The bathmat squelched like mud. A sensible beige bra hung off the towel rack.

This should all be hers. Judy's reflection blurred. *This should be ours.*

Jesse was in the kitchen making coffee when she emerged.

'Sorry.' He noticed her raw eyes. 'I wanted you to meet them.'

Judy waved her hand. 'I cry about twenty times a day. Don't take it personally.'

'Sorry.' Jesse set a mug in front of her. 'It's just instant. You probably get better stuff in Sydney.'

'Probably.'

'John said you like it milky and sweet.' He glanced at her furtively.

'I added some Jim Beam, but. In Paulina's honour.'

'You *didn't*.'

Jesse smiled, shrugged. 'Try it.'

Judy blew on the coffee, tentatively sipped.

'You didn't.' She narrowed her eyes. 'Please tell me she *didn't*—?'

'Nay.' His eyelashes cast shadows on his cheek. 'Jus' one time. She skipped work so I could give her a tattoo, then—'

'*Tattoo?*'

'Sorry. I never told you?'

'No,' Judy said fastidiously. 'You didn't.'

'Yeah. Um.' He opened the pantry. 'She wanted a tramp stamp.'

'Oh gawd.' Judy wiped her eyes. 'Of course she did.'

'Ha, yeah.' Jesse pulled out a packet of biscuits, arranged them on a plate with shaky hands. 'We didn't go through with it, obviously. She was … scared. Of the pain, I guess.'

'Oh,' Judy whimpered. 'Poor baby.'

'Yeah.' Jesse turned away abruptly. 'She was such a baby. She always called me a baby for being younger, but she was such a baby, eh.'

'Poor baby.' Judy covered her face. 'Oh. Baby girl.'

'Yeah.' Jesse placed the biscuits and a pair of mugs on the tray. 'Anyway, I'll just take these out. I think Jess's showing your old man where we grow our weed. Seemed pretty interested.'

'Oh gawd.' Judy laughed helplessly. 'Thanks for that.'

Alone in the kitchen, she had another cry, then took her mug out to the porch. The sun hurt her eyes. She stared through it, anyway, at the boy who should've been her son-in-law or maybe her lover, and the plain-looking woman he was married to, and the half-naked child who should've been hers to hold, and the stooping-tall man who could never make up for it all, no matter how hard he tried.

'Sorry.' Jesse reappeared on the porch. 'John wants to get blazed. Is that alright?'

Judy raised her eyes heavenward. 'I s'pose. It's a special occasion.'

He went back in, returned with a carved wooden box, a grinder, papers. Eyes lowered, he sat across from her and placed a dried green nugget in the grinder. Judy watched his hands working, his arms, until he caught her watching.

'Sorry,' she mumbled, cheeks colouring.

'Nay.' He reddened. 'You're good.'

She followed his fingertips as they lifted the lid from the grinder, lined up the green flakes on a slip of rolling paper. Again, he looked up.

'Sorry.' She shook her head. 'Just … your hands.'

Jesse looked at his hands and understood. Playfully passed them through the sunbeams.

'Oh, Jess.' Judy sighed, charmed to the point of exasperation. 'You know, you really broke my heart for a while there.'

'Yeah?' He met her eyes. 'It goes both ways.'

They looked at each other, looked at each other looking, for so long and with such intensity, she forgot time, death, everything.

'It's good to see your face,' he said after a while, and looked away.

'Yes.' Judy lowered her eyes. 'You too.'

Time resumed its beat inside her chest. She heard Jessica raking the compost, John's footsteps. She was ready with a smile when he stepped onto the porch.

'Homegrown, brudda.' Jesse offered him up a fresh-rolled joint. 'Enjoy.'

John grinned like a twelve-year-old. 'Groovy.'

'Gawd, you're a dag.' Judy cringed as he sat, circled her shoulders, and sparked up. When he offered her a toke, she refused. 'That stuff messes with your head.'

Jesse blinked. 'Paulina used to say that.'

'Well, good. I taught her something.'

John returned the joint to Jesse.

'Here's to you, Mrs Novak.' Jesse toked. 'Or, wait: is it something else now?'

'It's still "Novak".' Judy sipped her lukewarm coffee. 'And it's still "Ms".'

'I had a hard enough time getting her to the altar.' John tucked Judy's hair behind her ear. 'She was quite happy living in sin.'

'I was happy,' Judy agreed. 'I'm still happy.'

Jesse stood up abruptly.

'You're a really nice couple, eh.' He relinquished the joint. 'All yours, brudda.'

Jesse ducked inside, smoke dispersing in his wake. John inhaled, wheezed a little.

'You're such a dag,' Judy repeated, resting her head on his shirtfront.

They sat quietly in the sweet-smelling fug, listening to the rake, the wind whispering through the kentia palms. Jesse emerged from the house with a sketchpad.

'I knew I had it somewhere.' He opened it in front of Judy. 'This's the design she wanted. It took me ages. She was really picky, eh.'

Judy's eyes blurred. 'Oh?'

'She told me, "I want something that symbolises the void and that'll look cute above my butt".'

'Stupid girl!' Judy cried. 'It's perfect, Jess.'

John peered closer. 'Great work, mate. Really.'

'Can I buy it off you?' Judy looked up at Jesse. 'Please?'

'Your money's no good here.' Jesse wandered back to his seat; peeked at her through his thick eyelashes. 'You nay want something more permanent?'

'Jess!' Judy shook her head. 'I'm too old for a tramp stamp.'

'Aye. Probably.' Jesse traded a glance with John. 'I could do it somewhere else, but. If you're worried about wrinkles. Somewhere close to the bone.'

'Close to the bone?'

'Here, for instance.' Tentatively, he reached across the table, turned her palm upwards. 'The skin's tighter.'

'My wrist?'

'It's tighter, near the bones.' As his fingers circled her wrist, she recognised the scar where he'd almost taken off a tip. 'It can be pretty painful, though. There's not much to soften—'

'You think *I'm* afraid of pain?' Judy interrupted. 'Me? Paulina's mother?'

'Nay.' His grip tightened. 'Not you. Never.'

Under his thumb, her pulse quickened. Sunlight swarmed her veins.

'Go on, then,' she whispered. 'I'm waiting.'

ACKNOWLEDGEMENTS

The Newcomer would not exist if I hadn't first had the privilege of visiting the island that inspired it. Thank you to the Neilma Sidney Literary Travel Fund and its round-two judges — Rachel Bin Salleh, Emily Bitto, and Angela Meyer — for seeing promise in my proposal. *Kingdom by the Sea* never did get written, but it got me on the right flight (and its title lives on in chapter 21).

The moment I glimpsed the rock's famous greens and blues through the plane window in June 2018 was love at first sight. My love has only deepened with successive visits. I hope that this love shines through the (often intense) darkness. My gratitude to the people of Norfolk Island who welcomed me, gave me lifts, taught me things, or even just looked at me askew. See yorley again soon — if you'll have me.

Thanks also to the City of Melbourne for awarding me the 2020 Boyd Garret Residency. In ordinary times, this residency would've been life-changing. In COVID times, it was life-saving. I am incredibly privileged to associate 2020 with sunlight on red carpet, and sparse city views, and space, and time. I'm privileged to live in a city that supports the arts.

It's been a pleasure to work with Scribe again for my third (and best!) book. Thank you, Marika Webb-Pullman, for always taking care with my words, and for being such a wise and intuitive presence, on and off the page. Laura Thomas, for another stunning cover (the perfect little sister to *TLOABM* and *BR*). Cora Roberts, for your warmth and realness, which makes the prospect of publicity slightly less terrifying.

I wrote this book in the spaces around my day-job. Thank you to my fellow pro bullshit artists in the QA team for making these days bearable. I hope you'll appreciate the ownership statement + seeks permission on page 160 (among other things). Love yas.

In the early stages of writing this novel, my body put a violent halt to the writing process. Thank you to the staff at Royal Melbourne ICU for bringing me back. Thank you to beautiful Ben, whose face was the first I saw, out of comaland. Thank you to my family, who were with me the whole time in comaland, and have always reminded me that (duh) there are more important things in life than books. I wouldn't be who I am, without you.

Thank you to my friends for all the wines, coffees, dumplings, brunches, bows and arrows, laughs, vents, honesty, and goodness. This scene, and this world, are easier to navigate in your company. Thank you for getting me out of my own head and sharing what's in yours.

I'm extremely grateful to the booksellers who advocated for my previous books, and grateful (in advance) to those who hand-sell this one. And, of course, to the readers — especially if you've made it this far.

Finally, Kirill. Thank you for having the infinite patience of staying married to me despite every third sentence out of my mouth for the past two years being some variation of, 'On the island, blah blah blah.' You're my rock. You're my island. I'm so happy to spend my days with you.